## PRAISE FOR *STAMPI*

*Shortlisted for the British S*
*for Best N*

"His most ambitious novel to date. A major nov... unique multicultural perspective, his political and economic acuity, and his skill at developing characters fully grounded in history have long deserved a major audience, and his skill in building a fully SF world, never quite so clearly in evidence as here, may finally help bring that audience to him."—*Locus*

"A bona fide classic."—*Publishing News*

"Grimwood imbues his creations with startling psychological complexity. . . . He has produced, imago-like, an inspiring butterfly of humanity and hope from a hard shell of despair."
—*Guardian*

"This is a virtuoso lesson in bringing artistic unity to radically dissonant elements. It is also the novel of a writer with real heart."—*Time Out*

"Forget *The Matrix,* this is far more sexy and sophisticated. Mind-bendingly good."—*Cosmopolitan*

"Turning the idea of the past determining the future upside down, this thriller takes an attempted assassination of the U.S. president and an emperor awaiting his death in distant China and creates a riveting ride."—*Esquire*

"The best book this talented author has yet written."
—*New York Review of Science Fiction*

"One of the most forceful and iconoclastic writers at work today."
—*Crime Time*

"Grimwood has written some of the best SF in the world over the past five years and *Stamping Butterflies* continues his journey to greatness."—*SFX*

"This is nothing less than a monumental achievement. A novel to which you willingly and joyfully devote your total attention, and which is even more satisfying on multiple readings."—*Vector*

"Futures near and far collide. Three stories intertwine tantalisingly, their resolution shocks."—*New Scientist*

"A novel which explores high concept ideas from a human perspective, which features beautifully tragic and broken characters, which evokes a powerful sensation of being somewhere else through gritty and detailed imagery and description, and which is frequently witty and always clever... like its characters it is smart and appealing."—*SF Crowsnest*

"If you like William Gibson at his wildest; if you're comfortable with a root uncertainty and the chaos-fraught nature of the universe; if you enjoy a lush story fractally and poetically told—this is a novel you will not want to miss."—*SciFiDimensions*

"Fast yet humane, hip yet bizarre, futuristic yet embedded in the absolute present moment of the world, Jon Courtenay Grimwood's novels read like thrillers but maintain a kind of caring irony and clarity of political vision which not only make him one of the best of the new UKSF writers but suggest new directions for every kind of writing."—M. John Harrison, author of *Light*

"Ambitious, deft and accomplished—confirms Grimwood's place amongst the very best of contemporary SF authors."
—Iain Banks, author of *The Algebraist*

"Jon Courtenay Grimwood is a critical, crucial voice in modern Science Fiction."
—China Miéville, author of *Iron Council*

"A masterpiece. Jon Courtenay Grimwood is British SF's best kept secret. Now you can find out why."
—Charles Stross, author of *Accelerando*

"Clever, wise, and enigmatic, *Stamping Butterflies* has great relevance to the times in which we live.... The writing achieves a clarity most writers die trying to achieve."
—Jeff VanderMeer, author of *City of Saints and Madmen*

"A mature, often alarming, deep and admirable work of fiction."
—Adam Roberts, author of *Salt*

## PRAISE FOR THE ARABESK SERIES

## *PASHAZADE*

*Shortlisted for the Arthur C. Clarke Award, the British Science Fiction Association Award for Best Novel, and the John W. Campbell Memorial Award*

"Raymond Chandler for the 21st century."—*Esquire*

"Dazzling, seductive and pointed."—*Independent*

"A provocative hard-crime novel, Arabic alternate history, and literary page-turner all in one."—*Entertainment Weekly* (A-)

"All brilliant light and scorching heat... Grimwood has successfully mingled fantasy with reality to make an unusual, believable and absorbing mystery."—*Sunday Telegraph*

"Set to cement his position in both critical and public opinion. With four previous books behind him, Grimwood started well and has steadily improved, honed, and entertained.... The pacing of this book is near perfect."—*Murder One*

"Blends alternative SF and hard-boiled mystery... Grimwood artfully unveils the changed world that has developed in the many decades since WWI ended differently. Ashraf, a lifelong underdog and pawn, emerges as a resourceful and deadly foe, adapting quickly to survive in a game where the rules and the playing field shift repeatedly. SF and mystery fans will be pleased."
—*Publishers Weekly*

"A good example of cross-genre fertilization—in this case, setting a cleverly constructed whodunit within the larger context of a vivid, thoroughly imagined alternate history... the result is a substantial entertainment that is alternately violent and touching, exotic and strangely familiar. Grimwood's El Iskandryia is a place worth visiting. The next two installments, *Effendi* and *Fellaheen,* can't appear too soon."—*Washington Post*

"Utterly compelling. Ashraf is mysterious without being remote, and his quest to solve the dual mysteries of the book makes for fascinating reading. Grimwood has built a solid alternate history, completely plausible in every detail and peopled with characters as unique as El Iskandryia itself."
—*Romantic Times* (4.5 stars, Top Pick)

"A mature balance between sensibility and action in what's essentially a rite of passage story allied with a detective thriller—deftly told and laced with neat ideas."—*Time Out*

"A convincing portrait of a man shaking off the demons of his past and becoming, finally, the person he was meant to be . . . a well crafted and absorbing novel."—*SFSite*

"Reading *Pashazade*, a vibrant and living city is evoked. . . . This rich, exotic setting provides a background for Grimwood's story in which excitement and adventure are inevitable. . . . When it comes to winding up the tension, [Grimwood] is certainly no slouch."
—*SFRevu*

"Unpredictable, unputdownable slice of city life."—*New Scientist*

"Multilayered characters, social comment, humanism and heaps of gadgetry from one of the most exuberant cyberpunk writers around."—*Guardian*

"All the makings of an excellent film—producers, take note."
—*Locus*

"The extraordinary depth and complexity of the plot is matched by the prose style... cannot be recommended highly enough."
—*Interzone*

"Satisfyingly unstable territory . . . The prose implodes and reinvents itself, echoing the chaotic narrative every step of the way."—*Publishing News*

"Jon Courtenay Grimwood is a step ahead of his contemporaries. He sees the world through unforgiving eyes, yet his style is razor sharp, his prose is biting and his vision unique."
—*Ottakar's Online*

"Cool, crisp prose . . . richly evocative of a future just out of reach. Five stars."—*SFX Magazine*

"The story line increases in complexity as it unfolds and Grimwood's hard, pithy style is gripping to the end."—*Focus*

"A novel which pulls you in and doesn't let go . . . If this is SF, then bring it on, I can't wait for the next installment."
—*South Wales Echo*

"Intelligently written and compulsive... *Pashazade* is a delightful hybrid of detective fiction, SF and alternate history, dusted with the street lyricism of Jeff Noon and a hint of Angela Carter–like magic."—*Coldprint*

"Here we have the definite step forward in the evolution of Jon Courtenay Grimwood as writer and literary stylist. *Pashazade* is definitely and by definition his best to date.... A deeply original work, carrying within it the seed of Grimwood's vision of an alternate future... Strange indeed, and quite wonderful."—*Ariel*

"Well imagined and evocative... Jon Courtenay Grimwood writes fast-paced, absorbing cyberthrillers, and he does it well. Buy this book, read it, tell your friends. 10/10."—*Starburst*

"Fast, furious and compelling."—*Company*

## *EFFENDI*

*Shortlisted for the British Science Fiction Award for Best Novel*

"If you're not reading Jon Courtenay Grimwood, then you don't know how subtle and daring fiction can be."
—Michael Marshall Smith, author of *Spares* and *One of Us*

"An intriguing cross-genre premise that allows for a lot of fun."
—*Observer*

"JCG has emerged over the last few years as one of the more interesting newer British novelists.... No one else is doing anything like it—or even trying to. Grimwood actually seems to have been in the places he makes up."—*Locus*

"A head-trip of a mystery novel... *Effendi* is the second of JCG's examinations of the relationship between the West and Islam through an outsider's eyes. Unsteadying, fast-paced and furious."
—*Big Issue*

"One of the finest novels I've read in some time... such a treat."
—*SFSite*

"*Pashazade* and now *Effendi* reeled me in within the first few pages.... Fast, furious, fun and elegant, the Arabesk trilogy is one of the best things to hit the bookstores in a while."
—*SFRevu*

"By turns affecting, engrossing and bewildering, so that great anticipation is created... these books go straight into the tiny to-be-read-again-as-soon-as-possible pile."
—*Interzone*

"If *Pashazade* was a success, *Effendi* is a triumph. JCG has taken the direction he embarked upon with the first book, mirrored and echoed the narrative structure therein and pushed his writing to another level."—*Third Alternative*

"It's specific and detailed and as immersive as hell.... Essential reading for anyone who read *Pashazade*. And if you haven't, go and buy it, then buy this."—*SFX Magazine*

"The dazzling *Pashazade* was always going to be a hard act to follow, but it comes as little surprise that the prodigally-talented Grimwood has pulled off the trick. His way with a sentence has a baroque finesse that makes these unclassifiable novels as elegantly written as they are rich in imaginative energy."
—*Publishing News*

"Grimwood's alternate history setting of the city of El Iskandryia (reminiscent of the exotic location, politics and intrigues of Lawrence Durrell's Alexandria Quartet) is wonderfully realized, as are the characters." —*Vector*

"*Pashazade* was, quite simply, the best SF novel I read last year, and *Effendi* is a worthy successor.... All of Grimwood's trademarks are present here in spades: edgy, streetwise prose, a fiendishly and rewardingly complex plot, plenty of black humour and his usual immaculate pace."—*Outland*

"Details are what JCG's books are all about. A wealth of them, building up to a world that sucks you in... It's a suitably gripping setup and Grimwood doesn't waste it."—*Starburst*

"There's futuristic technology here, and an intriguing framework of alternate history. But the heart of *Effendi* lies in the mysteries of each character's past. Sorting them out, and watching the tough-minded Ashraf Bey bring the multiple stories to a satisfying resolution, is marvelous fun." —*Cleveland Plain Dealer*

## *FELAHEEN*

*Winner of the British Science Fiction Award for Best Novel and shortlisted for the August Derleth Fantasy Award for Best Novel*

"A major landmark in JCG's career... The only real heavyweight work of orientalist post-cyberpunk fiction ever written and I am green with envy... If you have time to read just one trilogy this year, get the Arabesk books. Otherwise you're missing out."
—Charles Stross, author of *Iron Sunrise*

"[Grimwood] once again delivers his trademark mixture of vividly realized characters and evocation of place.... By turns a political thriller, a murder mystery and a search for identity, *Felaheen* is SF at its most inventive. Grimwood's spare, hardworking prose evokes a richly-textured world, which we sense extending beyond the edges of the page. The truth remains elusive until the very end, and even then we can't be sure of everything. But the journey is well worth travelling, and the scenery is spectacular."
—*Guardian*

"With the Arabesk books Grimwood, quite unfairly, pulls off five genres; SF, fantasy, crime, literary and noir. On the back of my copy it says, file under SF, but this is just silly since he can write as well as Dave Eggers and could engage with fans of Inspector Rebus."—*Big Issue*

"An action thriller that has the unusual distinction of appealing to fans of several fiction genres... This could well be the year of Jon Courtenay Grimwood."—*Bookseller*

"It seems entirely reasonable to regard the series, taken as a whole, as perhaps the most important SF trilogy of the past decade to remain unpublished in the United States."—*Locus*

"A fascinating blend of the traditional exotic and the futuristic noir punk... a must read." —*Sci Fi Weekly* (Editor's "A" Pick)

"Literary SF is a field full of writers who can handle big plot lines. Few though have Grimwood's way with a sly observation or careful metaphor.... Closer to greatness with every single novel."
—*SFX Magazine*

"Rounded characters, Byzantine plot lines and deft, streetwise prose mark JCG as one of the finest writers in the genre today.... Well worth the wait."—*Ottakar's Online*

"The back alleys and courts of North Africa come alive in JCG's *Felaheen*.... Food, violence and the exercise of intelligence." —*Time Out*

"As always, Grimwood has created a rich, vivid tapestry of plot and character, from the apparently mundane death of a chef to Raf's macabre and brilliantly depicted trek across the salt fields. Highly recommended."—*Starburst*

"He is a one-man Condé Nast, his world so rich, stylish and exotic that you want to buy a holiday there.... Grimwood writes a line to make all other writers in the world sick with envy." —*Big Issue*

"*Effendi* was one of the best novels of 2002, *Felaheen* equals it and perhaps even surpasses.... More, please!"—*Dreamwatch*

"Delve into the mysterious world of *Felaheen*.... An inventive hybrid, mixing the best elements of thriller, romance and SF." —*Company*

Also by
Jon Courtenay Grimwood

9TAIL FOX
FELAHEEN
EFFENDI
PASHAZADE
REDROBE
REMIX
LUCIFER'S DRAGON
NEOADDIX

# STAMPING BUTTERFLIES

Jon Courtenay Grimwood



BANTAM BOOKS

STAMPING BUTTERFLIES
A Bantam Spectra Book

PUBLISHING HISTORY
Orion edition published 2004
Bantam Spectra trade paperback / September 2006

Published by Bantam Dell
A Division of Random House, Inc.
New York, New York


Cover art by Stephen Youll
Cover design by Jamie S. Warren Youll

---



---

Library of Congress Cataloging-in-Publication Data
Grimwood, Jon Courtenay.
Stamping butterflies / Jon Courtenay Grimwood.
p. cm.—(Bantam spectra book)
ISBN-13: 978-0-553-38377-5
ISBN-10: 0-553-38377-9
I. Title.

PR6107.R56S73 2006
823'.92—dc22
2006042766

Printed in the United States of America
Published simultaneously in Canada

www.bantamdell.com

BVG 10 9 8 7 6 5 4 3 2 1

For Sammy, same as it ever was . . . and Jams.

"When the truth is replaced by silence, the silence is a lie . . ."

*Yevgeny Yevtushenko*

# STAMPING BUTTERFLIES

## KEY:

 **now**

 **then**

 **the future***

*Future dates are given by number of emperor and years reigned. So *CTzu53/Year7* means 53rd emperor (Chuang Tzu), 7th year of reign.

# PROLOGUE

## *Paris, Monday 26 March*

*Beijing outraged . . .*

Someone had taken the fate of the world and tossed it onto a chair and somebody else had dumped it under a table, where it remained until a thin, grey-haired tramp picked up the paper, wiped off the worst of the grime and spread it out.

Forty-one degrees in Cairo. Snow in Cape Town. Russia's president-for-life had just re-invaded Chechnya, the Chinese navy was blockading Taiwan and the current occupant of the White House had announced his intention to become the first president since Truman to visit North Africa.

It was five years since the tramp had read a newspaper and within three paragraphs he remembered why. His life was messy enough without adding complications from the rest of the world.

"Monsieur?"

This was his cue to order a coffee or leave. Counting his coins without taking his hand from his coat pocket, the *clochard* nodded. "Espresso," he said. He didn't blame the boy. There'd been that summer he arrived as the shutters were opening and stayed until the old woman, the one who was now dead, shooed him out onto Rue du Temple so she could finish mopping up for the night.

Leaving a handful of coppers, mostly to prove he could, the tramp began to fold his paper. That was when he first noticed two young men going from table to table, both dressed in the default cool of New York or London, black T-shirts hanging loose outside black chinos, expensive shades and simple shoes.

It was the dress of urban anonymity. One that spoke of hurried lives and the need to blend into a certain stratum of city life. In Paris, where T-shirts got tucked over even the proudest bellies and dressing alike was the preserve of *banlieue* dwellers or *bon chic/bon gen* couples with five-button blazers and Rue St. Honoré frocks, such foreignness shouted trouble.

At least it did to the tramp in the tweed coat. And shouted it loud enough for him to push back his chair, stand up and squeeze past a German tourist, who promptly checked her pockets, then frowned, wondering if she'd just been perved.

The men caught up with him later, probably by accident, at a food stall in the Marché des Enfants Rouge, where he sat scraping chicken tagine from a pot while he watched a Sudanese boy argue with a thickset girl who looked half Arab, half something else.

Both the girl and boy knew he was watching; neither minded.

A triangle, made up of Rues St. Paul and de Turenne to the east, des Archives to the west and the river to the south defined the edges of his world, within which the tramp was known and obscurely famous.

No one talked of the heroin, the cheap brandy, the nights he never quite made it back to a derelict, fifth-floor room overlooking Passage St. Jacques. The Marais district was a very private place. So private that many of the tourists who now roamed its narrow streets barely noticed it was there.

"I'm looking for Jake Razor," one of the men said, no introduction and no politeness, just the bald statement and the expectation that this would be enough.

The man in the old tweed coat looked blank.

"Jake Razor."

"*Pardonnez-moi?*"

They stared at each other and there it might have ended, except that the first of the Gap-clad men signalled to the second, who pulled up a chair. "*Nous cherchons pour Jake Razor. Le mathématicien et guitarist punk . . .*" From his jacket he retrieved a press card and a letter from some editor at *Rolling Stone,* dumping these beside an old photograph of a bare-chested, snarling boy in black jeans.

"*Avez-vous* seen him?"

"He's dead," said the tramp, checking the name on the card. "Years back. There was a fire. It was on the radio."

Bill Hagsteen sighed. "That was Marzaq," he said. "The Arab kid."

Marzaq al-Turq had been born half German and half Turkish, as his name suggested, but the tramp didn't bother to point this out. "Even if Jake's alive," said the tramp, "what makes you think he moved to Paris?"

"We have information," said Bill Hagsteen.

"There's a family trust," the other said. "It bought an apartment in Rue St. Paul, roughly fifteen years ago."

"But no one from the family uses it. In fact, none of them have been anywhere near this city in all that time." They were like an old married couple, finishing each other's sentences without even noticing.

"No problem," said the tramp. "Give me the number and I'll take you there."

"If we had that we could find it ourselves."

"We shouldn't even know about the apartment," added Bill Hagsteen. "The trust doesn't take kindly to enquiries from the press."

The man in the tweed coat thought about this and then thought about it some more. Pulling a final sliver of flesh from his chicken bone, he pushed away his empty bowl. "Maybe I can help," he said.

The steam bath was at the southern end of Rue St. Paul, and the tramp enjoyed seeing his new friends strip to their towels and sit sweating on tiled benches as they watched every man who entered for signs that he might once have been lead guitarist with Razor's Edge.

"Where now?" Bill Hagsteen asked, which the tramp took as an indication that he'd had enough of watching locals shift uneasily under his gaze or glare right back. They ate brunch at the Cajun place next to the Arts, less than a minute from the steam bath. And then Bill had the idea of checking if Jake had ever rented a room at the hotel. So their guide went in by himself and came out again seconds later.

"Fifty euros," he said.

"Twenty-five," said the other.

Bill Hagsteen pulled fifty from a crocodile skin wallet and handed it over without comment.

Folding the euros into his hand and pocketing them before he even reached reception, the tramp smiled at the woman behind the desk. He was smarter today. Still wearing his tweed coat, but with a pair of trousers which looked almost clean.

"Sorry about that," he said, "forgot something."

The receptionist gave him the rate card he asked for, explained about weekend deals and then looked at him more closely.

"I'm babysitting Americans," he explained. They'd nodded to each other in *Le Celtic* a few times though never spoken.

"You're American." She said this as a fact.

"I've been many things."

Outside, on the pavement, the tramp regretted that no one resembling Jake now rented a room at the Arts Hotel, although a New York poet had lived there for years. Unfortunately he'd died.

"Did you get a description?"

The tramp shook his head. "Before her time."

They stopped to look at the opium pipes in the window of the Buddha shop, crossed the road to cut down Rue Charlemagne, with its blue plaque naming Charles as "Emperor of the West" and rejoined Rue St. Paul via a *passage,* old buildings rising six storeys on either side of the narrow walk-through.

A black woman at the only free till in Monoprix looked briefly at Bill Hagsteen's old photograph and shook her head, her attention already on a man waiting impatiently behind them. Visits to the *tabac* and the English bookshop produced much the same result.

"Tell me," said their guide, "how good is your information?"

"Sixty per cent," said Bill Hagsteen. "Maybe less."

"I hope it didn't cost you too much."

"It cost nothing," the other said tartly.

"Could be," said the tramp, as he pocketed their fee, "that's why it's worthless."

She was young and pretty and very scared. And 150 euros was what it took to get her delivered to Passage St. Jacques in an uninsured taxi, driven by a boy without a licence. Her name was Zeinab and she was shocked to find that the tramp spoke her language, and more shocked still that his bed turned out to be a mattress on a metal balcony.

He was, after all, paying a sum she could barely imagine.

"I like fresh air," the man said. And watched Zeinab smile doubtfully as she glanced around his filthy attic room, with its torn leather chair facing an untuned TV, which she imagined to be broken, but he knew replayed proof of the Big Bang, dancing snow from the birth of the universe.

"Three years," he told her. That was how long he'd been clean.

Another smile twisted the teenager's lips without ever reaching her eyes. Ahmed had made it very clear about what would happen if the tramp had been lying about having money. About what would happen if he got Zeinab back damaged. She'd been there when her pimp took the man's call, so it was small wonder that her hands wouldn't stop shaking.

Ahmed had been the tramp's dealer in the early days, before he sweated out the darkness and his addiction on a mattress, dragged onto the balcony and never returned, an endless reminder not to go back.

"Until midnight," Zeinab said.

The tramp sighed. He'd told Ahmed that for 150 euros he wanted a girl until sunrise. "I'm not walking you back at midnight," he said.

Zeinab shook her head. "No," she said, voice firmer. "Mr. Ahmed's coming to collect me." And then she lay on her front, as the man instructed, though first she removed her clothes.

Sometime between the tears and midnight, darkness attempted to take over, announcing its arrival with a sudden pressure at the back of the tramp's skull. He heard the girl gasp as his fingers tightened on her shoulders and then she was crying, with those blind unconscious sobs of the truly afraid.

"Okay," he said, "it's okay." Not knowing if he was talking to her or to himself. And withdrawing from the tightness of her body, he rolled off and sat with his face to the night wind, listening to his breath steady and the sounds of the city reappear.

"Monsieur..."

She knelt behind him, apologising for her terror. Alternating between broken French and a stream of Arabic, which trailed into silence as he turned to face her.

"No," he said firmly. "Not you, me..." And he helped Zeinab to her feet and indicated that she should dress, but she shook her head, eyes huge. It was Ahmed, he realized; the kid was terrified that he might complain to her owner.

"It's okay," the man insisted, but he didn't stop Zeinab when she sunk to her knees in front of him, wiping her lips with the back of her hand. After a few minutes he lifted her up again and kissed her on her forehead, smelling unwashed hair and panic.

The darkness and he had a clear agreement on what was and wasn't allowed. Reading a paper had been pushing it. The young whore with her olive skin, dark nipples and fear-enhanced eyes was so far outside the rules that the man knew whatever happened next would be bad.

"You know," he said, as he watched Zeinab eye her clothes. "You should leave now." Her breasts were too small to need a bra and the tramp wondered if her slip was Ahmed's idea, or something she'd owned before she became the sadness she now was. It was only when Zeinab climbed into her jeans and pulled on a jacket that he realized the slip was not a slip at all but some kind of transparent shirt.

They waited for Ahmed under the arch where the *passage* met Rue St. Paul, five floors of other people's lives stacked over their heads. And when her pimp finally arrived it was in the taxi which had dropped Zeinab at the apartment.

"Jake."

The tramp shook his head. "We've been through this," he said. "I'm not Jake."

"Whatever..." Checking Zeinab with a quick glance, the pimp appeared satisfied. "Behave herself?"

"Yeah," said the tramp, watching the young girl climb in beside Ahmed's driver. "Good as gold." The pimp looked pleasantly surprised.

"Okay, then," he said. "We're done."

"Not really," said the tramp. "We agreed until morning."

"No." Ahmed shook his head. "I agreed nothing. You asked, that's different. Still..." Dipping his hand into a suit pocket, he produced a small paper bag. "Here," he said, "for old times' sake." There were five of them, tiny tubes like a doll's toothpaste, each with a short needle where the cap should be.

The ultimate painkiller. Battlefield heroin.

A full moon reflected off the river, inlaying its surface with jagged slivers of silver. A cat, hunting along the cobbles, detoured around the tramp in a long looping path when it saw him crouched at the water's edge. A cemetery owl from Père La Chaise swooped low overhead, skimming branches before returning the way it came.

The man who was not Jake Razor considered all of these things as he shucked off his tweed coat and rolled up his sleeve. The River Seine looked almost flat and yet it was not; the river was whatever shape the banks and bottom made it. And the moon, that too looked flat, but only if one thought in two dimensions. *Or four,* the tramp reminded himself. Sometimes the darkness made him think thoughts which were not entirely his own.

It was only on his way home, early next morning, with AMERICAN PRESIDENT REFUSES TO SIGN SPACE ACCORD WITH CHINA, BEIJING OUTRAGED clutched almost forgotten beneath one arm, that the darkness finally gave the tramp his orders. He was passing Rue Charlemagne at the time, with its blue sign, "Roi de France, Empereur." And maybe this was what nudged the darkness into naming its price.

The tramp must kill again. And the person he should kill was the occupant of the White House, Charlemagne's heir, the new Emperor of the West.

# CHAPTER 1

## *Marrakech, Saturday 12 May*

President Gene Newman liked visiting new cities. In fact, he liked it so much he took the trouble to have one of his interns write up brief histories for each city he was about to visit. The note for Marrakech, named for *Marra Kouch,* and peopled mainly by Berbers, being North Africans in direct descent from a prehistoric Ibero-Mauretanian culture, had run to five pages and been crammed full of similar facts.

When challenged, the intern informed the President that she hadn't been allowed enough time to make her essay shorter and he should try harder with the history. She was allowed to say things like that. Ally was his only daughter.

"Enjoying yourself?" the US ambassador asked.

The correct response was *Yes*. So Ally nodded, despite midday heat which had sweat running down her spine and was already making embarrassing stains under the arms of her T-shirt.

Most of Marrakech had turned out to watch the new American President, his daughter and their bodyguards trudge across the sticky expanse of Djemaa el Fna, North Africa's most famous square. They were accompanied on this walk by a very senior minister of the Moroccan government and the US ambassador, who was doing his best to look unruffled by the jellaba-clad crowds who pushed against hastily erected barriers.

Gene Newman was here against the advice of his own staff, mostly to prove that he was not the previous incumbent, a man given to calling up generals for advice while playing *Command and Conquer* on his PSP. So said Ally, who'd got it from another intern who had it from a woman on the switchboard. It was a good story, even if untrue.

Marrakech was the reason Ally had joined him on the North African section of this trip. She'd seen the Medina featured in an old Bond film and wanted to experience the crowds and the chaos of the Old City for herself. The President could tell from Ally's expression that she'd been expecting more. That was the big problem with being fifteen, emotions showed on your face. Hypocrisy came with age, at least it did in his experience.

"Maybe that stuff was just for the film..."

"Ally?" The President bent his head.

"There were monkeys," Ally said. "And bald men juggling knives. Someone had a camel to give rides."

"We have snake charmers, medicine men and belly dancers." The Moroccan minister had to lean across Gene Newman to explain this. "And those people ringing bells in red with the huge hats are water sellers. But sometimes film companies want more."

Ally nodded, yet still managed to look doubtful.

Her black jeans and long-sleeved purple T-shirt, tied-back blonde hair and huge dark glasses to protect her eyes from the sun had been carefully chosen.

Demure enough to impress those behind the barriers who'd grown used to seeing the daughters of *nasrani* tourists wear little more than tight shorts or low-cut vests, but not so much of a compromise that her outfit played badly with hard-core liberals and redneck critics back home.

A scarf had been suggested by the Moroccans and politely rejected. No one really expecting their proposal to be any more than that, a simple suggestion made for form rather than anything else.

The man speaking to Ally Newman was a first cousin of the King, or maybe it was second. Gene Newman knew his name, he just wasn't able to pronounce it, at least not with sufficient confidence to use it socially. So he called the minister "my friend" and hoped he wasn't causing too much offence.

Although his very presence in Morocco had already caused offence to many, Gene Newman understood this. He'd read the digests and then demanded sight of the CIA originals on which the digests were based. It was touch and go whether this visit would cause more good than harm.

Gene Newman sighed.

"You also wanted to see the Barbary apes?"

His Excellency looked anxious. As if he should have realized that a thousand years of history was not enough.

"I've been here before," admitted President Newman. "After college. It's every bit as impressive as I remember... No," he said, shaking his head. "Just forgot to call my wife last night. Not clever."

"Ahh." The other man looked sympathetic. "You could do it immediately after this?"

"You're right," said Gene Newman. "And we probably do need to turn back."

This last was addressed to his daughter. A nod to the nearest Secret Service agent told the man that the President was done, while an equally quick nod to his daughter, followed by a glance at His Excellency, told Ally exactly what was expected of her.

"Thank you," she said with a smile. "It's been really interesting."

"Interesting" was a Newman family word for boring, but the minister didn't know that and this was just as well, because Ally could see from her father's frown that she should have said something different.

"I mean it," she said hastily. "It would have been neat to see monkeys but this is really, really..." Ally gestured round the vast square with its jellaba-clad crowd now spilling out onto flat roofs and filling the upper balconies of a long café behind them. "It's really something," said Ally.

"You like?" The minister sounded pleased. Although why the cousin of a king should care what a fifteen-year-old American girl thought Ally wasn't sure.

"Oh yes," she started to say. "I really—"

That was when the first bullet hit the dust beside her, and an agent she'd barely noticed before slammed Ally to the dirt, breaking a floating rib on her left side as he rolled over her, putting his bulk between the girl and the direction of the shot. "Stay down," growled his voice in Ally's ear. "There might be another."

The rifle was an old Kropatscheck rechambered for 8mm. It had seen service with the Vichy forces in North Africa and then—a decade later—been wrapped in oilcloth and stacked in the corner of a cellar for a further fifty years, half hidden and almost forgotten.

Until today.

Wiping vomit from his lips, the man who was not Jake fumbled the rifle into its component bits, cleaned the bolt with a scrap of rag held between shaky fingers, ejected seven unused bullets from the tubular magazine and haphazardly wiped down both magazine and bullets while he waited for the police to find him.

He had failed and for this he would not be forgiven.

The darkness had suggested the minaret of La Koutoubia as an ideal place from which to shoot the President, but this proved to be out of the question, because uniforms of every hue had begun locking down the area around Djemaa el Fna before the tramp even remembered where to find the rifle.

Actually, a minaret from any of the other three mosques overlooking the massive square would have done just as well, as would the roof terrace of Café Argana or even Les Terrasses de l'Alhambra, which hadn't been there when he first knew the city.

In the end he'd been reduced to climbing the scaffolding on a building site off Rue Zitoun el Oedim. "Shit choice," said the man.

And the ghost at his back had to agree.

Ridiculously beautiful with his honey-dark skin and huge eyes, the teenage boy was arguing with a bare-kneed girl on a roof that no longer existed, but which the tramp could just have seen, had the dog woman's house not fallen down in the years since he'd been away.

Neither the girl, the boy nor the man who remembered them had any doubt about the fact that the boy was losing. And even now, with the Kropatscheck reassembled in his hands and darkness still using his eyes, the bearded tramp could summon up Marzaq al-Turq's thin face and that of the red-haired girl, all rounded cheeks and down-turned mouth, which only levelled out on the rare occasions when she smiled.

"Please," Moz said, as he combed lemon-juice highlights into the hair of a girl called Malika. "This is important."

Back then, the house had belonged to the English woman and it sat on the corner of Derb Yassin and a nameless alley, in the old Jewish district, in the days when the Mellah still held more than a handful of *Yehoudia*. Once, of course, there had been nearly forty thousand Jews living in the Mellah, but the foundation of Israel and the Arab–Israeli conflicts had put an end to that.

When begging didn't work, Moz tried blackmail. "Look," he said, "you have to—"

"No," said the girl, "I don't." Her patience had gone, her voice was tight. If Moz possessed more sense he'd have paid attention to Malika's warning signs.

"You would," Moz insisted, "if—"

"If what? *I loved you?*"

Moz nodded.

"You know," Malika said, "my mother warned me about boys like you."

It was a bad joke. The woman was long dead and there *were* no other boys like Moz in Marrakech, nor girls like Malika either; that was what they told themselves. Moz and Malika were what Marrakech had for punks, a half-English waif given to wearing men's shirts instead of dresses and a half-German boy in jeans, with newly dyed black hair and shades stolen from his employer, Jake Razor.

Sat there on the roof of Dar el Beida, at a time somewhere between noon and the next call to prayer, an hour when the city panted like an old cur under the weight of its own exhaustion, and only cats and occasional hippies were stupid enough to roam the maze-like streets of the Mellah, Moz finally realized that Malika wasn't going to do what he wanted.

Beyond a certain point friendship broke. As for love, it seemed that was more fragile still.

"I can't," said Malika, as she took back her comb.

Moz poured away the saucer of lemon juice in silence.

"And I won't," she added.

"Then I will," said Moz. "And I'll do it by myself."

Their fight was about whether Malika would help him deliver a package of drugs for Caid Hammou and about the fact that Moz wanted to get his hands into Malika's pants and Malika wasn't entirely sure she'd let him.

The year was 1977.

Wreckless Eric had signed to Stiff, Television's LP *Marquee Moon* was ripping apart the souls of all who heard it, Sheena was a punk rocker. The Sex Pistols, about the only good thing to come out of the jubilee of Queen Elizabeth II, had got to number one in the UK charts and been banned from Woolworth's. Neil Young was two years away from the greatness that was *Rust Never Sleeps*.

Despite their clothes, Malika's attempts to bleach her hair and the shades hiding the tears which now hung in the corner of Moz's eyes, none of the above names meant a thing to either of them.

## CHAPTER 2

### *Marrakech, Friday 25 May*

Charlie Bilberg's brief was simple: extract the maximum amount of information with the minimum amount of Amnesty International outrage and clear the Marrakchi case off his section chief's desk before the end of the third week in July.

Charlie's section chief had not specifically tied this end date to the beginning of Ramadan, that month when all devout Moslems fast during the hours of daylight, but the young agent was bright enough to make the connection for himself. There was no point igniting an already flammable situation.

A military court had been convened and the fact that Colonel Borgenicht had yet to hear any evidence was not enough to stop Fox News and a number of the tabloids reaching their verdict in advance. The only thing seemingly still open for discussion was how the execution should be carried out.

Agent Bilberg was there to sift advance evidence.

Actually he wasn't there at all. He would be arriving in Marrakech next week and staying at a flat in Gueliz arranged by the US consul on behalf of the American ambassador.

This week he was on leave, that was what it said on all official records. Which was how Charlie Bilberg found himself sleeping at a Hivernage tourist hotel in the New Town, surrounded by package-tour Austrians who descended on the morning buffet and cleared it of cheese, sausage and sliced meat before Charlie had finished his first cup of coffee.

He'd been careful to do holiday things, spending two mornings at a café just off Djemaa el Fna, drinking mint tea at a plastic table, while hard dance from a tiny machine shop opposite competed with the café's choice of soft rock, which often switched between French, English and Arab, mostly in the same song.

And both times he'd paid for his mint tea with a twenty-dirham note, one black with grease and smelling of ginger and cinnamon from the thousands of previous owners who'd eaten only with three fingers and their thumb.

As night fell he'd wandered the oily smoke of Djemaa el Fna's famous barbeques and watched belly dancers, covered from head to toe in thick white dresses which were sewn with golden chains that perfectly accentuated the fullness of their breasts and the divide of their buttocks.

A man in a loose jellaba had grabbed his own balls and jiggled them up and down in Charlie Bilberg's direction as Charlie turned away from the belly dancers, and he still didn't know if this was a deadly insult or an offer to come back to his hotel in Hivernage.

And in between all this, Agent Bilberg had sat at a desk in his first-floor room and listened to the recording of an interrogation which was every bit as unhelpful as he'd been led to believe.

* * *

"Okay," said a French-sounding voice. "When did this start?"

"Yesterday morning, about five."

The man answering wasn't CIA. An interrogator trained at Langley would have said "O five hundred." The agent listening to the recording while simultaneously skimming a transcript to check its accuracy was glad of that. A few of the things the voice had been saying made Charlie very nervous indeed.

On a pad in front of him sat his notes. Little more than a handful of words and none of these rang any bells. A folder from the office stood open next to the notepad. The only memo inside announced that the CIA, the FBI and the NSA had no record of this man's fingerprints but that searches at a local level were being instigated. Interpol had also been alerted, a P13 going out to all European forces.

The hotel room was larger than Charlie had expected, with a bathroom off to one side, a simple desk in the main room and a television that managed to get half a dozen channels, most of them in Arabic.

"And what happened at five?" The French accent probably counted for little. Almost every doctor who spoke English in North Africa spoke it with a French accent, such were the accidents of history.

"Oh," said the American voice. "We injected another thirty milligrams of psilocybin…"

Downing his fifth coffee of the morning, Charlie Bilberg skimmed the next fifteen pages of transcript, barely reading the medical examination and the part where the doctor gave her permission for "Prisoner Zero's" interrogation to continue. (So someone at the Langley press office had thoughtfully labelled their captive. Charlie had his own views about giving catchy labels to criminals. As far as he was concerned it only encouraged them.)

Charlie jumped the recorder forward to the last intelligible block of answers and lit his first cigarette of the day, drawing smoke into his lungs.

"Who helped you?"

"Malika."

"Who's Malika?"

"Someone Moz knew."

Both names were currently being fed into the NSA system. If this produced no leads then the names would be passed to the

European database in Brussels. Charlie was in favour of releasing them now at local level, but this had been overruled by Paula Zarte herself, everybody's new boss at Langley.

Two odd numbers added together always made an even. Two evens added together never made an odd. If a number is divisible by eleven the sum of its alternate digits is always equal, say 121 (apart from when zero messed up the sequence). It was irrelevant if the first 119 decimal places of vacuum energy exactly cancelled because it was what happened with the 120th that mattered...

There was no end to the information that Prisoner Zero apparently wanted to share. Speed-dialling a contact he'd been given at the NSA, Charlie zoned out a block of pure cracker-box maths while listening to his cell phone go unanswered.

"Chosen of what?" said a voice, when Charlie tuned in again.

"Of heaven..."

A sound, like someone sighing. "And what exactly is that supposed to mean?"

The silence which followed was broken by the flick of a lighter, the old-fashioned kind, and an animal-like howl.

"Well?"

"Incomprehensible" read an anonymous, hand-scrawled note next to the relevant section of transcript. Not that Charlie Bilberg needed this. The exact time of each statement was printed in the margin. A gap of eighteen minutes occurred between that question and its answer. The hand-scrawled note recorded that the prisoner was conscious during this entire period and was not undergoing any additional form of heavy questioning.

The time track was designed to make sure any taped confession would stand up in court. The Agency could do without some judge throwing out key evidence on the basis that most of it was cut and paste.

Personally, Charlie thought that using a time track was an excellent idea, although he was in a minority. He wasn't hopelessly naïve, however. Agent Bilberg had a good idea of exactly what had been done to Prisoner Zero before the man arrived at a point where he was prepared to make his statement.

Not all of it involved violence.

Running back, Charlie listened carefully, one hand against his ear to cut out noise from the room's overhead air-conditioning. "Chosen of heaven," that was definitely what the prisoner said.

On his wall behind the dressing table was a socket labelled

"5-star hotelNet," so he plugged in his Sony Vaio and waited for the little laptop to recognize the connection, then he fed in his room number and Amex details. The price was a hundred dirham a day, about ten dollars.

Google gave him a Baptist site, chapter five of *Ivanhoe* by Walter Scott, some mediocre poetry, a ministry dedicated to the New Holy Cross of the Rosy Dawn and a handful of references to assorted verses from the Old Testament, none of which looked likely.

Shutting down his laptop, Charlie went back to the recording, matching what was said word-for-word against the transcript in front of him.

"Like Equal of Heaven, only that's the monkey..." The answer, like the question, was in English, its slurring most probably explained by the medical prescriptions stapled to the back of the transcript.

Three hallucinogens, two sedatives and a painkiller mostly prescribed in childbirth but also used for lowering inhibitions. One of the sedatives and all of the hallucinogens were illegal in the US, which was fine because this wasn't the US and the various doctors who'd signed the prescriptions were not American. Charlie Bilberg had been careful to check.

"What makes you Chosen?"

"I'm not..."

"You just said you were."

The reply, when it came, was too muffled to make out, the transcript using a row of Xs to show that this line of dialogue was beyond deciphering.

"This is pointless," said a voice Charlie hadn't heard before. "The man barely knows what he's saying."

"More chance of getting the truth."

A snort, but the voice fell silent as the first man went back to his questions. "This group of yours, who leads them?"

"Group?"

"Who leads the Chosen of Heaven?" The way the interrogator snarled this question made clear his belief that CoH were terrorists on a level with al Qaeda, the Baathist Party or the Taliban. "Well?"

"Only one person is chosen," said Prisoner Zero. "And only the darkness knows how he is selected."

The silence which followed this made clear that it was not the answer the interrogator had wanted or been expecting.

## CHAPTER 3

## *Marrakech, Summer 1969*

The summer Moz turned seven a stray word crawled into his ear and ate its way to his brain, where it set up a nest that spawned questions, which tunnelled into the jellied ignorance inside his head, changing the way he thought and saw and smelt things.

He began to see patterns behind the patterns to be found in *zellije* work on the walls of mosques and public fountains. Certain tile formations repeated and mirrored themselves in ways people did not at first realize. A beating from an imam taught the one-armed boy that not everyone wished to have this general ignorance pointed out, so he learnt to lie.

From a scrap of guidebook found behind a bush on the edge of Jardin Aguedal he learnt that his home was seventeen hundred feet above sea level and forty miles from the High Atlas, whose peaks rose another twelve thousand feet. Eight miles of wall circled the Red City, broken by twelve great gates, each *bab* giving its name to a *quartier* of Marrakech. The circling wall was made of *pisé,* mud mixed with lime and straw. Moz wasn't too sure what miles and feet were, so he added this to his list of questions that needed answering.

Shit smeared the page, but Moz didn't mind. Having scraped the square of paper clean, he washed it in a fountain and pegged it on his mother's clothes line to dry in the sun. These days it lived in a small cardboard box under his bed along with three Spanish coins, a plastic Biro that no longer worked and an Opinel knife with a broken blade.

No one he asked knew how long a mile was.

Moz forgot to do the jobs his mother gave him and cared so little that he barely noticed her irritation turn from anger to worry. He ate less, slept less and tasted nothing. Eventually he ran out of people to ask. That was when he realized his world was really quite small.

It was Sidi ould Kasim, the old army corporal who lived on the ground floor, who told Moz he'd been infected. Sat on his wooden stool outside the tiny house in Derb Yassin on the edge of the old

Jewish quarter, he scowled at the one-armed child and sipped at a tea glass which contained three mint leaves floating in neat *marc*, brandy distilled from little more than pips and skin. Everyone in the Mellah knew what his glass contained but no one mentioned it. The Corporal's temper saw to that.

Corporal ould Kasim, Malika, Moz's mother and Moz lived in the same narrow house, where the dark alley of Derb Yassin intersected with an even tighter passage, one too decrepit and dark to merit a name or even appear on a map. The Corporal and his daughter occupied the downstairs while Moz and his mother occupied both of the rooms upstairs and everyone shared the roof as somewhere to dry washing or store furniture so worthless as to be unsellable.

"I said," ould Kasim demanded, "who told you about miles anyway?"

No one told me, Moz wanted to say. I discovered them for myself from a *nasrani*'s shit scraper, when I was meant to be collecting *skhina*.

*Skhina* were the pots of eggs, meat and vegetables which got baked every Friday for the *Yehoudia* still living in the Mellah. Moz worked odd days for Maallan Mohammed, a master baker who owned the nearest bread oven and the maallan charged double for Jews.

This was not a reply Moz could give and besides, feet and miles were just unspecified measurements he'd stumbled over and kept stumbling, as Moz always did until he found his answers.

"Are you deaf as well as stupid?"

There were some who said ould Kasim was a police informer and a few who believed he was nosy by instinct. Most just thought he'd never recovered from his wife catching a fever. Because Leila was dead, when something went wrong he hit his daughter instead.

"He's not stupid," Moz's mother said, coming out to collect her son from where he stood in the street, too afraid to walk past the old Corporal. "He just sees things we don't..."

Sidi ould Kasim could not understand why Moz's mother would not marry him. She was foreign, ill and poor, a German woman who no longer even wrote to her family. Whereas he had a pension from Paris, a city he'd help liberate, and owned a *Croix de Guerre* as proof. It was a small pension by French standards but more than enough to keep a man living in this city. Certainly enough to ensure that any woman he married would never need to work again.

All the same, Dido kept refusing and the old man with his stool, filthy jellaba and frayed boots took her refusals badly. He blamed Moz and in this ould Kasim was right. If not for her son Dido would probably have married the Corporal to get away from what her life had become.

"All he does is dream," Sidi ould Kasim told the woman. "Dream stupid dreams and make up lies."

Moz shook his head.

"And what's that he's got now?"

"Just a magazine," Moz protested. "I found it."

"American muck," the Corporal said crossly. "Soon you won't be any use at all." Taking the magazine from Moz's hand, he opened it at random. A half-naked negro with her brat, a man wearing a glass helmet and a boy holding a Molotov cocktail.

"You shouldn't let him read this," he told Dido, tearing that week's issue of *Time* in two. And so Moz missed knowing that Apollo had reached the moon and famine had killed thousands in Biafra while violence stalked the slums of Northern Ireland.

Later, when his mother had gone out to work and ould Kasim was back on his stool, watching boys scrap and small girls hurry home with wild snails for that evening's soup, Moz clambered over the edge of the roof, dropped onto a pile of crates stacked against the side of their house and jumped from here to the ground. All this he did one-handed.

Most of his magazine was gone, used to set a fire in the grate of ould Kasim's kitchen, but what little was left Moz took to a bench in the Jardin Aguedal, working meaning from the letters by the light of a dying sun.

From where he sat, Moz could see a stork's nest set like a turret on the city walls. The comforting smell of warm dung rose from two donkeys tethered under a tree behind him. There were other smells warming the air, charcoal from a bread oven and grilled meat, goat probably. He could almost taste the greasy smoke as it drifted from a house on the other side of the gate.

And then Moz put his hunger aside and turned to the scraps of magazine. There was a wall in China so big it could be seen from space. This wall was in urgent need of repair. Solid objects were not really solid but made from vibrations. Clever people believed more worlds than one might exist. And one day machines might be smarter than humans (although the person writing said this was unlikely).

Even after he'd laboriously spelt words out one letter at a time, saying them aloud to the darkening sky, many remained hard, but their meaning could sometimes be guessed from simpler words on either side.

And so the parasite entered his brain and changed everything. It changed how Moz saw life now that he knew nothing was as it seemed and the wall on which the storks nested, his roof and the scraps of torn magazine in his hand were made of spaces between vibrations which moved around each other, attracting and repelling.

This knowledge ate out the certainties of his life and kept eating until it changed the way things felt beneath his hand. Somehow everything in the Mellah became less solid and more ghostlike than it had been before.

He talked to a Sufi at the mosque near Dar si Said, where Rue Zitoun el Jedid met an alley that cut through to Rue Zitoun el Kedim. It was a small mosque and not as important as La Koutoubia or the mosque in Quartier Berima, which was nearer but also opposite the Royal Palace.

The Sufi was one of a circle of old men who sat cross-legged on a bench outside, talking quietly among themselves. It took Moz three weeks to summon the courage to approach the man because Hajj Rahman was the oldest and wisest of those who met each day.

Like Marrakech's famous red walls, La Koutoubia and many of the city's older buildings, the sides of the little mosque were pocked with square holes left by wooden scaffolding from when it was built many years before. The city's pigeons and doves had been squatting in them ever since.

"Please . . ." Moz said.

The Sufi looked up to see a small boy with an empty sleeve pinned crudely to the front of his jellaba. "What is it?" he demanded.

The one-armed boy shuffled his feet and tugged at the neck of a threadbare gown. He had flour on his fingers and a chunk of bread bulged from his pocket, neither of which was appropriate for the place in which he found himself. In between shuffling his feet and glancing at the Sufi, the boy seemed to be matching pigeons to their holes in the wall.

"Are you in trouble?" Boys were sent to him for punishment, mostly by mothers who believed he could change things he could not. "Well?" demanded the Sufi.

"No more than usual..."

Hajj Rahman smiled, examining the boy properly for the first time. His hair was dark blond, which was not unusual in the Atlas. He had the sallow skin of a Berber and cheekbones to match, but his eyes were almost black. The Sufi could not remember having seen him before.

"What's your name?"

"Turq."

The old man shook his head. "Your name," he said, "not where your father comes from."

"That's what people call me," the boy answered, his voice apologetic.

"And your father," the Sufi asked, "does he call you Turk?"

"No," said Moz, "he left."

"Your mother then." For a second the man looked thoughtful. "You do have a mother?"

Moz nodded. "She calls me Moz."

"Short for what?"

"I don't know," said the boy. "She's German," he added, as if one might explain the other.

"And your father was Turkish." Hajj Rahman nodded to himself as everything fell into place. He knew of this boy, whose mother sold *majoun,* cakes of marijuana, to foreigners on Djemaa el Fna and sometimes went to their beds.

"Tell me why you're here," said the Sufi, but Moz just stood there. A couple of times his mouth opened and then he dropped his eyes and turned away.

"I said, tell me."

"It was a stupid question," said Moz. "I'm sorry."

"Let me be the judge," ordered the Sufi.

There are some who believe there are no stupid or unnecessary questions. Hajj Rahman was not one of those. Almost every major question which could be asked had already been answered, either in the Holy Qur'an or the Hadith, the sayings and case law of Islamic wisdom or by the Sufi masters.

"I've been trying to find out about things."

"Ah," said the man, "I see..." Tugging at his beard, Hajj Rahman adjusted his jellaba until he could sit more comfortably. "What things?"

The Sufi treated the boy's question with great dignity. A far greater dignity than he would have shown to someone twice the boy's age.

Moz gestured to the crowded street and to those wheeling carts or riding past on tiny motorbikes or dodging this traffic, then he included himself and the old man with the white beard.

"Ah." Hajj Rahman smiled. "You wish to know about God."

"No," said Moz, as politely as he could. "Mostly I want to know about atoms and how long a mile is."

"Whatever they are," said Hajj Rahman, "the one made the other." At the sight of the boy's puzzled frown, the old man gestured that Moz should join him on the bench.

This the boy did, awkwardly.

"There are ninety-nine names of God," explained the Sufi. "The Merciful, the Subtle, the Apparent... These are written. Without knowing it, we all search for the Hundredth Name."

Moz didn't mean to be rude. He was just too surprised to remember to be polite, even to a hajj. "Says who?" he asked.

"It's agreed," said the Sufi. "And everyone is looking, including you."

Glancing at the boy, he saw matted hair and broken nails, fingers grimed with dirt and flour and an oversized jellaba that was filthier still. And then he looked beneath this and saw hunger, of a kind not fed by food.

"This word," said Moz.

"Which one?"

"The name."

"Who said it was a word?" Hajj Rahman asked.

"You did."

"No," said the Sufi. "That's not what I said at all. It could be a sunset or a perfect number. A pattern of tiles so beautiful that suicides decide to live. Not having found it, how can anyone know what this name might be?"

"It could be a *number*?"

"Of course," said the Sufi. "It could also be a perfect note, a falling leaf. There are seventy-two paths open to humanity." He gestured to the mosque beside them. "Beauty is only one of them... You know what writing is?"

Moz scowled. Of course he knew.

"Everything is written," said the Sufi.

If all things were written, then... "I don't understand," said Moz, "everything is decided in advance?"

"No." The Sufi shook his head. "*Everything* is written. All paths and all possibilities, but you should not worry yourself about this." He smiled at the boy, face thoughtful. "In fact," he said, "many people do not worry about such things at all."

It was only after Moz had thanked the Sufi and left that he realized he still didn't know the length of a mile.

## CHAPTER 4

### *Marrakech, Thursday 7 June*

Prisoner Zero had been tried in his absence. The blond CIA man had been careful to explain that international law allowed this to happen. He'd been tried by a military commission, found guilty and condemned to death, which translated as five thousand milligrams of penthanol, followed by a hundred milligrams of pancuronium bromide.

In handing him over, the Moroccan government was merely meeting its legal obligations. A military commission had tried him because his attack on the President was deemed an act of war. And his confession had been accepted as sufficient proof of guilt.

Prisoner Zero knew this. It had already been explained to him by an official from the Interior Ministry, a fat Souari in a crumpled suit who ended his brief visit by asking if Prisoner Zero wished to appeal directly to the King. (On the birth of his son in 2003, Hassan VI had freed 9,459 prisoners and reduced the sentences of another 38,599.)

Taking Prisoner Zero's silence as a negative, the official breathed a sigh of relief, introduced the man beside him as an American agent and hammered on the door, demanding that the guard outside let him out of the cell. He didn't bother to say goodbye to Agent Bilberg or Charlie's new prisoner.

Only when the official was gone did Charlie Bilberg introduce himself. The suit Charlie wore was charcoal, but cut from summerweight Italian wool, and his white shirt had single cuffs which displayed enamel Langley cufflinks. He looked, he hoped, as the new breed of CIA operative was meant to look.

"Charles Bilberg," Charlie said, his voice tinged with old Boston. "I'll be going with you to the airfield." If he was surprised that the prisoner he'd come to collect was naked and shackled by a length of chain he didn't let it show.

Staying in the fetid cell long enough to explain to Prisoner Zero that he was about to be moved, such explanations being part of Langley's latest policy, Charlie retreated to the governor's office and suggested Prisoner Zero be hosed down and found an old jellaba, shoes and dark glasses. Only then would he be relieving the governor of his burden.

So now Charlie sat on the rear seat of a battered Peugeot 306, seven cars back from a prison van with blackened windows, while a silent Moroccan police officer hunched behind the *petite taxi*'s steering wheel and cast glances at Prisoner Zero in the driver's mirror.

"It's fine," said Charlie, tugging at the handcuffs which attached the prisoner to his left wrist. "Stop worrying."

Getting this job was a good sign. It showed the Agency had faith in his initiative and work skills. The fact Marrakech was a Berber city and he was the only person in the section to speak rudimentary Chleuh, the side effect of a not-so-long-gone summer spent hiking in the High Atlas, was purely coincidental. Charlie Bilberg knew this, he'd been told so by his section head.

Charlie was hot, the *petite taxi* lacked anything as sophisticated as air-conditioning, his summer-weight suit was beginning to look as if he'd slept in it and the edginess of the small Moroccan at the wheel was making him nervous. "Look," said Charlie, turning to the prisoner shackled to his wrist. "Maybe we can do a deal."

Since Prisoner Zero had already been condemned to death, this seemed less than likely. Anyway, the prisoner was far too busy concentrating on a Yamaha 125 stalled in the traffic to pay the agent's words much attention.

He'd had a dirt bike very like that when he was a kid. An older model, obviously, but not that much older. It seemed there were still sidewalk mechanics in Avenue Houman el Fetouaki who could machine replacement parts for cars and motorbikes most people in the West had forgotten even existed.

What made this bike interesting was its rider, a boy in a black leather jacket and open-faced Shoei despite the blistering heat and the fact that no one, but no one, in Marrakech ever bothered with helmets or protective clothing.

The Yamaha was a two-stroke, single cylinder. One of those sit-up-and-beg bikes with long forks and all-terrain tyres, its exhaust tucked beneath the saddle. Originally shipped as 125cc, some kid from the tanneries had obviously rebored the pot and stripped off the mudguards.

So now, on a good day, the bike whined like a wounded wasp and spat oily smoke. Unfortunately it also overheated, choked and died on a regular basis. Which was how a suicide bomber with enough ex-Soviet C4 wrapped round his waist to take out an armoured van found himself on the approach to a roundabout, frantically trying to kick start a dead engine as his target drove past, police bikes to the front and rear.

"You listening?" Charlie Bilberg said, glancing at his prisoner. Only Prisoner Zero just kept staring after the rider now disappearing behind them.

"Guess not," said the man.

Up ahead the crawling prison van was being beaten with fists like some recalcitrant donkey. A crowd hammered against its slit windows and twisted at the handles on its rear doors, the noise of their fury lost beneath the frustrated howl of sirens from stalled police bikes and the low thud of a helicopter overhead.

"Aren't your people going to do anything about that?"

Charlie didn't know the name of the driver who glanced back at this question and smiled, but he knew the man's rank and it was high enough to have Charlie worried. Brigadiers made for unusual chauffeurs, even at such unusual times.

"Relax," said the small man. "This is for show only. I have my own men in the crowd."

"Where?" Charlie demanded.

The Brigadier grinned. "Who do you think's hammering on that van?" They were now three cars back from the decoy, which actually translated as them, plus another two completely innocent *petite taxis,* three donkeys and at least five mopeds, a cheap scooter and three cycles: because that was how most people in this overhot and dusty city seemed to travel, on foot or on two wheels. Charlie Bilberg was still trying to work out if private cars were banned inside the walls of the Medina or if no one could afford them.

All he'd seen were *grande taxis,* which went everywhere, *petite taxis* that seemed to be local, small flatbed trucks grafted to scooters and more donkeys and mopeds than he knew existed.

Colonel Borgenicht's plan, created in conjunction with the Brigadier, with Charlie Bilberg assisting, was that the decoy took the flak should there be an angry crowd, while an AH-64 overhead ostensibly kept an eye on the black van but actually protected the *petite taxi* in which the man was held.

Charlie still found it hard to think of the silent figure shackled to his ankle as Prisoner Zero, although this was how news stations across the world were now referring to him, so Charlie thought of him as "him." The man who slotted a fifty-year-old bullet into a hundred-year-old rifle and tried to put a quarter-ounce of copper-jacked lead through the head of the President of the United States over a distance that even a fully trained sniper would have found near impossible.

There had been incumbents of the White House who Charlie Bilberg could understand complete strangers wanting to kill, some of them quite recent, but Gene Newman was different. For a start, this President was honest, intelligent and able to walk, chew gum and talk foreign policy at the same time.

Add a PhD in physics and an MBA from some fancy economics school in London and three languages, two of them fluent, and the guy was a dream ticket. So why, given that President Newman was currently demanding that Tel Aviv get its tanks off the new Palestinian premier's lawn, should some deadbeat Arab want him dead?

Charlie Bilberg was damned if he knew.

"If this gets ugly, you die," said Charlie, wincing at the banality of his words. It was catching, talking like this. A fact his girlfriend had taken to pointing out on a slightly too regular basis.

A new-issue Colt automatic lay in Charlie's lap, its make and model unrecognized by the Brigadier and completely unknown to Prisoner Zero, who sat blank eyed, watching jellaba-clad boys run towards the van up ahead. A split to his lip had opened again, where he'd worried an old scab with his teeth, and dark blood now trickled into his beard.

"You got that?"

"Yes," said the Brigadier, "he's got that. And he's not going to answer, believe me. If he was going to say anything useful he'd have said it already. Now put the gun away before someone sees it."

Charlie Bilberg sighed. A Pentagon official was on record as insisting the prisoner spoke English, French and Berber, as well as Arabic, but so far there was no sign that this shell of a man retained the ability to speak any languages at all.

Mind you, the same Pentagon official also had him down as a brilliant strategist, terrorist banker and crack shot. Slightly begging the question why, if he was so brilliant, he'd tried to shoot the President from too far away with a broken-down antique.

"We could still cut a deal, you know," said Charlie. "You give us the Chosen of Heaven network and the CIA will do what it can do to get your sentence commuted. Maybe you could serve your time here, in Morocco."

"Agent Bilberg..."

The gaze of the man in front flicked towards the driving mirror, frown lines blossoming around his dark eyes. Silence was in order and no one was to speak, behave oddly or draw attention to themselves. All this had already been agreed. In fact, Rabat had insisted on it.

But escorting Prisoner Zero from a Marrakech jail to an already secured landing site beyond Jardin Aguedal, while the van headed for a duplicate site in the huge groves of Oliveraie de Bab Jedid, was Charlie's first really big job. Getting information on the network which ran Prisoner Zero would make Charlie with the Agency for life.

"Talk to me," Charlie insisted, ignoring the scowl in the mirror. "Let's see if we can't work something out..." Beside him the prisoner nodded, the movement so slight as to be instinctive. And just as Charlie got ready to feel elated, he realized that Prisoner Zero was actually nodding to a small dirt bike which drew alongside and then surged past the *petite taxis* in a trail of oily smoke, horn blasting.

Weaving round a donkey cart, the rider dodged between a *grande taxi* and a younger boy on a bike, slid himself between two old men frozen in the act of trying to cross the road, accelerating right up to the point he slammed his bike straight into the back of the prison van.

Thirty-two pounds of Soviet C4 ripped apart the bike, finishing off not just its thirteen-year-old rider but a dozen of those who'd been hammering angrily on the sides and rear of the van.

The van itself was flipped over and tossed onto a police outrider, crushing man and bike utterly. Unable to escape from his buckled cab, the van's driver burned up in front of a suddenly frozen crowd. Those in the back were already dead, flame withering their corpses as surely as it stripped paint from the twisted carcass of the prison van.

"*Merde,*" said the Brigadier.

Charlie glanced from the burning van to his driver, then realized the Brigadier was actually watching vapour trails rip towards the Apache helicopter overhead. The Peugeot's roof stopped Charlie seeing which one connected with the AH-64's tail but he felt the impact, the whole of the Medina felt the impact, and then the combat helicopter was tumbling over itself on the way down.

Given that the Apache had been hovering almost directly over the prison van, it was perhaps inevitable that it should hit one of the palm trees lining the route, about a hundred paces from the site of the bomb.

"We leave," said the Brigadier, and spun his wheel, the *petite taxi* splintering a donkey cart as the Peugeot slammed into reverse, executed a quick turn and raced away from the screaming crowd. A loud thud said that a pedestrian hadn't got out of the way in time. After that, everyone stepped well back.

"Where are you taking us?"

"Back to the prison."

"No." Charlie Bilberg was adamant. "We take him to the landing site. The area's already secure. There's a 'copter waiting."

"If that's what you want." The Brigadier had just seen a $17.5 million AH-64 attack helicopter brought down by a handful of ex-Soviet ground-to-airs. If the young CIA man couldn't see the flaw in his own logic, then too bad. Anything that got Prisoner Zero out of Morocco was fine with the Moroccan authorities.

Plus, and this was what mattered, anyone watching would believe Prisoner Zero dead, ripped apart by the bomb, and within an hour most of the world would have joined them.

All the Brigadier had to do was drive his vehicle into the Medina, out through the gate at Bab Agnaou, run it round a short section of Marrakech's famous red walls and drive calmly to the Jardin Aguedal.

"Okay," he said. "Let's do it your way."

Caid Hammou flicked shut his Nokia and frowned. What the immaculately suited old man wanted to do was stand up, stamp over to a small group eyeing him anxiously through the doorway of his shop and slap them silly for unbelievable stupidity. Instead he sipped slowly at a glass of mint tea and smiled at a tourist couple sitting opposite, revealing one gold tooth.

The English were pink and wide eyed. Slightly anxious to find themselves sat on a bench discussing prices when they'd only intended to browse.

"My wife," said Hammou, putting down his cell phone, "always wants to talk. Now. You like this one? Very beautiful. Made in Switzerland. It says so on the back." The replica Rolex was assembled in mainland China, had a dial printed directly onto white metal and used a cheap quartz movement held in place by a white plastic ring.

Hammou watched the Englishman scowl, then peer at a narrow second hand which jerked forward, second by second, instead of sweeping cleanly as it would if the watch were really automatic.

"That's quartz," the Englishman said.

"Or maybe this?" said Hammou smoothly, pulling out a watch at random to find himself holding a garish copy of a small Cartier dress watch, the bezel decorated with twelve "diamonds" too cheap even to be cubic zircon. "For your beautiful wife... Buy two watches and I can give you a better price."

Sipping again at his tea, which he'd sweetened with a block of sugar the size of his thumb, the elderly man smiled as the Englishwoman instinctively sipped at her own and winced at its bitterness. Somehow tourists never seemed to understand that mint tea was meant to be sweet and sticky.

"You like this?"

Hammou watched the man discard the fake Cartier without a second glance and turn over the Rolex to examine a cheap crown stamped into the clip of its metal strap. He was shaking his head.

"I tell you what," Hammou said, "for you I get something better." He waved in the general direction of the group outside. "My cousins. You have a look round here, while I find you something special. It's all right, I trust you. But if someone else comes in, you make sure you make a sale, okay?"

The English couple laughed dutifully and Hammou let himself out, heading straight for a shop across the passageway. As if on cue, those waiting outside followed him in.

"Okay," Hammou said, "where is he?"

"In a *petite taxi* headed towards the gardens."

"So why haven't you got him?"

"He's got company."

"The blond American." Hammou nodded like this was obvious. "We expected that," he said. "I still don't see the problem."

"Abbas." The boy who spoke was thin-faced, his teeth bad and his gaze turned inwards to something dark and lonely. The boy on the bike was his brother, both boys from a family that owed Caid Hammou a serious and hitherto unpayable debt. Glancing uncertainly towards a thickset, rather dapper middle-aged man, he waited for the man to expand on this explanation.

"Brigadier Abbas is driving the taxi himself," said Hammou's nephew. "We didn't know what to—"

"Okay," Hammou said, voice tight. "I understand." He wanted to add, *let me think,* but to do so would reveal weakness. So instead he told the youngest to make mint tea and began to sort through a tray of Hong Kong replicas, all of them stamped "Swiss Made."

The downing of the helicopter would result in arrests, beatings and probably swift and violent bouts of illegal, unauthorized torture. America would demand results, and even without their demands Sécurité would rip apart the Medina if that was what it took to find answers. This was to be expected.

To kill any member of Sécurité was something else again. Direct challenges were answered by direct action, this was the North African way. And killing the city's Head of Sécurité, to target the Brigadier, was asking for Marrakech to be locked down. It had happened before.

Glancing up from the tray, Hammou realized they were all watching him, their faces expectant but less worried than earlier. His mere presence absolved them of responsibility for what came next.

The choice was his, such as it was . . .

"This one is automatic," said Caid Hammou. "Look, you can see inside." The old man, who had no need to work in any shop, even one of his own, handed over a replica of a Patek Philippe. The crocodile strap was actually plastic and the view glass at the back was Perspex, but through it could be seen a working mechanism.

"You move it from side to side," Hammou said, matching a gesture to his words, "and the watch winds itself, no batteries needed. And it keeps perfect time. Well . . ." Hammou paused, as if to think about that. "Almost perfect," he amended. "Maybe you need to adjust it by a few seconds every week or so."

He smiled and nodded as the Englishman examined the dial and then turned the watch over to look at the tiny gilt hairspring, beating like a heart. "Is good, no?"

The man nodded and then the bargaining began, but not before Hammou called to a passing boy for another tray of mint tea.

"Show them your pass," suggested Charlie Bilberg and Brigadier Abbas tried not to sigh. He knew Langley liked the fresh-faced look but still wished the CIA would stop recruiting children.

"If I show them my pass," he said heavily, "then they'll know we're not really a *petite taxi*... And so will everyone else." His nod took in those crowding a sidewalk, itself something of a novelty in that part of the Medina, where many streets were surfaced with little more than cracked blacktop over beaten earth and passing taxis or donkey carts forced those on foot to retreat into doorways rather than get crushed against crumbling walls.

"Take a look," the Brigadier suggested.

Agent Bilberg did. Seeing old men in jellabas and young men in T-shirts, teenage girls with their hair hidden beneath scarves and a few, better dressed, with their hair tied back and gazes defiantly bare. Small boys stood in a huddle around a slightly larger boy who clutched a radio.

"What do you notice?"

"The lack of small girls...?"

The Brigadier sucked his teeth. Maybe the CIA man was not as stupid as he'd thought. "You're right," he said, "they're at home helping, but that wasn't what I meant. What else?"

Scanning the crowd waiting to pass through a roadblock, Charlie Bilberg thought about it. He'd been trained to look for anxiety and for a certain tightness around the eyes or studied blankness of expression. An otherness, but no one looked out of place. There were a few elderly men standing alone, but none who looked as if he were an outsider to himself or this society.

"Nothing," he told the Brigadier, when the silence stretched too thin. And that was the truth. Charlie Bilberg could see nothing remotely out of the ordinary. It was like finding himself in a killing house where every pop-up was civilian.

"Exactly," said the Brigadier. "Ninety-five per cent of people in Marrakech are happy with the way things are run. Well, their bosses, heads of family and caids are happy, which is the same. The other five per cent look like everyone else . . . We wait in this queue."

The roadblock was perfunctory. From the top of Bab er Robb a single stork watched two uniforms on the road below halt cars and demand papers. When the taxi containing Prisoner Zero drew close, Charlie Bilberg realized the men weren't even Sécurité. They were traffic cops or maybe gendarmes, bussed in from outside, something local.

A quick glance assessed the suited foreigner, the Arab driver at the wheel and the silent man with a greying beard, a copy of that week's *Al Sahifa* open on his lap. Only the driver got asked for his papers, which he gave willingly and took back with a respectful nod.

According to these he was a taxi driver called Hamid, who had a room in a house near Place du Moukef on the other side of the Medina.

"Okay."

Slipping the Peugeot into gear, Brigadier Abbas passed through the Agnaou Gate and out of the Old City. A long way behind him a plume of grey still billowed into the hot summer sky and sirens still sounded, though it was hard to tell if these were ambulances or police cars. Maybe they were both.

"Try the radio," Charlie Bilberg suggested.

The death toll was currently thirty-one, including the outrider on the leading police bike and the three occupants of the prison van, two guards and Prisoner Zero. That Prisoner Zero was dead the news flash took for granted.

"Interesting," Charlie Bilberg said.

"Not really." The Brigadier's voice was dismissive, his demand for silence either forgotten or no longer relevant. Steering his vehicle between the edge of the road and a donkey cart turning right, he headed around the walls towards a distant grove of palms and the beginning of a track.

Ornamental shrubs lined both sides of the track, but these were brown and shrunken, victims of a drought that had lasted for five years.

"That's an official station," the Brigadier explained. "It says what we need it to say. You want to find out what's really happening, try this . . ." Spinning the dial, he located a burst of something hard-edged and thrashy, in pointed contrast to the *al-Ala* featured on the previous channel. Calculator-cheap beeps took over when the Rai ended, signifying a news flash.

Brigadier Abbas knew the young CIA agent spoke little Arabic but still made the man wait for a translation until the DJ signed off, frenzied words giving way to a thrash of Casablanca nuRai. Even from his seat in the back, Charlie Bilberg could tell that the Brigadier was amused about something.

"What?" he demanded.

"The bomb," said Brigadier Abbas. "You ordered it."

"I ordered—"

"The CIA."

"Believe me," said Charlie Bilberg, "we don't do stuff like that. Not anymore."

"Of course you don't," Brigadier Abbas said smoothly. "It seems you persuaded an elite force from Israeli intelligence to do it for you." The Brigadier's laugh was as sharp as a dog's bark. "This is good," he added, "very good."

"What's good about it?"

"First, it's absurd, so we can dismiss it easily. And second..." A jerk of the Brigadier's head indicated Prisoner Zero sitting silently behind him. "This one is already dead, think about that. No trial, no fuss, no media. You just take him somewhere and extract every last piece of information. With pliers if necessary, and if you don't have the stomach I know people who do."

For a second, as the Brigadier slowed at the sight of a roadblock up ahead, he considered suggesting that he join Agent Bilberg in the helicopter, then the Brigadier had a better idea.

"Leave him with me," he said. "We'll share anything he knows. Who'd object?"

"My bosses," said Charlie Bilberg, shaking his head. "They know he wasn't in that van for a start." And then the agent's eyes flicked to the soldier approaching their car and the pump-action shotgun in his hand.

"Hey," Charlie said. "Those aren't—"

He was right. They weren't.

Exploding glass sandblasted flesh from the Brigadier's face. And by the time Agent Bilberg understood he too had been hit by flying glass, one of the Brigadier's eyes was sliding like broken yolk from beneath his fingers.

The injured Brigadier tried to say something but the windscreen had pierced his throat and the words were drowned beneath a froth of blood.

Charlie's own fingers came away red and sticky. His eyes were both there but his fingers could touch tongue where they should have found cheek. When he checked his prisoner he found the man curled beside him on the seat.

*"Put down your gun."*

The words were aimed at Agent Bilberg, who suddenly realized he'd picked up his own Colt and was now holding it to Prisoner Zero's head.

I don't think so.

That was what Charlie tried to say. He wasn't sure how much of it the man in the expensive suit with the swept-back hair and dark glasses actually understood. Keeping his gun firmly in place, the young CIA man reached into his jacket and retrieved a tiny cell phone, which he flicked open, speed-dialling a number. The machine stayed dead.

Charlie Bilberg glanced towards his Siemens and tried again, checking from the corner of his eye that he'd punched the right button. When nothing happened he tried it on vocal, his broken voice ordering it to dial seven.

Again nothing.

Agent Bilberg was still trying to work out what he was doing wrong when the rear door yanked open and Caid Hammou's nephew Hassan leant across Prisoner Zero and took the gun from Charlie's right hand. Two of the agent's fingers broke as the man twisted the Colt from his grasp.

The lock knife in Hassan's other hand was French, the blade a mix of high-carbon steel, chrome and molybdenum. He held it strangely, jutting from his fist, so that he could reach in, twist away the gun and cut the CIA agent's throat all in one go.

"*Nasrani,*" Hassan said dismissively. "They get lost when their toys don't work." Picking up Charlie Bilberg's cell phone, he tossed it to a thin-faced teenager. "Dump it," he said. "Somewhere beyond Ben Guerir." The town he named was on the road to Casablanca, about an hour north of Marrakech.

"Turn it back on," he added, "just before you dump it. Oh... and lose this as well." Reaching into his pockets, Hassan produced a small box, then hesitated. "No," he said, tossing it to the brother of the suicide bomber instead. "You," he said, "lose this where it won't be found."

"Will do." The boy stripped off his stolen battledress and shrugged himself into his own jellaba, stuffing his uniform into a Nike holdall. He placed the cell-phone jammer on top and zipped the bag. "The debt is paid?"

Hassan nodded his head.

"What about that?"

"Someone else can deal with him. Hurry it up." He watched the boy walk towards a clump of palms, while he waited impatiently for the second teenager to change out of uniform.

"Come on," Hassan said. "They'll be wondering where their *petite taxi*'s gone." He meant the Americans or the Moroccan army or Sécurité... Whichever mix was waiting two kilometres ahead for a car so anonymous it contained no tracking devices.

A minute later, both foot soldiers were gone, their absence marked by the high whine of small dirt bikes.

"Well," said Hassan. "You've really fucked up this time." He scowled at the prisoner and then at the dead CIA agent on the seat next to him. "Let's get this over with. What did you tell them?"

"The truth," said Prisoner Zero, in a voice that sounded like wind through broken pines.

"And what did they do?"

"Kicked the chair from under me and started all over again." The prisoner smiled, and as smiles went it wasn't entirely sane.

"So what did you tell them then?"

"Nothing."

"So then they demanded the truth?"

"Which I told them."

"So they kicked the chair from under you and started all over again?"

"You know how it goes," said Prisoner Zero.

"Want to tell me what brought you back to Morocco?"

Prisoner Zero thought about this and then thought some more. Finally he looked at the man who'd so recently cut Agent Bilberg's throat and shook his head. "You wouldn't believe me anyway."

"What wouldn't I believe?"

"The truth..."

"No," said Caid Hassan, nephew of Caid Hammou and de facto boss of the city's biggest crime family. "Probably not."

Retrieving Agent Bilberg's Colt, the elegantly dressed man dropped out the magazine and thumbed away all the bullets but one, then gave the gun back to Prisoner Zero and nodded at Brigadier Abbas.

"Feel free," he said.

# CHAPTER 5

## *Zigin Chéng, CTzu 53/Year 20*

A circle can be begun at any point. The brush is held upright in one hand with the wrist held clear of both table and paper, the circle being drawn swiftly and confidently in one clean stroke.

A circle may begin at any point. He had been told this as a child. It can begin far away in a strange land, where sun-bleached palms fill a tired grove and smoke rises from an ancient vehicle or it can begin closer to home, just outside the walls of the Zigin Cheng, or within the Forbidden City itself. It can begin with a word or a kiss, in flames or ice or the cold darkness of a night sky with the stars looking down on things that should not be seen.

Although he was tired to the bone and restless with waiting for death the fifty-third Chuang Tzu was nothing like as old as he felt. He was, however, exhausted. And he had been fighting with himself for longer than he could remember and was still not sure who was winning. So while he wrestled with his darkness and watched butterflies flit across the walled garden from where he sat under a tree, he considered something rather miraculous.

A killer was coming, the merest slip of a youth with barely enough life lived to cast a shadow. The Chuang Tzu was not sure whether to be upset or glad.

Beneath his cloak, the Emperor wore a *chao pao,* a formal court robe. In his case this robe was blue and decorated around the neck, across the shoulders and above the hem with embroidered five-toed dragons, conforming to the regulations for a first- or second-rank prince.

It was a wholly unsuitable garment for a man destined to wear imperial yellow and in choosing it the Chuang Tzu had offended almost everyone who was not already offended by his recent behaviour.

He had tried and probably failed to change history. He had fought battles within himself that those outside never saw. And he had fought against the rules laid down by the Library. For any Chuang Tzu to be killed would be shocking and the shock of his death would be felt through the empire like reverberations through a hollow drum.

All the same, there would be many who felt such an end was to be expected and that, on balance, the fifty-third Chuang Tzu deserved no less. The Emperor himself was one of these.

Settling back against a willow, the Emperor took a deep breath and let fear flow with the breath from his body. To live or die, the choice remained his. A single clap of the hands would be enough to summon General Ch'ao Kai to the edge of the gardens.

Once instructed, the General would post guards around the inner pavilions and the outer, around the Forbidden City and even in the two surrounding cities where the ambassadors and servitors lived.

And the General had enough guards. Chuang Tzu had seen them exercising in front of the Wu-Men, a gate so vast that an entire army could muster in its shadow. Although why an assassin should want to kill the ruler of the richest, most cultured empire history had ever known was a mystery that Chuang Tzu hoped soon to have unravelled, once the two of them met.

In the meantime he had his dreams.

Dreams of a far stranger assassin arrested on the point of failure and put to questioning. It happened in a place of walls like the walls which surrounded Chuang Tzu's city, only these were of beaten earth, lime dust and straw and the sun overhead was hotter than the one Chuang Tzu knew.

The streets of this city were dirty and the trees lining the wider roads were shrivelled from drought and burnt along the edges of their fronds, but the walls of both cities had one distinct similarity, despite their difference in magnificence and construction.

Both were red.

Because the Chuang Tzu knew that meaning could be found within coincidence and his daydreams were as significant as any which came in the night, he considered this point seriously and decided that the redness of the walls was probably important. And there was a chance, not a good chance admittedly, that he might come to understand this significance before he was killed.

It would be a short reign, merely twenty years, and an inglorious one. And its end would be as strange as its start, which began with a butterfly and a small boy being sent to bed without supper.

Mirrored eyes had swallowed the sight of endless, utterly identical small boys, a million Zaqs. The butterfly who stared at him was red, the size of a small plate and had fat black spots on each wing, though when Zaq looked closely he realized the spots were somewhere between purple and ultraviolet, their edges both fractal and recursive.

There was a difference, apparently.

Zaq had never met a butterfly the size of a bird. Actually, he wasn't sure he'd ever met a bird.

"In the Carboniferous period," said the butterfly, "even mayflies had wingspans this big. Mind you, back then there was so much oxygen in the atmosphere that forests burned when wet..."

That was when Zaq knew he was dreaming.

"Yes and no," the butterfly said.

It rested on the edge of Zaq's bed, which was actually a door that was held off the ground by rocks at each corner. A hundred or so holes had been drilled in the door, a hand-breadth apart, so that Zaq's mattress could breath. His brother Eli was very proud of this.

The butterfly looked around.

And what it saw, kaleidoscope-like through the endless facets of its silver eyes, was what it expected to see. A shitty little shack built from sheet plastic and cheap blocks of polycrete, roofed with a rancid canvas awning in what had once been a landing pad for hoppers.

There were two ways the butterfly knew this. The first was that a faded "H" could still be seen etched into the ledge on which Zaq's mother had built her house, the second was that the butterfly could remember when Rip had briefly been fashionable. In those days tiny silver hoppers had buzzed around the non-world like blowflies.

Opinion was divided on Rip's exact provenance, but then opinion in the 2023 worlds was divided on most things, with a sizeable minority believing that the thousand-kilometre jumble of steel and extruded ceramic was an art form and the Razor's Edge, that long scar down its side, a statement about futility.

The hoppers were toys for the rich in worlds where such definitions had become meaningless, because poverty was an abstraction and hunger a life choice, like living dangerously, monogamy or dying of natural diseases.

That was the theory, anyway.

"You don't have the faintest idea what I'm talking about, do you?"

The small boy shook his head.

Of course he didn't. New emperors rarely did.

When Zaq awoke he was lying in sunlight and such was his fear of the unexpected brightness that he rolled straight off his bed and underneath a table, crouching in the safety of its shadow. Somehow the whole of Rip had revolved, so that the glassed-over rip within which Zaq's village squatted now faced a gap between the worlds above. Their village had become desirable overnight.

Eli had tousled his hair, let him play with the rat and laughed at him, and when that didn't work his mother sent Zaq to bed without supper. Since the shack had only one room, food was a rarity and what with there being no front door and holes in the roof and no one would be sleeping that night, this was more for show than anything else.

"Zaq..."

Morning came broken. And only the butterfly understood how Rip kept to its new orbit beyond the edge of the 2023 worlds, but then the butterfly knew why gravity still held long after the electricity was gone and most of the food boxes stopped producing food. There had been a systems failure on Rip forty-eight centuries earlier, four thousand eight hundred and three years to be exact.

"What?"

Zaq looked at his mother.

"Four-thousand-eight-hundred-and-three..." She said the words without understanding because the highest number Maria knew was twelve, which had been her age when she met Eli's father: A scavenger with scars older than she was and hard connections, the kind that paid him in knives, medicine and food.

After Gabriel had come Eddie, who traded metals for food.

"Scrap," Zaq said, looking at the apple she held.

"You miss Eddie?"

For Zaq the question was meaningless. Eddie had been with his mother for less than eighteen months, leaving one morning to strip copper from level fifteen of the Rip and that had been it, Eddie never returned. Zaq had absolutely no memory of the hard-eyed man who fathered him and how could he? It was six months after Eddie's disappearance before Maria began pulling afterbirth from between her legs, while Eli cut the cord and wiped slime from the new baby with his hands. This had been Zaq's introduction to life and many on Rip had introductions far worse.

"Four-thousand-eight-hundred-and-three," Zaq said, tasting the size of the number. It sounded like something the ghost mothers might say. "*The day is gone, the night comes in and my baby is lost . . .*" Zaq knew all about the ghost mothers. Eli knew many scary stories and they stuck to the inside of Zaq's head like flies to tar-paper.

"Here," Maria said. "This will make you feel better."

Across the hut, Eli froze. He was older than Zaq and had first choice of all the food. "Me," he said.

Three paces took the boy to where his brother sat with an old blanket pulled tight around him against the shivers. On Eli's shoulder sat the rat he'd rescued from a shaft off the lower levels. Null had fallen through a hole and been unable to scrabble out.

Maria hated the animal, but it was hard to scold Eli when he returned from most trips with a fistful of copper wire or a circuit tray which changed patterns every few seconds. She'd once swapped circuitry for enough slab meat to feed all three of them for a month.

"Me first," said Eli, his eyes fixed on the apple.

"There's enough for everybody," his mother said.

Maria was lying. A third of the apple was already rotten and most of what was left was mottled with bruising. She'd taken it as payment in the dark, realizing too late that the sticky sweetness on her fingers was a sign of corruption, not quality. Maria had never seen fruit before, but the man who gave it to her had sworn it would make her both clever and lucky.

The tiny bugs living in its flesh were guaranteed to change her whole life for the better. Of course, the man had said, she could always give it to one of her sons, say the younger. The man's voice had been soft when he said this, as sweet as ever Eddie's had been.

"Take a bite," she told Zaq.

He looked doubtful.

"I'll have it," Eli said.

"Zaq's ill," Maria insisted. "He gets first bite."

"I'm not," said Zaq, shaking his head, mostly to stop his mother from putting her hand to his forehead to see if he had a fever.

"Burning up," she told him. "Eat it now."

"I've got a fever too," announced Eli, but his brother had already bitten into the fruit and over-sweet juice was running down the small boy's chin.

"Yuk . . ."

"It's good," Maria promised.

"I feel sick," said Zaq and passed the apple to Eli, who immediately took a bite before Maria could stop him.

"You have some," Eli suggested, seeing anger tighten his mother's eyes.

Maria shook her head. "Give it to Zaq," she said.

She was a good mother who shared her food and only ever stayed out nights if it was impossible to get back. Never once had she thought about selling, killing or abandoning either of her children, no matter how tired they made her. There were, however, limits and both Eli and Zaq understood that these had just been reached.

So Zaq did what he was told and ate everything, including the core, in silence, then licked his fingers and went with Eli to find fuel, anything that might burn. "Magnesium would be good," said Zaq, but his mother was asleep and Eli was outside, lying on top of a girl Zaq had never seen before.

The next morning Zaq woke with a rash, feeling sick and muttering about M-theory, Zero Point Energy and the luxury of oblivion. So Maria did something she'd never believed herself capable of doing. She took the gold ring Eddie had made her from circuitry, his lucky lump of black glass which she'd stolen and what was left of her beauty down twelve levels, looking for a medicine woman.

What Maria found was Doc Joyce, a shambling figure dressed in rags and old sweat and what he wanted was none of the above.

All he required in payment was a metal bolt Maria wore strung on a cord between her breasts. She didn't stop to consider how he knew this talisman existed or where she kept it hidden. The ragged man was obviously a shaman, how could he not know? Waiting patiently, she stood as he undid the buttons on her dress and stared impassively at the hexagon of grey metal.

Other men had gazed in rapture at her breasts. Not for some years, it was true, but even where she lived in the cold thin air that fed the upper levels of Rip, strangers would occasionally stop, catch their breath and wonder fleetingly—in between lust and the promise of forgetfulness—about the twists of life that gave a perfect ass, breasts and hips to a roofwhore with two children and a scar which disfigured half her face.

Doc Joyce barely noticed her body as his fingers closed around the hexagon. The bolt was warm and would remain warm long after it was taken from between her breasts. And were he to pass electricity through the hexagon and introduce it to the cold then the object would remain cold even if Doc Joyce hung it on a cord and tucked it under his own rags. And the Doc always wore rags when visiting the intricate maze of shafts, narrow levels and hangars that made up this part of Rip. It helped to blend in with the scenery.

The Doc had been hunting for a scrap of metal such as this for most of his life, which was already twenty times longer than that of the girl standing in front of him. His vision had been augmented to scan beneath life's surface layers, his sense of smell was acute enough to distinguish illness from anxiety and he could taste the presence of a hundred different metals on his tongue.

That was how he'd known this was the moment he'd been waiting for. A taste on his tongue unlike all others.

"Button your dress."

The girl looked so offended that Doc Joyce almost smiled. Every society had its own social currency, even one as fractured as Rip. She traded on her beauty, he traded on his intelligence; there wasn't that much difference between them, no matter how impossible she would have found that thought.

"My small boy," she said.

"How old?" Doc Joyce asked, firing up a medical core. Something Maria saw only as a quick blink and sudden concentration on the part of the man.

Maria told him.

"You're rather young to have a child that old," Doc Joyce said, reading off her biological age. It was a comment made without thinking.

Maria looked puzzled.

"Eli's older," she said.

## CHAPTER 6

### *High Atlas, Monday 25 June*

Ghosts hid among the holm oaks and cedar trees. Aged and almost transparent with exhaustion, they had been driven into the High Atlas by disbelief and fundamentalism, the last being a *nasrani* term for long beards and a rigid belief.

The ghosts had learned to distinguish those who disbelieved from those who objected by their clothes. Disbelievers wore jeans and T-shirts mostly. Blue jeans, sometimes black and mostly tight, although a few of the girls now wore trousers that flapped round their ankles like sails starved of a breeze.

Objectors wore three, sometimes four fists of beard, when in the old days two would have been considered sufficient. Like the disbelievers, they also refused to accept the ghosts, albeit for diametrically opposite reasons.

So the djinn wandered the city hungry and lonely, spilling into absence with every new breeze. Those who could, the ones freshly fed on belief or fear, headed for the dry woodlands of the High Atlas, where their kind were still welcome and if not welcome then at least accepted for what they were.

The man rough plastering an arch in a half-finished kasbah on the slopes of a valley had no trouble believing in ghosts; but then Prisoner Zero had little trouble believing in most things, except himself.

"Nobody's worth that much," said Idries, tossing his newspaper to the floor of the kasbah. The dust it raised stuck to the lower edges of a freshly plastered area, extracting a sigh from Prisoner Zero.

"You know how much it is now?" Idries demanded.

Prisoner Zero didn't.

"Twenty-five million dollars. You have any idea how much that is in dirham? You want to thank God you're among friends." There was a tightness to the small man's voice that the prisoner might have found worrying had his mind been less locked into flashbacks of ghosts, burning cars and the falling 'copter.

It was nearly three weeks since he'd shot the Brigadier. A time spent working himself half to death in Hassan's kasbah, unable to summon up the doubt he needed to make the ghosts vanish, while lacking enough faith to deny their existence.

A doctor had been introduced the first morning, a clean-shaven young man who arrived blindfolded in the back of Idries's jeep and who dressed the burns on Prisoner Zero's stomach, listened to his heart and peered deep into the back of his eyes using a cross between a flashlight and a magnifying glass.

"It will take time," the doctor said.

"What will?" Idries asked.

"For the drugs to leave his system."

"Drugs?" That was Hassan. At least Prisoner Zero thought it was; he had trouble remembering.

"This man is drugged," said the doctor. "Surely you knew?"

"Is he?" Hassan's laugh was bitter. "I'm surprised you can tell."

"Aren't you going to answer that?" Idries asked eventually, after Prisoner Zero abandoned his arch to drag a metal ladder into the hall, signalling Idries to bring a bucket full of rounded stones.

"Answer what?" Prisoner Zero demanded.

"Your mobile." The rat-faced man held out a cell phone he'd spent the previous week trying to make Prisoner Zero carry round with him.

"I don't think so," said Prisoner Zero, putting his ladder into position.

Seen from above, Idries looked every bit as unprepossessing as the prisoner remembered, maybe even worse now that a thin skim of hair was all that covered the man's narrow skull. Prisoner Zero tried to recall who'd first called Idries *rat boy* and gave up.

It didn't really matter. As a small child, Idries had been weaker than the others, or so Prisoner Zero had been told. So what he lacked in strength he decided to make up for in guile, but his mind wasn't quite as fast as the others' either. That was why Hassan eventually gave him a knife.

The next boy to pick on Idries got his cheek opened in a single slash. There were two things Hassan told Idries to learn from that incident.

The first was that skin stretched tight over bone splits easily and bleeds more than seems possible. The second was that their uncle Caid Hammou was right. There are some things in life that need to be done only once. Almost everybody left Idries alone after that.

It was just after dawn and Prisoner Zero was already tired. He'd started early, partly because, these days, his dreams were even more complex than his life and sleep had become a tougher choice than polishing the walls; but mostly he'd started early because whole areas of the hall still needed to be soaped and until his *tadelackt* plaster was sealed it remained vulnerable to just about everything.

He knew that Idries found his ability to plaster both comic and disconcerting. People like him weren't supposed to acquire the skill. Such jobs were meant to be left to those who grew up with them. And the trick of working in *tadelackt* was something handed down from father to sons, a family secret retained by generations of plasterers in Marrakech, Fez and Rabat.

Yet all it really took was a smattering of basic chemistry. At least, that was all it took for Prisoner Zero.

Produced by burning limestone contaminated with clay, *tadelackt* was different. The silico-aluminates from the burning combined with water to produce a plaster which allowed for hydraulic setting. Although the real skill, not to mention the hard work, came when the finish needed polishing. This had to be done by hand, using the force of a flat pebble to control crystallization. As for the soap, that was required to seal the surface and impede chemical reactions, allowing a finish as hard and smooth as polished marble.

"What's going to happen?" Idries said.

"I'm going to finish polishing," said Prisoner Zero, "then start with the black soap..."

That wasn't what Idries meant and Prisoner Zero knew it. Hassan's rat-faced cousin was there because Caid Hammou had given him the job of babysitting Prisoner Zero.

It was typical of Hammou and Hassan to combine keeping their guest safe with making him work for his keep, a very North African combination of exploitation and obligation which Prisoner Zero still found strange after all these years.

There were twelve bedrooms in Hassan's new kasbah, four bathrooms, five reception rooms and a kitchen, built around a central courtyard with a fountain as yet unattached to any source of water, and Prisoner Zero got the feeling Hassan intended to have him plaster them all. Idries had not even seemed surprised that first morning to find Prisoner Zero alive when all the papers were busy reporting him dead.

He'd just turned up, as ordered, in a jeep laden with lime plaster and released Prisoner Zero from the chair to which he'd been tied. That was when Prisoner Zero first realized that being driven out to the half-built kasbah didn't necessarily equate with being shot.

"What are you smiling at?"

"Your boss."

Idries looked worried. "What about him? No, wait..." The rat-faced man held up one hand, common sense changing his mind. "Don't tell me. I don't want to know."

"You think he's going to kill me?"

"Caid Hammou?" As if Prisoner Zero might mean anyone else.

"Yeah, your uncle, *the boss*."

"No," said Idries. "If he was going to do that then you'd be dead."

"And this house would never get finished."

"There are other plasterers in Marrakech," Idries said flatly.

"Thousands of them," agreed Prisoner Zero. "So why doesn't Hassan get someone else? I've got other things on my mind."

Like ghosts and dreams and a nagging, insistent feeling that something kept looking at the world from behind his eyes and not liking a single thing it saw. A feeling which manifested itself as a low-level headache in the back of Prisoner Zero's skull where the darkness lurked.

"Hassan believed you were long since dead," said Idries. "We all did."

Prisoner Zero thought about his final months in Amsterdam, the squat overlooking the canal and the fire. "I was," he said. "Then I went to Paris."

Idries made a sign against the evil eye, his reaction so instinctive it operated below the level of conscious thought. "You shouldn't say such things."

"You weren't there," said Prisoner Zero.

"But you came back to Morocco."

"Yeah." Prisoner Zero smiled. "That's one way of putting it." Two days on a cheap coach, a ferry crossing from Alicante and a week of sleeping under flowering almond trees, walnuts and finally palms as he hitched south, doing his best to avoid anything that looked like authority. The heroin lasted from the real Paris to Paris sur la Mer, otherwise known as Casablanca, leaving him sick and sweating.

"And before . . ." Idries skirted around the incident in Djemaa el Fna, yet they both knew what he meant. "Hassan asked around. Apparently you were plastering an old brothel at the back of Maison Tiskiwine. For food . . ."

"For keep," said Prisoner Zero, "there's a difference."

"Ahh."

Prisoner Zero smiled and let Idries think he meant sex, though that wasn't it. He'd enjoyed seeing Leila's girls pass by in their thongs or camiknickers but he was there for anonymity, to be regarded like an old piece of furniture, comfortable and useful but consistently invisible. A woman in a souk had been talking about hiring a plasterer when the man who wasn't Jake had interrupted, offered his services.

"You've done the work before?"

"Of course."

"Where?" Leila's eyes were bright, openly suspicious.

He named Riad-al-Razor, near Bab Doukkala.

"Never heard of it."

"It was a while ago."

The rate Leila mentioned was so low that even Prisoner Zero had raised his eyebrows, only accepting when he realized she was about to turn back to her conversation.

"Look," Idries said. "You need to answer that."

"No," said Prisoner Zero. "I don't. So stop bothering me."

Idries began to shrug, looked at the man he was there to watch and smiled, understanding spreading slowly across his thin face. "You're not meant to answer it," he said. "It's a signal."

Prisoner Zero said nothing. He handed his polishing stone to Idries, climbed down from the ladder and walked slowly to the window, stopping while he was still in shadow.

Ghosts and the memories of things still to happen were waiting for him out there. And yet by next spring there would also be a garden of small palms and ornamental bushes, a fountain fed by water piped from higher up the valley. Pegs already marked where the beds were to be dug and foundations had been laid for a road to run from the gate to a parking area along one side of the kasbah.

Prisoner Zero tried to imagine what it would be like to own such a house and found he couldn't. It was years since he'd owned more than his memories and the clothes in which he stood. Even the flat in Paris was owned by a family trust, his tiny allowance for food, electricity and gas unchanged since the day it was first paid.

"I need some cigarettes," he said, turning back from the window.

"You don't smoke."

"How would you know?"

Idries sighed. "I'll get some tomorrow," he promised.

"Now," Prisoner Zero said. "I mean it. I can't finish this until I've got some." He indicated the area of wall he'd been polishing with the fist-sized lump of agate. It had a dull shine like poor quality marble.

"What kind?" Idries asked.

"The cheapest you can find. Try the village."

The village was six mud-brick houses, the crumbling, white-domed tomb of a local saint and a *téléboutique* used by every family within a five-kilometre radius to make calls, collect messages, buy cigarettes and gossip. There was no mosque as such, so the men held Friday prayers in the whitewashed tomb.

Ties of kinship being what they were, seven other villages had connections to this one and together the eight made up a holding which originally owed obligation to the caid of a valley fifteen kilometres distant. All of the houses in the eight villages followed the same simple design but their colours varied from village to village, depending on the mud from which the bricks had been made.

An ancient path passed the walls of Hassan's new kasbah, leading down a gravel slope to the village in the dip below. Another path crossed this one near the kasbah's gate and headed uphill towards an abandoned village on the plateau.

Choosing this spot was Hassan's way of making it look as if his kasbah had been there forever, a meeting point for paths and part of the valley's history. The pretence would work better when the concrete blocks making up the gate had been plastered over and the garden had been given a chance to settle in.

It was into this valley that one of Maréchal Lyautey's brigades had limped in the spring of 1916, tired and near defeated from fighting the tribes south of the High Atlas. Instead of attacking as expected, the leader of the tiny village, a descendant of the local saint, gave the French shelter and food, ammunition and replacement horses. When the brigade left, their major promised the chief that he would be made caid, ruler of the whole valley.

Hassan claimed that his uncle was the bastard of that man's bastard, the grandson of a slave and a man whose name was to become enough to make other villages surrender without a shot being fired.

"Look, if you won't go to the village, I'll go myself."

"No way," Idries said. "You know what the boss ordered. You're to stay in the house, you're not even to go near the windows. Anything you need, I get."

"Fine," said Prisoner Zero. "Get me a packet of cigarettes."

If ever a house needed ghosts it was this one. The breeze-block shell of the kitchen was hungry for feasts yet to be cooked, there were basins upstairs where no one had washed and bedrooms where no man had sulked and no woman cried herself to sleep. No one had died in their beds because there were no beds. And thus no girl had ever spread her legs to make sheets for a boy she hoped one day to love and no babies had been born of such blind and necessary optimism.

All this Prisoner Zero knew, just as he knew that ghosts had fled to this valley from Marrakech and that he might just have saved Idries's life by sending him to buy cigarettes that no one would ever smoke.

With Idries gone, Prisoner Zero picked up his cell phone and turned it off, tossing the thing into a bucket of newly mixed plaster where it slowly but certainly began to sink. Viscosity, density and displacement, he filed all three away to consider later. If there was a later.

Finding a rag in the kitchen he rinsed it under water from a standpipe in the garden and headed for a half-built stable block. Horses were still considered a sign of wealth in the Atlas and Hassan had a stallion and four mares on order, pure-bred Arabs every one. The black jeep currently occupying what would become the end stall was an old diesel, running round the clock for the second time. Its treads were worn almost bare and a bang had scraped paint off one door.

Sacks of lime plaster still sat in the back, so Prisoner Zero moved these first and then began to wipe down the vehicle. Once the doors were free of fingerprints, he climbed inside the front seat and began, as quickly as he could, to remove all trace of Idries.

He wiped down the steering wheel and gear stick, the rubber pedals and handbrake, smeared his rag across a length of plastic dashboard and then wiped down the insides of both doors. Clambering out, Prisoner Zero reached for the mats and almost ran to a half-dug flowerbed, shaking both free of gravel and dirt.

All clean, he sat himself back in the driver's seat and changed gears, running rapidly through a whole sequence. After that he turned the handles which wound down the windows and put the handbrake on and off half a dozen times. As an afterthought, he wiped down the lever that put the jeep into four-wheel drive and worked that back and forth for a few seconds.

Then he got out of the jeep and promptly leant back in again to shake dandruff from his filthy hair on to the driver's seat. All that remained was to wipe down the sacks of plaster he'd carefully unloaded.

This wasn't what Prisoner Zero was meant to do if his mobile rang and it was probably pointless, but he did it just the same. He was meant to head for the high plateau where a goatherd would meet him near the top of the path. And he was to take Idries with him.

Idries didn't know this because he hadn't been told. That was the way Caid Hammou worked. The only people to know were the goatherd, who was meant to meet Prisoner Zero near the abandoned village, and Prisoner Zero himself.

Obligation and the repayment of debts could be a very complex thing in Marrakech.

There was a certain strength and logic to Hammou's plan, but a weakness also and it was the weakness which had always undercut his family's ideas where Jake Razor, Malika and Moz al-Turq were concerned. Caid Hammou and his nephew consistently ignored the obvious, which was that some people had real trouble doing what they were told.

The bolts on the cedar front doors to the kasbah were as long as Prisoner Zero's arm and as thick as the wrist of a child. They were brass, as was traditional, although chrome had become fashionable for riads in the city.

Prisoner Zero, very intentionally, left the main doors unlocked but the soldiers still came in the windows, smashing half a dozen simultaneously to toss in stun grenades. Even with torn strips of cotton in his ears and his hands protecting his head, the shock waves made Prisoner Zero feel sick.

Dropping to a crouch, he found a wet rag he'd prepared and slammed it over his mouth and nose, shutting his eyes against the tear gas and keeping his breath shallow.

"*You, down!...*"

The words were shouted in English, followed a second later by a bark of Arabic and then French, same meaning, different voices. As Prisoner Zero was already crouched in the middle of the hall, he simply tipped on his side and stretched out on his front, the rag still held to his mouth.

"Hands behind your head."

Prisoner Zero assumed the position and waited. He could see feet... Well, boots really. Mostly black boots although one pair was green, made of canvas with thinner laces. That was the pair which stopped directly in front of him, shuffling back and forward. For a moment Prisoner Zero thought those boots intended to kick him in the face.

"Roll over... No... Keep your hands where they are."

Prisoner Zero rolled, and found himself looking up at a handful of US marines, a Moroccan liaison officer and two men from an elite regiment raised in Fez. They all had guns, even the liaison officer, and all of the weapons were pointed at him. It was like being... Prisoner Zero wasn't quite sure what. A fish maybe. Pulled out of the water, finally seeing the owner of the net.

"You going to shoot or not?" Prisoner Zero asked.

"Nothing so easy," the liaison officer said. And as if a signal had been given, one of the others stamped on Prisoner Zero's leg. A kick to the head followed and Prisoner Zero tumbled into somewhere else.

## CHAPTER 7

### *Zigin Chéng, CTzu 53/Year 7*

"What are you looking at?" demanded Zaq.

And while he was still wondering why his jade-framed mirror refused to answer, the young Emperor remembered. He'd promised to smash the glass if it ever spoke to him again and, as he'd pointed out at the time, neither of them could afford that much bad luck.

General Ch'ao Kai stood in front of the huge glass. Almost as if protecting it from the teenager's latest tantrum. The General was doing his best not to look disgusted.

Zaq had just returned from the Ambassadors' City, his disguise strewn on the floor behind him. No one was interested in plotting to overthrow him. They were interested in body modification, who'd lived the longest and which world was the richest, most highly cultured or threw the best parties. Politics seemed beyond them.

The week before, Zaq had trawled through the back alleys of the Servitors' City, in the clothes of a cook, searching the inns and brothels for co-conspirators. Needless to say he found none. Both cities were in agreement that the Chuang Tzu's existence was beneficial to the well-being of the 2023 worlds. So certain of this fact had tonight's group been that most ambassadors at the party had trouble even understanding his suggestion.

"Morons," Zaq said, wiping off the last of his make-up with the back of his hand. Outside his window rain lashed the glass and hammered pregnant drops against the roof, always a sign that the Emperor was upset. And who wouldn't be? Zaq had returned to his pavilion expecting to be allowed to sulk in peace and found five naked concubines arranged artistically on his bed.

"Kill them," the boy ordered.

Zaq was back in full costume, complete with court sword, his hair pulled into a black ponytail and tied with ribbon. Only servitors wore queues and although visiting ambassadors were told that the tradition carried over from ancient days when servitors still believed they might be lifted to heaven by their plaits, this was untrue. The Manchu had demanded it. A sign of servitude. One that had allowed the heads of the Han to be dragged easily across the chopping block.

He knew this for a fact. The Library had told him.

"Kill them," Zaq said. "I mean it."

General Ch'ao Kai tugged at the edge of his padded silk jacket, always an indication that he was worried. Any minute now the leopard's tail hanging from his ceremonial lance would start swinging in rigidly controlled fury. He'd served five emperors and Zaq was his least favourite. The old man would never be unprofessional enough to say so but he didn't need to.

The old man's anger was very convincing.

*"Do you want me to do it myself?"* Zaq's voice was hard, his face set.

This wasn't meant to be a difficult question, although it became obvious from the turmoil in General Ch'ao Kai's eyes that the old soldier was having trouble working out the right answer.

The Emperor sighed.

That is, Zaq sighed. And because Zaq was in his seventh year as the Chuang Tzu, when he sighed it was as Emperor and so he was watched by forty-three billion people, a figure that rose rapidly as others realized what might be about to happen.

At the age of eleven Zaq had his favourite poet thrown to the wolves. The man was skilled in verse, diplomatic to a fault and Zaq liked him. So, as tantrums went, this was not particularly sensible or even original. A drunken Muscovite had done something very similar more than five thousand years earlier and gone down in history as Ivan the Terrible.

In fact Zaq got the idea from the Library while skimming the life of Ivan Vasilyevich, a man who seemed to have inherited his throne from his father. This seemed so unlikely to Zaq that he considered asking the Librarian if the Library might have got it wrong.

Only the Library never got anything wrong. It was the single most accurate data source in the 2023 worlds and its content had the status of law. The fact its core was alien was regarded as a good thing; because whichever race created the Library had long since died and this meant the Librarian had no in-built allegiance to any one world, species or cultural grouping.

In fact, its only allegiance seemed to be to the concept of Chuang Tzu and this it displayed, first and foremost, in a ruthless and sometimes cruel adherence to the truth.

The Library's core could talk to Zaq directly, but the Librarian could manifest in any of the mirrors scattered through the Forbidden City, although there were many of these.

The poet hadn't been real, of course. No one in the Purple City was real except for Zaq, but he hadn't realized that back then. In fact, he'd only realized it within the last three days, but the more Zaq thought about it the more he knew it was true. The others were just puppets and backdrop, so much bleeding meat controlled by the multiple mind that was his Library.

The Library was to the Librarian what Zaq was to the Chuang Tzu, the reality behind the façade. Zaq wasn't sure if he was meant to have discovered this.

Year of the dragon.

Season of the bitch.

This morning, his thirteenth birthday, he'd been pulled from sleep by a polite cough and come awake to find himself surrounded by five naked concubines. A present from the Librarian presumably.

He'd sent them away and returned from the Ambassadors' City to find all five in his bed again, arranged picturesquely under the sheet. Sloe eyes and high cheekbones above hamster cheeks, hair as dark as obsidian and perfect breasts tipped with nipples as rare as unflawed amber. Having taken a long look, Zaq shut his own eyes and realized he couldn't remember a single thing about any of them.

All he got were generalities.

A sense of beauty.

An awareness that if he sent them away another five would probably take their place, as anonymous and as beautiful as those he'd just dismissed.

"Get me a knife," Zaq told the nearest concubine.

Huge eyes watched him, impossibly large. When she spoke it sounded like water running over rock.

"What kind of knife, Excellency?"

*Any kind* was what Zaq was about to say but he changed this, fighting for specifics. "A sharp one," he said, although that should have been obvious.

Without another word, the naked girl slid from under the sheet and padded across the marble floor towards a doorway. Zaq tried to remember how the room next door might look and decided it was gold, green and red. Most rooms in his palace were gold, green and red.

"Excellency..." She held out a long steel blade fixed into a mutton-fat hilt, topped with a ruby the size of a quail's egg. For a moment Zaq debated telling the concubine to stab herself. His only problem being that she'd do it. In the seven years that had passed since Zaq left Razor's Edge to become Chuang Tzu he had run out of unreasonable demands.

Everything he asked for was given.

"Turn around," he told the girl.

The General was watching now, his glance slipping between the blade, Zaq's face and the perfect back and buttocks of the girl, as if a line existed between the three, invisible but unbreakable.

"And again."

The order was intentionally ambiguous, obscure. But the concubine instantly did what Zaq wanted her to do, confirming for Zaq that the girl now turning to face him, her bare mons as flawless as her buttocks, was nothing more than a fleshly manifestation of the Library.

A mere aspect of the palace. Soft furnishings.

He could sink his knife beneath one of those upturned breasts or slice open her perfect stomach. There were other things, perverted things, that he could do but even Zaq tired at the banality of those thoughts.

"You may go," he told the concubine.

Her eyes flicked towards the main door and Zaq nodded, wrapping his cloak tight around him until he was almost completely buried in its yellow folds.

"You too," he told the others, meaning all of them. And they went, one by one, their eyes dark and devoid. "And don't let them come back," Zaq shouted after the General. "You hear me?"

He stamped across his room and stopped pointedly in front of the mirror. "Tell the Library I'm going to kill the next person to come in here." To make his point, Zaq hurled the long blade at the glass but it just bounced off the wall, its handle shattering when it hit the floor.

For five days Zaq refused to leave his room and his audience drifted away until all that remained was a small core of the old and aimless, those who lived almost exclusively through the butterfly life of one much younger and infinitely more fragile.

That was the deal. The Chuang Tzu lived in absolute, terrifying splendour for the length of his natural life and, in so doing, absolved all others of the need to consume quite so conspicuously.

As each emperor burnt out within one natural life (this also being part of the deal), those watching got to see eight, maybe more Chuang Tzu be selected, raised to the Dragon Throne, grow old and die. Of course, this applied only to those who retained their corporeal bodies. The cold eternals had mostly seen maybe twenty or more emperors come and go before even this became too little to make remaining alive attractive.

## CHAPTER 8

## *Marrakech, July 1971*

On the afternoon that two hundred and fifty army cadets, many from the Ahermoumou Military School, invaded the Moroccan King's forty-second birthday party at Sikharat and machine-gunned ninety-two of his guests, accidentally killing the leader of their attempted coup in the process, a fight between two Marrakchi boys broke out behind La Koutoubia. An event so utterly insignificant that it took a foreign hippie to notice it.

Four generals, five colonels and a major faced a firing squad following the two-and-a-half-hour battle at the summer palace, which was only ended by the coolness of the King, who stared down the rebels following the death of their leader.

And as rumours of the confrontation brought the souks to a sullen halt and men spilled onto the alleys in groups to discuss what little they knew, Hassan, Idries and two boys whose names Malika did not know chased Moz through the gathering crowds, cornering him in the gardens behind the mosque.

The first punch split Moz's eye, the next snapped back his head and spun the garden around him. Blue sky, palm trees and a distant sixteenth-century tower all watching him fall.

Getting up again fast was hard with only one arm, but Moz managed it. And as he wiped blood and dust from his face, he stared round at the boys who'd pursued him from Place Abdel Moumen around the back of the mosque and into the dusty gardens.

"*Fatah*."

"*Teazak*."

"*Ibn haram*."

"*Hmar*."

The insults were meaningless. Merely words overhead—"foreskin," "arse," "bastard" and "jackass"—ready warmed from their use by others.

"Hit him again." Idries was cheering for Hassan. Self-preservation made this the rat-faced boy's default position in everything. The other two Moz didn't recognize, although he noticed they watched Hassan impatiently, waiting for the killer blow. Their conversation was with each other, low-voiced and private.

Only Sidi ould Kasim's daughter watched in silence.

It was a year since she and Moz had last said a word to each other. Malika still hadn't forgiven Moz for the fact his ma had refused to marry her father. He watched her though, each night, through a crack between the tiles in his bedroom floor. A thin girl with reddish hair and bony shoulders, whose buttocks were as scrawny as any goat.

"Are you still fighting," said Hassan, his question contemptuous, "or have you given up?"

Moz punched him. The only blow he'd actually managed to land. "I don't give up," he said, watching Hassan put a hand to his face and find blood. "Don't you know anything?"

It was the first of three fights with Hassan, and the one Moz would remember best; not for its violence or fierceness or even how it ended, but for the noise that suddenly crashed through the open window of a yellow van parked, quite illegally, in the shade of a half-dead palm behind them.

The boy whose nose had just been broken was all of eleven and a whole head higher than most of his age, making him taller by far than Moz. "I'm bleeding," said Hassan, examining his fingers.

"Here." Idries pulled a blade from his pocket. "You can borrow this." He held his knife out to Hassan, who shook his head angrily while the nameless boys said nothing, just watched and waited to see how Hassan would react.

And then, suddenly, as if sound-tracking their expectation came music like no other.

*Won't get fooled again...*

Crashing chords and a language Moz barely understood.

Only he would get fooled, Moz knew that. He wasn't clever enough to stay out of trouble or fast enough to run away. Hassan and he fought over a packet of tissues. A small, locally produced packet wrapped in cellophane and printed with the name "Kleenex," because this was a make the *nasrani* knew and recognizing what they bought made foreigners happy.

Moz had been warned not to work Idries's patch, but everyone who knew him agreed he was bad at listening. And Moz was better at selling the tissues than Idries, because the *nasrani* only had to look at his empty sleeve and torn jellaba to begin reaching for coins. Idries was good at looking sad but he couldn't compete with that, no one could.

Hassan didn't actually sell the tissues. He just took a cut from Idries and half a dozen other boys, none of them as good at selling as Moz.

Moz grinned.

"I'm going to kill you," Hassan said quietly.

"He is," agreed Idries.

The older boys remained silent.

And behind them all stood Malika, as if not quite part of what was happening. She was still scuffing one bare heel in the red dirt when Moz struck again. Only this time he kicked, as hard as he could, one toe breaking as he caught Hassan between the legs.

No one said anything as Hassan crashed to the ground, writhing around in the dust like a beetle with half its legs torn off, although even the two older boys looked vaguely impressed.

Stepping forward, Moz stamped on Hassan's stomach.

"*Hey,*" someone shouted from the door of the van. "*That's enough.*"

The *nasrani* wore a thick coat, this was the first thing Moz noticed about him. In the height of summer, the man wore a goatskin waistcoat with a fur collar. Moz was so surprised by this that he forgot to keep an eye on Hassan. Not that it mattered, the older boy was still in the dirt, clutching his stomach. The second thing Moz noticed only when the foreigner came over to help Hassan to his feet. The coat stank.

"You have a name?" he asked Moz.

Moz nodded. Of course he did. "I'm Hamid."

"Call me Dave," said the man. "And I mean it. You really shouldn't fight." The *nasrani* spoke English, which meant Moz was the only one able to understand him. The boy waited politely to find out why he shouldn't fight but the blond foreigner merely smiled. As if the statement was enough.

"What did he say?" Hassan demanded.

"That we shouldn't fight."

The older boy snorted, his battle with Moz temporarily forgotten. Dusting himself down, Hassan came to stand beside the smaller boy. "Ask him if he's got cigarettes," Hassan ordered.

The man pulled a crumpled packet of Gauloise from his jeans and handed them over as if this was nothing. Moz passed them to Hassan, who flipped one from the packet and stuck it in his mouth.

"Use this." Dave Giles tossed Hassan a plastic lighter and waved it away when the boy tried to give it back. "Keep the thing," he said. "I've got another."

"What did he say?"

"It's yours," said Moz.

Hassan looked doubtful, shrugged and he pocketed the lighter anyway. When the man said nothing, Hassan grinned.

"See if he's got Coca-Cola."

Before Moz had even begun to translate, the foreigner was walking towards his yellow van. And when he returned it was with a white box, a blue and red logo printed on either end.

"Pepsi," said the foreigner. Handing them each a can, he dropped to his heels and settled into an uncomfortable-looking squat. "Learnt to sit like this from an Ethiopian," he told Moz. "Met him at the Gare du Nord in Paris. Cool guy, begging. He gave me this . . ." The foreigner pulled a silver cross from inside his shirt. "It's very old."

"And what did you give him?" This seemed important because foreigners didn't always understand the rules governing the giving and receiving of gifts. "You did give him something?"

"My watch." Dave shrugged. "I never really liked it anyway."

"Was it a good watch?"

"Well." The man thought about it. "Depends what you mean by

good. Not gold, if that's what you mean. And it ran on a battery." Until then Moz hadn't known watches could be made from gold or run on batteries. He looked at the foreigner, wondering whether to ask his next question.

"Where's Paris?"

"In France."

"Where's France?"

"You always ask so many questions?"

"Always." Moz nodded. Of course he did. How else was he going to learn anything?

"North of here," said Dave, then smiled as Moz opened his mouth. "Wait," he said, "I'll get my atlas." And he was gone before Moz had time to ask him what an atlas might be.

The first thing Moz noticed about the picture of France were parallel lines along the bottom of the page, each with a 0 at one end and 1000 written at the other, as a number, not as a word. One of them said "kilometres," while the other was labelled...

"*Miles*," he said.

Dave nodded.

There was no secret, miles were just fatter kilometres. Looking closer, Moz realized you got eight of one for five of the other.

In the end, Hassan grew bored with waiting and that meant Idries got bored too. So when Hassan crushed his can and stood, nodding abruptly to the foreigner, Idries did the same.

"Time to go," Idries said.

"I'm staying here," said Moz.

"Coward." It was the first thing either of the silent boys had said in the entire time since Moz was cornered. And as soon as the boy opened his mouth Moz knew why he'd been silent. What with every radio claiming a new war with Algeria was inevitable.

"You're Algerian."

"What of it?"

"Nothing." Moz grinned at Hassan. "Can't you get any real friends?"

"I'll see you later," Hassan said. He jerked his head at Malika. "Come on, time to move."

The nine-year-old looked from Moz to Hassan and then at the white box which contained the Pepsis. "I'm going to stay," Malika said.

# CHAPTER 9

## *Washington, Wednesday 27 June*

"You *can* help . . . ?" Gene Newman sounded almost doubtful.

"We'll see," said Professor Mayer. "Let me send you Katie Petrov. You'll like her. Very bright. Try not to like her too much . . ." Only Professor Mayer would have dreamed of talking to the President like that or got away with it.

"Okay, Petra," he said, "we'll talk later." President Newman put down his phone and flicked shut a little black book in which he kept those numbers which mattered to him. Old friends, ex-lovers, big-budget contributors and his old tutor. The fact he dialled these calls for himself drove his staff wild. That was one of the reasons the President still did it.

Gene Newman had a problem. On the desk in front of him was a telegram from the new Pope congratulating him on the capture of Prisoner Zero and asking him to rescind the death penalty.

A telegram was how the *Washington Post* described it, although the reality was more a list of tightly argued points, some of which were pretty good, particularly the one about not making martyrs. Unfortunately that suggestion didn't seem to be playing well in Kansas.

The letter from the Prime Minister in London was more mealy mouthed but it said more or less the same. Now might be a good time to commute the sentence and avoid making more martyrs than were strictly necessary.

Gene Newman loved that last bit.

"Mr. President . . ."

Gene Newman's secretary walked the long way round to his desk. Even after two years in the job, Isabel Gorst didn't feel right stamping across the eagle that glowered at her from the centre of the Oval Office carpet.

"Isabel."

The President wore black out of respect for those killed in the Marrakech helicopter crash, for the guards in the prison van and for the CIA agent and Moroccan officer whose bodies had been found in a burned-out car. Black tie, black suit, Stars and Stripes enamel badge. He'd been wearing the same outfit for almost a month.

"What have you got there?"

The President asked his question without looking up from the Pope's telegram. All the same there was a warmth to his voice that had the elderly Hispanic woman smiling. She knew it was mostly a side effect of memory.

For much of his early twenties, Gene Newman had earned his living with that voice, still did if he was honest. It had taken him from a local soap to prime-time comedy drama inside of three years. And from there to Hollywood. And his trick, the best he'd ever pulled, was to retire at the height of his earning power.

There'd been no big announcement, just an easing off of public appearances and a reluctance on the part of his agent to forward scripts that weren't original, thoughtful and immaculately written. Since these were rarer than hens' teeth, Gene Newman made two films in his eighteen months in Hollywood, won an Oscar for each and then bowed out so gracefully it took even his agent a year to work out what had happened.

"Edvard asked me to give you this."

She put a thin report on the side of his desk rather than overbalance the unstable pile that was his in-tray.

"It's breeding," said President Newman. He meant his in-tray.

"Let me handle it."

The President looked at her.

They'd been through this before, many times. The President's habit of trying to read everything that passed through his office was regarded with tolerant amusement by his friends and as a sign of paranoia by his enemies.

His wife, who seemed to spend more time than ever in the gym and rarely bothered to read anything before signing it, viewed it as a simple quirk and expected no less from a man who'd thrown in a high-level Hollywood career for three years at Harvard, two years at Oxford and ten months at the Sorbonne.

A number of stories circulated about his reasons for leaving Paris, and in his defence the President would only point out that he was still married and to his first wife, which made him something of a statistical rarity.

"Is that what I think it is?"

Isabel Gorst nodded.

"You read it?"

She looked as shocked as she felt. "It's from the National Security Advisor," she said.

"Just asking."

"Is there anything else, Mr. President?"

"Coffee," he said. He had kitchen staff to do all this, of course, but the First Lady had taken them aside and corrupted the lot of them. Told them about his kidneys, caffeine and the night sweats. So now he got decaf with soya milk as well as only one whiskey a day, more ice than alcohol. Payback for being a little too free with the chemicals in his teens. A fact he'd happily deny on anything except a Bible.

"You know, I'm not sure—" Isabel Gorst began.

"Look," said the President, opening the file. "I'm about to find out exactly why some guy tried to shoot me. I deserve a coffee."

When the cup finally arrived, weak, more milk than coffee, Gene Newman was still coming to terms with the fact that, far from now having his reason, it seemed the entire might of his intelligence services was unable to give him a name, nationality or political persuasion for the man.

"Paula." Gene Newman caught his CIA chief as she was putting on her coat for a meeting on the Hill. "I've got a question."

Paula Zarte waited.

"Why do you think he wanted to kill me?"

She smiled. "You're the President of the United States of America."

"Yep." President Newman nodded. "I've been told that already, but it's not an acceptable answer. Think about it," he said. "*Is* that an answer?"

"It works for me."

"Let them wait," Gene Newman said. "Let's take a stroll."

They walked in silence, Paula waiting as the President watched a bird swoop beyond the Rose Garden. "You know," he said, "Ally wants a cat."

"You don't like cats?"

"Of course I like cats. And dogs and horses, cows, pigs, mules, turkeys, especially turkeys. I even love coyotes. But that's not—" He stopped suddenly. "Did I leave anything out?"

"Eagles, sir."

Gene Newman frowned. "Let's take that one for granted."

"So what's the problem with cats?"

"They kill birds and they make me sneeze."

"Didn't you have a cat in—?"

"Two," he said. "Siamese and Persian. One lilac, one blue. They belonged to the director's mistress. You remember the nose job I was meant to have got done just after I left the show?"

"It's been mentioned."

"That wasn't rhinoplasty, that was how I looked when not suffering from histamine overload."

"Is there something I can help you with, Mr. President?"

"Yeah," Gene Newman said, "there is. There's something Ed's not telling me. I need you to find out what."

"I love this garden . . ."

The CIA operative standing next to a twisted crab apple nodded. He was wearing tortoiseshell glasses and a very good Italian suit, probably better than the one the President was wearing.

"This whole area used to be greenhouses. Did you know that?"

"No, sir."

"Well, it was, before that monstrosity was built." Nodding over his shoulder Gene Newman indicated the lighted windows of the West Wing and the still-open door to his office. "You know what was here before the greenhouses?"

"No, sir."

"Jefferson's pavilion. The one he had built in 1807."

The agent looked blank and Gene Newman sighed.

"You knew Charlie Bilberg?"

He saw the answer in the set of the young man's jaw.

"And you were present when Prisoner Zero was retaken?"

"Yes, Mr. President." Michael Wharton looked like he wanted to add something but restrained himself and Gene Newman smiled.

"I know," he said. "You led the capture, only you didn't because it's not our country, so officially you were there as an observer. An unnecessary question but we have to begin this conversation somewhere. And that was it."

They were standing, shoulder to shoulder, at the far end of the Rose Garden, the President's bodyguards safely out of earshot but firmly within view. Gene Newman was resisting the First Lady's latest suggestion, that he have himself microchipped for safety like some dog, and he'd threatened her with a state visit to Belgium if she dared mention the idea again.

A bit of Gene Newman wanted to ask the boy if he knew who first planted roses on this site and when, but it was unfair to expect everyone to have his own interest in the minutiae of White House history.

"What was Charlie Bilberg like?"

Agent Wharton hesitated.

"This is off the record," said the President. "In about two hours' time, when you've got sufficiently bored being shown Mrs. Roosevelt's china collection by an intern, my Chief of Staff is going to bring you into the Oval Office for thirty seconds so we can go through the rigmarole of being introduced all over again. That will be the first time you've ever met me. Is this clear?"

A quick nod.

"Good. Now tell me about Agent Bilberg."

"He would have made a good officer, sir."

"But he wasn't there yet. Is that what you're saying?"

"He spoke Chleuh."

"What?"

"It's the language of the Atlas, one of them anyway. Charles spoke a little and intelligence suggested Prisoner Zero spoke it also."

"That was why he was sent?"

Agent Wharton almost shrugged, but caught himself in time. "Someone obviously thought—"

"Someone?" the President said sharply.

"Yes, sir."

"But you don't know who?"

"No, sir. I don't have that information."

Gene Newman sighed. "No problem. I'm sorry about Agent Bilberg."

"Yes, sir, so am I."

"He was a friend?"

"No, sir. We barely knew each other."

"Well," said the President, "that was quick." He was still in the garden, thinking about Thomas Jefferson, slave owner, drafter of the Declaration of Independence and third President of the new United States of America.

Paula Zarte's smile was a full-on dazzler and revealed perfect teeth, the kind Gene Newman would never have dared possess, even when he was in Hollywood and certainly not now he was in his late forties. Mind you, for all he knew they were real and untouched by cosmetic dentistry.

"I did what you asked."

"Good," said the President. "That's what you're there for."

Paula paused, decided his comment wasn't serious and risked a mocking smile.

She was beautiful, Gene Newman thought in passing. A full ten years younger than he was with the body of someone ten years younger than that. Full breasts, slight hips and curved buttocks, her skin almost purple in a certain light. The President couldn't help himself, he noticed the same things, every time.

Paula Zarte also had the nerves of a poker player and a brain so sharp he paid it the respect due to an edged weapon.

"Maybe we should go in," Gene Newman said, "before someone starts talking."

They sat in the West Sitting Hall, by a window which overlooked the Executive Office Building. Yellow curtains behind them, eau-de-nil walls and a dado rail and door arch painted in a hue his wife's Italian designer insisted on calling duck-turd blue.

"Is something wrong, Mr. President?"

"A madman wants to kill me and no one can tell me why. The Republicans are targeting my son's girlfriend. My wife thinks I need a trip to the vet. The coffee around here tastes like dishwater. Apart from that everything's fine."

The black woman smiled. "I've just called in the transcript of the very first interrogation, the one when he was first asked why he tried to shoot you."

"And what was his answer?"

"He was listening to the rain."

"What?"

"That's what he said. 'I was listening to the rain.' We're not talking conspiracy here. We're talking lone nutter. That's what Ed doesn't want widely known. Conspiracy plays better."

"And what was he hearing?"

Paula looked puzzled, then understood. "Who knows?" she said. "Something else, I guess . . ."

"You want to be my excuse to order some coffee?"

"Sure," Paula said, amending it to, "that would be good."

The First Lady might not approve of caffeine but she approved of Paula Zarte even less. It was down to the business in Paris. And then the President appointed Ms. Zarte head of the CIA over the head of the obvious candidate. The First Lady wasn't the only one still deciding what she thought about that.

"What do you want?" Gene Newman asked, when the coffee had been brought and a woman from the kitchens had shut the door behind her.

"I'm sorry?"

"I want to win the next election," said the President. "That's short term. Long term I want to walk out of here in six years with some of my self-respect still intact. I want Ally and Bill to be happy. And if I make a small difference to the safety of this country and the world, then that would be good too.

"And if I can't go down in history as a good president then I'll settle for not being a bad one. That's what *I* want. Prisoner Zero risked his life to try to kill me, so that's what *he* wants. Now what do *you* want?"

"My version of what you just said," said Paula. "To be good at this job. Not to screw up. Not to end up with another divorce."

"You guys having trouble?"

"Only the usual," Paula said. "The hours are too long. We're never in the same city at the same time. We buy breast fillet, sugar snap peas and portobello mushrooms every Friday evening and throw the lot out a week later because even when we're both there neither of us has the time, energy or slightest inclination to cook."

"I'm sorry."

Paula sighed. "It gets worse," she said. "Mike's having an affair."

The President had known Paula for most of her life. That was one of the reasons why Paris had been such a mistake. He could still remember the girl she'd been, a spindly army brat off to college. Their families had known each other and the President knew she wasn't telling *him*. She was telling the late twenty-something he'd been back then. Old enough to give advice and not so old it was like talking to someone's father.

"God," Gene Newman said, "when did Mike tell you?"

"He didn't."

He looked at her then.

"Oh yeah," Paula said. "I'm completely compromised."

"You had him followed?"

Her nod was slight.

"By someone you trust?"

"Every day, with my life."

Which had to mean the Puerto Rican woman waiting anxiously in an area now reserved for the bodyguards of those visiting. One of the First Lady's more interesting ideas.

"Felicia?"

Another nod.

"Who is Mike seeing?"

"One of your staff."

The President sighed. "You probably shouldn't have told me that," he said. "You want me to end it?"

"How?"

"I'm sure we need an ambassador somewhere. You stay, Mike goes . . . You can write the closing script nearer the time. Meanwhile think about redeploying Felicia. Make it a promotion."

"And me?"

"You?" The President tipped his head to one side.

"Should I expect to be redeployed?"

"No." Gene Newman shook his head. "This job belongs to you for as long as you want it." He was working on the basis that Paula knew she'd got the job in spite of what happened in Paris and not because of it . . .

"Paula was here." The First Lady's comment was not a question.

"You're right," said the President. "So she was."

"And *that's* why you're sitting in the dark?"

"It's the overload of caffeine."

The First Lady looked around at the sitting room. "Did Paula have anything interesting to say?"

"The man who tried to shoot me had been listening to the rain."

"I can think of better reasons."

"Yes. I'm sure you can."

"Is Paula about to become one of them?"

"No," said Gene Newman, and there was a firmness to his voice which his wife hadn't heard in months. Being shot at seemed to agree with him.

# CHAPTER 10

## *Zigin Chéng, CTzu 53/Year 11*

It was one of the more elegant ironies of immortality that memory could be captured within the lattice of a diamond and that this lattice could be produced by burning and compressing the body from which that memory was taken.

Zaq wore all of the emperors who'd gone before him on his cloak and their memories were his memories, their ennui and hatreds were his also, as were their passions, loves and foibles. It made for a complicated sense of self and some days he would forget who he was and think of himself as just another memory.

An actor in an old-style Beijing opera with a cast of one and an audience of billions.

Other days were different, sometimes very different. On the morning of his fifteenth birthday Zaq decided he was alone, that the audience didn't really exist and never had, he was alone in a pavilion with an uncertain and ever-changing number of rooms, surrounded by smooth-faced eunuchs, almond-eyed concubines, ponytailed warrior guards . . .

All beautiful in their way, all elegant, all fake. As fake as the ambassadors in their city beyond the purple walls.

He was alone.

Zaq found it next to impossible to believe that no other emperor had realized this, so he skimmed their diamonds faster than was safe and ended up on his knees in a corridor, watched by a Manchu guard, vomiting soft-shelled crab onto pink marble. He had been right, though; none of them had realized.

"If it is a truth."

The voice in his head came on his seventeenth birthday, in the evening when hunger was no longer quite so amusing and Zaq was beginning to wonder if he should have sent all his guards away. Retaining one of them might have made sense, except then he wouldn't have been alone and being alone was what this was about.

"Well," Zaq demanded. "Is it true?"

Even as a child he'd spoken rarely to the Librarian, preferring to trust in himself. Nothing in the years which had passed had changed his mind.

"That depends."

Surprise me, thought Zaq.

"Remember that concubine?"

Of course he did. The long blade still lay on the tiles, covered with dust and surrounded by bits of its broken handle. His room had remained his alone since that morning, untidied and inviolate, four years' worth of dirt crusting the floor and griming carved panels until the dragon frieze around the wall looked as if it had been painted with velvet.

"The girl died."

"She wasn't alive in the first place," Zaq said.

"Starvation," said the Librarian. "She starved herself to death in the Restful Gardens."

"In the what?"

A map of the Purple City came into his mind and then Zaq realized it wasn't a map at all, it was an aerial view, showing the three state pavilions, slung out along a north-south axis, with his own quarters, three identical but smaller pavilions to the north of these.

And to the north again, carved out of a sprawl of lesser pavilions, gates and temples was a walled garden he'd forgotten was even there. On the grass, next to a mulberry bush, lay a girl, her eyes closed and hair freed from the pins which had held it in place.

"You know," said Zaq, as he bent to retrieve the dusty blade. "I could have saved you the trouble." Checking its weight, Zaq brought the blade up, waited on the moment and tossed it lightly at the wall, hitting a silk hanging of some mountain pool, the kind with a path skirting the water's edge and a small wooden bridge on which stood two children.

The only thing remotely unusual about the hanging was that rain sleeted from the top left corner, endless stitches of drizzle.

"Was that necessary?"

"You can mend it," Zaq said. "Hell, just make another..."

The Librarian shook its head. There was no other way Zaq could describe the feeling.

"Why not?"

"Because everything in this room is original."

"Including me?"

The Librarian sighed.

That evening rain lashed the Ambassadors' City, flooding a

thousand pavilions and forcing fifty to be abandoned completely. It fell at a slant, roughly left to right, and whole districts which had never been anything but temperate found themselves cowering under slate-grey skies and wondering if the sleet would ever end.

Such weather was rare. In fact, even the cold immortals who made a point of knowing everything had to admit that a storm such as this was unknown. It was understood, because this was taught as a fact of verifiable truth on all 2023 worlds, that life around Star One relied for its very existence on the presence of the Chuang Tzu.

No emperor/no climate, the equation was that simple.

Few alive could still remember the arrival of the first colony ships. Immortality had been perfected, at least in its non-biological forms, but insufficient attention had been paid to the boredom of eternity and the corrosive nature of the ratchet effect which demanded ever sharper, stronger and more intense sensations to maintain something like the same level of satisfaction.

Living forever turned out to be much like long-term sex, psychologically tricky; which was why what killed the original colonists was not hardship but boredom. This became the second crisis to hit the worlds.

The first happened no more than a decade after the colonists landed, when the original Chuang Tzu died. No one was watching the Emperor then because these were still early days in the life of the 2023 worlds. He died in the night, peacefully and in his sleep, having told the Librarian that this was what he wanted to happen because he was now very old and very tired.

On fifty-seven worlds, which was the number then inhabited, colonists woke with headaches that got worse as the day went on. By the following week, half the children had nosebleeds or ruptured ears. While tens of thousands panicked, an elderly Indian scientist ran an analysis on the atmosphere, using a semiAI that had been out of date when her grandmother had loaded it onto the ship which brought her family from Calcutta. The answer was surprisingly obvious.

The oxygen-nitrogen mix which the colonists had assumed was natural to all 2023 worlds was thinning, creating elegant day-glow where ultraviolet interacted with oxygen in the upper atmosphere as it leached away into space.

The worlds were dying.

It took a Tibetan monk to solve the problem and that he bothered at all required compromises with his conscience. Historically, at least, the Chuang Tzu represented everything the man hated about Han imperialism and cultural arrogance. All the same, the monk took a small child whose mother had recently died and presented it to the palace, walking right into the Celestial Chamber to leave the child on the throne, like a screaming sack of rubbish.

The palace was empty, the guards gone. The monk was careful not to enquire where... He wasn't afraid of dying, of course. He'd died a hundred times before and could remember most of his lives; at least those of his lives that had happened since he came close to the gates of enlightenment.

Depositing the child, the man explained in simple terms the laws of reincarnation, paying particular attention to the rules governing the appointment of new lamas. He didn't actually tell the silent air around him that emperors came under similar rules or that the ancient Chosen of Heaven had shared such selection procedures with the throne of the Dalai or Panchen Lama, but he might have suggested it.

And he was careful to present reincarnation as real, inasmuch as anything could be real in a quantum universe where facts were both true, false and linked simultaneously.

So now emperors came and went, living out their short reigns in the gaze of those who lived far longer. Maybe this transience was the inspiration for the butterfly cloak or maybe the butterflies had been taken from the mind of the very first emperor, a newly promoted commissar major who'd been nicknamed Chuang Tzu by his grandmother and not as a compliment.

It was hard to know and probably irrelevant, but at some time during the centuries which followed the dreamer's death it became a tradition for each new incarnation to be visited by a butterfly at night.

## CHAPTER 11

### *Marrakech, July 1971*

Something of the desolation and misery of the *esclave* clung to the walls of Criée Berbere and unnerved those who came in search of bargains from the rug merchants who had taken the slave auctioneer's place.

The buying and selling of people had lasted well into the twentieth century and at one time the going rate in Marrakech was two slaves for a camel, ten for a horse and forty for a civet cat. Those days were gone but there were children in the souks whose grandparents and sometimes even parents had been owned by someone else.

The passage behind Criée Berbere was narrow, high-walled and thick with smoke from a makeshift grill. The height of its walls trapped the grill's thick haze and forced all who used the passage to pass through a cloud of thyme, onion and burning charcoal.

And as the coals over which the skewers of lamb cooked were still a little too hot, the boy behind the grill offered that afternoon's customers cheap paper tissues as protection for their fingers.

He was doing his best not to look at the Englishman.

David Giles sat in a locked doorway, near where the alley turned a corner. His Afghan coat was missing, the Tuarag cross was gone from around his neck and someone had pulled one jeans pocket inside out. He smelt a lot worse than when Moz last saw him but he'd been alive then, that was the difference.

The previous afternoon, Call-me-Dave had been wandering fairly aimlessly from stall to stall in Djemaa el Fna, asking people if they knew somewhere inexpensive he could sleep. Since the second of the day's calls to prayer had barely finished echoing from the square's three minarets this seemed odd to Moz, but the man was a hippie and foreigners were odd by nature.

"What's wrong with your bus?"

It took Dave Giles a second or so to work out that the boy meant his VW Caravette. "The police towed my bus away," he said. "I've got to pay a fine."

"For using the mosque garden?"

Dave Giles shrugged. "They didn't say," he said. "But I need somewhere to stay while my family send money."

Malika's father had offered the man a space on their roof for ten dirham a day, which was nothing for a foreigner, but David Giles turned it down. He was looking for a place with a television. When ould Kasim asked Moz what was wrong with Derb Yassin, he told the old soldier that the foreigner wanted hot water.

It seemed easier.

A dozen heels must have brushed past the *nasrani* as people slipped between the leather and carpet souks and stepped over his outstretched feet while pretending not to notice he was there.

Glancing round, Moz dropped to a crouch beside the foreigner and slid his good hand quickly inside the man's shirt. He was definitely dead and his wallet on a string was gone. An irregular circle of white around one finger revealed he'd also lost his puzzle ring.

In Call-me-Dave's back pocket, however, Moz found a comic—*Galactic Warrior*—which he pocketed before turning to the boy with the grill, who was dicing onions on an upturned tile.

"How long?" Moz asked.

"How long what?"

"Has the dead man been here."

The boy peered at him from under badly cut hair, his face suspicious. "Which dead man?" he said and went back to his onions.

It took courage for Moz to talk to a policeman, even the kind who wore khaki shirts and carried only small guns. And by the time he found that courage a whole café full of officers knew the small one-armed boy wanted to talk to them.

The café was just outside the gates of the Medina. A place of metal chairs, Formica tables and tiny floor tiles that felt like studs under feet. The walls hid behind sheets of reconstituted local marble better suited for public baths or cheap graves. Café Nouveau had been built in the last decade of French rule in a style that was already out of fashion on the mainland. The police used it because no one else did. Or maybe it was the other way round.

"What do you want?"

The one-armed boy didn't answer the sergeant who spoke. He chose instead an officer with a kinder face, a man younger than the others at that table. So it was only by accident that Moz found himself talking to the most senior police officer present. A graduate who'd taken his degree in Paris. Which might have been enough to cause Aboubakr Abbas endless problems, except for the fact that his uncle had only just retired from the force and he'd spent a childhood hanging around staff canteens in the Hotel de Police in Gueliz.

"What?"

"I've found a body." Moz's words came out so quiet that he repeated them without being asked. "In a passage behind Criée Berbere."

"Man or woman?"

The sergeant was waved into silence by Major Abbas.

"A hippie," said Moz, answering anyway.

Major Abbas sighed. "What's the name of this street?"

"It doesn't have one," said Moz.

The Major nodded. There was nothing unusual about that. A hundred different passages in the Old City made do without names and even the most modern government-produced maps left blank whole areas of the Mellah and much of the inner souk.

"And you," said the policeman, "do you have a name?"

"Al-Turq," Moz said, without thinking.

Major Abbas shrugged, he'd heard stranger. Finishing his mint tea with a single gulp, the Major nodded to the others, half farewell and half to say they could stay where they were. "Show me," he said.

## CHAPTER 12

### *Lampedusa, Thursday 28 June*

It was sweat and dirt, not heredity, which gave Prisoner Zero's hair its texture. Something the marine specialist cutting it understood because her boyfriend was black, while her Lieutenant and the Pentagon official standing beside him were not.

After three swipes either side, Prisoner Zero was left with a greying Mohican, a fact that raised a half smile so private it never reached his face. And then the Mohican was gone, buzzed away in a clatter of cheap blades. The clippers were local, garishly chromed and came with five attachments, one for each setting. At the moment the blades were naked, resulting in a crop fine enough to draw blood when they caught a mosquito bite on the back of Prisoner Zero's neck.

It was his first morning at Camp Freedom and beyond the Mediterranean headland dawn was transmuting sullen waves to mercury, while a shoal of flying fish turned unseen to slivers of silver. No fishing boats were allowed near the Punta dell'Acqua, and the tiny cove below the headland had been closed with a chain across its entrance, much as might have happened five hundred years earlier.

The mostly German tourists who originally occupied the hotel had been shipped to other resorts on Lampedusa or sent home.

Where once Turkish raiders landed war parties and Sicilian princes banished their enemies the USS *Harry S. Truman* was now anchored. For the first time in months, pregnant Tunisian *clandestini* weren't staggering through waves or crawling up narrow beaches, too tired even to beg for asylum. As a local Forza Italia spokesman said, sometimes good came from bad.

"Now the beard."

More clippers, starting on Prisoner Zero's jaw, at a point just below his left ear. Once again the hair came away in coarse strips, greyer than before. The marine wielding the clippers finished the left side and started on the right, leaving the man handcuffed to the chair with a long goatee that was almost a cliché of how a terrorist should look.

Examining her handiwork Marine Stone shrugged, took a fistful of the goatee and switched her clippers back on. The prisoner's face was pale from lack of sunlight and sallow, almost olive. He didn't look like an Arab to her, but what did she know?

She was just there to do what she was told.

Lieutenant Ashcroft and the civilian were arguing security arrangements and it seemed to be the man in the suit who was making most of the complaints, all of them idiotic.

The island of Lampedusa was seven miles long and two miles wide and its nearest land mass was North Africa, a mere seventy-one miles away, whereas Sicily, the island to which Lampedusa belonged in spirit if not geographically, was twice that distance. At its peak, during high summer, nine hundred North African asylum seekers a month washed up on what was Italian soil.

"Body hair," ordered the civilian and Specialist Stone glanced at her lieutenant for confirmation, realizing too late that this was a bad move. "Got a problem with that?" the civilian demanded.

"Yes, sir." Her voice was flat. "I have, sir."

"And your problem is what?"

"He's handcuffed to a chair. And wearing clothes, sir."

They shackled the naked prisoner to a bench in the hotel gym, face up, wrists fixed to the legs at one end and ankles to the legs at the other. "They" being Master Sergeant Saez and the man from the Pentagon. None of the current round of visitors wearing suits and shades had bothered to introduce themselves to Specialist Stone; she was only some lowly peon in marine intelligence.

Maybe it was need to know.

Clicking on her clippers, Specialist Stone took the suit at his word and removed all of Prisoner Zero's body hair, starting with his lower legs. When she got to his genitals she just kept going, moving aside his shrunken prick with casual insouciance before starting on his stomach and then chest, around the nipples and under his arms.

Prisoner Zero stank, there was no doubt about that, the kind of stink she remembered from weekend visits to the Chicago Zoo with her father. Even the suit was close enough to notice it.

"He needs a bath," said the Lieutenant.

"No," the suit said. "What he needs is a shower."

"This is de-licing, right?" the Lieutenant asked, when Master Sergeant Saez had finished hosing Prisoner Zero down with water taken from a fire point.

The suit shook his head.

"Then why shave the body hair?"

"Why?" The suit smiled at Lieutenant Ashcroft as if he were a child and a particularly simple one at that. "I'd have thought that was obvious," he said. "We're making it easier to attach electrodes."

Lieutenant Ashcroft wasn't the only one to hope the man was joking.

The first reference to Lampedusa occurred in a letter from Pope Leon III to Charlemagne, Emperor of the West, informing him of a battle between the Byzantines and an Arab army. In 1436 Alfonso of Aragon presented the island to Giovanni de Caro. In 1661, its owner, Ferdinand Tommasi, received the title of prince from the King of Spain. Seventy-five years later, when the English Earl of Sandwich visited the island, he found only one inhabitant.

None of this the Lieutenant had known the evening before, as he piloted a helicopter across the darkening waters of the Mediterranean, with its cargo of three men in suits, five marines and one manacled prisoner.

He had orders, a flight chart downloaded from the Italians, a map reference and GPS positioning in case he still couldn't find the place. As it was, all he actually needed to do was play spot the Nimitz-class aircraft carrier.

There'd been a suggestion that the USS *Harry S. Truman* should be positioned off Lampedusa's south-western tip, between Punta dell'Acqua and the Tunisian coast, but this was felt to be unnecessarily insulting to Tunis, and anyway everyone from the President down knew there was nothing the USS *Truman* couldn't do equally well from the Sicilian side, thirty miles to the north-east...

"Get to it," the Master Sergeant had told a corporal as Lieutenant Ashcroft released the doors and the corporal had nodded at two marines. Together they'd manoeuvred the blindfolded prisoner into the doorway, down some steps and onto a small patch of withered lawn.

Away to one side, a dozen SLRs whirred and a Fox Network reporter began her spiel to camera. Stating the obvious, as always. No one rushed forward or jostled for position. The rules for journalists had been set out in advance, in triplicate, to be signed by department heads.

They were the chosen, flown by the Pentagon to a tiny island in the Mediterranean owned by Italy. And the Italians had been delighted to loan its western tip to the Pentagon. It said so on the press release.

"Walk," demanded the Master Sergeant and Prisoner Zero did, while two marines on either side gripped his upper arms. The swathe of crepe hiding the man's eyes was held in place by a strip of duct tape that circled his entire skull. Plastic cuffs locked his wrists behind his back and a short length of shackle secured both ankles. His shoes were gone and so was the ring he'd worn on his little finger.

Some of the finest linguists at the Pentagon were currently failing to come up with a translation of the flowing script engraved into its red stone, despite using the latest in translation software. This was because it was written in an old form of Persian. Prisoner Zero had no idea what it said either.

He understood colloquial French, that much was now confirmed. A quick and dirty CAT scan having produced language recognition patterns for this, Arabic and rudimentary Berber.

That he spoke English was known from his interrogation.

If Prisoner Zero now failed to acknowledge a single order it was because he chose not to rather than because he didn't understand what was being said. Master Sergeant Saez had his own opinion on that but had been told to keep it to himself, especially while the press were around.

* * *

"So," said the small man, walking over to where Prisoner Zero stood shivering and naked in the early morning light. "This is our man, right?"

As if it could be anybody else.

Lieutenant Ashcroft sighed, mostly at the fact that the Pentagon's representative had excused himself the moment the lawyer came through the doorway and begun to introduce himself. Behind Miles Alsdorf stood Colonel Borgenicht, commandant of the newly named Camp Freedom. He was looking less than happy.

"Yes, sir. This is Prisoner Zero."

Both Colonel Borgenicht and the lawyer paused to examine the man, water dripping from his naked body.

"What happened to his hair?"

"I shaved it off, sir." The answer came from a Marine Specialist so short that she barely stood level with the White House lawyer, who had a career's worth of Cuban heels and hand-made suits behind him, even back in the days when he couldn't afford them.

"And why exactly did you cut it off?" asked Miles Alsdorf. He was holding a very expensive briefcase in one hand and wore this year's Rolex Presidential. Given what the White House was paying for his counsel on this matter, he could easily afford both.

Specialist Stone looked towards Lieutenant Ashcroft. Only the Lieutenant was busy not meeting her eyes.

"Because those were my orders, sir."

"And who gave this order?"

"A man in a suit, sir. He didn't give his name."

Miles Alsdorf's frown was usually reserved for opposing counsel. "You do know, don't you," he said, speaking to the Colonel, "that the President himself is taking a personal interest in this case?"

"So is the Secretary of Defense," said Colonel Borgenicht. The current spat between the White House and the Pentagon was their business. He was a career officer and hoped to keep it that way.

The corridor leading to his cage Prisoner Zero drew from memory, scratching it into the skin of his arm with a thumbnail. The only problem with this was that his map kept fading.

At the end of the corridor was a door and through that door could be found the hotel's swimming pool, its showers and changing rooms. Two marines had been in the process of emptying the pool, using an electric pump, when Prisoner Zero was marched by. Maybe they expected him to try to drown himself.

He currently wore a pair of trousers made from coarse orange paper, designed to fasten with a cord. The cord was also made of paper and broke easily. The prisoner knew this because he'd broken it.

He'd received four injections and been told he'd get antibiotics three times a day with his food. The cigarette burns on the inside of his thigh had been cleaned without comment by a marine paramedic, swabbed with some antiseptic and then dressed with a strip of synthetic skin. They were taking remarkably good care of him for someone they intended to kill.

And they did still intend to execute him, because more lethal injections were scheduled for two weeks to the day, Thursday 12 July. Although, as Master Sergeant Saez had pointed out, if the Pentagon was allowed its way, Prisoner Zero would already be up against a wall.

Fittingly enough, the wall Master Sergeant Saez had in mind was the one Prisoner Zero first noticed when Specialist Stone ripped free his blindfold the night before, and the prisoner found himself staring at a tourist hotel.

Almost pink in the twilight, the wall was meant to look as if it had stood forever. Only a workman had plastered the thing too soon, certainly before the mortar holding the breeze blocks had had a chance to dry, and angular cracks now indicated stress points in the structure underneath.

In the wall was a wrought-iron gate. This had been padlocked and sheeted on both sides with steel plates which were held in place by bolts. Next to the gate was a flowerbed and this had been trampled down. After the wall, the door and the flowerbed, the next thing Prisoner Zero had noticed was a curl of dog shit on the earth, turning to ash with age.

As Prisoner Zero scratched maps into his arm, Specialist Stone got busy painting out a window opposite Prisoner Zero's cage. Obliterating a stretch of ragged cliff with blue sea beyond, the dissonance between ochre rock and the utterly flat blueness of the Mediterranean an indication of the depth of the drop.

In one dimension, the blue was so close as to be part of the same, while in another it was obviously and entirely separate. As it was in the dimension beyond that.

Gulls, dark-headed and greedy, spun on the thermals above the edge of the cliff and then dropped away, like bit parts in some conjuring trick. Butterflies danced beyond the glass and then they were gone, along with the cliff, gulls and his sight of the sea, whitewashed away with a heavy brush.

It had all been very beautiful, in some ways more real than anything he'd ever seen, and yet Prisoner Zero had trouble working out what all this had to do with him. He should have been elsewhere. In America, most probably on the lawn of the White House with the latest rifle and laser sights. Saving the future from itself.

"Are they treating you well enough?"

Miles Alsdorf must have been told what to expect because his face expressed no surprise at finding his client held in a cage made by welding together huge sheets of steel mesh. The big surprise for Miles Alsdorf was that he'd won his fight for daily access.

The cage had been welded into place in the middle of the hotel weights room, which had been cleared of dumbbells and a pair of dual-stack multigyms, although mats were still piled below a large window; now whitewashed, padlocked and covered with mesh left over from welding the cage.

"Colonel Borgenicht's just been explaining it to me," Miles Alsdorf added, stepping into the room and shutting out the guards behind him. "They don't want to lose you."

Silence greeted this comment but he kept smiling all the same. He'd defended New York cop-killers, three black teenagers accused of raping the daughter of a Texas senator and a self-confessed baby-smotherer, a twenty-three-year-old from Kansas too deep into heroin even to remember how she got pregnant. And once, about fifteen years before, he'd defended the butcher of Lyons, an octogenarian Nazi whose senility stopped him from even knowing that he'd committed the crime.

"I'm Miles," said the man, "Miles Alsdorf, remember? I've been retained as your lawyer. We need to appeal," he added. "And the sooner the better." Lifting his briefcase, he looked around for a place to put it and realized too late that there wasn't one. So he put it down again and squatted on one side of the wire, while Prisoner Zero sat, his knees tucked up under his chin, on the other.

Pulling a Dictaphone from his pocket, Miles described the cage in short, clipped sentences, making particular reference to the fact that the prisoner's slop bucket had no lid and that visitors such as himself had nowhere to sit. And then something else occurred to him.

"How are you supposed to know where Mecca is?"

Prisoner Zero stared at him.

"I thought people like you had to pray five times a day?"

Like me?

*Only if they believe in God,* Prisoner Zero wanted to say, but he didn't; believe in God or say it either. He believed in cold equations, Quantum Foam and in time, which he knew had two mutually compatible shapes. The first spiralled out like an ice-cream cone, widening in circles from a single point at the bottom, the other was spherical.

He'd chased down some of the equations twenty years before, thinking about little else towards the end and always reaching the same conclusion. Time was a marble.

A book had held his proof. A cheap notebook mostly full of songs, with tattered corners and a vomit stain across the back. Its final pages were brittle and wavy from cat pee, where Miu had got trapped indoors one weekend and been reduced to pissing on Prisoner Zero's notes and a pile of *New Scientists* in one corner. The nearest thing she could find to a litter tray.

That would have been the last summer in Amsterdam. The year Johnny Thunders issued *Hurt Me* on the New Rose label. The year of *New England.*

## CHAPTER 13

### *Zigin Chéng, CTzu 53/Year 13*

Emperors had killed themselves before, not often admittedly, although one famously threw himself off a cliff during a thunderstorm. And it was felt by many that the Librarian should have realized the cliff incident was about to happen, given that the old man had spent the previous week working himself up into thunder and lightning.

At which point, someone offered the belief that the Librarian had known exactly what was about to happen and chosen not to interfere. The resulting discussion about the nature of free will lasted for roughly eighty years and led to the colonization of a new world as a third of the inhabitants on a world in the equatorial belt took themselves off into exile.

No emperor had ever tried to starve himself, if this was what was happening, and there were arguments about that too. Some believed the latest Chuang Tzu was ill and should be treated or helped, and the feeling among these was that the Library should reach into the young man's mind to send him to sleep, working its magic while the Emperor was unable to harm himself. Others saw what was happening as a battle between the new Chuang Tzu and the Library itself. Although what they were fighting over and exactly what weapons were being used was open to debate.

And so Zaq found himself sitting with his back to his bed, the blade and tang held loosely in one hand. He'd taken to pissing against a pillar, as if he'd forgotten or no longer cared that an audience of billions might be watching. And while it was true that he still hid for the more serious ablutions he went to the commode alone, with none of the ceremony or retinue of attendants which usually accompanied him.

It was into this stalemate that a man climbed, scaling the outer walls of the Purple City as if he'd been practising all his life. He wore green trousers and a red shirt, black gloves and no shoes, the soles of his feet having been modified both to increase his grip and do away with the need for footwear. His hair was black and worn tied back, much like Zaq's own.

The man was in his twenties. A mere child in the eyes of most who watched his climb. Hardly anyone in the Servitors' City paid much attention to him at first. All the important people had been summoned by the palace master to discuss what could be created that was exquisite enough to bring the Emperor out of his depression.

As expected the first concubine, chief cook and head musician had very different opinions, although not one was able to suggest something that hadn't been tried a dozen times before.

And so the man walked between the low houses traditional to the Servitors' City until he reached the Manchu Gate, which led through the City of Ambassadors to the Tiananmen and Wu Gates, the last of which guarded the entrance to the palace.

In fact, "palace" was really a misnomer for a complex of temples, courtyards and yellow-roofed pavilions, surrounded by a wide moat which lapped gently against a walkway that ran along the bottom of the walls.

There were a thousand courtyards and nearly ten thousand rooms within the walled space of the Zigin Chéng, otherwise known as the Forbidden City. Of these, six pavilions, three gates and two bridges were significant and all of those were slung out along a north-south axis like fat weights on a fishing line.

The first of the important pavilions was the Qianquing, known as the Dragon Gong. It had a two-tiered roof that turned up at the corners and its walls were cinnabar red, both inside and out, while the wooden beams which supported its yellow-tiled roof were painted green and red, again as propriety required. At each corner of the roof, carved dragon *acroteria* protected the Chuang Tzu from evil spirits

Behind the Qiangquing was the Jiaotai Gong, where imperial seals were stored and the empress received homage. A small pavilion with a single roof lay behind this, where the empress slept and received the emperor, when there was an empress, which there wasn't.

These three pavilions made up the imperial quarters and were copies of larger, ceremonial buildings further south. And whereas the private buildings were raised from the ground on a simple marble platform, the great ceremonial pavilions of Preserving Harmony, Central Harmony and Supreme Harmony stood upon a triple platform. So that the very first brick of Supreme Harmony, the greatest of the halls, was four times the average height of an imperial soldier.

Begun in the fifteenth century, Earth era, on the site of an earlier city and laid out to strict Confucian lines, the original Forbidden City had taken fourteen years to build and required the toil of a hundred thousand artisans and the enslavement of a million Chinese peasants. No one knew how long it took the second Zigin Chéng to grow. There were a few who believed that *acroteria*, followed by yellow-glazed tiles, had twisted out of the ground like shoots from a seed.

And there were others who believed that the city formed itself overnight while the first Chuang Tzu slept: Although these were divided into those who believed the outer city was formed new and fell into disrepair and those who believed it grew ready-aged, some walls already crumbled and courtyards fallen into disrepair.

As with most things, the majority of the 2023 worlds' 148 billion inhabitants never gave the matter a single thought. The City of Ambassadors and the Servitors' City had been wrapped around the palace for over forty-five centuries and the palace had been wrapped around the beating heart of the emperor's pavilions for just as long.

Two hundred paces along the walkway, to the east of the Wu Gate, a sluice in the purple walls let through the Golden River, although iron bars closed off this route to all living creatures larger than a ten-year-old carp.

"Not for us." One glance at the bars and the man kept walking, his gaze on a corner turret a hundred paces beyond that. It was impressive, triple-tiered and almost a fortress in its own right. In its shadow, three fishermen in court robes were busy climbing into a flat-bottomed boat.

The man dressed as a servitor smiled at them politely and turned the corner, passing the East Gate, where a dragon arch fit for an emperor was flanked by a phoenix gate for his empress, with lesser entrances for everyone else, beginning with squared porches for civil and military administrators and ending with a simple wooden door that let such as him go about their business.

Nodding to a guard, the man walked on. Several hundred paces further along the walkway was the north-east corner turret.

"Right," said the young man, "this looks like it." On his shoulder sat a large rat, eyes full of panic. It was bred for night work in tight spaces and the walkway and wide moat gave the animal agoraphobia. So the rat didn't really care which turret its owner chose so long as he took them somewhere darker, preferably with a roof and walls on all sides.

The young man assumed his pet ran some kind of simpatico system but the truth was stranger: an ancestor of the rat had been coded for basic language skills. To say that Null understood more than it said was ludicrous because—obviously enough—the rat said nothing; but Null could comprehend a vocabulary of about fifty words and construe probable meaning from the tone of many others.

"Up here, I guess..."

Long lengths of bamboo scaffolding fat as a child's leg had been erected against the north-east turret and lashed together at the cross points with rope. When the young man got closer, he realized that the uprights actually grew from the dirt while the crossbars were held in place by vines which had grown up the side of the scaffolding. A barge loaded with roof tiles had been tied to a wooden pontoon.

Climbing the rig was simplicity itself, so while the rat shut its eyes the young man made his way to the top, walked a plank between scaffold and crenellations and dropped into a different walkway, one that ran from corner turret to corner turret around the walls of the Purple City.

Below him were the eastern pavilions, storehouses and the Qianlong Gardens. Walled areas within other walled areas within the walls of the palace. A vast and elderly eunuch waddled from beneath an arch and stopped to watch a gardener's child roll a hoop from one side of a tiny courtyard to the other. Behind the chamberlain came two younger eunuchs, probably not much older than the man watching from the top of the wall, although both had the soft, child-like faces of those who'd been castrated at least a year prior to reaching puberty.

And though none of these three looked up to where the servitor stood on the upper walkway, a billion or more watchers saw him reach out to soothe his rat, explaining his plan in simple words until the rat began chattering to itself.

As far as the Library could tell, the Emperor was not aware of this rise in interest from those watching, which in itself was worrying, not because sulking was unknown to emperors but because the Librarian expected a stronger link between the watchers and one raised to the Celestial Throne.

Yet, with Zaq, this link was no stronger than the link between those watching and the young man now walking calmly into the north-east turret, smiling to a guard and starting down the tower's great wooden stairs.

Since it was impossible for a servitor to manifest the same level of empathy as the Chuang Tzu, the Librarian dropped this anomaly down a level, allowing a subroutine to extrapolate all possible reasons simultaneously and arrive at no single explanation logical enough to pass back.

"See?" said the young man. "Nothing to it."

The rat wisely stayed silent.

Man and rat might as well have been invisible to the inhabitants of the Forbidden City, for all the attention they attracted as they left the turret and crunched along the wide stretch of gravel between the boundary wall of the eastern pavilions and the northern wall of the Forbidden City itself. Two minor eunuchs even stood aside to let the servitor pass.

"Thank you."

"You're welcome." It was clear from the ennui in the taller eunuch's voice that he'd barely registered the existence of the man for whom he just stepped aside.

"Whatever..." Tucking the rat into the sleeve of his coat, the man cut through the north gate of the Imperial Garden, exited through the southern gate and passed under an arch into the Emperor's inner court, at the centre of which stood a marble dais and the three private pavilions.

As with all areas within the Forbidden City, the inner pavilions were circled by their own walls. Only these walls were formed by a continuous line of offices, bedrooms for concubines, a kitchen and endless store-houses for gifts from the various ambassadors, mostly unopened and some going back ten or fifteen centuries.

A chef was waddling towards him so the man stepped hastily back, out of the chef's line of sight. Then he counted to a hundred, which he managed by counting slowly to ten and then counting to ten again and again, starting with the little finger of his left hand and finishing with its mirror image on his right.

"Where's the Master Chef?"

The servitor fired off his question the moment he stepped out of the steam, materialising beside a bubbling cauldron of crab broth, into which a tall sous chef with a hollow face dropped intricately wrapped dim sum.

"It's just," continued the servitor, "that His Celestial Excellency requires something to eat..."

Chang San, whose unfortunate nickname was Old Rat, blinked and disdain gave way to shock, followed quickly by envy and finally careful consideration.

"I'll arrange something," he said, as over his shoulder another half a billion watchers understood instantly that this was exactly the chance for which the sous chef had been waiting. "You can go," he told the younger man, "leave this to me."

"I'm afraid not." The young man shook his head, appearing almost contrite. "I'm to take it to His Celestial Excellency myself." He glanced into the copper pot boiling on a range beside Chang San. "Shrimp?"

"Pork," said the sous chef.

"They look perfect," said the servitor. "Guaranteed to touch any emperor's heart."

Shrewd eyes watched the younger man. "You will tell His Celestial Excellency that Chang San prepared the dim sum, won't you?"

"Of course," said the servitor. "You have my word." He looked beyond the boiling cauldron to busier cooking ranges. Chilli and ginger sharpened the air, while dancing flames flash-flared like furious ghosts above red-hot woks and oily smoke caught in his throat.

All possible meals were being prepared at all possible times. Unfortunately it was weeks since the Emperor had eaten any of them.

"I'll need a tray," the servitor said.

For a second it looked as if Chang San might simply yell across the kitchen to one of the boys, but though the chef opened his mouth to shout he thought better of the idea. Nodding to himself, Chang San told the servitor to stay where he was.

When he returned it was with a tray edged in red-lacquered ebony and inset across the base with a thin, almost completely translucent slab of mutton-fat jade.

"Treat this carefully," said Chang San, handing his prize possession to the waiting servitor. "It belonged to the previous Chuang Tzu."

## CHAPTER 14

### *Marrakech, Summer 1971*

Major Abbas waited for a cart to get out of his way and then stepped over the legs of a beggar as if she didn't exist. The boy beside him stopped for a second, but only because the Berber woman was feeding her child, pendulous breast sucked hollow by the infant's appetite.

On the western edge of Djemaa el Fna, where orange-juice stalls lined the sticky blacktop, Moz risked a glance at a fruit seller and then flicked his eyes sideways, his gaze drawn by a passing handcart piled high with dates, *dragut noir* from the look of them.

"Hungry?" Major Abbas asked.

"Thirsty," Moz said.

The police officer pushed his way through the crowds to the

nearest stall. "One juice," he said, then indicated a French tumbler blown from greenish glass, bubbles suspended in the sides. "Make it large."

And together Moz and the police officer waited in the gathering dusk as the stallholder pulped half a dozen oranges and strained the juice through a plastic sieve. Smoke from a recently erected rotisserie stall competed with red grit to fill the air. As ever, tables and chairs were being set out in the busy centre of the square, arranged around kitchen carts, their hand-scrawled menus taped to metal posts that kept overhead canopies in place.

Drugged cobras, outlandishly dressed water sellers and Berber medicine men occupied a patch of dusty ground to one side of the stalls, while round the edge of the square, like wagons protecting an encampment, stood the inevitable juice stalls. Always the first thing anyone saw, whether they were local, hippies or just tourists.

"How much?" Major Abbas asked.

"To you, Excellency, nothing." The small man waved the policeman's coins away with a broad smile.

Major Abbas nodded. "*Bismillah*," he said, handing the glass to Moz.

"*Bismillah*." Moz took a gulp and then another and would have finished the glass if he hadn't suddenly caught the policeman's wry expression. "Sorry," Moz said, holding out his tumbler. "Here."

The policeman shook his head. "Sip it," he said. "Otherwise you won't taste the orange juice properly."

The juice was bitter but sweet at the same time and cloudy with fragments of pulp which had evaded the sieve. Some of these ended up stuck to his lips, like fragments of sunburn.

"How does it taste?"

"Sweet and bitter."

"Like life," said the Major. His glance at the boy was thoughtful. "Why did you come to tell someone about the body?"

"It's my duty."

Major Abbas laughed. The Interior Ministry had been running a radio campaign to remind ordinary people of their duty to the country. It was simple, even mundane. A straightforward repetition of the obvious. Obey the law and all would be well. Disobey and...

Well, everyone knew what happened to those who disobeyed.

"You want a cake?"

Moz grinned.

"It's for the policeman," he told a stallholder, pointing to a pile of sticky pastries and then nodding at the man who stood watching. In Moz's hand was a pile of small change, coins given to him by Major Abbas.

"I hope His Excellency enjoys it." Dead eyes stared at the boy, utterly emotionless; so emotionless that no emotion was necessary. Quietly and quickly, Moz made a sign with his fingers and the man blinked, his gaze flicking to the policeman who stood oblivious.

Moz had no idea what the signal meant, but he'd seen Hassan use it to an older boy who let Hassan pass without trouble. It only worked in the souk and around this edge of Djemaa el Fna. Moz had been using it a lot recently.

"Take care," said the man.

Moz nodded.

"Here's your change," Moz said, as he offered the Major a handful of tiny five-franc pieces. A hundred francs made up a dirham and everyone was meant to call them cents now but nobody did. Moz had already pocketed a third of the coins for himself, which was what he imagined the cake might cost. It was hard to tell; he'd never bought anything in Djemaa el Fna before.

"Keep it," said the policeman.

When they got to the passage behind Criée Berbere the body was gone and all that remained was the ghost of old ammonia and a treacle-like stain where the man had sat.

"He was here," Moz protested.

"I'm sure he was," Major Abbas said. "So let's find out where he's gone."

Hammering on the door of a workshop, the policeman waited a few seconds for his answer and then hammered again. Whatever the weaver intended to say got swallowed when he recognized the uniform of the man standing outside his door.

"There was a body," Major Abbas said. It was not a question.

The man nodded.

"Where did it go?"

"The dog woman took it."

Both men looked at each other.

"She insisted."

"Where was she taking it?"

"To hospital."

"She was taking a dead man to hospital?"

The carpet maker nodded and the police officer sighed.

"Who carried it?" he asked.

"I don't know," the carpet maker said. "She asked me to lend her Hamid but I refused. She's not clean."

Major Abbas wasn't sure if the man meant in a spiritual, religious or physical sense. Not that it mattered. Lady Eleanor Devona slept with spaniels on her bed, rarely washed and shared her life with Elsie Strickland, a woman ten years younger but infinitely more decrepit. Any form of uncleanness would have been appropriate.

"You know the way?" Major Abbas asked Moz. "To the dog woman's house," he added impatiently, when Moz looked blank.

"Of course."

Her door had a huge brass dolphin as its knocker. Maltese, the woman told them when she noticed them looking. A dolphin door knocker and nothing else. No handle, no visible hinges and none of the usual broad-headed nails found on Medina doors.

"Come in," she insisted. "Don't mind Molly, she doesn't bite." Nodding beyond a yapping spaniel to an elderly woman who leant on two canes, all hips and twisted pelvis, Lady Eleanor added, "That's Elsie. She doesn't bite either."

Major Abbas smiled. It was the smile of someone trying very hard to take shallow breaths.

"So," said Lady Eleanor, slamming bolts into place behind them. "You've come about the body." Being the dog woman, she said this in English and when Major Abbas spread his hands to reveal his lack of the language Lady Eleanor sighed. "*Le corpse*," she said loudly. "*Le cadavre*."

"*Elle a dit vous venir au sujet du cadavre*." Moz spoke quietly, tugging at the Major's sleeve for attention...

"Such a clever boy," Lady Eleanor told the Major, opening the door to show them out. "Such a pity he's only got one arm."

Moz didn't bother to translate, although he touched his hand to his heart, mouth and forehead, bowing deeply when she slipped a five-dirham note into his jellaba pocket.

"Come back sometime," she told Moz. "You can take Molly for a walk."

"Can you believe it?" The Major had to be talking to himself because Moz was five paces behind him, head down. They were getting near the boy's street. Major Abbas recognized all the signs. It wasn't fear of his parents which made the boy so jumpy but fear of being seen by his friends in the company of a policeman.

Some things were harder to live down in the Mellah than others.

"Your name?" Major Abbas demanded suddenly. The notebook he took from his pocket was regulation issue, cheap paper that tore beneath the nib of his pen. "Hurry up..."

The last was said loudly enough to be overheard by two boys watching from the entrance to a nearby alley.

"Al-Turq, sir."

"Your real name."

"I don't know, sir."

Major Abbas frowned. "You must have a name."

"Marzaq," said the boy.

"That's what your parents named you?"

"I suppose so," Moz said. "My mother anyway. I don't know about my father. She doesn't talk about him."

"And she calls you Marzaq?"

"Not often. She calls me honey." She called everyone honey; sometimes Moz suspected that anything else was just too complicated. His mother hated complications.

The Major could hear a snigger from where he stood. So he looked up from his pad and glared at the two boys still watching. One of them stared back, but when he stepped towards the alley's entrance both slid away. Small fish retreating in an aquarium gloom.

"Where do you live?"

"Near here," Moz admitted. "Just behind the old mosque. The one with the broken roof. Three doors from the *tabac*."

Major Abbas wrote it down exactly as given. "Your mother's a hippie?"

"She's German," said Moz.

"But she speaks Arabic?"

The boy shrugged. "A little," he agreed, "also some French, not much though."

"And your father?"

"Dead," Moz said. "At least I hope so."

Major Abbas flipped shut his cheap notebook and looked around him. The walls of the alley were peeling, scabs of plaster littering the ground. Even the feral cats were thinner than elsewhere and for the Mellah that made them almost dead. Ribs like cracked twigs and fur matted with dust. The place stank of shit, human and animal, and with the heavy taste of blood from a nearby slaughterhouse. Jewish maybe. Most of the usual slaughterhouses were on the edge of the Medina.

"Your arm," Major Abbas said to the boy. "How did you lose it?"

Moz looked down at the empty sleeve pinned to the front of his jellaba, so that it couldn't flap free.

"I didn't," he said, "it's still there."

The Major stared at the boy's face but it was free of irony or insult; in fact, Major Abbas doubted that the small boy even knew what irony was. As for madness, how could anyone tell? But the boy's huge brown eyes were clear and his gaze firm. The kid had the longest eyelashes of anybody he'd ever seen, Major Abbas realized, then looked away, suddenly embarrassed.

"What do you mean it's still there?" The words came out harder than he'd intended.

"It's there," Moz said. "Wait, I'll show you." Without pausing, the boy unbuttoned the neck of his jellaba, dragged the garment over his head with his one good hand and discarded it in the dirt. "See?"

He stood naked, his body thin as a kitten and every rib visible for counting, legs thin like a stork's and genitals small as a lost acorn. Turning, Moz presented his scarred shoulders and thin buttocks to the man who hardly saw them, he was too busy looking at the arm twisted behind Moz's back and tied in place with cheap twine.

"Why?" Major Abbas asked.

"I use the wrong hand," Moz said, his voice matter-of-fact. "All the time. Mostly to eat. You know, my dirty hand."

Everyone Major Abbas knew ate with their right hand only. And in Paris it had been a shock to see his French friends, people he regarded fondly, tearing at their baguettes with both hands and lifting fruit from bowls with whichever hand was nearest. All the same . . .

"Your mother does this?"

The boy shook his head. "Malika's father."

"But your mother lets him?"

"He owns the house," said Moz, as if that explained everything and perhaps it did.

"So," Hassan said later. "You're friends with policemen now."

Moz shrugged.

"Tell me," insisted Hassan. "What were you talking about?"

"Nothing."

"He walked you across Djemaa el Fna and bought you cakes for nothing?" There was a slyness to his voice Moz hadn't heard before.

Idries sniggered.

"I'm going home," Moz said firmly.

"What a good idea," said Hassan. "We'll come with you."

Twisting to check his escape route, Moz spied the two Algerian boys leaning against the wall about ten paces behind him. Both were smiling. He knew what was coming and was obscurely glad that Malika was not there to see it.

"Catch me," Moz said, jinking around Hassan and cutting down an alley so tight a toddler could have touched both sides at once.

They did.

## CHAPTER 15

### *Lampedusa, Saturday 30 June*

The office was tiny, stacked with boxes. On one wall a work roster gave duties to Antonio, Marc and Gus, bar staff who'd long since been sent back to their villages. A marine artificer had bolted a steel grill across the room's only window, reducing the daylight to baroque shards which ran across the top of a desk as if escaping from a painting.

An electric fan on a small filing cabinet swung back and forth. Every time it reached hard right it glitched, clattering noisily as it stripped plastic gears, before beginning to swing back again. Prisoner Zero would have liked to fix it but both his feet were shackled to a chair.

"Have they been treating you well?"

Prisoner Zero looked at the redhead in the doorway and then flicked his gaze to the marine and the suit behind. The suit wore black Armani, with a red tie and white shirt. His shoes were expensive but dusty, the side effect of not being senior enough to rate his own jeep. On his little finger was a graduation ring. It looked expensive.

"Doesn't he talk?"

The suit's question was addressed to his military escort. The man was a civilian so Master Sergeant Saez didn't bother to answer.

"I'm Katie."

Stepping towards the chair, Dr. Petrov held out one hand and waited. When the prisoner didn't take it, she kept her hand extended, apparently counting off the seconds behind watchful green eyes. At a point known only to herself, Katie Petrov dropped her hand and nodded.

"I'm Bill Logan," said the suit. "And this is Dr. Petrov. She'll be asking you some questions."

"Everything you tell me will be in confidence." Katie's voice was firm and the glance she gave Bill Logan was heavy with meaning. "I want you to know that."

"I'll leave you with him then."

"That would probably be a good idea." Turning to the desk, Katie picked up a manila file and flicked it open. Inside was a single piece of lined paper, blank on both sides. She usually used a Psion Organiser to record her notes and then downloaded them to her laptop, but this was different.

"Undo the shackles," she told the marine. "And then let me have the room to myself."

"The shackles are to stay on, ma'am," Master Sergeant Saez said. "And I'm to stay here."

"Not a chance," said Katie Petrov. "I don't talk to patients in front of third parties. It's unethical."

"For your own safety, ma'am."

The psychiatrist smiled. "I have a black belt in jitsu," she said. "I work out for two hours a day. Look at him..." She nodded at Prisoner Zero who sat, head down, staring at dust that danced in the shards of sunlight, his body encased in a filthy orange jump suit. "Do you really think he's a threat?"

"He tried to kill the President."

"With an antique rifle," said Katie Petrov, "from almost half a mile away. And I'm not the President, thank God."

"All the same," said the Master Sergeant. "My orders are to stay with the prisoner."

"Really?"

Master Sergeant Saez nodded.

"Then we have a problem," Katie told Bill Logan. Shutting her file with a snap, Katie ignored the marine, nodded politely to Prisoner Zero and prepared to vacate the room designated her office.

"Where are you going?" Bill Logan was media coordinator for this operation, his temporary release from CavourCohen Media coming after a brief call to Max Cohen from someone unspecified at the Pentagon.

"Where do you think?" Katie said. "If you can fly me out to the middle of nowhere then presumably you can fly me back again."

She eyeballed the man in the black suit, gaze firm. She knew exactly who Logan was and how he'd made his reputation, but since the man hadn't bothered to introduce himself properly Katie chose to think of him in the abstract, as a hanging for expensive clothes and limited outlooks. Doing this made it easier not to feel worried by her decision.

"We'll get another psychiatrist," said Bill Logan. "That won't be hard. And you're only here because you went to college with the President's son. In fact, we can make a virtue of this. Announce that you felt compromised by your knowledge of the First Family. Unable to assess the maniac who tried to kill—"

"Except that's not what *I'll* be announcing," Katie said, "is it?" She put her folder back on the desk and turned to face the man. Without even realizing, she fell into a combat pose. A fact not missed by Master Sergeant Saez, who took a second look at her, reappraising.

"What I'll announce," she said, "is that I turned down this assignment because you refused to give me proper access to Prisoner Zero. A man who is quite obviously drugged. To this statement, I'll add a rider. That, in my personal opinion, flying me out to this godforsaken island was nothing more than a cynical media exercise by the Secretary of Defense designed to keep the White House quiet..."

"Okay," said Katie. Picking up her pencil, she wrote "30 June" at the top of her piece of paper, then added "Isola di Lampedusa" and "Session One."

If in doubt begin at the beginning.

Under that, Katie wrote "Question One."

Beyond the window, marines continued to crunch their way across gravel, coming to the end of a path and then starting back, their swivel a rasp of stone against metal. The sound reminded Katie of her childhood. Not that she'd spent her childhood on military bases. Her father had owned a gold Dunhill lighter, the kind with a revolving pillar built into one corner. Turning the pillar made steel grind against flint to create the spark.

She'd loved that lighter.

"Tell me about your childhood," Katie Petrov said.

It was the question few clients could resist. Occasionally some patient would throw a tantrum and flatly refuse to answer, which was an answer in itself. And often Katie found herself explaining that just because something bad had happened didn't make it significant. As for the number of times ex-lovers had lain there in the dark, still burning from the afterglow, to paint the night with their *when I was young* . . .

Looking up from her sheet of paper, Katie found the prisoner staring at her. For a second she thought Prisoner Zero was looking at her breasts and then she realized, even as she blushed and grew angry with herself for blushing, that it wasn't her breasts which interested him but the 2b pencil in her hand.

"You want this?"

The pencil was entirely black, little more than a stub, with "Calvin Klein" written in script down one side and a black rubber at the top, slightly chewed.

"From an old boyfriend," she said. "A fashion journalist. We didn't last long." Men talked about themselves when they felt insecure, women when they were at their most confident. And Katie worked on the basis of information exchange; not everyone in the profession approved but it worked for her.

Prisoner Zero's eyes never left her hand, his gaze animal and hard. Working in prisons had taught Katie that almost anything could be used as a weapon. This was why her pencil was short and blunt. Too short really to hold properly, which made the thing too short to be used as a weapon. At least Katie hoped so.

"You want it?"

The man nodded.

"Then say so."

Prisoner Zero transferred his gaze from her hand to her face. He looked younger than she'd been led to expect and strangely vulnerable now that his beard and tangled hair were gone. It was hard to reconcile him with the bug-eyed fanatic featured on the front of every paper.

"Say yes," said Katie, "and you can have it. At least until the end of the session."

The man simply stared at her.

"I know you understand."

Holding out his hand, the man waited. And Katie had to force herself not to gasp at the lacerations across his palm.

"They did that to you?"

Was that a shake of his head? Katie Petrov wasn't sure. All she knew was that the man's hand remained out and his gaze had returned to the pencil.

"Okay," she said, "why not?"

Prisoner Zero tore the pencil's eraser from its sheath with his teeth and bit flat its hollow black tube. Then he ripped open the front of his orange jump suit, slid his arms from the sleeves and began to drop his trousers.

"What are you—?" Katie was about to hit the attack alarm she'd been given and which hung on a paper ribbon around her neck, when Prisoner Zero sat down again and began to use the flattened metal tube to scratch rapid lines into his thighs, blood beading the middle of the lines where his improvised blade dug deepest.

When the map was finished, Prisoner Zero flipped round the pencil, sucked blood from the edge of the metal and then used the pencil's point to sketch an identical map on the inside of his jump suit. Only then did he stand up, almost as if nothing had happened, and shuffle his arms back into the sleeves.

"Put it on the desk," said Katie. "If you've finished with it."

So he did, placing the pencil parallel to the edge, with its blunt lead just touching the corner of the manila file. This was to stop the pencil from rolling away. The ripped-free eraser he balanced on end just below the point of the pencil, like the dot on an exclamation mark.

Katie now knew three things about Prisoner Zero. He manifested self-destructive tendencies, he was anal, in the broader, less accurate sense of being meticulous and he was uncircumcised, which was definitely culturally counter-intuitive. He was also either unashamed of his nakedness or oblivious, because nothing in his recent behaviour suggested exhibitionism.

Actually, Katie knew four facts, although it took a few seconds for her memory of the needle's spoor to sink in. He'd been a drug addict at some time in his life, which undoubtedly meant he had a previous criminal record. And that should make it marginally easier to pin an identity on the man.

"I've been told you speak English," Katie said. "But if you're not comfortable with that then I also speak French and a little Arabic..."

Nothing. Just those eyes, as empty as deep space.

"You've lived in the US?" Katie Petrov glanced at her notes from habit and remembered they were blank. "Nationality?" she wrote at the top, adding her question mark as an afterthought.

"Tell me about your mother."

No answer.

Prisoner Zero watched while the woman made a note.

"What?" she asked, when she finally looked up. "Why do you smile?"

*That pencil, the paper,* Prisoner Zero wanted to say. He suspected, inasmuch as he thought about it, that they were intentionally old-fashioned to make him feel secure. As if a laptop might somehow be too foreign, too American.

In this he was wrong.

She'd demanded and got doctor-patient confidentiality in all matters except any directly affecting Homeland Security, which she was duty bound to report immediately, and Katie Petrov didn't want some spook with a Van Phrecker sat next door recording every keystroke she made, so she used a pencil and paper. It was her own attempt to keep the interview secure.

## CHAPTER 16

## *Zigin Chéng, CTzu 53/Year 13*

The first of the imperial pavilions was simpler than the servitor had expected. Still vast, but simpler. A double-eaved hipped roof rested on red walls, while fretted shutters that hinged from the top were held open by ropes, the windows below being surprisingly ordinary and papered from inside. An empty bed, built from brick and covered with a silk mattress, stood against one wall. The silk was crumpled and scrolls lay unopened next to it on the floor.

A Tartar bow and a quiver full of arrows gathered dust on a gable high overhead. Not having seen a bow before, the servitor imagined it was some kind of single-stringed musical instrument.

The tray was his passport through the pavilions of the inner court. An ebony and jade passport laid with a glass cup, squat iron teapot and pre-warmed gold platter on which sat five types of dim sum, each one representing all that was best of the cuisine of the original Middle Kingdom.

Sous Chef Chang San had been careful to tell the servitor the significance of each morsel and how it related to the others on the plate. As well as *jiaozi* dumplings, Szechwan *huntun* and *char siu bao* (steamed buns with roast pork), there was *har gao* and, obviously enough, the sous chef's special pork dumplings.

The young man doubted if the sous chef really expected him to explain this to the Emperor. Failing that, however, there seemed little reason for Chang San's manic intensity or the way he demanded the servitor repeat back the descriptions to prove that he knew which of the slowly congealing lumps of food was which.

"You won't forget?"

"Of course not."

Chang San smiled thinly. "Be sure you don't." He wouldn't put it past the young man to claim the cooking as his own. There was something untrustworthy about the servitor's eyes, which were much too wide apart and possessed an unsettling insolence. Worse than this, his nails were filthy and Chang San found it hard to believe that any previous emperor would have been willing to take food served by someone with dirty hands.

"So," said the young servitor, as he casually broke a piece of crust off a deep-fried *huntun* and fed it to his rat, "what do you think?" But Null merely wrinkled its whiskers and looked round for more.

After the rat had dined on the oily edges, its master ate what was left of the filo base and most of the chilli and chicken filling, chewing the food with interest as he slid the rat back into his sleeve and rearranged the dim sum so that the plate still looked full.

"For the Emperor," he told a guard, and the man stepped back from a gold, red and green arch which was decorated with calligraphic banners praising the Chuang Tzu as the intermediary of heaven.

"For the Emperor..." Having called out these words, the man slammed his halberd into the tiles so hard that the weapon almost bounced out of his hand.

The interloper expected to find more guards in the Hall of Union but instead he found himself alone, facing a wooden throne. The throne was gilded, flanked by four lesser thrones, two on either side and all positioned a pace behind the throne of the Emperor. For reasons which were not immediately clear the lesser thrones were hidden under silk. Only the central one was uncovered.

It fitted him perfectly.

*"You shouldn't be sitting there."*

"Tell me about it," said the servitor and the voice in his head laughed a little sadly, or maybe it was bitterly. The servitor had always known that it was not really a voice, merely what his mind translated as a voice. It had been a long time since he'd expected other people to hear the things he heard.

Directly over the dais on which the throne sat was a panel painted with cryptograms representing *Wu Wei,* the fundamental Taoist principle of responding spontaneously and fluidly to any circumstance.

Above the panel hung a ceiling so ornate it made the servitor's head spin just to look at the intricacy of the gilded carving. He could make out endless dragons and, he thought, a phoenix, but most of the central carving was geometric, endless repetitions of a simple form.

A pale silk carpet covered the dais but the actual floor of the pavilion was dark stone pitted with age and scuffed with the feet of nearly five thousand years of ambassadors presenting their credentials.

The twenty-seven most commonly used seals rested inside a glass cabinet, some were soapstone, a few sandalwood but most were jade. All but three were in Manchu, one of those being in a language no one had ever identified.

Watched by at least a billion the servitor carried his tray across the courtyard to the third and last of the private pavilions. Heavenly Purity housed another, significantly more important, seat of power, the Lesser Throne from which the Emperor greeted ambassadors on their first arrival.

It was in this pavilion that his concubines should live, in eighteen bedrooms, arranged nine on both sides, each bedroom containing three beds, fifty-four in all.

All but one were deserted.

And it was this last that the Emperor had made his own. Neither the servitor nor the billions watching knew which room housed the Chuang Tzu because the feed was strangely imprecise about this.

"For the Emperor," said the servitor.

The officers who moved to intercept him wore scale armour

made from star-shaped pieces of what looked like steel sewn at the points to a silk jacket, each attachment being protected by the body of the star next to it. An intricate and time-consuming way to create armour. Except that the officers' armour was summer-weight, carbon-based and required no tempering. It still swallowed the light, though, and presented itself with a solidity belied by its actual lightness.

"From the kitchens," the servitor said, lifting his tray slightly higher. Stepping between the guards, he swept through a door that opened as if his entry was expected and found himself in an anteroom, facing another guard in armour even more light-swallowing than that of the men he'd just left behind.

General Ch'ao Kai watched the young man walk towards him across an unlit floor, while outside drizzle cut across Rapture's sky and a cold wind slid through the pavilion and ate into his bones, more potent than fear.

"Everything's going to be all right," the servitor said, and then he nodded, repeating himself in little more than a whisper as billions of watchers begged leave to disagree. He spoke, of course, to the rat now frozen within his sleeve, liking the darkness but made fearful by the levels of anxiety radiating from its master.

"Food for His Celestial Excellency."

The General inclined his head just enough to include the young man within his gaze. He was hereditary leader of the guard, custodian of the inner door and an elder clansman of a lesser banner. It was true he commanded few fighting troops but with no enemy these were unnecessary. Quarrels might happen between the 2023 worlds but the worlds themselves could not fight each other, since each was dependent on all others for the fine gravitational balance which kept them in stable orbit.

One of the earliest of the Chuang Tzu had made this clear. Besides, in an empire of plenty where was the need for violence? No single culture had ever monopolized all 2023 worlds but a constant homogenization now more or less guaranteed the cultural equivalent of convergent evolution. The smallest differences might still seem massively significant, but major differences had long since been etched smooth by familiarity and time.

"What do you have there?"

The servitor glanced down at his tray. Now seemed a good time to state the obvious. "Five different kinds of dim sum," he said. "This is *har gao* and this Szechwan *huntun*, that's *char siu bao* . . ."

He counted off the tiny offerings one at a time, silently giving thanks to the absent sous chef.

In the end it was the tray rather than the food which persuaded General Ch'ao Kai that the man spoke the truth. Inlaid ebony and a single slab of flawless mutton-fat jade. Only an emperor would be served on such a tray.

"Are you expected?"

"I couldn't say."

"You . . . ?"

"How would I know?" The young servitor shrugged and General Ch'ao Kai suddenly got a sense of having seen the man before. As the palace was as full of servitors as it was of eunuchs and the General made a point of paying less than zero attention to either, this seemed more than likely.

"Put down the tray," General Ch'ao Kai demanded, "then face the wall with your legs apart and your hands clasped behind your head."

"No," the servitor said. "I couldn't possibly do that."

"Why not?" General Ch'ao Kai was so shocked by the answer that he forgot to be furious, although a thin sliver of his mind retained the insult and readied itself to be offended.

"Because it would upset my rat," said the servitor, "that's one reason." Shaking his sleeve, he waited for a narrow white face to show its nose and whiskers. "This is Null," he said. "Unfortunately his sister died."

"Sister?"

"Void," said the servitor. "There's another reason," he added. "Slightly better. I'm not allowed to let this tray out of my hands."

"You're not—"

"In case the food is poisoned." His shrug was slight, an acknowledgment of the absurdity of this suggestion. "The order was very clear."

"And who gave this order?"

"The Library itself," said the boy, pretending not to notice a slight widening of General Ch'ao Kai's carefully kohled eyes. Only the Emperor spoke directly to the Library, its voice being the one single element missing from what watchers were allowed to experience of the Emperor's life inside the Forbidden City.

It spoke to the worlds, but only through the Librarian.

"You spoke to the avatar?"

"No, sir." The servitor shook his head.

General Ch'ao Kai had two choices. He could strike the servitor down for blasphemy or he could open the door. As well as being undignified, striking him down seemed unwise, particularly if the servitor was telling the truth.

Fifteen billion people held their breath.

"In you go then." General Ch'ao Kai made his decision sound like a command. "Don't let the food go cold."

The servitor glanced wryly at the congealing filo parcels but kept silent and just nodded to the ornately armoured General as the door opened and he stepped into the dirt and chaos that was Zaq's room.

"Here," he said. "I've brought you some—"

What he brought went unannounced because Zaq catapulted himself naked from a sunken bath, scooped his long knife off the floor and spun round to face his visitor, just catching a glimpse of General Ch'ao Kai's shocked face before the door closed itself and he was alone with the intruder.

"Wait," the servitor said, backing away.

Thunder shook the sky outside and lightning lit the windows. And as Zaq slashed with his blade, a howling wind ripped blossoms from cherry trees and toppled the spire of a distant pagoda.

"*Wait!*"

The voice belonged to the servitor and it was in Zaq's head, echoing around the darkness that the Chuang Tzu contained within him. This shouldn't have been possible because no one was allowed in Zaq's head except the Library, and he resented even that.

"Get out," he screamed, as fire split an oak outside, cleaving five hundred years of careful nurture. "Go now."

"Zaq," said the man.

"You mustn't call me that." Zaq's voice had risen to a howl to make itself heard over the roaring wind outside and tears blinded him, the blade in his hand feeling wrong since he'd smashed the handle six years before.

Opening his mouth to shout for General Ch'ao Kai, Zaq shut it again. He'd banned the General from entering this room. Come to that, he'd banned everyone. Here was where he was meant to be safe.

"Out," he demanded, and blinked as a rat jumped from the stranger's sleeve.

Instead of backing towards the door as Zaq expected him to do, the servitor casually tipped the tray sideways, spilling dim sum, cup and squat iron teapot onto the tiles. This done, he gripped the now-empty tray by one corner and swung the thing hard towards Zaq's wrist.

If the blow had hit flesh, both bones in Zaq's forearm would have broken because the Chuang Tzu had no codes that added strength to his simple, calcium-based skeleton; in fact, he had no physical enhancements at all.

Such things were rendered unnecessary.

As the edge of the heavy tray neared Zaq's wrist, smoke streamed up his spine, across his shoulder and down his arm, setting hard as steel and dark as jet. So unobtrusive was the Emperor's symbiont that the armour was in place before Zaq even realized he was wearing it.

Ebony split and mutton-fat jade hit the floor, the base of the tray mixing with earlier fragments from the knife handle. Without hesitation, Zaq slashed with his blade, his armour adding strength to the blow. Razor-edged steel met unprotected flesh and sliced deep, silencing the servitor's scream with the scrape of a blade across larynx.

Zaq's coat splattered red and then the servitor pitched forward, hitting the floor on his knees. It was, Zaq had to admit, all very convincing. The headless body at his feet gasped at him like a dying carp, shat itself and shuddered its way into oblivion. The blood on Zaq's cloak was suitably warm and when Zaq tasted it he got salt and a sweetness that reminded him of something just beyond the edge of memory.

"Librarian."

"Highness."

Zaq sighed. Sulking might not be quite the way to describe how the Librarian behaved after he'd been out of contact with it for more than a day but to Zaq it seemed to come close. In this he was wrong. The speed at which the Library lived was quantum, simultaneously past and present. What Zaq saw as a retreat into formality was merely a side effect of temporal distance.

On one level, the absence of a few weeks was sufficient for the Library to have had several billion thoughts, many of them relevant. On another, a few weeks was less than a single thought in the mind of a creation so old it could remember time changing direction at least twice.

"Send cleaners," said Zaq, his voice bored. "I need someone to clear up this mess."

"Tell the General."

"No."

A few years back, Zaq had worked out that the Librarian always knew what he'd decided to do before he did. And when he'd challenged the Library on this, it had admitted this was true, while insisting there was nothing sinister in the fact. Apparently this was a design flaw in the unaugmented human brain, a lagging of consciousness behind intent.

The Library had sounded almost amused while it explained this; as if Zaq was somehow missing the point.

"You summon help," Zaq said, looking round at the chaos of his room. "After all, everything's you really."

"Me?"

"All of this." Zaq gestured at the body at his feet, then at servitors sweeping away floods in the courtyard below.

"That wasn't me," the Library said. "You want to know why he was here?"

"Does it matter?" Zaq asked.

"So you don't want to know who he was?"

"He was you," Zaq said. "Like everyone else in this place. You know that as well as I do."

"No," the voice in his head said, sounding almost sad. "You're wrong. That was you, more or less..."

# CHAPTER 17

## *Marrakech 1975*

The house at the end of Moz's alley remained empty. No one had lived in it since the dog woman died and her companion went home to England. So now it was to be sold, but before this could happen the place needed repairing, otherwise it couldn't be sold to a *nasrani* and no one but a foreigner would be willing to pay the price the dog woman's family in England had decided it was worth.

"Ask Hassan," Malika insisted. Caid Hammou decided who got building work in the Mellah, and Moz needed money because his mother needed medicine. He knew this because Malika had told him so.

"Hassan won't—"

"Ask him," she insisted, and then she smiled as the jellaba-clad boy shuffled his feet in front of her. "If you don't," she said, "I'll ask him for you."

Smashing down an internal wall and carrying away the rubble was Moz's first real job. He was thirteen, ould Kasim had agreed his hand could be untied and he got the work because Hassan found it funny that Moz was asking for his help.

"You want what?"

In the background Idries smirked.

"Dar el Beida," said Moz. "I heard they need someone to help re-build the dog woman's house."

"And you understand building?"

"I can learn."

It wasn't until later that he discovered that Hassan was taking not just ten percent in commission from what little Moz earned. The older boy had also been given a handful of dirham by his uncle, who hired the foreman who actually employed Moz. He had to give another ten per cent to the foreman for the hire of a sledgehammer.

Moz laboured for the whole of that autumn, far harder than he'd ever worked in his life. And at the end of each day his body ached and clear liquid bled from the blisters on his hands and fingers, but Moz kept working and did as he was told, pissing into a bucket to help temper concrete for the maallan and always remembering to let the urine run over his fingers first, so that their blisters would heal and he could move the rubble faster...

It made no difference in the end.

The ring was gold and had an inscription around the inside, "all my love always." It took Moz most of that winter to find someone who read Turkish and in the end it was only bloody-mindedness that made him try the cigar seller in Gueliz.

There was a second ring; this was fatter but had the same words around the inside and Moz found it inside an envelope sealed and hidden at the back of a drawer stuffed with bras his mother had long since become too thin to wear and knickers washed to a faded and ghostly greyness.

He put those back where he found them.

In the same drawer was a make-up bag stuffed with names Moz had seen on advertisements in shop windows in the New Town. The bag was plastic and had a broken zip. A line of words pressed into the clear plastic read "Made in Hong Kong." Moz had no idea where Hong Kong was but then he hadn't known Dido owned any make-up.

Dido was what his mother insisted he call her.

For a while, when he was younger, he'd decided this was because Dido wasn't his real mother. He'd mentioned this theory to ould Kasim, Malika's father, trying to catch the man out. All ould Kasim had done was grin sourly, take another gulp from his cracked tea glass and grin again.

"You'd be so lucky."

A rabbi and his son buried Moz's mother in the Jewish cemetery. Moz would have preferred to have her interred in the New Town in the cemetery off Boulevard De Safi but the priest to whom he spoke wanted money. So Malika went to her rabbi and told him that Moz's mother was Jewish and so the man agreed to bury her in the cemetery next to Bab Rhemat and pay for it himself.

Malika and Moz had agreed she should tell the rabbi that Dido had married a gentile and been cut off from her family. Moz knew the meaning of gentile, and that Jews only liked to marry each other, from when he'd run errands for the maallan who owned a bread oven on the edge of the Mellah.

In the event, the rabbi just asked if she was certain about his mother's faith and then took over the rest of the arrangements. Twenty-four hours later it was done. Malika's father drove the rabbi away with drunken curses and threats of violence when he came calling a week later to see how Moz was coping with his grief. The rabbi came a handful of times after that but Moz was never there, and when the Jew left the boy a letter ould Kasim tore it into pieces and threw them in a gutter.

"You found her?"

Moz nodded. He was sitting on the roof with his face to a cold sun and his body throwing an impossibly etiolated shadow across the dirty red tiles behind him. Malika stood backlit in front, a black space where the winter sky should be. All he could see was a man's shirt washed so thin that even if the light had not been behind her Moz would probably have been able to see her legs silhouetted through the cloth.

The shirt came from a suitcase that once belonged to her mother, like everything else Malika ever owned. Malika was twelve that year. Moz was one year older.

"It's hard," Malika said. "You know, things like that. I remember."

What Moz wanted was for Malika to go away and leave him in peace but she'd never been very good at that. So while he was still doing his best to ignore her, Malika dropped to her heels in front of Moz and reached out to tap his knee. The briefest touch.

"That your bed?" Her nod took in a single blanket and an old pillow stuffed with feathers up against the wall that ran along the back of their flat roof. His other jellaba lay in a discarded heap next to the pillow. It was the one he'd worn for his mother's funeral. Malika had washed it for him. She'd done it without being asked.

"Obviously."

If Malika heard the sharpness in his voice she pretended not to mind. "It'll rain soon," she said. "You'd be better coming back inside."

Moz looked at her. "It hasn't rained in two years."

"Soon," she said, "it will. You can't sleep up here forever."

Moz wanted to say that he could, he would sleep where he wanted and nothing she could say would change that. She wasn't his . . .

"It hurts," she said. "I know that."

Holding his head against her bony shoulder, Malika let the boy cry himself out and then pretended not to notice when he pulled away and shuffled sideways so she could no longer see the tears on his face.

"Do you want me to do it?" There was, it seemed, no limit to the number of questions she could ask him. And as she always pointed out, Moz was not in a position to complain given the number of questions he asked himself.

"What?"

"The room."

Moz shook his head. "I'll do it."

"When?"

*When I'm ready,* that was what he wanted to say. Only he would never be ready. Her illness had been getting worse for a long time and Malika had been the one to realize the end was approaching. Not saying anything, but offering to fetch shopping for Dido or carry her bread to the local oven until even Moz understood what was happening and went cap in hand to Hassan for a job.

They had the autumn, three months in which Moz learnt more about Dido than he'd ever known before. She still refused to tell him where his father had gone or why, but Moz learnt that his mother's father was English and had married a German woman after the war. He wasn't sure which war and Dido was too tired to explain properly, but he asked and kept asking until he found a man in the Mellah who'd fled Germany and he told Moz what the boy needed to know.

"Come on," Malika said, climbing to her feet. "We'd better do it together."

It made Moz feel sick to go through his mother's few possessions. And only the fact Malika was there stopped Moz from giving up. He offered Malika the green dress and Dido's red skirt and the shoes, both pairs.

"You could sell them at the clothes souk," she told him.

"Keep them."

"It might upset you." Malika's face was serious, her mouth screwed into a smile that made her look sadder still. She was holding the shoes in one hand and looking between these and the boy who was on his knees emptying a cardboard box.

"If you want them, keep them," Moz said crossly.

Things like that didn't upset him, or so he told himself. There were letters in the box and an old passport which showed his mother looking young and pretty, her hair curled and cut close to her head. She wore a dress open at the neck and smiled at the camera. There were other photographs in a fat paper folder, some of them showing the same dress. She was pretty in all of these too.

Maybe she'd stopped having her photograph taken when her prettiness faded or maybe she stopped being pretty when whoever took those photographs went away. Moz found it hard to recognize his mother in the girl who smiled at him from almost every shot.

"Keep them," Malika said, when Moz began to tear the pictures in half. "And keep that." She nodded at the passport.

"You like them so much," said Moz, "you keep them." Carrying the box to the door, he threw it onto the landing and went back to his roof.

When he came down again, the room he shared with his mother had been cleared of everything that might remind him of Dido and Malika had stripped the bed and taken Dido's sheets for washing. And the next morning, when Moz met Malika in Djemaa el Fna with Hassan and Idries, she behaved as if clearing out his room had never happened.

## CHAPTER 18

## *Lampedusa, Sunday 1 July*

Concrete stabilized the cliffs on which the Hotel Vallone dell'Acqua now stood. Money for shoring up the cliffs came from an EU budget. There had been billions of lira in the fund originally but every time money passed down the line from government to regions, from regions to cities, from cities to towns and villages some of it seemed to get siphoned off.

People assumed it was the Mafia. In Sicily, when funds went missing, people always assumed it was the Mafia. In fact, it was everybody else, the politicians and council members, the police chiefs, administrators and town leaders.

So by the time the money actually reached Vallone dell'Acqua in the middle of the 1970s there was only just enough left to do the job it was meant to do, shore up a kilometre of crumbling cliff beneath Pasquali's chapel. A tiny seventeenth-century church built by a local saint who was convinced that Lampedusa, not Malta, was the island on which St. Paul had been wrecked. That a hotel was later built near the chapel was coincidence.

Had anyone on the island decided to take their cut, the job could never have been done. Only no one did, because even the fascists understood that saving Pasquali's chapel was more important than a new fridge, money under the mattress or a stove that lit itself.

This was, of course, a time when cash regularly went missing, ministers turned up in the boots of cars, bankers miraculously tied themselves up and then jumped off bridges and newly elected but unpopular popes suddenly woke up dead. It was a time of exploding railway stations, murdered magistrates and hijacked trains.

*Un momento di corruzione.*

Italy was different now, respectable again. It was the front line against *clandestini,* a bastion of Catholic light facing a sea of darkness. Italians knew this, they'd had a prime minister who kept telling them so. Of course, the fact he owned most of the country's TV stations made this easier than it might otherwise have been.

Situated just outside an *Area Riserva Naturale* which protected a large and rocky swathe of Lampedusa's southern coast from tourist development, Hotel Vallone had its own glass-sided funicular that ran down to a private beach where turtles sometimes stumbled ashore and guests could bathe naked, secure in their exclusivity.

The guests were gone and the funicular was out of commission. It had taken all the manager's tact to persuade a large and seemingly intransigent marine sergeant that he didn't want to wrap plastic explosive around a high-tension wire and cut the lift free, this being what Master Sergeant Saez had been in the process of doing when the manager arrived.

Now the manager was holed up in someone else's hotel, drinking Peroni from the minibar and watching stripping housewives on RTI. He felt safer that way.

Hollow clay blocks lay between upturned T-joists. Of the six surfaces in the weights room the ceiling should have been the most promising and would have been if only marines hadn't been using the room above.

The sound of heavy footsteps overhead had given Prisoner Zero that information.

Without a watch, Prisoner Zero had been reduced to judging time by changes in the slit just about visible under the weights room door. If he was right, the time was somewhere after midnight and before first dawn.

"Now," said the darkness.

Hunting down something sharp took time, so the darkness suggested Prisoner Zero shut his eyes and run his fingers over each side of the cage in turn. Which the prisoner did, plucking silent notes from plastic-coated mesh in his search for a way out.

When this failed, Prisoner Zero swept his hands under the bed and up the corners of his cage, where the sheets of mesh had been soldered together.

Above the lintel of the hatch Prisoner Zero found a vee of mesh not properly welded to the frame and began to twist, counting elephants until he reached forty-nine and the wire came free in his hand, so hot at the fracture point that Prisoner Zero heard his fingers hiss as they touched the break.

Whoever had originally tiled the weights room had smeared a sand and cement mix across the entire floor and then scraped it clean with a plastic blade. And they'd lacked enough cement to get a good mix because most of what Prisoner Zero cut from between his practice tile beneath the mesh was sand, the kind which hadn't been washed before bagging.

He was humming to himself as he worked, a song he hadn't thought of in years; three lines from the three-chord wonder which was "Lost in Mythik Amerika." The three lines leading up to the bridge...

> *I was watching you smile and seeing you cry,*
> *Lost in Mythik Amerika,*
> *Lost in the lie.*

Even after he cut the grouting from around a tile, the wire mesh on which he knelt would prevent him from being able to lift the thing. Prisoner Zero knew this and would wait for the darkness to tell him how to cut his way through the wire.

Two of the half-dozen interchangeable marines woke him at dawn and fed him and told him how many days until he died, which was ten. The Sergeant who'd first punched him was missing or at least busy with other duties, although his absence made little difference.

They still spat in his food, kicked over his slop bucket and did the things all guards had done for centuries and would do for centuries still. And when he was fed and his bucket was righted and the floor wiped clean, the marines unlocked his cage and took him to see Miles Alsdorf, one at each arm.

At the door of the weights room they were met by Sergeant Saez and the small black woman with the scowl. The two with their thumbs dug into Prisoner Zero's upper arms carried Colt 1911s holstered at their sides, as did Specialist Stone, who led the way. Only the Sergeant carried a rifle, its muzzle grinding into Prisoner Zero's neck at the point where his skull met vertebrae.

It was seven paces from his cage to the weights room door, fifty-four paces from the weights room to the door of the health club where his lawyer had been given a room as his office. Fifty-four paces, plus one right turn and then a left.

Originally given over to colonics, Miles Alsdorf's room had been cleared of couches, water tanks and tubes and furnished with a cheap desk and two simple chairs. Iron bars had been set crudely into its only window. One window and one door, the rooms on either side occupied by marines. Prisoner Zero was beginning to see a pattern.

"You're late," Miles Alsdorf said, but his words were aimed at Specialist Stone.

The marine shrugged. Her mother had scrubbed floors for a man like him. So far as she was concerned, Miles Alsdorf could whinge all he wanted, she answered only to those directly above.

After shackling the prisoner's feet together, the marines stood back. "We'll be outside the door," said Master Sergeant Saez, managing to make it sound like a threat.

"Whatever," Miles Alsdorf said.

The door closed with a bang and the lock was turned noisily.

"We need to talk," said the lawyer. "And talk now."

As ever, Prisoner Zero said nothing.

Sipping from a plastic cup, Miles Alsdorf dragged one hand across his immaculately cut hair and dried his fingers discreetly on the leg of a Brooks Brothers summer-weight suit. "You've got ten days," he said. "And that's it... Always assuming you're not going for some dramatic last-second reprieve?"

Again, that blankness.

Miles Alsdorf sighed. "I really do suggest you sign this," he said.

It was a power of attorney and under it rested a second piece of paper, actually two pieces. "And this is our request for a retrial," Miles Alsdorf added. "A civilian trial, you understand? A proper trial." He pulled a pen from his pocket. "All I need," he said, "is your signature."

Taking the platinum Montblanc from Miles Alsdorf's hand, Prisoner Zero unscrewed its top and carefully began to stab his wrist, keeping his back to the lawyer after Miles Alsdorf lunged to retrieve his pen. After the seventh dot, Prisoner Zero stabbed a double to mark the door, then methodically stabbed himself another fifty-four times.

Only then did he return the pen.

"The easiest way to get rid of me," said Katie Petrov, "is to talk to Mr. Alsdorf, your lawyer." She smiled, as if the comment was funny.

Raw scabs ran the length of Prisoner Zero's lower arm. Either an indication of self-hatred, in which case he should be on suicide watch, or a crude attempt, according to Miles Alsdorf, to give himself a prison tattoo.

The lawyer was relying on her to tell him which.

Katie Petrov sighed. Nodding to a bowl of pastries on her desk, she indicated that he should take a piece and tried not to worry when she got no response at all.

"When you're hungry," she said.

The talking to herself was intentional and something Katie used often. Everything about Katie's approach to this case had been thought through in advance, from the net curtains she'd recently put up to stop the man from losing himself in the Mediterranean beyond her window to the Sicilian sweets and the clothes she currently wore. A selection so neat and anonymous that even she had to look at them to remember exactly what she was wearing.

There'd been a suggestion, from her as it happened, that Prisoner Zero might respond better to a male psychiatrist. It had been made in the panic following her first meeting with the man and she'd had the sense not to push it when Petra Mayer disagreed. Having seen how Prisoner Zero shut down in the presence of Miles Alsdorf, she could only concede that the Professor had been right.

"We're going to do it differently today," said Katie. Actually they were going to be doing it differently every day until she finally hit on something that worked. Dr. Katie Petrov knew all the reasons why consistency was good. She'd done the lectures on building trust without establishing dependency. Hell, she'd written some of them, but he was running out of time and elective autism was a poor defence.

It was surprising the number of attorneys who assumed that a sudden descent into silence by their client would pass for evidence of mental trauma. Every half-bit stalker with a knife and a grudge, every thirty-something sleazebag who saw kindergarten gates as the entrance to heaven...

She was getting angry, mostly with herself, Katie realized. A sign of helplessness and very unlike her. Katie didn't get emotional at work. Not even when working with anorexic adolescents and statistically they were more likely to push industry professionals over the edge than anyone else.

"The thing is," Katie said, "you've only got ten days. I don't know if anyone's explained that?" She caught it then, a quick flicker behind his dark eyes. "Oh," said Katie, as she picked up what looked like the bag for a laptop, "I see. Everyone's told you that, have they?"

A cricket outside her window gave the only answer.

Opening the case, Katie pulled out a small silver box that trailed a mains lead. "I'd like to use this," she said. "It's not compulsory but it would help me help you." She held out the device. "Do you want to take a look?"

Sixty seconds later Katie let her hand drop.

"Electrodes," she explained, extracting a tangle of wires from the small case and putting them carefully on her desk. "This is a basic electroencephalograph. I use it mostly for kids with Ritalin dependency. It helps them learn to normalize certain brain patterns. Obviously that's not what I want to try with you..." There was a pause, the expectant kind. One Prisoner Zero was meant to fill.

"No problem," said Katie. "Would you like me to put them on for you?"

Outside her door waited two marines. Tall men with aubergine skin and cropped skulls, a rifle each and fat body armour. In their right ears they wore single black beads, button mikes were taped to their throats.

Either one would have held the captive down while the other helped Katie glue electrodes to his skull, and they'd have done it willingly and probably regarded Katie in a better light afterwards. Katie found the fact she wanted that approval unnerving. Almost as unnerving as realizing it was prompted by an unspoken fear that the marines regarded Katie as somehow against them.

"I'm here to help," Katie said. "I can do that better if you wear these." She nodded to the spider's web of wires. "All the box does is measure brain activity. It won't tell me your secrets or let me look inside your head." She spoke as she might to some drug-addled gang-banger in need of a quick and dirty court report. Casual did it, anything else and most of them retreated into a carapace harder than any which nature could produce.

Katie was still trying to work out exactly why she got this gig. At twenty-seven she was young to be doing this kind of analysis and her pro-bono work for Médecins Sans Frontières was well known. She'd been the only specialist prepared to go on CNN and say the outbreak of unquestioning patriotism which followed the attempt to shoot the President was bad for America's health.

It made her an obvious choice when Petra Mayer, President Newman's unofficial conscience, began looking for an independent expert to balance the expert already produced by the Pentagon. While at the same time rendering her opinion worthless to most of the Supreme Court, the majority of whom had been appointed by the previous incumbent.

So was her evidence meant to be taken seriously or had she been hired to jump through hoops? And, if so, was her old tutor part of that plot? There were levels to this Katie couldn't begin to imagine, she knew that. And rumours enough to keep conspiracy theorists busy for years.

That Prisoner Zero was the First Lady's bastard brother was one of the best. A slightly less fanciful one had the Pentagon knowing exactly who he was but refusing to tell the White House.

Whatever the truth, she'd been handed a poisoned chalice that might still turn into one of the decade's plum jobs. How many psychiatrists of her age could say they'd been retained to evaluate the mental state of a man on trial for trying to kill the President? Come to that, how many of any age...

Picking up the wires, Katie reached for a tube of surgical glue and smeared an electrode, sticking it to one side of the prisoner's skull. When Prisoner Zero didn't complain, Katie stuck another to the opposite side. His lack of complaint was a benchmark. The moment he shrugged her away was the point Katie would stop fixing the wires.

It helped that Prisoner Zero's head was recently shaved. Most of the kids she handled pro bono had hair twisted into topknots or cut to some gang pattern. For a few of the more vain, deciding whether or not to let Katie fix her wires took longer than they put into deciding their plea.

"Okay," Katie said, when the last wire was in place, "I'm going to say words and you're going to tell me the first thing that comes into your head. It can be a memory or reaction. Something from childhood or something from now."

So slow were the pupils which watched her that for a second Katie was worried the marines might be drugging him, but then the breeze lifted a corner of the net she'd pinned in place and, as Prisoner Zero's head flicked towards the movement, his pupils collapsed like stars swallowing themselves.

"Mother," Katie said. "What does that word suggest to you?"

*A bottle empty on a table.*

"It's all right," said Katie, "you can tell me."

Checking a readout on her EEG, Katie noted how high one of the columns had gone. Someday some genius would work out how to translate results into direct evidence and half her job would disappear overnight. "Okay," she said with a sigh, "let's try another... Cat."

*His lover at a pavement café feeding scraps from her plate to a sack of bones then shooing away the ragged child who came trying to beg coins. Amber eyes hurt in the twilight.*

"Sun."

*Brightness lancing through cracks in a study door and burning a thousand planets of dust, spinning and chaotic, tied by laws he was only just beginning to understand.*

"Water."

*A skin of liquid on the underside of an Amsterdam fountain clinging to the marble's hard bone and curving away into its own event horizon.*

"You."

"What?" demanded Katie, leaning forward. With an effort she made herself sit back and move on to the next word. There had been something there, something the man wanted to say, Katie was sure of it.

"Feathers."

*A dream-catcher made from a boa found in a biscuit tin. Celia left it on the wall when she went.*

Katie wrote "You" on her notepad and put a tick next to the word.

She often did that, let the questions move on and then make notes for a moment which was gone. Putting pencil to paper the instant something of interest arose sent out the wrong signals and that was something Katie tried to avoid.

"Let's try something else," she said. "Something simpler." Folding a piece of paper in two, she dripped red ink into the crease and neatly folded together the two sides, so that the colour oozed between the pages. And then she peeled them apart again.

"What do you see?" said Katie. "You can tell me."

And without a word Prisoner Zero stood up and shuffled to the door, shackles dragging and wires still trailing from his skull, the tiny EEG box scuttling through the dust behind him like some exotic household pet.

# CHAPTER 19

## *Darkness, CTzu 1/Year 0*

A circle may begin at any point. For the 2023 worlds the circle began and ended at Year Zero, in many ways a completely arbitrary choice.

From one and a half million miles away the darkness looked like a slowly turning shoal of shadows with odd and ersatz quasar tendencies. Most astronomers regarded this as a misreading of old data; those who didn't varied in their interpretations as to what the object might be.

One view was that the dark shoal was actually an asteroid belt wrapped stranglehold tight around an unimportant, type II yellow star, one with an energy output of roughly Earth strength.

No one thought the system valuable enough to visit.

Each of the 2023 sections of shell cast a vast area of darkness that swept across the emptiness of space, followed by a narrow fan of sunlight. This was, of course, an entirely humanocentric interpretation of the energy data.

Most of those who later wrote about the arrival of the first Chuang Tzu did so from the comfort of one of the 2023 worlds, and as few ever moved beyond that comfort or felt the need to examine their lives from outside, many now regarded existence beyond the worlds as myth and the arrival of the SZ *Loyal Prince* as an improving, morally enlightening fairy story.

Had the sun-circling sphere been solid instead of made up of 2023 potentially locking but currently unlocked sections, the area created would have made a single continent over 650 million times the entire area of the Earth. As it was, each of the 2023 sections had nearly three hundred thousand times more living space than the world from which the crew of the SZ *Loyal Prince* originally came.

Zaq knew all this, of course, because the great, glorious and correct knew what the butterflies knew and the butterflies knew what the Library showed them.

From one side of the unfinished shell to the other was 298.2

million kilometres, which was actually fractional in a galaxy that contained several hundred billion stars and stretched a hundred thousand light-years from rim to rim. All the same, many chose to regard the distance from one side to the other of the 2023 worlds as beyond imagining.

It simplified life.

Once the area around the sun had been occupied by planets. Three, maybe four solid bodies filling what became the emptiness between the 2023 fragments of shell and its star, with another five, mostly gas giants, slung out along the same plane beyond where the shell now hung.

The inner planets would have been iron rich, because this is the nature of inner planets of their age; while the outer planets would have been mainly hydrogen, with helium, water vapour and methane. Now all were gone and only the 2023 worlds remained.

So it was believed by those who held that the sun was natural.

Those who held that the sun was as manufactured as the worlds which surrounded it refused to accept the existence of the missing planets. In answer to the question, "From where did the matter to make the worlds come?" they asked another, "How could the breaking of nine planets possibly produce sufficient matter to create 2023 worlds?"

Such argument came later and had no relevance to the crippled Chinese freighter that limped out of an asteroid storm and settled near the underside of a slab of flat black glass a million kilometres thick. *Loyal Prince to the Heavenly Ruler of the Celestial Kingdom of Great Peace* was originally a single-engined, ShenZhou-class battle-cruiser, retrofitted as a refugee ship. She'd been drifting for fifteen generations Earth time.

For much of this period SZ *Loyal Prince* had been broadcasting a distress signal. Throughout the first five hundred years the signal had been in Mandarin, changing to standard English for the century following this. And then, when Colonel Commissar Lan Kuei finally brought herself to accept that her distress call would never be answered, she changed it back to Mandarin.

It was a matter of pride.

Her navigator, Lieutenant Chuang Tzu, was really called something else. He was one of those single sons, the little emperors, spoilt beyond belief but also bowed down under the expectation of his maternal grandparents, who had adopted him after his parents died.

Between the spoiling, the expectation and the impossibility of appreciating one sufficiently or meeting the demands of the other, the boy had fallen into a world of dreams, hence his nickname.

He was also one of the few crew members awake when the *Loyal Prince* fell into position beneath the edge of a glass slab so enormous that the entire Chinese Republic would have made but a splash on its surface.

"Take us in," the Colonel Commissar ordered.

From far off the line of sunlight between one impossibly vast slab of glass and the next looked knife-blade thin as the SZ *Loyal Prince* rose steadily towards it. And it was only when her navigator rechecked the distances that Colonel Commissar Lan Kuei realized the gap was actually wider than the distance from her own planet to its moon, easily large enough for an entire fleet of cruisers.

"Steady as she goes..." The Colonel Commissar watched Lieutenant Chuang Tzu smile at her order and pretended not to notice. The boy was useless but very pretty. Besides, being useless was hardly a handicap for the post of *yuhangyuan* aboard the *Loyal Prince*.

The ship more or less steered itself.

Once into the gap, the edges of the vast glass slabs seemed claustrophobically close, even though all readings indicated that the nearest was still a hundred thousand kilometres away.

"Shit," said Lieutenant Chuang Tzu.

The Colonel Commissar had to agree.

Besides the Colonel and her navigator there was only one other member of the crew still awake when the SZ *Loyal Prince* slipped between two worlds and found itself within an almost oppressive shell of matter. This last was Dr. Yuan, who died too soon after this to be properly remembered.

There were, of course, other members of the crew. Although whether they were sleeping or dead was open to interpretation. The Colonel Commissar's view was that they were sleeping. Her navigator, who despite his Chuang Tzu nickname was less of a dreamer than the Colonel Commissar imagined, was of the firm opinion that they were dead. He based this on the fact that some of them had begun to smell.

"Distance?"

"One hundred thousand, Madame."

She'd meant the distance until they reached the upper edge of the vast glass slab, but the Colonel Commissar didn't bother to correct the boy. She was asking questions for the sake of it.

A tall woman with broad shoulders, Colonel Lan Kuei hated her given name, which meant little orchard, and walked with a stoop unless in uniform, when she'd throw out her substantial chest and stride down the half-lit corridors.

She was in command of a dying ship with her effective crew reduced to one. A rip had opened the double hull of the *Loyal Prince* and their oxygen was leaching away through gates which were designed to be airtight. It was only a matter of time before the atmosphere became too thin to breathe and in deciding to enter the broken puzzle of the sun-circling sphere the Colonel was choosing a place for her ship to die.

Colonel Commissar Lan Kuei wasn't sure that her navigator understood that. They'd lost the last of their gravity on the approach, when the acceleration of their ship slowed and the floor of the SZ *Loyal Prince*'s crew quarters slid through a quarter turn to drop parallel to the keel rather than remain aligned with the engine.

The intention, of which the Beijing University of Astronautics had been very proud, was to replace the pseudo gravity of acceleration with resource-draining G-loops, positioned beneath the cabin floor and to be used on the last stages of the trip only.

Unfortunately the G-loops had never been fitted, largely because no one could get them to work, and by the time their inventor had confessed his error and suffered a punishment fit for the crime, the living quarters had been constructed to swing through a quarter turn once the ship's speed fell below a preset level, whether this made sense or not.

"The Doctor is dying."

Lan Kuei stared at the one remaining male crew member: That was how she thought of the boy, as her last remaining male crew member. There were regulations regarding the situation they were in but she'd already broken them. Standing orders stated that in the case of this kind of emergency the SZ *Loyal Prince* was to be put in stasis and the working crew must join the others in hibernation.

This would have been fine if most of her crew had not already been "sleeping" and her cargo deck stacked with frozen 'fugees who took what little power the generators still produced. Sometime soon, Colonel Commissar Lan Kuei would have to decide whether or not to turn off that power. Unless, of course, she did nothing and then time would take the decision for her.

"What do you want me to do?" The boy stood waiting for orders Colonel Commissar Lan Kuei no longer felt qualified to give.

She and Lieutenant Chuang Tzu had been lovers briefly and she'd found the boy surprisingly gentle. Lan Kuei wasn't used to her lovers being gentle. Usually men took one look at her huge breasts and buried themselves in fistfuls of flesh, twisting and kneading her skin.

The navigator had been different. Approaching each time as if it was the first and he'd never seen a woman naked before. All the same, fucking him had been a mistake. Something she'd never have done if the others hadn't already been dead.

"How close?"

For a moment Navigator Chuang Tzu thought his Colonel Commissar meant how close was the SZ *Loyal Prince* to the wall outside but then he realized that she was talking about the Doctor. "Minutes," he said, looking at a readout. "It may already be too late."

"Freeze her," Lan Kuei said.

"I'm not sure I know how."

The Colonel Commissar stifled a sigh. "Skip the preparation," she said. "Go straight to the freezing... That's an order," she added.

Chuang Tzu nodded gratefully. It was Lan Kuei's way of relieving him of responsibility for potentially killing someone he admired. Lan Kuei liked the Doctor too, in her way. Although their backgrounds were very different, Lan Kuei's as poor as Dr. Yuan's had been rich.

When Yuan volunteered for the mission her father had offered his newly graduated daughter her own house in Xicheng, one of the most fashionable districts of Beijing, if she withdrew her application. Colonel Commissar Lan Kuei's mother had asked how much of her bounty Lan Kuei intended to give the family and then nodded grudgingly when her daughter replied that she would give it all.

Lieutenant Commissar, Major Commissar and finally Colonel Commissar. Every time an officer refused to wake from cold sleep Lan Kuei found herself promoted. Now she could call herself Commissar General if she so wanted, but Lan Kuei didn't. She was bored with gluing new patches to her shoulder, particularly now there was only the boy to notice her new rank.

The freezing pods were three decks below the bridge and the Doctor was in her cabin on the deck above, which either meant Navigator Chuang had to manhandle an unconscious woman through eighteen hatches and along two kilometres of narrow corridor or else he could cheat.

Chuang Tzu decided to do it the quick way. Sometime during the first hundred years a bored engineer had thought ahead to life aboard the SZ *Loyal Prince* in zero gravity and decided to weld handles to all the walls in what he considered strategic positions.

These changes made so little impact on the fifty members of Engineer Li's shift that most of them never noticed; and the Commissar General only became involved twenty-three years later when Engineer Li woke for his next shift and decided to reprogram the spiders to repaint every wall a different colour.

He might even have got away with this if only his programming skills hadn't been so sloppy that the spiders ended up overpainting every surface, including all hazard signs and internal windows.

On file was Li's defence, still attached to his execution order. This stated that since up and down were abstract concepts in zero gee, the best way to adapt the human mind to cope with weightlessness was to paint each wall a different colour. So that instead of thinking up, down, left and right, the mind chose between red surface, green surface, blue and yellow.

Whatever, it worked.

Grabbing a wall handle, Lieutenant Chuang Tzu flipped open a ceramic grill and slid into an air vent, kicking off like a swimmer from the side of a pool. He handled himself well in zero gee, his racing turn against a far wall coming close to aerial ballet. Suicidal ballet, but ballet all the same.

Away from his Colonel Commissar, Chuang Tzu was different; more awake, less dreamy. Somehow just more competent. He had the Doctor on a length of monofilament behind him, her arms bound to her sides and her legs lashed together at the ankles so she wouldn't snag on her way through the shafts.

All went well, despite the speed at which Chuang raced along the air vent. And though he slowed into the final turn, his kick off was more flamboyant than ever and his exit through the vent so fast that he had to use his own body to cushion the Doctor's impact against a wall.

"What was that?"

"What was what . . . madame?" Chuang added the honorific as an afterthought. Conditioning overriding his desire to vomit.

"You gasped."

"I'm sorry. It was nothing." His comms link was open, something he should have realized and dealt with. Summoning the setting with the touch of his fingers, Chuang Tzu chose a level where the comms link registered as functioning but carried almost no signal.

There were a dozen red pods hungry and waiting. One for the Doctor, another for him, one for the Commissar Colonel and nine ever-empty pods for those vaporized while trying to repair the boosters. Tapping the nearest, Chuang watched it open, waiting while the semiAI ran a self test.

"Functioning," the pod announced as a glass square lit red. "Preparing for Koebe process." Slots opened on the inside of the pod to reveal simple claws; attached to those claws were clear tubes already filled with oily liquid. "Please enter phenotype."

"What?"

"Enter phenotype."

"Human," Chuang Tzu said. The animals were long since dead.

The glass square turned orange. "Enter seven-digit genotype," demanded the pod.

"Shit." Chuang Tzu ripped open the front of the Doctor's blue uniform, looking for dog tags. "I don't know it," he said. "It's not for me."

"Enter seven-digit genotype."

"You'll have to do without," Chuang Tzu told the machine.

The ceramic blade the Lieutenant produced from his pocket was strictly illegal. As compact and functional as befitted someone who'd grown up on a farm, but still illegal. Slicing the monofilament which bound Dr. Yuan's hands, he spun her round and sliced between her ankles.

"Prepare to receive the body," he said.

On the side of the pod the orange square reverted to red as the semiAI reset itself. "Functioning," the pod announced. "Preparing for Koebe process. Please enter phenotype."

"Stupid fucking—" Chuang began but stopped himself. "Promote me," he said loudly, simultaneously reopening his comms channel.

"What?"

"Promote me," Navigator Chuang said fiercely, "while there's still time to save the Doctor."

Two decks above, Colonel Commissar Lan Kuei sighed. Sleeping with junior officers always produced these kinds of problems. "*Madame,*" she said firmly. "You address me as *madame*."

"Promote me, *madame*." Chuang Tzu tried to put anger in his voice but it came out as petulance. He never had been any good at standing up to authority. "The pod won't—"

"Major," Lan Kuei said, "as of now."

Chuang Tzu dimmed his comms channel without signing out, a tiny act of rebellion, and turned to the pod.

"This is Major Commissar Chuang Tzu... Prepare to take a body," he told it. The semiAI would have to cope without a DNA reference for the flesh it was about to receive. Dr. Yuan was dying, the status light on her suit already down to a slow flicker.

The pod did as it was told.

In an ideal world, the pod would have had time to read Dr. Yuan's genotype, pre-plan fixes for any physical imperfections and replace all of the Doctor's blood with a mix of cryoprotectants, mainly glycerols. Only the SZ *Loyal Prince* was anything but an ideal world and Major Commissar Chuang Tzu wasn't sure he even knew what a genotype actually was.

On the breast of Dr. Yuan's uniform below a patch which showed cogs and ears of wheat framing a small rocket ship, a button alarm had started beeping.

"Chuang..."

"I know," he said.

Gripping his knife, the newly promoted navigator began to cut open Dr. Yuan's regulation tunic, trying not to notice one nipple becoming bare as he did so. The Doctor was impossibly beautiful, everyone agreed on that; at least they did back when there was an everyone to agree on anything.

"How's it going?" The voice in Chuang Tzu's ear was worried.

"Slowly," he admitted.

"Work faster," said Colonel Commissar Lan Kuei and was gone.

With the Doctor's tunic half open, Major Commissar Chuang Tzu gave up not looking and hacked at the cloth until he reached the waistband. This cut, he peeled the tunic from Dr. Yuan's torso and turned his attention to her trousers. There was a buckle, something elegant and strictly not regulation. Chuang Tzu cut this away without even noticing, keeping his hand between the dying woman's abdomen and the point of his blade, hesitating only when one knuckle brushed body hair.

All of this he did in zero gravity with one foot hooked under a wall handle and a thousand minor muscle adjustments every second to keep him steady. Beijing had chosen only swimmers for their deep-space missions and the navigator had swum every day as a child.

Yanking unsuccessfully at Dr. Yuan's trousers, the Major Commissar tugged again, only realizing on his third attempt that the doctor was still plumbed into a tiny waste unit attached to the back of her belt. It was smaller than standard and looked expensive, but then anything better than regulation looked expensive to Chuang Tzu.

"Disengage," he told the box.

Nothing happened.

"Do it," he ordered, which was pointless. All personal systems on the ship operated on owner order only. Not because that was all these systems could manage but because the original Commissar General believed in direct culpability. All ship-based systems, including personal ones, recorded all orders, which had to be direct.

That way, if something went wrong there was never any question as to whom could be held directly and unequivocally accountable.

"Major..."

The Colonel Commissar's voice was there again.

"Madame?"

"Your life readout."

The tiny diode below his breast badge now burned a dull orange. "Oxygen deprivation," said a readout on his wrist.

"What are you doing?"

"Preparing the Doctor for cryo."

"Still?" The Commissar Colonel sounded exasperated and, below that, she sounded scared. "What's the problem?"

"Dr. Yuan's wearing a waste box."

"Too bad." Lan Kuei's voice was cold. "Chill her down as she is. Then get yourself up here and renew your converter."

"Yes, madame." Chuang Tzu looked from the half-naked woman to the waiting pod, its lid open and ready. He knew that to freeze the Doctor as she was meant death. An event which would never intrude on Dr. Yuan's fragile consciousness. And this mattered to Commissar Major Chuang Tzu because it was his grandmother's belief that a death not met was no death at all.

Slicing up and around the top of each trouser leg, the Major Commissar removed both, then hacked up towards the Doctor's groin. When necessary he flipped the woman over, turning her this way and that, like an old-fashioned tailor shuffling cloth or a fish wife filleting carp.

Chuang Tzu worked quickly until all that remained was a floating box tethered directly into her spine. From the bottom of the box fed two narrow tubes, one entering her anus, the other splitting in two, the first catheter entering her bladder, the second her womb. Dr. Yuan's mistake had been to prepare herself for hibernation instead of cryo.

"Look at your light."

Chuang did. Orange, going on red.

"Is the doctor safely frozen?"

"Yes, madame."

"Then get yourself up here."

"On my way."

Sliding the Doctor's body into its pod, Major Commissar Chuang Tzu slammed the lid. All that remained to do was run the sequences necessary to chill it. "You know how to do this?" he asked the machine.

It lit for yes.

"Do it," he said.

The pod next door opened as ordered, lights dancing through a start-up sequence. Slots in the side revealed themselves and the snake-like tubes, which were really something else altogether, blurred into smoke and became familiar: clear tubes ending in long needles.

Chuang Tzu stripped effortlessly, hooking one foot under a handle to steady himself. The jacket he removed was an improvement on Kevlar, self-cleaning, airtight but willing to let his skin breathe in everything except vacuum.

"Major Commissar Chuang Tzu," he told the pod.

"Confirm."

The young Chinese officer put his hand on a ceramic plate and felt nothing as it lit briefly then darkened just as swiftly.

"Preparing for Koebe process."

"Proceed," he told the machine, pleased to discover that his voice was almost steady.

The needles were waiting for him. One entered his arm at the elbow, pumping in sedative, followed almost immediately by an anaesthetic. And then sleep came in a crash of waves and the smell of summer skies.

Major Commissar Chuang Tzu was swimming in a waterfall on the slopes above his grandfather's farm when the pod's first blade cut his throat, a small incision wide enough to take a tube. A second blade opened the femoral artery and pumping began, glycol entering his jugular as blood drained from his groin. Chuang Tzu's stomach was then pumped and his lower bowel flushed clean.

In all the process took three minutes.

And while Colonel Commissar Lan Kuei gave orders for the SZ *Loyal Prince* to draw closer to the nearest wall and wondered what had happened to the last remaining member of her crew, Chuang Tzu's pod reached the end of its preparations and flooded with liquid nitrogen, reducing its occupant to the fragility of glass.

# CHAPTER 20

## *Marrakech, Summer 1977*

"I did it." The boy's words were loud enough to turn every head in the police station. Behind the desk a man looked up. Moz didn't recognize his rank but Mustapha Zil was a sergeant on secondment from Tangiers, part of a plan to build bridges between the two cities. He'd been in Marrakech for three months and still found the heat unbearable.

"Tell me," said the Sergeant, running a finger under the rim of his collar, "what exactly did you do?"

"Took the watch."

Sergeant Zil raised his eyebrows. "Which watch?" he said.

Moz stopped, thought about it and started again. "You've arrested a girl," he said. "From the Mellah... She's called Malika," Moz added, forgetting her other name in his panic. It would have to do.

Sergeant Zil skimmed down a handwritten list. In Tangiers, all crimes were typed onto cards and filed. All the same, he found the entry.

"What of it?"

"She didn't take the watch."

The Sergeant looked at the boy. "You're saying you took it?" And Moz wondered why the man behind the desk sighed.

"Ahmed," Sergeant Zil called to a new recruit. "Take this boy to room three, then wait to see if they want you to bring him back again... Go with the man," he told the boy. "Don't be frightened."

It was a fairly stupid thing to say because everything Sergeant Zil had seen in his last twelve weeks suggested the boy should be very frightened indeed.

At the end of a ground-floor corridor, towards the rear of the police station, sat a row of interview rooms. Number three was the smallest, cloudy with cigarette smoke and already crowded. In one corner stood a young officer in khaki doing nothing. At a table sat two *nasrani*, a short-haired blonde woman in a silk blouse so sheer it revealed her breasts and a dark, hawk-faced boy with spiky black hair and some kind of hoop stuck through his ear.

Except for the difference in hair colour they might have been brother and sister, though the woman was less thin than the boy and wore white slacks to go with her blouse, while he seemed to be dressed entirely in black.

Standing opposite them was Malika, crying. A plain-clothes officer stood behind her, one hand gripping her neck.

"He says he took the watch."

Major Abbas looked round, obviously furious.

"This boy, Excellency." The recruit sounded apologetic. "He says he took the watch."

"Your name?"

"Moz," said Moz.

He watched the Major pull a nickname from his memory.

"The Turk," Major Abbas said and Malika looked up from her tears. No one had called Moz that for a while. Not since the afternoon behind La Koutoubia when he'd stamped on Hassan's stomach.

Moz nodded.

"You stole the watch?"

He nodded again.

"But its owner saw this girl steal it." Major Abbas gestured dismissively towards Malika. His hands now hung by his sides and Malika was busy rubbing her neck, trying to free it from the afterburn of the Major's grip. Opposite her sat the two foreigners looking unhappier by the second.

"Does someone want to tell me what's going on?" The blonde woman spoke English, her question hanging unheard in the smoky, overheated room.

"You're sure you took it?" Major Abbas looked serious, as well he might. Stealing from tourists was a crime treated severely in Marrakech.

The teenaged boy could get five years breaking rocks in a prison peopled with thugs three times his age. The city might have changed since the old days, when naked prisoners were sometimes made to impale themselves on broken bottles, but the change was not so great that the boy would come out the person he'd gone in.

"*What is going on?*" This time Celia Vere's question was loud enough to shock the interview room into silence.

"They're deciding how many times to whip her," said Moz, before anyone else had a chance to answer. He spoke broken English. "Which is unfair, because you've made them arrest the wrong person."

"Wrong . . . ?"

"I took the watch," Moz said.

"But Jake saw her." Celia Vere looked worried.

"No," said Moz, "he thought he did. The watch was already gone. Malika was taking food from your plate."

"Why?" said the thin boy with the weird earring, although when Moz looked carefully he realized the dark-haired foreigner was too old to be a boy and that he was wearing make-up. "Why take scraps from Celia's plate?"

The stare Moz gave Jake Razor was withering. One Moz had seen used by imams in the mosque when answers were wrong. "Look at her," he ordered. "Why do you think she was stealing food?"

Catching Malika's eye, Moz sucked in his cheeks and after a second's hesitation Malika did the same, standing there with hollow cheeks and tears drying on her thin face. A bruise closed one of her amber eyes, but that looked old.

"She's hungry," said Jake.

Moz turned to find Major Abbas watching him, a weird smile on his lips.

"Children in this city die every day," the Major said flatly. He spoke French, which only Celia understood, and his tone was such he could have been discussing the heat. "They die of hunger or lack of medicine, even of lack of schooling. You'd be surprised what can kill people in this city." He looked from Moz to the foreigners.

"You accept you got the wrong child?"

Celia nodded doubtfully.

"Okay," said the Major, "so we're releasing the girl." He spoke to Malika. "You can go," he said.

The girl just looked at him.

"Go," said Major Abbas, "before I change my mind."

When the door banged shut, the Major reached into a drawer

and pulled out a fistful of forms, dumping them in front of the *nasrani* couple. "You need to fill these out and make a sworn statement."

"Saying what?"

"That you were robbed. Without this we can't send the boy to prison."

Moz watched the woman's eyes trail from the pieces of paper to his face and then to the Major. For a moment it felt like he could look right inside her head, into the mind of a *nasrani*.

The two foreigners looked at each other.

"Life's too short," said the man.

"Plus I got my watch back." Celia Vere pulled back her silk sleeve to show a gold Omega. "And it was stupid of me to leave it on the table like that. I should stop taking it off when I make notes."

"You're a journalist?"

Something in Major Abbas's voice worried the woman. "Mostly a photographer," she said. "A little bit of writing, now and then. *Rolling Stone, Sounds, NME*. I even did a short piece on punk for the *Mail* last month, though I probably shouldn't admit that."

When Jake Razor grinned he showed broken teeth.

"We're going to leave it," said Celia, dismissing Moz, the interview room and Major Abbas with an all-inclusive wave of one hand. "I think we'll just find our hotel."

"Your decision," the Major said. "I'll still need to see your passports." One was American, the other British. The Major flicked through to check for visas and entry or exit stamps. The blue passport was new and had only one stamp, Casablanca. The red one was heavy with stamps going back several years, starting with Mexico.

"Everything all right?" For the first time that afternoon Jake Razor sounded something other than bored.

Major Abbas nodded at the passport. "Be careful," he said.

"About what?"

"About being here," the Major said. "About drugs and drink, about not offending people, about who you and your girlfriend accuse of stealing things . . ."

"But we really like this place," said Jake, and Major Abbas sighed.

## CHAPTER 21

### *Lampedusa, Monday 2 July*

"What's he doing?" said Specialist Stone, mostly making conversation. They were four hours into a night shift and her companion had spent much of this drumming his fingers impatiently on a table. He wanted his bed, MTV and oblivion. This shift was Master Sergeant Saez's way of telling the man he probably shouldn't have kicked the prisoner when Miles Alsdorf was there.

"Eh?" The thickset marine glanced up from his fingers and checked the screen. On it Prisoner Zero was knelt where his bed should be, his head almost touching the floor, his fingers scrabbling at something unseen.

"Reckon he's lost it?"

"Fucked if I know. When did this start?"

"About five minutes ago." Specialist Stone was lying. She had no idea when Prisoner Zero had begun this latest routine. She'd been too busy watching Corporal Thompson out of the corner of her eye.

"Wake the Master Sergeant," said Corporal Thompson, and Specialist Stone looked at him, then saluted. "Yes, sir," she said. Her smile lasted most of the way to the Sergeant's quarters.

At Miles Alsdorf's suggestion the marines had allowed Prisoner Zero a new mattress and blanket. Well, an old mattress really, stuffed with horsehair and worn down to its warp and weft along one seam. It was stained in the way old mattresses seem to get stained with a lifetime's worth of precipitous periods, spilt coffee, babies made, born and then grieved over.

Prisoner Zero wasn't sure why that mattress had been chosen. Maybe it was all the marines could find at short notice or perhaps Sergeant Saez really believed it was the most disgusting thing possible. If so, he should have seen the squat in Amsterdam.

The blanket which came with the mattress was US issue, the colour of goose shit and machine-sewn along all four edges. A label glued to one corner claimed it was made from recycled plastic bottles, thus helping the environment.

Since it was July and the room in which the cage lived had only one window and this was sealed shut, the winter-weight blanket was as useless as it was unnecessary; but Miles Alsdorf had demanded his client be given a blanket and a mattress and Colonel Borgenicht had seen to it that he had.

So tightly was the mattress squeezed between the sides of Prisoner Zero's cage that it could only be edged out a little at a time. The prisoner then had to lift free the metal frame which supported it, raising one end until he could manoeuvre the other away from the brackets welded around one end of the cage to support his bed. All of this he had to do in silence.

The floor beneath his bed was steel mesh, plastic-coated like the rest and soldered at the edges to the frame of the cage. The darkness had suggested he begin his tunnel under the bed, where four tiles met. To help himself remember this, Prisoner Zero had scratched a cross into his arm to mark the inner edges of the four tiles and then run a circle around that point to indicate the tunnel.

Having cut free the tiles, he would need to tear his way through the mesh on which he knelt before he could prise the tiles from their setting. This created so many problems that Prisoner Zero decided he'd better worry about them later.

The difficulty for Prisoner Zero was that he needed space to walk in order to focus. Itchy inside his own skin, that was how one girl had put it a very long time ago. Nail him down, sit him in a café with a latte, a spliff or that day's paper and he would drift away into dreams, complex interplays of events misremembered, rewritten memories and occasional flashes of something Prisoner Zero used to think of as genius.

In the days before he realized he didn't rate that word.

"You think we ought to stop him?"

Corporal Thompson reached for a can of Pepsi Max, ripped the tab and shook his head. "You heard the Sergeant. The guy's nuts. Get over it." Master Sergeant Saez had been and gone, barely stopping long enough to glance at the screen.

Staying with the picture for only as long as it took him to finish his Pepsi, Corporal Thompson switched his attention back to the DC comic in front of him, leaving Prisoner Zero to scrabble helplessly against the mesh of the floor.

"This is getting bad," Specialist Stone said, when another five minutes had gone. "We should pass it up the line."

"Feel free." Corporal Thompson nodded at the house phone. "I'm sure Sergeant Saez will be delighted."

Ten minutes after that Specialist Stone came to a decision. One that would have had her cleaning shithouses for the rest of her career if Master Sergeant Saez had found out about it. She telephoned the Lieutenant.

"Sir, it's the prisoner. He's trying to tear up the floor of his cage . . ."

"With his fingers, sir."

"No sir, he's not getting away."

"Yes sir, the steel mesh is still in place."

"The guards are still outside his door, sir."

"Why did I call you? It was my mistake, sir." Specialist Stone stood very straight as she said this, listening while Lieutenant Ashcroft provided his own answer.

"Yes, sir. Sorry, sir."

"Told you," Corporal Thompson said, passing her that week's issue of *Spider-Man*.

Inside the cage the prisoner was wrestling with the steel frame that supported his mattress, prior to dragging that mattress back into position against a side wall so it could hide the entrance to his tunnel. He'd cut free the grout from around the tiles, just as the darkness instructed, and made a start at worrying his way through the mesh.

All he had to do now was make sure no one thought to look under his bed and to do that he needed to put his captors off entering the cage.

"It's obvious," said the darkness.

And it was.

As Prisoner Zero stripped off his paper jump suit and squatted next to the doorway to his cage, he ran over the map of Camp Freedom he kept in his head. He was trying to work out if the *others* were here. He wasn't sure who the others might be, but he was pretty certain who they weren't.

The Corporal, the one who liked kicking him, had mentioned that dozens of Prisoner Zero's co-conspirators had been rounded up. Which was odd, because the prisoner was pretty sure the darkness had talked to no one but him and he had talked to no one at all.

In all, he'd known maybe five people in Paris and most of those had politely ignored him. A state of existence Prisoner Zero had worked hard to achieve and he was beginning to regret upsetting its balance.

All the same, thought Prisoner Zero as he began to smear shit onto the mesh, what choice did he have? And how could he possibly explain that lack of choice to the endless, interchangeable people who sat across tables from him and asked questions to which the answers had to be obvious?

The US President had to die because the future demanded it. Prisoner Zero knew this to be true even if he could no longer remember exactly why. And if Prisoner Zero could not go to the President then the darkness really did require that he persuade the President to come to him.

It had something to do with history.

# CHAPTER 22

## *Darkness, CTzu 1/Year 78*

In the beginning there was darkness. A cold inevitability that woke the ice, sending shivers through its body, each shiver a billion kilometres of glass reflecting aimlessly in space.

The darkness felt like electricity and tasted like strangeness. There was little in common between it and the mind which had woken into it and the darkness knew this.

Chuang Tzu slept.

And while he slept his icy sleep, something happened elsewhere. Lithium fissioned into helium, tritium and energy... Deuterium fused, as did tritium itself. When enough neutrons had been produced to create further fission Central Beijing vaporized, the resulting over-pressure expanding as shockwave and losing power as it went. Twenty-eight million people died almost instantly.

None of this Chuang Tzu or the darkness knew because it happened fifteen generations removed in a world which had long since lost interest in the SZ *Loyal Prince*. More ships and better had been built and launched and there were those who'd denied the SZ *Loyal Prince* was still out there and some who claimed it had exploded mere weeks after the mission began.

A whole cult had grown up around the idea that those chosen had been secretly executed or given over to experiments, that the televised launch had been stage-managed and the mission originally created to divert attention from war in Tibet. The darkness cared for none of this and though it tried to identify the small star venerated by the Chuang Tzu, whom it thought of only as *the ice,* this proved impossible. A fact the darkness understood to mean the star itself had been destroyed.

Closer acquaintance with the ice showed that in all probability it would not regard the destruction of a star as commonplace at all. It would probably regard this as very worrying.

And this the darkness found interesting, although not as interesting as the way the ice stored data, which was as interference patterns and reactions of chemicals, jumping sparks and webs of connections laid down as overlays on webs that had gone before.

A million permutations produced the fraction of one thought. In the end, irritated by the slowness of data extraction, the darkness took to deconstructing thousands of thoughts at once. And yet it still took decades for the darkness to realize that the data was fragmented and difficult to extract simply because it was not laid down in a coherent form.

So the darkness woke slightly and, having considered this, realized that the fragmentary nature of the data's extraction was a side effect of the coldness from which it had to be extracted. Which meant, it seemed to the darkness, that the very medium which held the data also hindered its use. An idea that made the darkness look beyond the ice to the nature of the material frozen.

The azimuth and angle of its looking was narrow and the fragment of the darkness designated to do the looking was less than one thousandth of the whole. But this was still sufficient for the darkness to realize that the ice was surrounded by separate and less coherent forms of data. Only the data in these forms was so corrupted that extracting it made mining the living ice look easy.

There was a distinction between the types of data, their containers and the ripped container within which they all floated. So the darkness began with the most dense of the data hordes, examining the SZ *Loyal Prince* and its semiAI, running millions of routines in an attempt to understand its origins.

A type II star, a sequence of nine planets (actually seven, as two did not rate that definition or, if they did, so did others not included in the nine), carbon-based life, relatively new, technologically simple. The darkness trawled opera from Peking, Rodin's *Kiss*, music by Brahms, the pyramids and Sphinx, the Great Wall of China and a painting of a soup can without understanding what any of them might be (or that they were carried under protest from Beijing, their mix chosen to reflect global levels of culture).

In the beginning there was darkness. A cold curiosity that waited for meaning, tasting numbers and extracting data from the chaos of eighteen hundred dead refugees, one rotting Colonel Commissar, a doctor frozen at the point of dying and a mind being slowly reclaimed from hibernation.

The darkness felt like electricity and tasted like strangeness. There was little enough in common between it and the hibernating mind and the darkness knew this.

So it reversed the process by which that mind became frozen.

Chuang Tzu woke.

Still strapped into position, his bladder cathetered, tubes entering his mouth and rectum and a claw from the side of the pod busy suturing a wound in his neck. The scream of the young Chinese navigator barely made it past the tube pumping whatever slop was being pumped into his stomach, passed through his colon and sucked from his body.

The whole level was in darkness. A vast impenetrable blackness that hugged the glass lid of his pod and swallowed floor, ceiling and all four walls. The emergency lights were off. More terrifying still, no lights showed on the panel controlling the pod, not even standby.

"Madame?" Major Commissar Chuang Tzu choked on the word and felt it return like an echo.

"*Madame?*"

"Who's there?"

"*Who's there?*"

"Help me," said Chuang, adding, "Please."

"Okay," said the darkness.

Chuang Tzu slept and dreamt of home. That he considered Grandfather Luo's farm home surprised him. He would have thought home was that flat in the Bund, the one he'd briefly shared with Wu. This was on the fifth floor of an ancient apartment block overlooking the harbour in Shanghai. And had the lift worked Wu's purchase of the apartment would have been impossible.

Although, to be honest, under the new rules no one owned anything outright in the Middle Kingdom. The flat was leased from Beijing for nine hundred and ninety-nine years, the payment for the lease charged over a period of twenty-five years. It was a common arrangement and open to easy abuse. Only one person was supposed to live in the apartment but two often did and sometimes three.

When Wu's sister came to stay and remained to live, muttering was heard from the concierge but that was mere habit. Had the concierge known about Chuang Tzu's friendship with Wu there would have been more than muttering. So Wu's idea that his friend should pretend to be close to his sister was a good one. It was just a pity that Wu found his sister and best friend together in bed.

He went back to Grandfather Luo's after that, saying nothing. Just turning up from the city with a case full of suits and the latest notebook semiAI, its case cut from a single block of hardened glass. The suits had been useless, too thin to wear in winter and too fragile to survive work on the farm. Ripping them up for rags had given Chuang Tzu's grandmother endless pleasure.

Wu's sister called him, and when her calls went unanswered she wrote a serious letter on rag paper full of regrets and fine sentiments. It was handwritten, in the classic *cao shu* style. Chuang Tzu never saw Madame Mimi, his grandmother, read the letter but everything changed after it arrived.

She no longer mocked his poetry or hammered on his bedroom door at dawn because the hens needed feeding. She fed him first from the pot and darned and mended his clothes herself. Girls from the village started to turn up unexpectedly and when her grandson showed no interest in farmers' daughters, the daughters and granddaughters of other exiles were invited to tea, or for supper or to stay the week.

In the end, because Chuang Tzu was growing up and had learnt how to handle his grandmother, he made friends with Lin Yao, a quiet girl from Xingjian. Her name meant jade treasure and she was tall and thin, with straight hair and tiny breasts topped with the longest nipples he'd ever seen. Although it took him eight months to discover these and he wondered later if they were the reason she'd been so unwilling to let him slide his hand inside her shirt.

For over a year the damp secrets of Lin Yao's body remained unseen; touched occasionally as they lay on the hillside in the spray of a waterfall, their notebooks open if unused beside them, but always unseen.

"You must taste the plum and split the peach," Grandfather Luo would insist, almost crossly. The man had been a great radical in his time. Too famous to kill and too dangerous to be let loose. His contempt for the timidity of the generations which had come after his own was widely known and had lost him many friends. "How else will you know if you want to keep the bowl?"

Madame Mimi had other views. As often happened, these conflicted not just with those of his grandfather but with themselves. A part of her was delighted that her grandson had found a girl traditional enough to wait for marriage. Another part suspected Lin Yao might be *Uighur*.

Larger than France, Germany and Italy put together, China's north-west province of Xingjian had long been Moslem, and though all China was now traditional Market-Leninist the old tribal ways continued, if quietly.

She tried catching the girl out but Lin Yao answered carefully, revealing little, as careful answers usually did. And in the end, having watched the black-haired girl for weeks which turned to months and then became a year, Chuang Tzu's grandmother decided that perhaps, after all, it didn't matter.

The girl lit joss sticks when required, ate pork dumplings if they were put in front of her and observed the important feast days. Sometimes appearances were enough.

And every afternoon, Chuang Tzu and Lin Yao climbed the lower slopes of Ragged Mountain, in whose shadow Grandfather Luo's farm existed, and walked together to the waterfall, their shoes crunching dry bracken underfoot or dragging through wet grass as the seasons bled into each other. Until finally even Madame Mimi was anxious for something to happen.

"I won't live forever," she told her grandson one breakfast, her face as creased as an old poem. "And before I die I want to see your children."

Flames danced over an iron griddle and buds blossomed on the fingers of a cherry tree in the farmyard outside. The kitchen was as perfect as his grandmother could make, far removed from the glitzy chrome of Shanghai or the lightweight adventures of holidays on the moon.

Most of those who visited Chuang Tzu's grandmother assumed her house was a bid for reassurance, like most retreats into tradition. This was to miss the point. The stone-built farm with its small meadows and old orchard, wild deer and pheasants was Madame Mimi's revenge. As was its décor of bamboo scrolls, paper screens and silk carpets.

It was her revenge for the Westernized years spent in exile in Paris. For the child she later lost to a New York taxi and the Rue St. Honoré frocks she left behind on their much-publicized return to Beijing.

She could remember the evening they decided to return. Sitting in the Chieng-Mai on Rue Frédéric Sauton, at one of those centre tables with a little glass screen on either side to keep conversations private. Two Americans in leather jackets had been sitting next to them, feeding a tramplike man who seemed more concerned with bolting his ground chicken and chilli than listening to what they had to say.

Chuang Tzu's father had been a baby then, his car seat slung on the floor beside their table. The Chieng-Mai was good like that. On the table between them lay a letter from the embassy offering her husband full immunity and the return of his family farm. All he had to do was come back to Beijing. They would not even try to control what he could say or limit his access to the Western press.

Of course, the letter didn't say there'd be no electricity or that the roads to the village would be allowed to become impassable and visas as good as prohibited to journalists wanting to visit the area.

It had been Grandfather Luo's choice. His decision.

Now she felt amusement and regret and small shards of resentment that caught her unaware like paper cuts. So she made her life in the shape of memories which had been old when she was a child and lived out her exile from Paris within another exile, this one.

When Chuang Tzu woke from the darkness for the third time it was to roll over and reach for the girl in his dreams. Only the girl was gone and the sheet under which he slept was hard and scratchy, a fact Chuang Tzu forgot as soon as she walked into his room both naked and smiling.

Neither of which was likely or even possible. The last time he'd seen Lin Yao had been by the waterfall, as she sat half naked on her heels in his shirt, slow tears sliding down her cheeks to fall on summer grass.

"You're leaving," she'd told him, back then.

"No." Lifting her narrow chin, Chuang Tzu kissed away the tears. It felt a very adult thing to do. "You're wrong." There was blood on the tail of his shirt, but much less than either of them had been expecting.

Their first attempt at sex had been brief and clumsy, her anxiety and his nervousness leading to relief only when they simultaneously decided that perhaps the time was not right.

"Swim?"

Lin Yao had looked so surprised at his suggestion that Chuang Tzu almost smiled. Neither one had braved the pool in all the months they'd been walking from the farm to the waterfall and back. And though Grandfather Luo's pig keeper said that snakes slept in its depths, neither Lin Yao nor Chuang Tzu believed him, any more than they believed that bathing in its icy water brought visions.

It was the pool's steep sides and the force of the waterfall that made them stick to the river that ran past the village.

"Come on," said Chuang Tzu, reaching for her hand. And that was what decided it. Lin Yao let her fingers lock around his and then, only half willing, she let herself be pulled to her feet and led to the lip of the pool. He undid her blouse and slid the sleeves down her arms, dropping her top onto the grass. Then he shrugged himself out of his own shirt and tossed it beside hers.

"How are we going to do this?" asked Lin Yao, shivering.

Chuang Tzu looked at her. "We jump," he said.

"And how do we get back?" Nodding at the long drop, Lin Yao indicated the problem.

"We climb," said Chuang Tzu, only then searching for the means to make this true. There were splits in the granite and narrow ledges, holes worn by water and the occasional bush busy clinging to the side. It should be possible, provided the first bit was not too slippery.

"There are handholds," he said.

Lin Yao was doubtful.

"Let me go first," suggested the boy. "If it's safe then you can go second."

Long black hair swept Lin Yao's naked back as she shook her head. "No," she said. "We jump together."

The drop was maybe twice their height, the depth of the pool unknown, and it wasn't clear to Chuang Tzu whether they were testing themselves or each other. Either way, Lin Yao twisted her fingers tight into his, stepped up to the lip and counted down from three.

"Lift off," said Chuang Tzu, and they jumped, falling forever until white water came up to hit them and the shock tore their hands apart.

"Cold," he gasped, voice frozen in his throat.

Lin Yao nodded, unable to speak because an iron band was being tightened by unseen fingers around her ribs.

Kicking towards the rock, the boy stopped when he realized Lin Yao had remained where she was. So he swam back, grabbed the girl's wrist and dragged her after him, only letting go when Lin Yao reached round him to grab at a crack in the rock-face.

"You go first," he said. "You're colder."

Lin Yao looked uncertain, as well she might. But she reached up and found a handhold, scrabbling with her toes as she pushed and pulled her body half out of the water. Her shoulders as she reached for a fresh hold were sharp as blades and her muscle stood out, root-like, beneath pale skin.

"You all right?"

"What do you think?" Lin Yao didn't say anything else, just found another crevice in the rock and then another, her toes scrabbling to keep their hold. And as she finally pulled herself clear of the icy water, Chuang Tzu reached for the handhold she'd used to begin her climb and pulled himself close to the rock-face.

"Keep going," he said. "Don't look down."

He was staring up at her, Lin Yao's whole body foreshortened into legs, buttocks and a narrow, almost hairless gash of sex.

Everything was a matter of perspective, Chuang Tzu realized. Ordinary things seen from extraordinary angles held their own meanings and messages. What her buttocks and sex said to him the boy was still working out when the girl scrambled over the lip of the pool and his perspective changed.

"Well, that was stupid," said Lin Yao.

Chuang Tzu shrugged. "Quite probably."

"That's all you can say?"

It was the climb, decided the boy. She must have known he was staring or else realized that not doing so was next to impossible.

"Here," said Chuang Tzu, picking up his shirt. He wrapped the garment around Lin Yao and then put his old jacket on top. "You need to get warm." They sat in silence after that. Which was to say that not a word passed between them, although icy water continued to roll over the lip of the fall and crash into the pool below while buzzards circled high in the sky overhead, their cry harsh and unlovely.

Down in the valley a boy shouted and army trucks ground their gears as they began to climb towards the pass. In short, the world continued around them as they sat, side by side, on rough grass in the weak sunlight of a late afternoon.

"I'm sorry," Lin Yao said finally.

Chuang Tzu glanced across. "For what?"

"Being cross."

It was the first time she'd ever apologized to him and the very fact she had gave Chuang Tzu a tiny, flawed advantage. "You weren't cross," he said, "you were furious."

When Lin Yao blushed, Chuang Tzu reached across and took her chin gently in his first finger and thumb, turning her head until she faced him. Their kiss was slow and tentative, her lips softening just as he was about to bring the kiss to an end.

"Love you," he said, the only time he'd said that to anyone. With Wu and Wu's sister it would have seemed clumsy and provincial and there had been no one else to whom he could say those words.

Grandfather Luo would have laughed at him and talked of selfish genes and bonds of affinity, while Madame Mimi would have grown tight-lipped and angry. Any talk of emotion within the family had that effect on her.

"What are you thinking?"

"About stuff," the boy said.

"What stuff?"

"Families. Children. Stuff like that."

Lin Yao's eyes went wide and for a second she looked shocked. Then she looked puzzled as if she might have misunderstood what he said. Which she had, but Chuang Tzu only realized that later and by then the SZ *Loyal Prince* was beyond the moon and he was accelerating out of her life.

Lin Yao let the boy lower her onto the rough grass and gently spread her knees. They began with Dragon Turns, in which the man lies between the legs of the woman. Missionary, Grandfather Luo called it. Suitable only for nervous young women and foreigners.

Chuang Tzu sucked the fingers of his right hand and carefully cupped her entire vulva, smoothing one finger between dry lips. Then he did it again, pushing the finger slightly inside her.

Sore from their previous attempt, Lin Yao tensed at his touch.

"I'll take it slowly..."

The boy waited for her to say no but she just looked at him. A third helping of saliva and Chuang Tzu knelt himself between the girl's legs. In the end it took two of them, Lin Yao spreading herself with her fingers while the boy used his own hand to position himself against her.

"Slowly," she warned.

So Chuang Tzu pushed forward, very slowly, feeling the tiniest jolt as Lin Yao's body opened just enough to let him almost enter and then tightened around him. Not knowing whether to push deeper or pull back and try that bit again, Chuang Tzu waited. With Wu's sister it had been easy. She just performed Jade Girl Plays the Flute and then jumped on top of him, there was nothing fragile about it.

In the end, Lin Yao solved the problem for him, pushing up with her hips. One wince and the thing was done.

They stayed so for a while, Lin Yao still wrapped in his shirt and coat and the boy naked above her with a cold, almost autumnal wind blowing across his bare back.

Eyes open and watching, they kissed and kept kissing until their eyes closed and the world disappeared. Lin Yao was grinding against him now, her teeth biting at his lower lip. So the boy bit back, hard and then more softly, feeling her body tense and her arms lock suddenly across his back.

A yelp like a wildcat released her. Lin Yao's head falling back, pillowed on her blouse and the rough grass. When her breath had returned and small tremors stopped running the length of her abdomen, the boy pulled back and then slid slowly in again, feeling an answering ache begin to build in his own body.

He should pull out, Chuang Tzu knew that. Spurt his hunger onto her thin belly or roll the girl over and release himself against the groove of her buttocks, but instead he gripped Lin Yao's arms and lost everything in the moment.

"You okay with that?"

Lin Yao nodded. She was sitting on her heels, Chuang Tzu's shirt still wrapped tight around her, a darkness between her legs where he'd so recently been. The boy could smell himself on her, the scent of sex rising like steam from her body, richer than musk and dark as gun-powder tea.

"We should get back," he said.

"Why?"

"Because my grandmother will be worried."

"And you worry when your grandmother is worried?"

"Of course." Chuang Tzu looked at her. "Don't you?"

"I don't live with my grandmother," said Lin Yao. And Chuang Tzu suddenly realized he knew almost nothing about who made up Lin Yao's own small household.

"Well, your mother," he said.

"My mother's dead." Lin Yao's voice was slightly surprised, as if she'd expected him to know this and perhaps he had.

"I'm sorry," he said finally.

"It was years ago," said Lin Yao, and Chuang nodded, although that hadn't been what he meant. And so they sat in silence for a few more minutes, while the sun snagged on a distant mountain like a lost balloon and the water in the pool changed from gun-metal silver to black.

"I need to go," Chuang Tzu said. "First I'll walk you home."

"Walk me home..." Lin Yao glanced at him, eyes wide. A thousand colours reduced to rust. "Am I going to see you tomorrow?"

"Of course... I promise."

"I don't believe you." Tears rolled down Lin Yao's beautiful cheeks and hid themselves beneath the neck of Chuang Tzu's jacket as she dressed in silence, with her back turned to him.

"Tomorrow," promised Chuang Tzu, when they reached the gate of her tiny farm.

Lin Yao shook her head.

It was late when the boy got home and later still when his grandmother gave him the letter which had arrived that afternoon from Wu. Only now, instead of a lieutenant, Wu was a major commissar and the youngest member of a panel headed by General Wu, his father.

Chuang Tzu's one-time friend wrote to say that great opportunities awaited those who joined the newly built SZ *Loyal Prince* and both Wu and his sister had taken the liberty of mentioning their friend's talents to the General, who was delighted with the suggestion.

Enclosed with the letter came a travel permit, a ticket for a government flight from Leshan to Wuhai and a letter, signed by General Wu himself, congratulating the young man on being chosen for the most important project undertaken since Qin Shi Huangdi ordered that slaves join together some small and rather useless defences to make the Great Wall.

Chuang Tzu left before dawn, dressed in the one good suit his grandmother hadn't reduced to rags and carrying an untidy sheaf of poems, a few of them dedicated to a girl who slept in a village twenty minutes' walk from the house he was leaving.

# CHAPTER 23

## *Marrakech, Summer 1977*

While the foreigners stood at the front desk filling out infinitely shorter forms which stated they weren't planning to fill out the forms required to report a robbery, Moz sat at the table in room three and watched Major Abbas make notes in his tatty notebook.

"Where did we first meet?" the Major asked suddenly.

Moz swallowed.

"Was it in here?"

"No." The boy shook his head. "There was a dead American."

"Ah," said the Major. "How could I forget? Only he was English, not American, and his father was a diplomat. It was all very irritating." The small man made a few additional notes in his book and then snapped it shut, inserting his pencil into a gap in its spine.

"You had one hand twisted behind your back."

Now he'd remembered the first meeting. The Major had problems removing the picture of a small boy casually stripping to show one arm tied into an impossible position, oblivious both to his nakedness and the bruises speckling his body like camouflage.

"What happened?"

Moz thought about it. "I started hitting back." This wasn't quite true. He'd got a job, the winter his mother died, but he wasn't about to tell the policeman that.

"For you," said the Major as he reached into his pocket. Peeling off a hundred-dirham note he glanced from the new note to the boy and sucked his teeth. Carefully replacing the hundred-dirham note, he extracted a handful of smaller notes, all of them scuffed along their edges and dark with grease from the fingers of those who'd handled them before.

"That's more like it," said the Major, but he was talking to himself.

The boy stared at the notes.

"Take them," Major Abbas said, his words an order.

Moz counted the money, to make sure it added up to a hundred. Ten notes in all, originally pink like the walls of Marrakech, with a drinking bowl on one side and a picture of the Sultan, as most of those who lived in the Medina still called King Hassan II.

Without being told, Moz folded the notes in half and then in half again, stuffing the money into the side of his shoe.

"What must I do?"

Major Abbas smiled. "Who said you had to do anything?"

In many ways, playing simple seemed the safest way to behave around this man so that was what Moz did. And besides, how could he not want something?

"You remember what I said last time?"

Moz knew word for word what the Major had said the time before. Moz was to bring him rumours. And there were always rumours, that the Algerians planned to invade or the Polisario, as the leaders of the Saharan tribes now called themselves, intended to thrust north and attack Marrakech. That one of the King's own ministers had been behind the last plot to kill the King.

In the fifteen or so short years of Moz's life, rioting students in Casablanca had been arrested, tortured and jailed, exiled trade unionists had been murdered in Paris, the old colonial companies had tried to bribe their way out of nationalization and two of the coups against the King had come dangerously close to succeeding.

Truth or rumour, these were not things that anyone sensible would repeat to the police. And besides these dangerous truths, there were lesser rumours of gangs and robberies, rapes, murder and infidelity. Only those were not what Major Abbas required.

He wanted only the first kind, the bigger and darker rumours. Moz was just unsure why the Major thought he might be the person to hear them.

"So," said the Major, "you'll keep in touch this time?"

Moz nodded.

"Good. Now take those two home." He jerked his chin towards the front office. "And suggest she wears something over that shirt." Flipping open his notebook, Major Abbas found the address. "They're staying at Hotel Gulera. You know where that is?"

The Major stopped himself. "No, of course you don't." He scribbled an address on a scrap of paper and handed it to the boy, who glanced at it once and carefully left the scrap on the table between them.

When Moz was gone, the Major made a new note in his book, upgrading the boy's usefulness from four to five. He'd always suspected the boy to be at least semi-literate.

"You realize," Jake said, shifting his rucksack, "that the little shit's probably a police spy."

"Jake!"

"I mean it. Look at him."

Celia shot a quick glance at the boy walking slightly ahead of her. He was staring up at walls as he passed, checking for street signs, she imagined.

"Looks just like a kid to me."

The spiky-haired man nodded heavily. He was wearing black Levi's and a Ramones T-shirt, his rucksack was made from black rubber. A pair of lizard-skin shoes seemed moulded to his feet.

"Not far," Moz said. His accent was a little more sing-song than usual and his words a little less clear. The Major obviously intended him to report back on these two and Moz wanted to put them at their ease.

Ignorance usually worked.

"That's what you said five minutes ago."

Moz shrugged and dodged neatly between a scooter and a cart laden with melons. When the couple didn't immediately follow, Moz waited.

"This thing's heavy," Jake said, shrugged his shoulders to indicate the bag.

"I'll take it." Moz held out a hand.

"Good idea," said Jake, as he began to shuffle his way out of the straps.

"Jake, you can't—"

"Yes, I can. He offered."

"The kid's half your size."

"So, he still offered."

"I carry it," Moz said. "You pay me when we get there."

"Welcome to Marrakech," said Jake.

They walked in silence after that, cutting down the side alleys that Moz indicated, passing through small souks, dusty squares which were anything but square and a market selling leather slippers made in the tannery in El Moukef.

"Over there," said Moz.

The entrance to that alley looked to Celia and Jake like all the rest. They'd been lost at least twice on the walk from Avenue Houman to Rue Bab Ailen, but the boy doubted if either of them realized that. Once they'd even circled past the same small mosque from two different directions and neither appeared to notice.

"Wait..." The woman was standing in front of a stall.

"We haven't got time!" Jake's voice was impatient.

"Yes, we have," Celia said. "Besides, I want to look at this." In her hand was a belt made from discs of leather laced in a row. Circles cut from hubcaps and beaten into a traditional Berber pattern had been stitched to each disc, their centres augmented with a five-peseta coin from the Spanish territories, each coin hammered flat and welded in place.

"They're amazing. Ask him how much... Go on." The woman was talking to him, Moz realized.

"*Ssalamu 'lekum.*"

"*Ssalamu 'lekum.*"

Civilities done, Moz pointed to the belt Celia held. "*Bshhal?*"

"*Khamsa ú 'ashren.*"

The boy almost choked. "Twenty-five dirham," he told the woman, who reached into her leather satchel for a purse. "It's way too much," Moz said hastily. "Offer five."

"Five?"

"*Khamsa,*" Moz said, turning back to the stallholder.

"*Ashrin.*"

"He says twenty."

"Okay."

"*La.*" Moz shook his head. "*Ghali bezzaf. Akhir Taman shhal?*"

The man scowled at the boy and told him to tell the foreigner how good the work was, how fine the leather, the quality of the silver used to make the circles and the fact that they were real Spanish five-peseta pieces. "*Akhir ttaman dyali huwa hada.*" A shrug closed the conversation. A shrug and a quick spread of the hands, universal gesture for *what more can I say?*

"He says twenty is his best price."

"That's fine," Celia said.

"No, it's not," Moz said. "Walk away... that way," he added, "towards the other side of the square."

"But I want—"

"Do it," Jake said. He might have been talking to Celia but he was looking at Moz and for the first time there was a smile on his face, albeit sour. "Go on," he told Celia. "Walk away. Isn't that what you do best?"

The stallholder sent a boy after them with the belt. Although he waited until they had actually entered a side alley.

"Fifteen," he told Moz.

"Nine."

"Fifteen."

The boy and Moz looked at each other. The kid was about eleven, Arab rather than Berber, small for his age and worried. Any smiles from his father were reserved for the customers, Moz could see that in the boy's eyes.

"Twelve," Moz suggested. It was an outrageous price for a belt, at least it seemed so to him. Very reluctantly, the boy nodded.

"Sixteen," Moz told the woman. He took the money from a purse she handed him, one note and six coins, counting the dirham carefully into his own palm. While Celia was busy putting the purse back into her satchel, Moz turned to the boy and put the ten and two coins into his hand.

"That's for the belt," he said. Equally quickly, he pocketed two coins for himself and gave the final two to the boy. "Yours," he said. "The price we agreed for the belt was twelve. Those are for you to keep."

"Thank you," said the boy, hand over his own heart.

"*Bessalama*."

"*M'a ssalama*." Returning the peace, the boy trotted back to his stall, a hand-me-down jellaba dragging behind him in the dirt.

"What was all that about?" Jake asked.

"All what?"

"The talking."

"We were saying goodbye."

"What?" Jake snorted. "You telling me everyone in Morocco is that polite?"

"I don't know everyone in Morocco," Moz said, reasonably. "But most people in Marrakech have manners."

Celia smiled at the boy still laden with Jake's rucksack. She found it hard to guess his age because everybody in the city seemed so small, but she imagined it was around fourteen, maybe a little older. She had a brother that age, away at school.

"You've insulted him," she said, transferring her gaze to Jake.

"Insulted him?"

"Yeah." Celia nodded. "You know. What you do best. You need to apologize."

For a moment it seemed like Jake might refuse, then he nodded grudgingly. "I can be a prick sometimes," he said.

Celia nodded.

"You know..." Jake Razor looked at the boy, face thoughtful. "Maybe you can help me."

"If I can," said Moz.

"You know where I can get some dope?"

"Kif?"

"Yeah." Jake laughed. "That's the man. You can get me dope?"

The answer was no but Moz nodded. "Of course," he said, making his voice slur like Jake's own. "Give me an hour."

## CHAPTER 24

### *Lampedusa, Tuesday 3 July*

The fact the Colonel could even name Pierre de Fermat surprised Dr. Petrov, that he could recognize proof of the mathematician's last theorem she found so staggering that she banished the thought from her mind. Something to be processed later, along with an unguarded comment he'd made while he was briefing her on their way to the weights room.

"You know why I got this gig?"

He didn't seem like a man who'd use "gig" in that context. But then he didn't seem like someone who'd ask that kind of question.

"Because of your record?" Katie had Googled him before leaving New York. Those ribbons on his dress uniform meant something. Mostly that he'd taken casualties and held his ground in some of the world's worst shitholes while other units were going to pieces.

"I'm black."

She looked at him then. A bull-necked man with cropped hair turning grey at the edges, flat eyes and a hard smile. He scared her and looking at him Katie wondered if he ever scared himself.

"I don't get it," Katie said.

"What's to get?" said the Colonel. "I'm black and so's he."

Katie glanced at Prisoner Zero and then raised her eyebrows. Sure, the prisoner had olive skin but half the men on the island were darker than this.

"He's not—" she began to say.

Colonel Borgenicht held up one hand, cutting dead her protests. "He is to the Pentagon and the Secretary of State."

The only equation Katie had been able to recognize smeared into the shit of Prisoner Zero's cage was $E=MC^2$. And if she was honest, Katie only recognized this because a boyfriend had bought her the T-shirt in her first year at Columbia.

"You want to tell me why you're doing this?"

The naked man didn't even bother to shake his head, just glared through the mesh with flat, light-swallowing eyes. Stubble now grew across his jaw and scalp, making him look like an off-colour recruit for the Aryan Brotherhood, all sneer and crudely cut tattoos.

Katie felt like calling for a marine doctor and demanding that Prisoner Zero's blood be tested. Only this would simultaneously compromise her integrity and independence. The first, by relying on a medical opinion she knew to be partisan. The second . . . Well, the second was obvious. Katie could imagine Colonel Borgenicht's response on being told that Katie Petrov believed the prisoner was being kept drugged.

That she might care what the Colonel thought was an interesting notion.

"Get me a local doctor." Katie tossed the order over her shoulder, then turned back to Prisoner Zero as if it never occurred to her a suit from the Pentagon might not do as he was told.

"We've got a doctor."

"I want a second opinion."

"On what?"

Katie did her own version of flat-eye. "His physical state," she said.

"Major Dutch is very good."

"Are you officially refusing me a second opinion?"

Katie heard the weights room door shut behind her. The suit would have liked to slam it but the door came fitted with one of those restraining springs designed to stop guests from injuring themselves.

"Now we're alone," said Katie, "you want to tell me why...?" She gestured at numbers cut into the shit which now skimmed a sizeable section of mesh. Letters and numbers, flowing equations and broken words, some of which Katie thought she half recognized and hoped she was wrong.

Disgust was a bad emotion to display in situations like this, so Katie tried to keep her face neutral. She'd been breathing through her mouth ever since Colonel Borgenicht had shown her into the cell. And the fact Katie had been notified at all was a miracle. At least one of the comments she'd overheard suggested the simplest solution would be to bring forward the date for the execution.

Mind you, Katie imagined she'd been meant to hear those.

Shit plastered the mesh. Not lumps of the stuff thrown at the sides of the cage in anger or smeared roughly across its floor, expressions of a furious disgust with life, and Katie had seen both in her three years visiting prisons. Nor was it the clumsy excretal smearing mostly found in dirty protests by those who regarded themselves as political prisoners.

This was a thin, almost translucent skim, completely flat and eerily similar in appearance to cloisonné, where a jeweller fills areas between welded wires with coloured enamel. Onto this surface the man had scratched his equations, using a tiny stub of wire that he still held in one hand.

The room stank and with every hour that passed it stank more. At some point the afternoon sun was going to reach the white-washed window and the smell would get even worse.

A paper plate had been folded to make a float and the stink of urine suggested Prisoner Zero had thinned his coating to get the right consistency. Speaking as someone who'd waited six weeks for a plasterer, only to have the man who turned up botch the job so badly that he left ridges all across her kitchen wall, Katie had to say that Prisoner Zero was achieving a very professional finish.

"They'll just hose it down," Katie told him.

This was untrue. Master Sergeant Saez had wanted to hose down the cage the moment he saw it, but the Colonel had other ideas, which boiled down to making Prisoner Zero live in his own mess. An approach that fitted Katie's perceptions of the man far better than his familiarity with Fermat.

Katie was expected to issue preliminary findings soon and had little enough to go on. Of course, put another way, she had more than enough to make her case. Sitting naked in a shit-smeared cell was not normal, even for those who made up most of her patients.

All Prisoner Zero had to do was start obsessively jacking off and she could leak to the papers that the man was mentally unfit to stand trial, never mind be executed. Meanwhile, she was stuck in the same shit-smeared cage, so what did that make her?

Pulling a cell phone from her pocket, Katie dialled Master Sergeant Saez. It took five minutes for him to send someone down to the weights room and only then did Specialist Stone discover the Sergeant had given her the wrong keys for the room.

"You finished in here, ma'am?"

Katie shook her head. "I just want to get some cigarettes."

"Good luck," said Specialist Stone. "You planning to walk into Lampedusa?"

"Can't I get some from the bar?"

"All gone and the PX doesn't stock cigarettes anymore."

"There's that vending machine in the lobby."

"Empty."

"Great," said Katie.

"You need them for work, ma'am?"

"Work?"

Specialist Stone nodded at the naked prisoner. "Something to do with him?"

Katie started to shake her head and then stopped when the woman standing in the doorway began to do the same.

"Is it to do with him?"

Katie nodded.

"Okay," said Specialist Stone. "I'm off in ten minutes. I'll take a ride down to the village." That was what the marines called the town, which most of the islanders called their capital. But it was hard for people grown up in Los Angeles and Philadelphia to take seriously a town with an area smaller than some of their malls.

"Not a big deal," said the woman, when Katie started to thank her. "I need some fresh air anyway."

The tobacco was black and the brand nothing that Katie recognized. All the same, she dragged the acrid smoke into her mouth, deadening the faecal stink of Prisoner Zero's cage. Into her mouth and out of her nose, familiar as breathing and almost as welcome.

Katie should have been cross with herself for cracking after five months, but all she felt was relief as nicotine broke the blood-brain barrier and her pulse began to settle. It wasn't that Katie had an addictive personality, she just liked the things.

"Isn't that Fermat?" Katie nodded at the cell wall.

A part of her had been working on the theory that the naked prisoner might react to a Western woman invading his space and perching on the edge of his mattress, openly chain-smoking cigarettes. A wiser part understood that he was unlikely to react to such crude provocation.

After all, Prisoner Zero was a ruthless killer busy playing games with authority. At least he was according to a file she'd just been given by a singularly unhappy Miles Alsdorf. Katie had known the Pentagon had their own choice of psychiatrist examining Prisoner Zero, she just hadn't expected him to reach his conclusion quite so quickly.

And the report made much of Prisoner Zero having tendencies, mostly sociopathic. Nowhere did the report suggest that he was an actual sociopath, because that might posit a degree of non-culpability on the part of the convicted. And anyway, how could she or the Pentagon's tame psychiatrist assert anything but generalities about the prisoner's internal state when he refused to talk?

It all came down to the confession.

"Shit," she said, not caring if the weights room was bugged. "How could you be so fucking stupid?"

Dark eyes held hers and then, as Katie sat frozen, Prisoner Zero reached across and stole her cigarette. Dragging deep, he rolled the smoke from between half-scabbed lips into flaring nostrils and handed the thing back to her.

"That confession," said Katie. "It makes things more difficult."

She knew exactly how stupid a comment this was. If she'd have been Prisoner Zero she'd have said whatever came into her mind as well. She'd seen the report of his injuries, written up carefully by the marine who first examined Prisoner Zero on his arrival on Lampedusa. All those unexplained burns, the torn fingernails and split lip, the lacerated tongue.

"Yeah," said Katie. "I know." Her smile was bitter. "Everyone confesses in the end."

# CHAPTER 25

## *Darkness, CTzu 53/Year 1*

*Let me out, please...*

His name was also Chuang Tzu. So said the butterfly.

Obviously enough, this was not Zaq's original name because that had been given up during the ceremony of rebirth. The fifty-third Chuang Tzu wore the very first on his cloak as a diamond buckle. Every emperor became a diamond eventually. It was one of the few advantages of living as a carbon-based life form.

All that was needed was death, cremation at fifteen hundred degrees and enough pressure to replicate geophysical forces found in the transmutation of soft carbon to intricate lattice.

There was a circular elegance to this solution which appealed to the Library on several levels, although it could explain its thoughts to Zaq on only three, the others being beyond the understanding of a small child.

The Library still used "darkness" when considering itself, because this was how the very first Chuang Tzu had thought of it. Now, however, it went by a number of names. The most obvious being "the Library." "My Librarian" had been the choice of an emperor, centuries before, who could not quite grasp that there was no Turk inside his mechanical box.

Zaq had little trouble imagining the darkness. So little trouble that he sometimes borrowed the name for himself, putting it on and taking it off like a cloak.

His mind had been full of monsters for as long as he could remember. And though his mother referred to the menagerie inside his head as imaginary friends, this was wrong on so many counts that Zaq merely smiled.

The butterfly who came in the night was just pretend. That's what his mother said and his brother Eli agreed. As for being the new emperor...

Breakfast was withheld, then lunch and supper. Three days later, with the boy protesting bitterly and frozen to his bones with hunger, Maria gave up being cross and went to see Dr. Joyce again, letting

Eli guide her down through the levels until she reached Razor's Edge. In a moment of unusual charity the elderly splice merchant suggested Maria prepare herself for the possibility that Zaq's claim was true.

One of the first things Zaq learnt after rebirth was how the very first Chuang Tzu awoke. With darkness and cold, small voices and words spoken without being understood.

*Let me out, please . . .*

**CTzu 1/Year 127.** He woke once when he died and again when he was reborn. Neither time did the young Chinese navigator understand what had happened to him, though what had happened was that the recently promoted Major Commissar was decanted into memory by the darkness and held there while his body was recreated.

The recreation of his physical self was an idea the darkness took from the young navigator. An interesting idea and not one which the darkness had encountered before because the darkness was immortal, at least in terms that the Chinese officer might understand and Chuang Tzu was only the second sentient being the darkness had encountered.

It being the first.

What the darkness took from Chuang Tzu's unfrozen body was not exactly the man's memories, nor was it a straight map of his neural connections or the chemical pathways established in his body. It was a collection of fragile associations. A collection it used to re-create the fleeting, ever-changing illusion of stability which the Chinese officer regarded as himself.

The darkness created Chuang Tzu's new body from its map of the original, taking time to modify a few design errors and make a small number of almost unnoticeable improvements. Inside the navigator's cells telomeres became semi self-mending, DNA began to zip and unzip without introducing errors. Minor things.

"Wake," said a voice.

Chuang Tzu awoke. And found himself in a painting. There was no other way to describe it. *Red Room at the Hall of Victory* was a very famous painting, one found as a print in doctors' offices, police stations and classrooms across the Middle Kingdom. Party members tended to keep a copy at home, displayed prominently.

Grandfather Luo, very definitely an ex–Party member, had kept his in the outside privy, nailed crudely to the wall. There were some advantage of being too famous to kill.

The Red Room in question was small, higher than it was wide and decorated with carved panels that flaked gold leaf to reveal a red undercoat beneath. There were five panels to the north and south walls, which was an auspicious number, and every panel displayed a dragon curling in on itself.

Li Xiucheng, the real loyal prince, had died here and been found in this room, stripped of his clothes, his seal of office and the jade rings he wore. All stolen by those who were meant to be guarding him.

Until he woke in it, Major Commissar Chuang Tzu had been of the opinion that the Red Room existed only as Party propaganda. And then, as he rolled over on a couch, Chuang Tzu realized that waking here now did not necessarily make that incorrect. He could be dead or hallucinating or even in the process of dying and lost to a vision induced by oxygen starvation and the shutdown of his higher brain.

Everything about the room was right and yet, at the same time, utterly wrong. When the young navigator tried to lift away the golden blanket covering his body he found it stiff like a board, fitted to his shape and so heavy that he was forced to heave against its weight.

"See?" Chuang Tzu said to himself. "You're hallucinating."

And with that the blanket became lighter, then floppy. And just as Chuang Tzu began to notice that its surface was still scratchy this also changed, until the material become so soft that it was as delicate as goose down.

"Too soft," said the navigator, only half to himself, and felt the blanket become like an emperor's blanket, comfortable and yet not impossibly soft.

"I should be afraid," Chuang Tzu told himself.

Waking in a painting that changed to match his thoughts... How could he not be afraid? Yet fear was the last thing Chuang Tzu felt because he had dreamed his entire life of a world where what he wanted just *was*...

Of course, the want itself changed.

At eight he'd been desperate to live underwater. And when Grandfather Luo had decided that paying a pig man to spread night soil on their fields was unhygienic and had a septic tank sunk into the bank behind their farm instead, Chuang Tzu's ideas changed and he wanted his own tank, sunk into the reeds by Sky Lake, with the fat pipe as an underwater entrance and the thin pipe reaching up for air.

This was Chuang Tzu's second year in the village when things were not at their best.

After the water came dreams of flying. He would swoop down the valley and beneath him spread Grandfather Luo's farm and the small village his family used to own before people became polite enough to forget such things. Wind would howl in his face, lifting him higher and higher until he was just a dot against the winter sky. It was always winter when Chuang Tzu flew, even when he dreamt in summer.

These were waking dreams. A world behind his eyes more real than the one which his father's death and Grandfather Luo's disgrace forced him to inhabit.

Fantasies, Madame Mimi called them, a waste of his life. Once, after she'd shouted at Chuang Tzu for not feeding the chickens, Grandfather Luo was instructed to beat sense into the boy. So he took the boy to the ice hut, a broad leather belt with a swinging buckle dangling from his wizened hand.

"I don't want to do this," the old man said.

"So don't," said Chuang Tzu.

Grandfather Luo smiled. "I don't intend to."

They sat on a log together, looking out towards the road bridge. Across the river they could see hills and beyond these the western mountains. The evening was heavy with monkey cloud and the far end of the valley was already half hidden in shadow.

Darkness came slowly, touching the mountains last. And still Grandfather Luo sat in the gathering gloom, watching the distant peaks turn purple, and said nothing. It was night before the old man rose unsteadily to his feet and straightened up, putting one hand to his back.

"I'm old," he said.

The boy nodded.

"And this night air is not good for me."

At dawn Chuang Tzu fed the chickens and set off for school before either of his grandparents came down for breakfast. When they did, they found a jug of fresh water drawn from the well, ready for Madame Mimi to make tea.

"You should have beaten him earlier," she said. "I told you it would work."

"So you did," agreed the old man. "So you did..."

At the age of eleven other dreams began. In each Chuang Tzu was a hero, brave beyond imagining and strong enough to fight his way through torrents and climb sheer cliffs. This puzzled the boy, who much preferred intelligence and cunning, until he realized that every dream ended with him rescuing a girl and that rescuing her somehow involved removing her clothes.

Beyond the window of the painted Red Room were mountains, a whole range of them, or so Chuang Tzu had always assumed. A smear of grey and a slash of black, narrow strokes like some childish exercise in calligraphy to denote fir trees. A wash of blue, overlapped at the end where the brush turned back on itself.

While beyond the window of the room in which he woke was... As Chuang Tzu watched, the blue deepened and the smear of grey swam through a rapid sequence of changes, like smoke in a bell jar. The calligraphy acquired roots and branches and frostings of snow. Only the sun stayed static, a glowing ember within a sharp, pen-edged circle.

"Weird," said Chuang Tzu and somewhere inside his head came a voice.

"Interesting," it said.

And as Chuang Tzu watched, the sun became brighter and its edge flared. At least he thought it did. Only by the time he began to notice this, the sun was already too bright to be stared at directly.

## CHAPTER 26

### *Marrakech, Summer 1977*

Moz stayed the night that first time he led Jake and Celia back to their hotel. Only Major Abbas was wrong, Jake and Celia weren't staying at Hotel Gulera. The *nasrani* couple had a pink-walled riad near Bab Doukkala, a rambling, four-storey town house slung around a small courtyard. And from what Moz could work out they'd bought the place, or rather Jake had, at a cost so insignificant it was less than his first electric guitar.

"Lost in Mythik Amerika" read the heading on a square of cardboard nailed to a wall in the courtyard. Four boys snarled from the album cover and it took Moz a minute or two to realize that one of them was the figure who pouted from the front of a dozen discarded magazines.

"Razor splits," said one. "Is this the end?" asked another. So many magazines were balanced on one corner of a half-emptied packing case that they'd slid over the edge onto the floor. When he looked again, Moz realized there were actually only two, *Sounds* and *NME*, but someone had bought at least a dozen copies of each.

"He must be really famous."

"Famous?"

"To afford..." Moz gestured at the guitar cases, a keyboard on black metal legs, a big tape machine. Resting against a huge Marshall amp was a black Triumph with silver mudguards and chrome pipes. Someone had wheeled it in from the alley, across a battered carpet in the hall and parked it behind a wooden pillar, one of four supporting an open balcony that ran around the courtyard, ten feet or so above their heads.

"All that belongs to his record company," said Celia. "I work for them, sort of."

"And the house?"

"Oh no," Celia said dismissively. "It was his idea to buy this shi—" Then she caught herself and smiled at the boy. "Let me change and then I'll show you round."

When Celia came back, she was wearing a silk shirt with the cuffs turned up once and the neck undone to the third button. And every time she bent forward to open a box or retrieve something from the floor Moz could see a flash of breast and a glimpse of nipple as Celia's shirt fell away from her body.

"Come on," Celia said. "This way."

They fed him something Jake cooked from a book. It involved chicken cut into small bits, unripe olives and yellow peppers. At best it was a distant cousin to tagine.

And having fed him, Jake handed him a Spéciale and watched while Moz sipped from the squat brown bottle and Celia rolled spliff after spliff on the back of Television's *Marquee Moon*, lining them up like little torpedoes.

Jake and Celia smoked three each, very carefully, not passing to each other, although they both offered to share with Moz.

"I should get back now," Moz said.

"In a while," said Celia, grinding out her roach. "You don't need to go anywhere yet."

Moz said it again about an hour later, when the square of sky above their heads had grown completely black and the night wind was restless enough to disturb the leaves which had dropped from a desiccated vine on the far side of the courtyard.

"It's too late," Jake said, "the streets won't be safe."

Moz resisted the urge to point out that he'd been wandering the Medina's streets after dark since he was old enough to walk. Something about Jake interested him, his casual attitude to life probably.

The boy knew exactly what interested him about Celia and he knew that she knew. Since discarding the jacket Moz had made her put on for their walk through the streets that afternoon, she'd worn a man's shirt, a gold jacket for supper and now she was back in that afternoon's silk blouse, side-lit by the light of a dozen candles, her breasts in silhouette beneath the thinnest silk he'd ever seen and her nipples erect with cold.

"You should stay," Jake said. "Go in the morning."

So the three of them sat in that half light until the candles burnt down to stumps and Moz couldn't shake the feeling that Celia and Jake were trying to outmanoeuvre each other.

"Okay," Jake said eventually, "I surrender." Picking up the last two spliffs, he stuffed them into the back pocket of his black Levi's, took a single copy each of *NME* and *Sounds* and headed indoors without saying goodnight to either Celia or Moz.

"Let him be," Celia said, when Moz stood up to follow. "He gets like that sometimes..." She patted the rattan sofa beside her. "We'll go up in a moment," she said. "But sit here first. I've got a proposition I think you'll like."

Even having looked the word up several weeks later in a dictionary which Celia kept on the kitchen table, Moz was still unsure which bit of what happened next she'd been talking about.

Jake was planning to rebuild, replaster and repaint the riad himself but he would be needing help. That was where Moz came in. Celia wanted Moz to introduce Jake to craftsmen willing to pass on their skills. Moz resisted the urge to tell Celia exactly what he thought of this idea. Instead he talked a little about when he worked on the dog woman's house, making his rubble-carrying, concrete-mixing and trench-digging sound more professional than it was.

And so Moz found himself being offered the job of houseboy and all-round helper and sometime in the hours to come he woke beside Celia in a vast bed, both of them naked and her arm thrown across his flat stomach.

"Shit," Moz said to himself.

Rolling onto his side, he slid his legs out of the bed and stood as quietly as he could. The first call to prayer had come and gone, Moz could tell that just from looking at the sky above Celia's balcony. If he moved now he could be back in the Mellah before Malika woke.

No one would believe him anyway.

"Shit," Moz said again. It was difficult to say how old the foreign woman was. Older than him and older than Jake, beyond that... Finding his jellaba, Moz turned it right side out and draped it over an old chair, looking for his shoes.

"Moz?"

He turned and a camera flashed, its light blinding. "I'm making a record," said Celia, "for posterity." She looked at the naked boy whose glance was flicking between the door, his clothes and her bare breasts. "Don't just stand there," she said. "Come back to bed."

The third fight happened in Café Georgiou in Gueliz two weeks after Celia first slept with Moz. Called for by Malika, who was angry at having been sent to do Hassan's bidding, Moz went reluctantly with Celia's salt taste still on his tongue, her ripeness sour on his fingers and the memory of her body heavy behind his eyes.

Nothing else mattered.

"You okay?" Malika asked finally, when Moz's silence began to outweigh her anger.

"Of course I'm okay," Moz said.

"You don't seem it."

"Believe me," said Moz, "life's never been better."

Celia screamed in a way he'd heard no woman scream and at night in the Mellah nothing was hidden. Moz had heard his share of sheets made and quarrels mended.

She ripped raw lines in his back and never turned him away. He took her on the warm tiles of the courtyard, in every bed of Riad al-Razor and bent over sacks of concrete in the hall. Jake only had to vanish in search of obscure building materials for Celia to hunt Moz down or Moz to come looking for her.

Once he'd followed her into a downstairs lavatory and taken her against the side wall before she had time to squat and relieve her bladder. And Celia hadn't known whether to throw him out or be furious when he came before she did.

He forgot his friends and ignored the first summons from

Hassan. Soon he was cooking for Jake and Celia and running errands, collecting mail from *post restant* and buying their provisions at the Thursday market. They never asked for their change and seemed surprised if he offered it.

One Monday he went to collect a parcel of clothes for Jake from the local post office. It had been shipped by a shop in London called Seditionaries and when Moz glanced longingly at the old jeans and Ramones shirt Jake promptly assigned to the bin, Jake waved one hand in easy permission and grinned at the sight of Moz scrabbling into black Levi's and a torn T-shirt.

Sex, clothes and free drugs. And for this Celia and Jake paid him twenty dirham a day. More than a grown man could earn working from dawn to dusk.

It was the summer of '77. The sky over the squat wall of Marrakech was the blue of Persian tiles and the afternoon heat was strong enough to fell stray dogs, until even the wildest hugged the shadows and lay as if dead in the red dust.

The war against the Polisario was entering its second phase, Johnny Thunders, the Heartbreakers and the Buzzcocks had recently opened the Vortex Club in London's Wardour Street. The US Senate was busy banning economic aid to Vietnam and Jake decided that now would be an excellent time to introduce Moz to cooking speed, the really cheap kind. But Moz was to remember that summer for a different reason.

His argument with Malika was short, pointless and entirely his fault. An argument he should never have won. He should never have won his fight with Hassan either. And it was the second that led to the first.

Having walked in silence, he and Malika had found Hassan waiting for them at a pavement table outside the café in Gueliz.

"You're late," said Hassan.

Moz shrugged behind his shades. "If you don't like it," he said, "I can always fuck off again."

Things went downhill from here.

Hassan needed Moz to do him a favour. Agreeing would go a long way to cancelling the obligations Moz owed to Hassan's uncle, Caid Hammou. The exact details of the favour would be revealed later.

"You don't really have a choice," Hassan said, when Moz said he'd think about it, meaning that he wouldn't...

"There's always a choice." Moz didn't actually believe this. In fact everything about life suggested that true choices were few and came rarely, but it was something to say and had the added advantage of upsetting Hassan.

"Not for you," Hassan said and gave Moz his stare, the one he'd learnt from watching his uncle. "Not with this."

"Why not?" asked Malika.

"Because Moz owes my uncle," said Hassan. "And Caid Hammou is calling in the obligation... Look," he added, his voice more gentle. Malika still had that effect on him, even now. "I'm just the messenger on this."

"That's all you've ever been," said Moz, scraping back his chair.

"Where do you think you're going?"

"To shit." Moz used a term so crude that a man in a suit at the table next door put down his paper and turned round.

Moz stared him out and the suit looked away.

"Make sure you come back."

"Of course I'm coming back," said Moz. "You think I'd leave her here with you?" He jerked his chin at the girl. Malika was still sulking about his silence on the way from Riad al-Razor.

The loo was modern. A ceramic standing pad with raised bits for his feet and a metal hose for washing himself afterwards. A maker's name at the top gave a company address in Paris. The door locked with a little catch that switched a sign outside from *occupé* to *libre*.

It made Moz wonder how much the coffees were costing Hassan. And that made him wonder why Hassan had chosen him. Hassan would have his reasons, of course. He was one of those people who never gave anything unless he wanted something bigger himself, usually help removing goods from where they belonged to somewhere they didn't.

Not this time, Moz decided. Things had changed.

Moz hosed clean the fingers of his left hand and pulled up his jeans without bothering to dry his fingers first, even though there was a towel attached to a roller on the nearest wall. Then he reached into the back pocket of his Levi's to extract a small polythene envelope that read "Lloyds Bank," with a silhouette of a prancing horse. The envelope belonged to Jake and so did its contents.

"Cooking speed," Celia called it, which made no sense at all until Jake explained that speed was amphetamine sulphate and cooking, used like that, meant common or cheap.

Cracking an off-white crystal between his teeth, Moz swallowed and felt its bitterness bite at the back of his throat. It took a handful of seconds for cold lines to begin to draw themselves around the tiny basin and the edges of the small window to become hard and luminous.

Moz liked amphetamines.

Half a dozen crystals and already he knew that chemicals which made his brain work faster were more fun than those which slowed him down. Hard tuning, Jake called it. Maybe Jake was right, maybe Moz should become Jake's roadie when they left.

Except, of course, there was Malika.

At the table outside and still in a sulk but sliding her gaze in his direction whenever she thought he wouldn't notice.

"Okay," said Moz, shutting the loo door behind him. "Let's get this over with..."

The café had a long zinc bar with a single beer handle for Spéciale, half a dozen ashtrays, olives in little saucers and a wooden drum containing Corona cigars. And behind the zinc stood Georgiou, an old Greek in a white apron, who only stopped staring at Moz when the spiky-haired boy finally rejoined Hassan and Malika.

"Where have you been?"

"Me?" Moz glanced from Hassan to the next table, where the man in the suit had gone back to his paper. "I told you. I've been having a—"

"Never mind," Hassan said hurriedly and for a moment Moz could have sworn that the older boy looked almost embarrassed.

Tough.

"Si Muhamed." Moz clicked his fingers for a waiter. "A beer and my girlfriend will have..." He grinned at Malika. "What do you want?" he said.

Malika asked for the first thing that came into her head.

"With ice," Moz added. "And lemon."

"Marzaq..." There was a tightness to Hassan's voice. At first Moz thought this was because Georgiou's was actually owned by Caid Hammou and Hassan was worried that Moz's rudeness might get back to his uncle. And then Moz realized the real reason. He'd just called Malika his girlfriend.

Well, double tough.

"It's okay," Moz said. "We haven't forgotten you." He nodded to the waiter. "His Excellency will have an espresso."

It was Moz's belief that Hassan didn't even like espresso and would have been happier joining Malika in a Coke or ordering mint tea, but espresso was what those who'd been educated in Paris drank, even now two decades after the French had gone.

Of course, Caid Hammou's nephew had never been to Paris, which probably explained his rigid adherence to the rules of those who had.

After Moz's beer, the coffee and Malika's Coke arrived and the customer in the suit had stood stiffly and stalked off in the direction of Place du 16 Novembre, Hassan sat back and stared at Moz.

"Okay," he said. "Idries will pick you up from the dog woman's house late tomorrow afternoon. I need both of you to be there when Idries arrives..." Hassan talked about his absent cousin as if the rat-faced boy was some employee, and maybe he was.

"What exactly," Moz said, "are we stealing?"

"It's a delivery," said Hassan. "Idries will give you the details."

"No," said Moz. "You. Now."

"Idries," said Hassan, pushing back his chair. "Tomorrow."

Moz also stood up. "Then it's not going to happen," he said, "because I won't be there. Jake's taking the car to Mogador."

"That's what you want me to tell my uncle? That your *nasrani*'s taking his bum boy to the beach?"

"Tell Caid Hammou whatever the fuck you want," Moz said, managing a sneer straight from the front of *Mythik Amerika*. "I'm out of here... Come on," he added to Malika. "Let's leave the little prick to his coffee."

A scrape of leather sole on concrete was all the warning Moz got of an anger so tight that Hassan tried to keep it silent.

Five... four... three... two...

Twisting sideways, Moz ducked. Only not quite fast enough because Hassan's left fist caught the side of his head and dropped Moz to one knee.

"Stop it!"

Malika's plea reached Moz through swimming darkness. And as Hassan positioned himself in front of Moz, the kneeling boy was faced with a flash of expensive clothes, smoky buttons on a cotton shirt. A belt of tan leather with dark spots in it. Black leather loafers that settled themselves and then moved again as Hassan prepared himself for a kick.

"No!" Malika shouted.

Indeed not.

Almost absent-mindedly, Moz reached forward and found the older boy's testicles, soft plums wrapped in silk. For a moment he was tempted to crush them but instead he made do with a cloth-creasing twist. And it was Moz who kicked, though first he had to force himself to his feet.

It was a blow weighted with years of anger, a fat crystal of cooking speed and frustration that Malika's sulkiness had somehow soured what Moz felt for Celia.

"*Moz!*" Malika said.

He heard her but Moz kicked just the same, feeling his toes curl as they sunk into Hassan's stomach.

Everyone in the street halted like God froze time and then Georgiou burst from the café, a cloth still in one hand.

"What are you doing?"

Moz expected Hassan to buckle over and fall to his knees, clutching his gut. And that later when Hassan had recovered, he'd round up Idries and some of the others and come looking for Moz, making the streets around Riad al-Razor a bad place to be for a few weeks, maybe even a month or so.

What actually happened was that vomit sprayed from Hassan's mouth. A fountain of black coffee, mint tea and half-digested cake splashing onto Moz and making Malika step back with a jump. And the stench as Hassan crumpled to his knees suggested this wasn't the only orifice to void.

"Shit," said Georgiou, suddenly sounding distinctly local.

"I reckon so," said Moz.

## CHAPTER 27

### *Lampedusa, Wednesday 4 July*

"Whatever." It would have to do.

Using a square of cigarette packet, Prisoner Zero smeared his stink along the base of a wall, filling the gaps. They were going to kill him before he had time to skim all the walls; the prisoner had worked this out around dawn.

"*Prisoner Zero.*"

It was a sergeant. One who didn't like him, as opposed to Master

Sergeant Saez, who actually hated him. Prisoner Zero found it hard to tell Saez and Kovacs apart because both had bull necks, cropped hair, skin ripe like midnight and similar thousand-klick stares. What Prisoner Zero saw when he looked at the two marines was not their scowls or skin tone, but uniforms.

They both wore a weird kind of jungle fatigue. Something mud-coloured, like it was designed for a forest where everything had begun to die. Unless, of course, it was meant to be desert camouflage, in which case it matched no stretch of sand or gravel Prisoner Zero had ever seen.

He was meant to stand now. This had been explained to him.

Master Sergeant Saez would come in first and shout his name, Prisoner Zero then had to stand, stare straight ahead and stay silent unless spoken to. This last part was easy enough. As for the rest... Sergeant Saez continued to demand that he come to attention but had long since stopped believing it was going to happen.

Knocking someone down was easy. Making them stand up to order was far more difficult.

"Attention."

Prisoner Zero turned his back on the noise of his cage being unlocked and concentrated instead on the square of cardboard as it skimmed over mesh in confident sweeps. Small rebellions were all he had left.

The outraged shouts never came. Instead Prisoner Zero became aware that someone stood right behind him, watching. Tossing aside his cardboard paddle, Prisoner Zero paused to admire the result. Something was still missing, that much was obvious. Unfortunately, he was having trouble working out what.

"Fermat," said Katie Petrov.

"You're right," a voice said, sounding impressed. The owner of the voice was a balding Italian in grey uniform. He was probably of normal build and height, but standing between Sergeants Saez and Kovacs, he looked both short and thin. Wire rim glasses magnified washed-out blue eyes.

"I'm Dr. Angelo," said the man in Arabic. "Have you finished?" Elegant fingers gestured at shit smeared across the wall of the cage. "If not, then please do."

Sergeant Kovacs had taken away Prisoner Zero's stub of wire the previous evening during an unscheduled search of his cage. This was one of the reasons the prisoner was behind. It had taken him most of the night to find a loose weld and work free a stubby length of wire.

Producing the wire from his mouth, Prisoner Zero slashed an equation into the lattice. It was famous and he used it only to fill space, adding a less famous equation (which was at least two centuries older) and improvised a third which linked the first two.

The fourth was something he'd stumbled over on his knees beside a canal. He'd lost his job by then, Prisoner Zero was pretty sure of it. There were some limits to life tenure, even at the University of Amsterdam. So much unfinished. He guessed God probably felt like that.

And so Prisoner Zero began to sketch. A circle, multi-layered, each layer actually a circle seen from the side so that it looked like a line, except each of these circles was really a sphere. Only he lacked the ability to express that extra dimension except in his head. So he drew another circle alongside the first and separated them with a vertical line to remind himself that they were the same but not.

He did this part mostly from the memory of a few pages at the back of an exercise book, the middle pages being taken up with chord changes for songs that never got written, much less recorded.

"What is it?" Katie Petrov asked.

"A butterfly," said the uniformed Italian.

"This is Vice Questore Pier Angelo," said Katie. "He's been asked to examine you."

"If that's all right?" said the Vice Questore. For a foreigner his Arabic seemed pretty good.

"I've worked for the UN," said the man. "In Baghdad and Damascus." Nodding to Master Sergeant Saez, who stood with a rifle clutched to his chest and a scowl souring his heavy face, Vice Questore Angelo added, "I'm also a Marxist, one of the few left. That's why your friend doesn't like me."

Katie Petrov smiled. "You want any help?"

"No." The balding man shook his head. "What I want is this room emptied while I make my examination." He had the face of a well-bred horse, with what was left of his hair swept back like a mane behind his ears. A wedding ring on his second finger said Katie Petrov's first impression was wrong.

"You don't need me to stay?"

"No," said the Vice Questore. "I'll need the patient out of his cage and the room to myself. I don't start until that happens."

"It's going to be a long wait," said Sergeant Kovacs.

Turning his back on their squabble, Prisoner Zero examined his work and discovered that it was already dead. The sketches, formulae and equations just looked what they were, simple cold equations signifying nothing. His map of space where ice held memories and the darkness spoke in miracles was gone.

"That's better," said the Vice Questore when the door to the weights room finally shut. Popping open his black leather bag, he extracted a stethoscope, a pair of surgical gloves and a small flashlight.

"Katie Petrov demanded a local doctor. Luckily I was in the area. Dr. Petrov and I came to a mutually advantageous agreement..." There was, of course, no luck involved at all. Vice Questore Pier Angelo took a look at the cage and decided it was every bit as bad as Rome had been led to believe.

"If you're happy with this?"

The Vice Questore paused to give Prisoner Zero space to reply. He'd already been warned by Katie Petrov that conversations were unlikely to be two-way events, but it seemed only polite.

"I'm a doctor," he said, "also a police surgeon. I opposed the Berlusconi government and for that I've been awarded a seat in parliament... Only in Italy," he added with a sigh. "Parliament has asked me to report back on your health, the levels of security to which you're subject and the conditions in which you're held. As you can imagine, Colonel Borgenicht is not happy."

The last thing the Vice Questore produced was a small Leica and a roll of 400 ASA Kodak old-fashioned film. "*La Stampa* is reporting that you've been tortured. Dr. Petrov believes you are being drugged. As Camp Freedom is sited on Italian soil I've been sent to check both."

Prisoner Zero's lungs were fine and his blood pressure surprisingly low for someone of middle age. His pupils reacted to light, his liver was unenlarged and when he blew through a white plastic tube the blue marker moved further than Vice Questore Angelo had expected.

"I'll need a blood sample," said the man, ripping foil from a disposable hypodermic. "And, when that's done, if you could just urinate into this." He handed Prisoner Zero a small plastic container.

When the actual tests were done and Vice Questore Angelo had added some chemical to the blood, dipped strips of paper in still-warm urine and spread a smear of shit over the bottom sheet of a glass slide, examined it under a small brass microscope and made notes in his book, he told Prisoner Zero to stand in front of his cage.

Camera flash lit the room. Only then did the Italian begin his examination for evidence of torture. "What are these?" he asked eventually, pausing at scars on Prisoner Zero's stomach.

Silence was his answer.

"Were they done here?"

The prisoner shook his head.

"Interesting," said Vice Questore Angelo. "Most people in your position would have said yes whatever the truth."

There were five burns in all, three on Prisoner Zero's left thigh and two on his abdomen. All of them less than two weeks old. Nodding to himself, Vice Questore Angelo discounted an old bruise at the base of the prisoner's spine and a pale cicatrix on the inside of one arm. "Who punched you in the kidneys?" he asked suddenly.

As ever Prisoner Zero said nothing.

"You test positive for blood in your urine."

When the prisoner stayed silent, Vice Questore Angelo shrugged, became aware that this was not very professional of him and decided that was too bad. He was getting to the bit covered in Dr. Petrov's off-the-record talk on their way in. "All right," he said, raising his camera, "now show me your hands..."

# CHAPTER 28

## *Razor's Edge, CTzu 53/Year 20*

Flash/no flash.

Doc Joyce claimed to be the man who'd fixed five miles of diamond-hard neon tube to the far wall of RipJointShuts and he refused to tell anybody how to turn the thing off. So it just sat there and illuminated the darkness with its message.

"Welcome to Tomorrow."

The interesting thing about this, apart from the fact the sign gave visitors something to head for in the gloom of the fourteenth level, was that it spoke to anyone who got close enough, repeating its mantra inside one's head.

A town of about three hundred (barely half of them recognizably human), RJS was old, marginally dangerous and had briefly been famous some years before when the newest emperor manifested in a hut several levels above and Doc Joyce, owner of the local bar and a cut-price slice merchant, went on the feed to announce that he'd birthed the boy, his brother and the mother.

He might even have been telling the truth.

A plaque at Doc Joyce's place (put up so visitors would know that this was the place the Emperor's mother came for advice), announced that RipJointShuts was the oldest inhabited shanty town on Heliconid, a thousand years being mentioned.

Inventive as the dapper little man was, he still got the scale wrong by a factor of four. People had been squatting in RJS for over forty centuries. Pretty impressive for a town that didn't officially exist on a sliver of steel that was meant to be uninhabited.

Near the bottom of the Razor's Edge, that endless tear down the side of Heliconid and a day's hike into the interior of level fourteen, stood an abandoned cargo container, in the shadow of the Tomorrow sign. This was Schwarzschilds, Doc Joyce's bar.

Few tourists came to drink and fewer still came back. Schwarzschilds made it into the guides but most of what was written was third-hand, hearsay taken from hearsay.

A smaller cargo pod, barely a tenth of the size, had been abandoned millennia before at the back of Schwarzschilds. Some of those who described the pod said it looked like a calf following its mother. Others, less whimsical, thought it looked like something the bar had shat.

It was inside this smaller container that a naked fifteen-year-old girl swapped half a kidney for a completely new set of shoulder sinews. Unusually, Tris did this before her own got ripped. She'd seen too many drop queens reduced to shuffling crabs on the level.

As having her shoulders rewired cost less than she'd expected, Tris used the other half to get her arms and legs restrung, ending up with all of her sinews upgraded to full-drop status with the tensile strength of the new sinews making a mockery of those they replaced, obviously enough.

Underestimating the obvious was to give Tris the most terrifying twelve hours of her short life. A week after the operation, with the original scars long since healed, Tris took an updraft to the top of Razor's Edge and dropped the full seventeen levels in a head-whirling handful of minutes, feeling her life zip through her fingers and across her back as she touched only twice, kicking off into nothingness and waiting until the last minute to use her diamond gloves.

The sinews worked perfectly. It was Tris's shoulder muscles which did a really embarrassing first-time-out crackle and pop.

"*Fuck. Fuck. Fuck.*"

If Tris had known a worse curse she'd have used it. All she could feel was white pain. A shock so absolute it was more or less indescribable. One that put all her previous experiences of feeling sick to shame.

She was inside her own pain. On the end of a rope.

And so began the longest night and morning of Tris's life. Crawl by crawl she made her way up the rope, knees locked tight and hands gripping on as best they could. It took eight hours to climb three levels and the rest of that day to reach Schwarzschilds.

"Hello, Tristesse," said Doc Joyce, when he finally bothered to look up from the mixing desk. "I wondered when I'd see you." Doc Joyce was the only person to call the skinny Riprat by her full name. The only person ever to stand up when she came into his room.

He'd done that the very first time she appeared in his doorway, wanting to know the prices. Tris had never forgotten. The Doc had still overcharged her but she could forgive him that. Doc Joyce overcharged everyone.

"You busy?"

The Doc snorted. "What does it look like?" he said.

A creature lay on the slab, completely naked but genital-free. All secondary sexual characteristics were also absent. The navel and nipples were gone, as were any breasts that might have supported them, always assuming the patient started out female. A completely smooth, hairless groin showed no sign of labia. In fact, it showed no signs of anything.

Two tiny horns budded from either side of the creature's narrow forehead and, in place of hair, its depilated skull was combed with corn rows of bone plate. It was a look Tris had seen often.

"Yeah," said Doc Joyce. He pulled up one eyelid, twisted the unconscious patient's skull from side to side, then shrugged. "Don't you just hate tourists?... What happened?" he asked as an afterthought.

"Slipped," whispered Tris.

The Doc's smile was not kind. "Sure you did."

Tris looked at the drugged tourist.

"God," said the Doc, "do I need to do everything?" Tipping the creature off the mixing desk, Doc Joyce patted the slab, dislodging a spider which had been busy behind the patient's ear. "Up you go."

On the floor the spider scuttled away to stand a few paces from the body. After a second or two, during which its metal legs quivered and reformed in restless twists of smoke, the spider sidled up to the tourist's skull and went back to work.

"Come on," Doc Joyce said, then took pity on the girl and tossed her a spider, letting it cut free her clothes. He left her knife where it was, taped to the small of her back. Minus clothes was one thing, defenceless was another, and Doc Joyce understood that naked meant different things to different people.

"Should have had the bones," Doc Joyce said. He'd tried to sell her a set of bird-weight legs, hips and shoulder bones and had run the maths for her as he pulled each one from its vat, suggesting skin flaps between her upper arms and ribs. Tris had been shaking her head before he'd even finished.

She lay on her front, because this was the way Doc Joyce wanted her to lie. It hurt just as much as lying on her back but had the advantage of letting Tris rest her face against the slab, which promptly adjusted itself to help the girl get as comfortable as possible. If she'd been face up, the brightness of Doc Joyce's ceiling would have stopped her doing that.

For reasons she never quite understood, Doc Joyce skipped the scolding that Tris had been expecting and went straight to work, his fingers cold on her skin.

She shivered.

"It's a mess, Tristesse," Doc Joyce said. "I don't need spiders to tell me that." Fingertips pushed into the pain across her shoulders and Tris found she was crying, racking sobs that only made her body hurt all the more.

Doc Joyce sighed.

When the girl turned up wanting replacement sinews he'd suggested she get her muscles upgraded in tandem and even given her a good price. This was prior to suggesting new bones. As the muscle swap would be invisible the kid's very vocal contempt for visible modification could remain uncompromised.

(It was noticeable that everything she'd ever had done was on the inside. Doc Joyce had his own theories on this, but then the Doc had a theory about everything.)

Out of the thousands who came and went he remembered Tris

because the very first time she came she wanted an augmentation so old-fashioned he almost did it for nothing to see if he still could. The kid had wanted her existing synaptic topology augmented with fullerenes to increase the speed at which connections could be made in her brain.

He pointed out that it would be far easier and infinitely more efficient just to replace her organic brain with a synthetic unit, maybe something with an open connection to the feed. The kid had been adamant. What she wanted was what she'd asked for.

In many ways the fact that Doc Joyce liked Tris was a triple bluff on himself. Everyone knew that the Doc was cantankerous, unreliable and avaricious. That was the description mostly given in the guides. *Cantankerous, unreliable and money-grubbing (this last being a specific form of avaricious).*

Those who knew him better understood that Doc Joyce was much less of the above than he first appeared; which was, of course, a cliché. In a feed novella he'd be played as a drunk who made good at the end and died heroically, his colleagues discovering too late that he'd secretly given up alcohol, drugs or whatever weakness the novella's AI had pulled off the shelf and nailed to him.

And the kicker would be that his last bottle of hooch, the one that shattered as he fell, its contents standing in for blood in the dust, this bottle would be unopened and the seal unbroken.

They'd both watched variations of that episode, several times.

The truth was different. Doc Joyce *was* cantankerous, unreliable and avaricious. He wasn't even a man, at least not on a genetic level. Although this had never made it into the guides because he'd done the op himself and done it long before most of the guides existed.

That secondary, half-hidden warmth and twinkle in his eye was as false as the first growl and snap. Only being golden-hearted was what the punters wanted and so that was what the Doc gave them, golden-hearted moments while his eyes twinkled, his mouth twisted into a rueful smile and he emptied their lives of anything interesting enough to catch his fancy.

It was a good act, convincing even, and Tris was his only weakness. Grinding his fingers into ruptured muscle, Doc Joyce watched Tris's head come up off the slab.

"Fuck," she said.

"Keep still," said Doc Joyce but the order was redundant, the kid had passed out with pain. The muscles he grafted were old stock, from a batch grown for a family on Turquoise who'd fallen one third of the way down Razor's Edge and decided to go easy on dangerous sports for a while.

When their houseAI queried the Doc's invoice for surgical-grade muscles, he sent by return a highly convincing and properly completed order, including an appropriate retinal scan for each member of the family. The house paid up after that and for a full set, everything from *biceps brachii* to *vastus medialis* for each family member.

He always managed to sell a surprising percentage of the tissue he grew on spec and if the muscles billed never quite matched the number actually used then these things happened. At least they did when you used a clinic as old and cranky as Doc Joyce's.

*The spiders were his crocodile.* He'd said this once to Tris, when she first came in to discuss brain rewiring.

And then, of course, he'd had to explain what crocodiles were and why alchemists in the old world kept stuffed reptiles hanging from their ceilings to impress their patrons. A loop of logic that forced him to divert through a definition of alchemy to a quick and dirty outline of human history. Doc Joyce was slightly shocked to discover that Tris was only crudely aware that most inhabitants of the 2023 worlds originated from the same species. And totally, utterly shocked to discover that Tris had no idea what he meant by the word "Earth."

"I still don't get it," Tris had said finally.

"What?"

"The stuff with the spiders."

So Doc Joyce had scooped up a handful, crushed them between his palms and then parted his hands to reveal a much larger spider standing in their place. His smile was that of a conjurer who'd just performed a particularly impressive trick. "You know how old these are?" he said.

Tris had shaken her head.

"Older than you."

"That's not so difficult."

"Older than me," added Doc Joyce, ripping the spider in two and dropping both bits on the floor, where the halves became spiders in their turn and scurried away, in exactly opposite directions.

"Really?" Tris said. She said it mostly because Doc Joyce seemed to expect a reply.

"Yeah," said the Doc. "Older than me, older than you, older than everyone in RipJointShuts added together." He smiled. "These days replicators are so small most people don't even know they exist. These came over on the SZ *Loyal Prince*."

"You're talking about smoke?" Tris looked puzzled. "You know, you buy time in a clinic and that smoke just rolls over you, mending as it goes..."

"Clinics are pointless," Doc Joyce said. "Most people are born already prepared."

"On the worlds?"

Doc Joyce nodded.

"So why do they come here?"

He'd looked at her, that time he was shaving her head to open her skull, slight smile twisting his lips as he wondered whether to say more.

"You can tell me," Tris said.

"You know, Tristesse," said the man, "maybe I can." He took a long look at the naked girl strapped to his mixing desk. "You remind me of someone," he said, then stopped himself. "When you get to my age everyone looks like someone else."

Tris could see the logic in that.

"People come to me," the old man said, "because they've tried everything else and because I have a reputation." The Doc shook his head, a gesture meant to signify his acceptance that this idea was absurd. "I don't cure them because they're not ill. I change them. Not always into what they want. That's what brings them here. The risk."

Imagine that someone has cooked thread noodles, the tiny almost translucent kind so that they are too flexible to snap like dry twigs but need another ten seconds or so to become properly soft. Then imagine that person taking a fat handful of those noodles and twisting, so that some pop, others half rupture and a few, mostly in the middle, stay whole.

This was the muscle inside Tris's shoulders.

The spiders worked swiftly at a level below human sight. First they cut away damaged tissue and then they knitted new muscle into place. It would have been possible to repair the original, but even with neural blocks Tris would be reluctant to climb until the stiffness had gone and by the time this happened the girl might be unwilling to climb at all.

A risk Doc Joyce felt reluctant to take. For his uncharacteristic kindness now had a price. It was obvious, at least in retrospect. The kid needed major repairs and he needed someone who could climb three klicks of wire and finesse open the hatch of a racing yacht.

*All Tomorrow's Parties* was currently berthed off the Chinese Rocks. Its owner was an off-world racer who owed Doc Joyce for a couple of complex augmentations, a debt he'd proved very bad at paying. In the circumstances Doc Joyce might even throw in some extra fullerene tubes.

The kid was going to need all the smarts she could muster.

## CHAPTER 29

### *Marrakech, Summer 1977*

In the days of the old Pasha a French general had been trapped in a Saharan fort under attack by Berber tribesmen. At lunch, when this attack began, the General was interrupted by an aide-de-camp who wanted to know his commander's orders.

"What are they armed with?"

"Cannon," said the Lieutenant, his face sombre. "And rifles. New model Martini-Henrys." This was a time when most tribesmen still carried muskets and swords, against which the stamped earth walls of the fort would have been completely secure.

"Thank God," the General announced. "I thought you were going to say fire hoses."

When Moz came by the house in Derb Yassin to make his peace with Malika he told the joke to Corporal ould Kasim and the old man had called it stupid. So Moz told it to Malika on their way across the street to Dar el Beida, where Moz was painting the entire place, very cheaply, for German boys who'd bought it from the dog woman's family and were moving out without ever having really bothered to move in.

Unfortunately Malika had needed the joke explained, which was embarrassing for both of them. And then, while Moz stirred paint in a plastic trough, Malika asked Moz who'd told him the joke.

"It was that Englishman, wasn't it?"

This was a sore subject. Almost as sore a subject as it was

between Moz and Sidi ould Kasim, who'd announced that this friendship with the foreigners was exactly what he'd expect from the son of a whore. Moz still wore a split lip from the brief and fruitless altercation which followed.

"What do you want from them?" asked Malika, and her voice was so strained that Moz wondered exactly what ould Kasim had been saying about him. "Look at you!"

Moz wore a pair of bondage pants from Seditionaries, with the straps cut so they didn't interfere with his work. Celia had been about to throw them out. And Moz's hair was now dyed black and spiked on top, the way Jake wore his.

"I like it," said Moz.

"Well, I don't." Malika scowled. "And those shoes are silly."

The shoes had crepe soles, fat laces and were made from red suede, brothel creepers, Jake called them. Neither of them mentioned the watch. The gold Seamaster was something else. Something beyond Moz's dreams. For a start Celia had given it to him.

"So," said Malika. "I suppose you want to say sorry?"

"That's unfair."

"No it's not," Malika said. She'd come with her red hair tied back, although she'd tied it so clumsily that it made her...

"And what are you staring at?" Malika added crossly.

"Just looking," said Moz.

"At what?"

"That ribbon, the shirt, your eyes..." Moz sighed. "And you're right," he said. "My shoes are silly. They're meant to be silly. They used to belong to Jake."

Malika wanted to say something about Jake, about Moz's story that Celia was Jake's sister because Malika didn't believe that for a minute. Only Malika didn't say anything because her mind was still stumbling over the first part of Moz's reply.

"What about the ribbon?"

He said nothing.

"Come to that," said Malika, "what about my eyes?"

Moz shrugged inside his ripped, oversized T-shirt and turned back to his trough of paint. Hassan would be coming before evening prayers to check how the job was going.

"I know what you want," said Malika. "And I'm not going to do it." She put down her broom and kicked a dustpan out of the way. "You don't really need me here anyway."

"Wait." Moz winced at the way his voice shot up. Although he was too anxious even to be embarrassed for long. "Don't go." He needed her help to do what Hassan demanded. Taking the parcel was the only way for Moz to make peace after his fight with Hassan yesterday and even that might not be enough.

"My eyes," Malika demanded, feet planted wide apart. "What about them?"

*You have the eyes of a cat,* Moz wanted to say. *Eyes so amber one could look for the whole of history to be trapped inside them.* They were many things, her eyes, but there were those in the Mellah who thought human was not one of them.

"Tell me..."

Malika was already too grown up to be wearing what she was, one of her father's old shirts as a dress. Pretty soon they'd stop being friends. At least the kind of friends they used to be. And this was probably the last summer they'd be able to talk like this. He'd seen the way Hassan stared at her. Moz knew what was coming and Malika knew also. Moz could see it every day in those eyes.

What Hassan wanted, Hassan got.

"They're beautiful, all right?" Moz said without giving himself time to think about the words or take them back. "And I haven't changed," he added crossly. "You only think so." Somehow it really mattered to Moz that Malika believed this.

"Yes, you have," Malika insisted. She didn't make it an accusation. Just a statement of fact. "As I said, look at you..."

"That's not me," Moz said. "Just clothes."

"Jake's clothes," Malika said. "I don't like Jake and I don't think Jake likes me." And suddenly the problem was out in the open.

Moz thought about it.

"You've only met him a couple of times," he protested.

"I don't need to meet people more than once to know I don't trust them," Malika said firmly and Moz had to smile. That wasn't entirely true. She'd changed her mind about him in the months after his mother died and stood up for Moz then, when Corporal ould Kasim tried to throw Moz out of the house.

She'd put on proper clothes, wrapped her head in an old scarf and gone to the little local mosque to talk to Hajj Rahman's daughter who dealt with family problems. Whatever the old Sufi said to the Corporal, Moz stayed, his world reduced to one upstairs room, the smallest. The beating Malika received from Sidi ould Kasim was terrible.

"Look," said Moz, "this is the truth."

Reaching for Malika's hand, Moz was slightly surprised when she didn't immediately pull away. "I'm not sure I trust Jake either, but he..." Moz hesitated. "Jake has books and a radio that gets stations from everywhere and he has newspapers every day. And a video."

Malika looked blank.

"Like film," Moz explained, "but it works on TV and the films come in a little box... It's Japanese."

"What films?" Malika demanded.

"'*The ancient sages say,*'" said Moz, "'*Do not despise the snake...*'"

He grinned. "It's from *Nine Dozen Heroes and One Wicked Man*. About a hero called Lin Chung... Jake's got films about himself too. He's a musician. Well," Moz qualified that, "he plays electric guitar and sings. He's famous. I'm sure you could watch them if I asked."

"So you're using him?" Malika's voice was thoughtful.

Moz didn't like the way that sounded. "Not exactly," he said. "We're using each other."

"Are you lovers?"

"*Lovers?*"

"The old man says Jake's fucking you. He says..." Malika hesitated. "That's why men like Jake come to Morocco."

Moz let go of her hand.

Malika was the one who talked to Idries when he arrived to see if Moz meant what he said in his message. That he and Malika really were going to do what Hassan wanted after all.

"When did Marzaq start going to the mosque?" Idries demanded, when Malika explained why Moz wasn't there.

"He wanted to talk to an imam."

Idries's smile was incredulous. "He's told you where we're to meet?"

She nodded.

"And Moz is definitely going to do this?"

"He'll be here any minute," Malika said, manoeuvring Idries towards the open door of the dog woman's house.

"See you later then," said Idries.

Malika found Moz where she expected to find him, still sitting on the roof. His back was to a wooden crate and his gaze was fixed on a stork's nest on top of what had once been a palace wall.

That the Jewish quarter bordered an area once occupied by the Sultans made sense because the craftsmen it contained were a valuable asset and the original wall around the Mellah had been as much to protect those inside as to lock them away.

"I brought some cakes." Malika held up a square of newspaper, the bottom of which had gone translucent with grease from the pastries inside.

"So?"

Dark glasses regarded her flatly.

"Where did those come from?" Malika demanded, realizing as soon as she saw Moz scowl how he'd take the question. Moz knew his anger was dishonest. Made worse by how close she'd come to the truth.

"From Jake, obviously enough. All I had to do was suck him off." Moz used the crudest term he knew.

"Look..."

"What?"

"I don't believe you fuck the foreigner."

"So why mention it?"

How could Malika tell him that ould Kasim was so certain Moz was selling his arse that he'd already told half the street? That the new imam had told the old Corporal to attend Friday mosque so that the subject of what to do with Moz could be raised and that even the police had come by...

It was the Major from the station asking for Moz by name which convinced Sidi ould Kasim that his suspicions were right. When even the police wanted to talk to Moz then it was obvious the boy was in trouble.

"People talk," she said.

"And they get it wrong," said Moz.

"Do they?"

Moz looked up at Malika and saw a girl in an old shirt backlit by sunlight. A hot sky the colour of his mother's eyes and Malika's hair burning like a halo. He knew, without knowing how, that in some way this was goodbye to their childhood.

Things change and they just had, he'd felt them shift.

"Sit," Moz said.

And when Malika began to settle herself beside him, Moz shook his head. "Not there," he said. "Here." And he patted his lap.

Hitching up her shirt a little, so her knees were free to go either side of him, Malika sat where he said and when their lips touched it was faltering, almost innocent. Not at all like the kiss with which Celia had set the precedent for Moz's nightly visits to her bed.

"We shouldn't," Malika said.

"You want to stop?"

Malika shook her head.

The next time they kissed, Moz's hand came up to grip the back of the girl's neck, pulling her closer. She stank like an animal, her reddish hair dirty with sweat and the lemon juice he'd combed into it earlier.

"What are you thinking?" Malika asked.

"That you're beautiful."

She felt him go hard as she kissed him back. Moz could see that in her eyes, which touched on his own and then slid away. He could see the doubt in her face and sense it in the way she shifted uneasily on his lap, not realizing that made matters worse.

Part of Moz wanted to help Malika to her feet and reassure her that everything was fine, maybe she should go home now and they'd meet later. Instead he just kissed her harder and yanked Malika's hips against him.

When she shut her eyes, Moz let one of his hands smooth its way down her leg until his fingers reached her bare knee and then he began to creep under the tails of her shirt.

"Moz," she said, then said nothing more.

What Moz wanted to do was lean her backwards slightly and slide his fingers between her legs. Instead he made do with reaching round to the small of her back, feeling her spine sharp beneath his fingers.

"You okay?" he asked.

Malika's nod was as brief as his happiness.

"You're crying."

The girl shrugged.

"I can stop," said Moz.

Malika shook her head, "No need."

On the ruined palace opposite, the solitary stork was preparing to bathe in the last of the afternoon's sun, shifting itself out of the shadow now that evening had begun to blunt the worst of the day's heat.

Moz kissed her again, more softly this time. And as Moz tasted Malika's tears on his own lips her hands reached up to twist into his hair, locking him into a long salt embrace.

Somewhere between the sadness and the settling to sleep of that solitary stork, Moz's fingers dropped from the small of Malika's back to the waistband of her white knickers and crept under the tired elastic.

She let his hand go where it would.

"Enough," Malika said finally. "We'd better get ready." And with that she stood, leaving Moz with a stain spreading across the front of his new trousers. He tried not to mind that she turned her back on him to adjust herself, fingers hooking between her legs to free crumpled cotton.

## CHAPTER 30

### *New York, Friday 6 July*

"So, let's go through this again. You met him where?"

Bill Hagsteen sat across the table from a man in a black suit, a spread of newspapers covering most of the space between them. About a quarter of these were American, the rest foreign. It was the foreign ones that seemed to upset the man in the suit most.

The man had not bothered to introduce himself but the fact two officers from NYPD's Sixth Precinct stood up when he came in told Bill Hagsteen all he needed to know.

The thickset officer had carried away Bill's iMac, his PowerBook, his PalmPilot, his digital recorder, his camera and his MP3, while the young one, the Hispanic kid with the cheekbones, had fastened the door to Bill's brownstone with a plastic seal the size of the Pope's fist and run a length of police tape across the bottom of his stoop.

After this, they ran him down to the Sixth and there he'd stayed. Occasionally people would poke their head round the door but that seemed mostly to take a look at him. Once someone offered him coffee and donuts and when he refused brought them anyway.

All of which changed when the suit arrived.

Bill Hagsteen was the journalist who'd put a name to the man in Vice Questore Pier Angelo's photograph. The man in the suit was not at all happy about that. Nor, it seemed, were Jake Razor's family, who had issued a press release, through a very expensive New York lawyer, informing the world that Jake had died in a fire in Amsterdam fifteen years earlier.

Unfortunately their press release coincided with Lady Celia Vere's interview in the *Sunday Times* in which she claimed to have recognized Jake instantly. Her reason for not recognizing Jake from the shot issued soon after Prisoner Zero's initial arrest was the same as Bill's . . .

Jim Morrison could have hidden behind that greying beard and hair and no one would have recognized him either. The man in Langley's original photograph looked like nothing so much as a flat-eyed and wild-haired Islamic fanatic. Since this had been entirely intentional, Agent Wharton found it hard to fault this bit of Bill Hagsteen's defence.

There were other parts to the journalist's story about which Agent Wharton was even less happy. "You wrote three versions of this article. In one of them you said it was impossible to be certain that Prisoner Zero was Jake."

"They were drafts," Bill said. "That was the second draft."

"What changed your mind?"

Bill Hagsteen shrugged.

"We'll find out," said the agent. "All your calls are being retrieved from the cell-phone company. We're busy re-creating all your wiped files. It would be much simpler if you just told us."

"Told you what?" Bill Hagsteen demanded. "That I changed my mind? It's Jake Razor," he said. "Deal with it."

A list of everything found on Bill's PowerBook was printed out on a long sheet which unfolded like stair carpet and tumbled down one side of the table, proof of guilt supposedly, although what kind of guilt was unspecified. There were perforations where each sheet could be torn. Bill Hagsteen felt like offering to do the job himself.

The agent didn't seem to have a very high opinion of Bill's capacity to tell the truth. Come to that, he didn't seem to have a very high opinion of Bill, period. And Bill couldn't help thinking this might be down to forensics finding those old spanking downloads on his Apple.

He'd thought at the beginning that the agent wanted to talk to him about the abortive trip to Paris, but something else seemed to be exercising the man.

"How long ago did you first meet Jake Razor?"

Bill Hagsteen shrugged again, which had been his default position to a number of questions since he'd been told that he wasn't being allowed access to a lawyer and that Miranda rights didn't apply.

"We'll find out," repeated the man in the suit. "So you might as well answer."

"I can't remember," Bill said, and watched the two uniforms glance at each other. "It was fucking years back," he added crossly. "How well can you remember the seventies?"

The Hispanic officer with the cheekbones sucked his teeth. "In the seventies," he said, "I wasn't born."

"Lucky you."

"Okay," said Agent Wharton. "Forget that. *Where* did you first meet him?"

"God knows," Bill Hagsteen said. "The Mercer Arts Center before it fell down. Max's Kansas City. The downstairs dive at the Palace flophouse... One of the regular places. Where everyone met."

"Everyone?"

"Johnny Thunders and Chris Stein, Terry Ork, the Ramones... Hell, Debbie Harry waited tables. That's just the way it was. Half the time you didn't get names, you just knew the faces."

"And you were the drummer in Jake Razor's band?"

"It wasn't his band," said Bill. "And I didn't play in it. We supported him once in London. We paid our own expenses and after the Rox deducted damage from the night's take we ended up owing the club. We never toured with them again."

"Of course it was Jake's band." The thickset officer looked so certain that Bill suddenly had a vision of the man hanging out at CBGB's in a different incarnation. "Jake Razor. Razor's Edge."

"He named himself after the band," Bill said. "Which fucked off a lot of people. The band's name came first."

"So," said Agent Wharton, "you knew the man well enough to know this. And yet somehow you couldn't recognize him when you spent a week together in Paris. Have I got that right?"

"I called you, remember?" said Bill Hagsteen. He was beginning to think this might have been a bad move.

"Only once it was too late." Agent Wharton held a fat file in his hand, but he held it carelessly and Bill Hagsteen could see from its reflection in the window behind the desk that most of the pages were blank. Some, however, were not blank and there were enough of those to be worrying.

On the table in front of the man were copies of photographs pulled from Bill's partner's camera. Endless mood shots of Parisian cafés, the slowly rusting pomp of the Beauborg Centre and the formal garden behind Rue de Rivoli. A couple of shots showed the steel shell of L'Institute du Monde Arabe and the man in the suit had been particularly interested in those.

Bill had tried to explain how pneumatic pumps shut huge steel irises against the brightness of the Parisian sun in a modern take on the Islamic arabesque, but he wasn't sure the man had been listening. By then Agent Wharton had moved on to the two photographs of a shabby and bearded tramp outlined against the silver waters of the River Seine.

"I'm telling you," Bill said. "I thought Jake was French."

"Did he sound French?"

"He did to me."

"And you met him on the street?"

"In a market. He was at a table scraping chicken stew from an old saucepan."

"And this meeting was prearranged?"

Bill Hagsteen shook his head. He'd have stood up and walked round the room but the last time he'd tried that Cheekbones had put his hands on Bill's shoulders and pushed him back into the chair.

It was becoming obvious that Bill should have contacted someone in authority before writing his piece. Certainly before the story was printed and hit the streets. It made a mockery of the US intelligence services if the people who finally blew the identity of the President's would-be assassin turned out to be a pair of middle-aged rock journalists.

Bill had been told this several times.

Not found, blew... He'd been constructing entire conspiracy theories and the proposal for a book around that one word.

"So," said the suit, "you didn't know in Paris. You didn't know when you wrote your second *draft*." He placed heavy emphasis on the word as if using the term somehow carried extra meaning. "What changed?"

Somewhere in the Twenty-third Precinct on the Upper West Side Jim was being asked identical questions. Bill knew that. He'd been told to which precinct his partner had been taken but not the actual location. Bill was meant to read something into this, only it was hard to know what. Apart from the fact they had him locked in an interview room on the Lower West while his long-term lover and ex–work colleague was being held on the Upper West.

And the thing that got Bill Hagsteen was not that Agent Wharton was furious, it was that the man was embarrassed.

*Not found, blew...*

Bill could feel the book deal turning into a miniseries. Other journalists might have been more worried but he'd been through the riots in Cleveland and marched against the second Gulf War. Besides his name was splashed across newspapers all over the world. In America there was no defence against mistreatment stronger than the threat of bad publicity.

"I got a call," Bill said. "That was the first thing."

Agent Wharton waited.

"Someone in London tipped me off about Celia Vere's piece for the *Sunday Times*. I still wasn't sure but I figured if Jake's ex-manager was going to put her name to it—"

"And the second thing?"

"His watch," Bill said.

The agent looked up from his file.

"Which watch?"

"He was wearing an Omega in Paris," Bill said, "gold with a white face, check the shots."

"Pretty odd for a tramp," said Agent Wharton.

"Pretty odd about describes him." Bill had taken to leaning forward, as if trying to include the agent in his story. "Jim enhanced the picture quality and matched the watch to one in the shots from Razor's last interview. He swears the watch is identical, right down to damage on the face. And then... you know... there were those photographs..."

Bill meant the ones splashed across the front of most of the papers, the shots the new Italian government had released without first alerting Washington. Agent Wharton knew more than he wanted to about them.

"He looked more like Jake in those. Kind of battered and sunburnt but the sneer was right and the way he stood, one foot forward and his arms folded. Maybe you had to know him to recognize it."

"Yeah," said the man with the suit. "And you did, didn't you? You spend a week with this man in Paris and the next thing that happens is he takes a crack at the President... What?" Agent Wharton demanded, glaring at the door as if he could see straight through it and kill whoever knocked on the other side with a single glance.

"You need to turn on your cell phone."

"What?"

The Sergeant who peered round the door looked the suit up and down, too battle-scarred and too old to give a damn for anyone who wasn't her boss or an immediate colleague. "That's what the message said, turn on your mobile."

She shut the door with a bang.

"Agent Wharton," said the suit into his phone. "What? You're shitting me..." Michael Wharton never swore and certainly not in front of uniforms from the NYPD. So he stared the Hispanic out for a few brief seconds, as if daring him to smirk, and went back to his call.

"Where?"

"Both of them?"

"Me?"

"Yeah."

Snapping shut his cell phone, Agent Wharton took a look at the printouts, the photographs and the mess of papers and prepared to walk away from the lot. "Wrap him up," he told the older of the two officers. "He's off to see the President."

# CHAPTER 31

## *Zigin Chéng, CTzu 53/Year 20*

The Emperor flinched at the sound of a lash, then flinched again and again until daylight pulled open his eyes and he woke to find himself in the Pavilion of Celestial Dreams, the smell of a distant city on his skin and ruined flesh burned into his memory.

He was exhausted by the effort of holding the dreams in his head.

"Saw two shooting stars last night."

Zaq looked around him for the source of the words. And miles above the Forbidden City particulate matter fell softly through the upper atmosphere. All that remained from a Casimir coil dumped by a racing yacht which had been stolen once to order and once again on something stronger than a whim.

*All Tomorrow's Parties* shed the first coil because that was what it always did at the halfway point of any race, once the vector was in sight and pit craft were waiting to cocoon it back into health. It took the decision on its own, based on precedent and extrapolation of all available data, which was rather less than it would have liked. The second coil it dumped because Tris told it to and she was holding a gun to its memory.

Where every emperor since the original Chuang Tzu had slept on a bed of solid oak, his head resting on a wooden pillow, Zaq bedded down in a corner of his room, wrapped in an old blanket and nightmares. He did this because it annoyed the Library and he had no need to tell the Library about the nightmares because it already knew.

They were the price Zaq paid for refusing to be Chuang Tzu. At least Zaq imagined they were. The war between Zaq and the Library was quiet and understated, but they both knew it was moving into a new and dangerous phase.

These days the darkness signed itself Rapture Library, the rapture bit being an old and bad joke at the expense of *Holy Ghost Guides Us,* a converted freighter fleeing from the world of the first Chuang Tzu, which stumbled through space and into the still-forming 2023 worlds.

Landing in the hills behind the embryo city, its crew imagined the world in which they found themselves to be deserted and it was only when a breakaway sect of fundamental polygamists began cutting down mulberry trees to the north of the Forbidden City that the Library disabused them.

The Boy Emperor had been forced to hide in his palace as thunder crashed hard enough to crack glass and lightning destroyed the tents of the polygamists with improbable accuracy.

Of course, Major Commissar Chuang Tzu was not really a boy, whatever the legends said, although all of those who followed after had been children, almost all adapting happily to their new name and lives. The fact the Library had begun to refer to Zaq by his pre-manifestation name was worrying because it seemed to suggest that what Zaq feared was true.

And the Emperor knew how problematic a thought that was,

how wrapped around with doubt, and this worried Zaq also...The Chuang Tzu was required to be solid in his certainty, representative of intelligence, knowledge and wisdom. He was, to quote the Librarian, the spiritual health of the 2023 worlds made manifest.

It seemed doubtful to Zaq that the Library had ever intended this to be the lesson learnt from its banishment of the polygamists. A short and rather frightening conversation between Zaq and the Librarian revealed that it had been the destruction of the mulberry gardens which angered it.

"Although anger's probably the wrong word... It is, isn't it?"

Assent came from inside Zaq's own skull. A place both suffocatingly close and infinite in its distance.

Applying human emotions to an entity already ancient before amino acids tripped into life half a galaxy away was not helpful. Although this didn't stop the amino acid's descendant from so doing. And it seemed, from a throwaway afterthought, that what really troubled the Library was not the physical destruction of the mulberry bushes or the threat this implied to the silkworms which gave the orchard its reason for existing.

The Library had been scared that the orchard's destruction might upset the fragile happiness of the young Chinese navigator, who was only just coming to terms with his own progression from ice to Emperor.

There were a few among the cold immortals who felt that the navigator and every emperor who came after were no more than pets for the Library. Zaq knew different. The Library had been created not to command but to serve and without someone to serve its existence had no meaning.

This alone was the reason it clung to its role as tutor to each new Chuang Tzu with all the ruthlessness of a court eunuch in the real Forbidden City.

"Bath," Zaq shouted.

As orders went this was entirely redundant. A bath would have been run by servitors the moment Zaq dropped out of deep sleep and into his half-waking haze of dusty alleys and hurt children. In the event that Zaq remained there, another bath would be run and then another and another.

Zaq never saw this happen. He just rolled out of his huddle, walked through a single door and found a steaming pool awaiting him. All of this Zaq knew in the instant he realized that he didn't, facts simply appearing in his head.

The only place where the Librarian kept its peace was in the walled Butterfly Garden, which was within a larger walled garden to the north of the three private pavilions. And Zaq knew this was only because the butterflies were in themselves manifestations of the Librarian, who was, of course, merely one manifestation of the Library, which was merely...

Boxes within boxes.

"Your bath." Tuan-Yu.

*Orthodox and Heaven Blessed.*

His title went unsaid. Although Zaq was willing to bet that the servitor in the crimson *changfu* with the silver embroidery had muttered it under her breath. Some mornings, particularly in the first month after he'd given the order that no one was to use any of his titles, Zaq had actually seen the girl's lips move as she swallowed her words. Only Zaq's further announcement that this would be regarded as the height of rudeness brought her mumbling to an end.

He was too old to be this childish, Zaq knew that.

"Does your—" The servitor stumbled over the mistake and blushed prettily. No one ever did anything in the pavilions but prettily or with grace and style, and even her apology was elegantly simple. "I'm sorry, sir... Do you wish me to bathe you?"

Her name was Winter Blossom On Broken Rock and the Emperor had named her himself. He called her "Broken" or "Winter Blossom" for short, names to which she answered with downcast eyes and a demure, almost coy smile. She was the fourteenth handmaiden to attend him since he killed the intruder and the first he found bearable enough to have in his presence.

Some days, Zaq still felt too raw to face anyone, but those days were fewer than they had been and were getting fewer year by year. It was the hope of finding a way out of his predicament that had made life less wearisome. At first he'd only wanted to step down from the throne. Now Zaq knew that his only hope was to abolish himself altogether.

"Sir...?"

He'd forgotten to answer her question.

Five years ago, she'd have stood there, dressed in her silk *changfu* and looking expectant until he noticed her or remembered for himself, but Zaq had put a stop to that. All queries were to be asked when they arose and the girl was not to wait for him to notice her.

He was still to be regarded as invisible beyond this room, that was unchanged, but in here... It had taken Zaq and the Library months and one of the worst battles Zaq could remember to work out this compromise. No one was to wait on his every word and no one was to guard him. He would walk the Forbidden City as he wished and except on those days when 148 billion souls absolutely had to watch him take a bath or a new concubine or offer respect to those emperors who had gone before, he would remain Zaq.

The boy who'd made the mistake of waking up one morning and mentioning to his mother that he'd been visited in the night by a butterfly.

Such rules were simple both to make and to enforce. All Zaq had to do was reach an agreement with the Librarian and all those in the Forbidden City knew instantly what was expected of them. Some days Zaq really believed he was the only emperor ever to notice that all of those who served him, the eunuchs and concubines, serving girls and palace guards, were interchangeable manifestations of the Library itself.

Oh, he knew they were flesh all right, Zaq could vouch for that. Flesh and blood, bone and sinew. Still merely animated, though.

"Come here."

Winter Blossom On Broken Rock looked pleasingly puzzled. She was already as close to him as modesty and politeness allowed.

"There," Zaq told the girl, pointing to a spot at his feet and she did as he said.

Eyes as dark as clouds on a winter night and hair that fell in a splash across her shoulders, black onto crimson, the silver butterflies and golden blossom of her silk robe glittering in the morning light. He passed her a dozen times a day in the outer gardens, at the table, standing mute in a corridor with eyes cast down as he staggered by under the weight of dreams and loneliness.

"What's your name?"

"Broken, sir."

Zaq waited.

"Sir?"

"Your full name."

"Winter Blossom On Broken Rock, sir."

"And before that?"

Once again the girl looked puzzled. So puzzled, as she sucked her cheek and chewed prettily at her bottom lip, that Zaq almost forgot to watch her eyes for signs of the darkness.

It was there, though.

Zaq was sure of that.

"You have my bath," he said.

She nodded and began to strip, moving to a line of melody heard only in her head. When Zaq's own expression stayed blank, her fingers suddenly faltered at the fastening under her right arm as if the tune had failed.

"Aren't you joining me, sir?"

"Why would I do that?"

*Because it would be fun? Because nothing else makes sense?* He could almost hear the answers in his own head as the Library whispered them to the girl.

"Hurry up," he said.

All pretence of fun was gone. She removed her silk gown swiftly but clumsily, yanking an undershift over her head and almost getting trapped as her pale arms caught in its short silk sleeves. She looked, as she always looked, elegant and vulnerable.

"Now wash."

Climbing into the marble tub, she sank into the steaming water and let it close over her shoulders until only her head was exposed.

"Free your hair."

She looked at him, eyes huge. In all the time since he'd noticed her Zaq had never asked this. Everything else had been offered or taken. He'd tried to find out if Winter Blossom On Broken Rock had a life when not with him, asking her endless questions and memorising her answers to see if they remained consistent, which they did over months and even years.

In the early days of his being Chuang Tzu, Zaq had crouched in a night-soil trench, trying to discover if the trench was really used. And sure enough, no sooner had he hidden himself than half a dozen servitors came in, laughing and chatting as they pissed noisily from the long bench above.

The Library was very clever.

A week later, bored with watching the trench, he wondered aloud whether servants ever fucked and less than a day later turned a corner in a vegetable garden to find a serving girl rutting noisily with a boy from the kitchens. So intent were they on providing him with proof that neither even looked round when he stopped to watch.

"Let me," Zaq said, unwinding the ornate knot that kept her oiled tresses in place. And the girl sat in silence while he did so.

* * *

The most important job in the known galaxy was his. Tuan-Yu. Orthodox and Heaven Blessed. Dreamer of Worlds. His very existence kept alive the 2023 fragments of the unformed shell and 148 billion people who had watched him untie the hair of a serving girl.

This was the figure to which Zaq always came back. It was a hard number to imagine, and he'd tried.

There were a hundred billion stars in the spiral. In other words, for every star in the galaxy there lived at least one person who owed her or his continued existence to Zaq. At fifteen he'd demanded that the Librarian show him a hundred billion stars and kept up his demands until his request was finally met.

So many lights coalesced inside his head that it was like looking at a single star, until Zaq looked more closely and distances emerged, large beyond imagining. It was like falling into infinity, except that the moment Zaq decided this the Librarian widened its remit to include other galaxies, each one circling a black hole that ripped light into darkness.

When Zaq awoke it was three days later and his skull echoed with thoughts of foam and simultaneous states of being and absence. A week later, while walking between the smallest of the private pavilions and the gate leading to the outer garden, he decided that something really had to change.

He'd been working on making the change ever since.

# CHAPTER 32

## *Marrakech, Summer 1977*

"You know about ould Kasim . . . ?"

Yeah, Moz knew. Idries had told him already. The old Corporal had been beyond angry when Malika finally got back to the Mellah, after helping deliver the parcel for Hassan's uncle.

Moz should have stayed around but Malika had insisted on making her own way back. At the time she'd seemed more furious about Moz changing his mind and agreeing to take Hassan's job than she did about him being the first boy to get into her pants.

Now Moz wasn't so sure. "You know where she is?"

"Haven't seen her."

"Really?"

"That's what I said." Hassan seemed anxious to be rid of him.

"Okay," said Moz.

The other boy shook his head as Moz wandered away, a Perrier bottle in one hand, his other deep in the pocket of khaki trousers ripped at the knees. Whoever had made them had sewn chain between the ankles, so that Moz looked like a hobbled camel.

That was fashion, apparently.

Hassan's own suit was Italian wool with a thin chalk stripe and five-button cuffs, double stitching on the lapel and on all of the button-holes, even those on the five-button sleeve. A tailor at Hotel Mamounia had made it to a pattern Hassan had seen in a magazine.

This, a present from his uncle, was fashion.

Also, in part, a disguise.

Malika was missing. Nothing else would have dragged Moz from Riad al-Razor back to Café Georgiou, the tourist café in Gueliz that Hassan would one day inherit from his uncle.

It was an irony not lost on Hassan that Moz, who wanted more than anyone he'd ever met to be *nasrani,* avoided Gueliz because this was where Hassan now spent most of his time.

"Me?" Moz halted outside the dog woman's house, taking in Corporal ould Kasim on his rickety stool surrounded by a sea of abandoned tabloids, a tray of pastries now reduced to a few sticky crumbs and a half-full tea glass which the midday heat was keeping blood hot.

"Of course, you. Who do you think I'm talking to?"

Raw anger was the only emotion Corporal ould Kasim ever expressed, all others, even cold hatred and icy contempt, seemed beyond him. As if his time in the French police had somehow scrubbed all subtlety from the palate of his emotions. An old-fashioned army truck forever stuck in first gear was how Moz's mother once described the man, in a voice so sad it spoke of broken hopes that a higher gear might exist, just waiting for her to find it.

"Yourself, I imagine . . ." said Moz. "I can't think of anyone else who'd be interested in what you've got to say."

"I need to talk to you."

"So?"

Sidi ould Kasim scowled. "Come here," he ordered, waiting for the boy to amble over. It didn't help the Corporal's temper that he was gathering an audience, beginning with the two hajj who lived next to the dog woman's old house. Cousins, they were forever squatting in their doorway playing backgammon. Their wives would also be watching, from behind wooden shutters that blinded two tiny first-floor windows.

In the Mellah one only had to sneeze and an old woman five streets away would immediately want to know what the doctor had said. The wives watched from behind closed shutters because houses in the Mellah were either too poor or too Jewish to have *mas-rabiyas*, those ornately screened balconies found across most of North Africa.

Jewish houses had windows at the front and shutters instead.

"Where's Malika gone?" The old man's voice carried a brook-no-argument, watch-yourself kind of tone.

"I don't know," said Moz, gulping from the Perrier bottle he still held in one hand. "Why don't you tell me?" The mineral water came from Celia's supplies at Riad al-Razor, obviously enough. He'd taken it along with some speed when he woke to find the morning he'd been planning to spend at the riad unravelling around him. Celia and Jake were locked into some argument and neither had seemed particularly pleased to see him.

Sweeping one hand through his spiky hair, Moz let his shades follow the old man's gaze towards the backgammon players.

"Do they know what you did to her?"

She'd left the house early on Saturday. The bread had not been made since, the floors went unswept and litter had begun to build up in layers around the old man's wooden stool. A random circle of dirty tea glasses stood going sticky and dust-encrusted in the heat.

"I did nothing." Ould Kasim's voice was contemptuous. "You're the problem. You and those friends of yours."

"Maybe you did more than just beat her... Is that what happened?"

"Watch your mouth."

"Maybe you buried her in the cellar."

"I'm warning you," said the Corporal.

"You're warning me?" Moz said. He looked the soldier up and down with all the disgust he could manage. "Maybe you should be the one worrying about the police. You pervert—"

Sidi ould Kasim stood.

It was meant to be frightening. A threat. *Don't make me stand up.*

*Don't make me come over there. Why do you bring these things on yourself?* Moz and Malika knew the litany by heart. And no doubt Malika's mother had known it before that, when she was still alive. It went with the unbuckling of his belt, the clenching of a fist, the twist of one shoulder, signals of what was to come.

Moz could almost taste his own fear. A miasma made from old memories and reactions that clung to his body like steam from a *hamman*. All the same Moz managed to make his shrug dismissive, he was proud of that.

And if he got hurt. So what?

A single graze on Malika's arm had always hurt him more than the darkest bruise on his own body. They were tied, connected in ways neither of them wanted to talk about. Sometimes, when Malika glanced at him, Moz could see that knowledge written in her eyes.

Their names began with the same letter, they lived in the same house, in rooms exactly above and below each other, they were born in the same month, a year and a day apart, both had parents who were dead, his mother had been *nasrani* and so, Malika insisted, had her real father.

And then there was ould Kasim.

They both hated the man and had talked about running away when they were small. As they got older, it became not running away but escaping to find a new life... He'd let her down. All that stuff with Celia. His hands inside Malika's knickers on the roof.

Finding Malika had become the only thing that mattered. Because Moz knew, as well as he knew his own smell, that Malika would not have run away without him.

"Where are you going?" The voice was a shout behind him. One that Moz chose to ignore.

"Don't you dare walk away from me!"

The sensible thing to do would have been to keep walking. Instead, Moz turned and began to walk back, throwing up one arm to meet the belt as he had a hundred times before.

Only this time Moz stepped into the blow, more or less by accident, and the buckle which came whistling down wrapped the leather around his wrist. So Moz grabbed the strap below the buckle and yanked, almost pulling ould Kasim from his feet.

Cardamom, cheap brandy and a lifetime's bitterness, Moz could smell them all on the old man's rancid breath. Now was the moment Moz had waited for, the one where he ripped the belt from

Sidi ould Kasim's hands and turned it on its owner, beating Malika's persecutor to his knees.

Malika and Moz had dreamed about this endlessly, in between making plans to run away, poison the old man with bad meat or wrap his drunken body in a sheet and drop it down a well behind La Koutoubia.

"Let go," Corporal ould Kasim ordered.

"Make me."

The backgammon players were on their feet now and the oldest of the wives had come to the door, bringing with her the smell of cheap rose-water and lamb tagine.

Stepping back, Moz yanked hard on his end of the belt, watching the old man stagger, then dig in his heels and yank back.

Moz grinned.

It was this more than anything else that stoked the old man's fury. Bringing up one knee, the soldier aimed for Moz's groin and when that failed he stamped the edge of his boot down the front of the boy's shin. Only Moz's foot was no longer there.

"Missed," said Moz. A very childish thing to say, but he didn't care.

The Corporal, the man who claimed he could reduce hardened prisoners to whimpering obedience with a single pebble and a short length of string, could no longer even knee someone properly. Moz wanted the group standing opposite to understand that.

"You know," Moz said loudly, "I haven't got time for this." Stepping back, he yanked viciously on his bit of the belt and watched the old man stumble, going down on one knee in the dust.

"See you," Moz said, dropping the belt.

And there it might have ended if only Sidi ould Kasim had let Moz leave. But as the boy turned away, already readjusting his shades and sweeping one hand through his hair, the Corporal regained his feet.

"No you don't," he said, swinging the belt harder than ever. The heavy buckle of the belt hit Moz's shoulder, bruising flesh as its metal tang pierced his shirt and lodged in his skin below the collarbone.

Odd, thought Moz.

Without further thought, he pulled the buckle from his chest, watching the underlying flesh pucker beneath cloth as the tang pulled free. The next thing he did was turn round and smash his Perrier bottle hard into the side of Sidi ould Kasim's head.

Two days after this, Major Abbas pulled Moz off the corner of Boulevard Mohammed V. The Major did this by the simple expedient of pulling up next to the teenager in a *grande taxi,* pushing open a door and ordering Moz to climb inside.

The boy would no sooner have refused than try to make a run for it, both of which were known to be very dangerous options where the Marrakchi police were concerned.

"Leave it," Major Abbas snapped, when Moz leant forward to wind down one window. There was something in the way he said this that scared the boy.

"You seen Malika recently?"

Moz shook his head.

"Anyone looking for her?"

"No." She was a foreigner's brat, Corporal ould Kasim's responsibility. No men from Derb Yassin were out searching through the narrow alleys of the Mellah, fired up on rumours and outrage. She wasn't worth the effort.

"You're Marzaq?" The new voice was sharp, like broken glass and edged with an accent which was new to the boy.

Moz nodded. Anything else would have been pointless.

The elderly *nasrani* who sat in the back of the *grande taxi* had improbably black hair and tortoiseshell shades which reflected Moz back on himself. A skinny punk in a torn Ramones T-shirt, his hair cut with kitchen scissors and held erect by a mix of sugar water and Vaseline.

"He doesn't look like an *Arab*."

The stress the old man placed on this last word was both ugly and contemptuous. On the other hand, he was speaking fluent Arabic, which was impressive in itself.

"Half Turkish," said the Major. "Quarter English, quarter German."

"*Merde,*" said Claude de Greuze, one-time advisor to the old Pasha and still on retainer from Paris. "What a fucking mix." A mirrored gaze slid over Moz's thin face and the boy shifted uneasily in his seat. "Maybe he's got something to be worried about..."

"No. The plastic's hot, that's all." Patting the cracked red vinyl, Moz mimicked snatching his fingers away. "Much too hot."

"You speak French."

"Yeah," said Moz, "and Arabic. You want a guide to the souk I'm the best. I can show you around all the best places. Get you good prices."

Slowly, very casually, Claude de Greuze produced a Browning from the inside of his jacket, pulled back the slide and put the muzzle against the side of Moz's head.

It felt warm.

"You think this is a joke?"

Moz stared back. Not defiant, just puzzled. He was good at doing puzzled. "No," he said finally, when the seconds had stretched too thin. "I don't think this is a joke at all. I was just offering to help."

There followed a rapid-fire discussion between Major Abbas and the stranger, which switched between languages almost every other sentence. This was the first time Moz realized the Major had been learning English and now spoke it better than he did.

Moz understood about a quarter of what was said and this was a quarter more than the Frenchman intended him to understand as the words "Malika," "necessity" and "school" tumbled between the two men.

"If you say so," said the stranger, lowering his gun. He glanced again at Moz. "Maybe I'll take him up on that offer," he said to Major Abbas. "Let him show me round the souk." Claude de Greuze's smile revealed a whole mouthful of nicotine-stained teeth. "He could show me some of his favourite cafés, while he's at it. He'd do that for me, wouldn't he?"

Moz thought about those words on his walk back to Riad al-Razor. Not so much what the Frenchman said as the way he said it. And Moz thought about the man's smell. Garlic, tobacco, sweat and ginger were common in a city where water was rare and most washing was ritual, at least for the people he knew.

The foreigner's smell was different. A sour reek which so completely filled the *grande taxi* that it was a wonder someone as fastidious as Major Abbas could stand it. That was when Moz realized something which was to change the way he looked at the world.

Major Abbas, the most feared police officer in the whole of the Medina, had no choice but to sit with the windows shut, while trying to breathe through his mouth because, for reasons Moz could barely comprehend, he could not afford to offend the old Frenchman.

It was a terrifying thought.

## CHAPTER 33

## *Washington, Saturday 7 July*

*Five things you need to know about Zero Point Energy*. A selection of tabloids lay open on Gene Newman's rosewood desk. A *New York Post*, a copy of the *Sun* from England, half a dozen others. The President hadn't bothered to check which contained the list, it could have been any or all.

The five points had been posted the previous morning on alt.sf.science by a top-end theorist from NASA, a man with a disgustingly cynical sense of humour. The tabloids had printed them straight.

1. Zero Point Energy is named after its inventor (the soon to be late Prisoner Zero).
2. ZPE uses Quantum Foam, which is so small you can't even see the bubbles.
3. A cup of Quantum Foam would be enough to boil all the seas on Earth.
4. An SUV running on ZPE would run from now until the end of time without ever needing to fill up.
5. With ZPE a spaceship will cost no more to fill than a lawnmower, but go much faster...

Gene Newman had no idea if a practical application for the Casimir force equations really had been scratched into the shit blasted off the mesh of Prisoner Zero's cage. It was impossible to tell, since some idiot had apparently decided to wash the shit, the equations and the scratched sketches away.

Whatever, serious scientists were talking about the possibility that Prisoner Zero had successfully tied a big pink bow around gravity, inertia, heat and electricity, with some throw-in about the shape of time which Gene Newman had given up trying to understand.

All he knew was that Prisoner Zero had gone from Arab terrorist, through psycho killer and ex-punk junkie to tortured American genius in a matter of hours. Which didn't stop the *New York Post* featuring a tasteful countdown chart to the man's execution.

Draining the last of his coffee, Gene Newman turned back to the tabloids. EINSTEIN ASSASSIN DISCOVERS ULTIMATE POWER—FORMULA FEARED LOST FOREVER. Actually, that was one of the broadsheets.

"You got the answers yet?"

Across the Oval Office Isabel Gorst shook her head. "I'll get on to it," she said. "Meanwhile here's the list of people who've called." She walked round the eagle on the carpet, as she always walked round the eagle, and put the list into his hand. Neither of them mentioned that his in-tray was bigger than ever.

"Petra Mayer?"

"Oh yes," Isabel Gorst said. "She's going to call in an hour."

"Okay," said the President. "Have Paula remind the Secretary of Defense that I'm still waiting for some answers."

Colonel Borgenicht was going to have to explain exactly what had happened at five a.m. yesterday morning at Camp Freedom and who thought using a fire hose to blast the twenty-first century's very own version of Newton's *Principia* off the mesh would be a good idea.

Rage had put most of the medals on Sergeant Saez's chest and the ribbons went right over the place where the rage hid. It formed a fist-sized chunk where his heart should be and had carried him out of the Philadelphia projects and into a life where he had two kids, a nu-school BMW complete with tinted windows, and a bunch of men who trusted him not to throw away their lives.

His kids lived with his ex-wife in a house he'd more or less built by himself, after buying a pull-down on the edge of Belleville. It was a good house and he tried not to be angry about living somewhere else these days.

Michael Saez knew why he was angry and his ex-wife knew why he was angry. So Sergeant Saez couldn't fault her logic in leaving. He didn't want the boys to turn into him either.

All the same, he resented being stuck on a desolate little island in the middle of nowhere. And resentment made him drink more of a bottle of Jack Daniel's than was decent and wake before the birds, still drunk and with a filthy headache, not to mention a marked reluctance to spend his morning guarding a cage covered in shit.

There were other things that made Sergeant Saez furious and these came out in the days following, when the damage was already done and most of the questions were more about filling in gaps for Colonel Borgenicht's paperwork than building a true picture of anyone's state of mind.

Not all of these made it into Dr. Petrov's rider to the Borgenicht Report, but the ones which did included the fact the Italians had been printing lies about how the marines were treating the Arab, the fact that the weights room had apparently begun to smell worse than a brick shithouse and Sergeant Saez's fury when the so-called Arab turned out to be American. Strangely enough, Saez never mentioned the fact his cousin had been piloting the helicopter brought down in Marrakech. Although Dr. Petrov included it anyway.

After the shit had been blasted from the mesh with fire hoses and the original blanket and mattress had been removed to dry in the sun, new bedding was brought in and Sergeant Saez woke the two embedded cameramen so they could photograph the newly clean cage. (One of them was from Fox News, the other had an uncle in the Pentagon Press Office.)

Sergeant Saez then climbed into the cage himself and made sure the two men photographed him as he knelt on the floor, pulling and twisting at the plastic-coated mesh until his hands hurt. Then he showed the cameras his own fingers, which were now raw from the effort and beginning very slightly to blister.

"You see?" he said. "The prisoner damaged his own hands trying to dig his way out." Even the man from Fox News looked doubtful.

While Master Sergeant Saez was busy bringing Colonel Borgenicht to the attention of the President, Prisoner Zero was having an early morning appointment with Katie Petrov, who was too busy taking a call on a hotel phone to notice that her patient was drawing a spaceship in the dust on the floor with his foot.

"Lower the blind."

"Why?"

Turning on her office's portable television, Katie zapped to the channel mentioned by Bill Logan, still on loan to the marines from CavourCohen Media and currently CCM's most famous VP.

"Shit." It was true. The helicopter off the edge of the cliff really had been hired by Amnesty and a long lens was focused on her window. She could watch herself staring out of a window at the very helicopter taking the photograph of her staring out of the window at the very helicopter . . .

It was recursive to the point of insanity.

And to make matters worse the channel was busy broadcasting the verbal warnings it received as it received them. So now the whole world knew that the marine Colonel in charge of Camp Freedom had just threatened to blow an Italian helicopter out of the sky.

As Dr. Katie Petrov walked back to her desk, she inadvertently scuffed out a sketch of a needle-like racing yacht which would have told her more about Prisoner Zero's grasp on reality than carefully logging his reactions to a hundred unanswered questions.

The prisoner was quite obviously aware of what went on around him and every CT scan suggested he understood exactly what was being said. And if even half the medical data Katie had on file proved accurate, then the man was actually busy answering her questions inside his head. She'd spent the last few days coming out of their sessions only to discover that Prisoner Zero's silence had been the shell to an entire world's worth of hidden speech.

"You do know," said Katie, "that you have only six days left to live?"

Dark eyes watched her and, to make matters worse, Katie could swear that her attempt to focus Prisoner Zero's mind on his fate only left the man amused.

"It doesn't worry you?"

Again those eyes. That blankness.

Not only was he waiting for death. He was unafraid of it. As Katie wrote this on her notepad she realized it was probably the first thing she'd written in over a week that struck her as unquestionably true. Yet little in his daily ritual suggested he was certifiably religious. Maybe it was a variation on suicide by cop.

One of Katie's earliest clients had opened fire on a police car from his wheelchair and been killed in the answering fire. It had been his fifth attempt in three years.

Possible, but unlikely.

She had, Katie was forced to admit, almost no real handle on Prisoner Zero, which made her no better or worse than the psychiatrist originally brought in by the Pentagon. And if Colonel Borgenicht was getting increasingly upset by Katie's inability to reach a verdict then she could only repeat what she'd already told him.

She'd rather be late than wrong.

Of course, she wasn't the one with helicopters buzzing round her head like flies. Well, actually she was but they weren't after her. They were after the men who ripped fingernails from a world-class mathematician; because, apparently, that's who Prisoner Zero was…

Katie put her head in her hands.

It got worse.

Her mentor, the renowned Harvard academic Petra Mayer, had taken a single glance at the Vice Questore's photograph, ignored the prisoner altogether and speed-dialled the NASA theoretician with the cynical sense of humour. After that she called a Chinese refugee teaching quantum physics at Padua University and Dr. Natalia Aziz in Cairo, who specialized in the mathematics of low probability/high impact events.

Each one agreed to report their first findings to her within the hour.

Authenticating the half code, proofs, theorems, fractured formulae and incomplete sketches visible in the background of Pier Angelo's photograph took a joint effort rare in academia and rarer than kindness in the paranoid world of high mathematics and quantum research.

And only when Petra Mayer had taken one shocked call after another did she pick up her own phone and speed-dial the President direct. A lot was made of this point. And though it wasn't so surprising to discover that half a dozen of Harvard's finest had Gene Newman's direct line only Petra Mayer had the number for his cell phone.

Petra Mayer had spent her mid-twenties in prison for hammering nails into a Montana redwood. Few states send people to prison for harming a tree, Montana included. Only the girl hadn't been trying to damage the tree, she'd been there to halt a lumber firm busy taking down five-hundred-year-old redwoods to sell as specialist timber.

The nail caught the chain of a power saw and stripped off its links, exploding the cutting belt like chain shot and taking off the fingers of a foreman overseeing the lumberjack.

The court case made headline news across America and Petra Mayer used her time inside to write a best-selling polemic on ecology, biodiversity and sustainable growth. Simplicity of style was one of the things which helped *Tao and the Way of Global Maintenance* to become a *New York Times* bestseller. The other was the fact she stuck all the biology, physics and economics at the back in an appendix called "Other Stuff," where it could be safely ignored by the bulk of her readers.

The President was one of the few who actually bothered to check her sums. So when his old Professor finally dialled the direct number, Gene Newman opened his cell phone, saw who it was and promptly stood up, setting off a chain reaction that had chairs scraping the floor all around the Situation Room.

"Thank you. That will be all."

Around the table half a dozen advisors, department heads and military chiefs nodded. "Thank you, Mr. President."

"Petra," he said, watching the door close.

"Mr. President?"

"You just saved me from my Defense Secretary."

The slightly disbelieving snort from the other end made it clear that Petra Mayer found this unlikely.

"You wanted to talk to me?"

"That's why I called," said the Professor. Only her age and the weight of her news excused the impatience in her voice. "You've got a problem."

"I've got dozens," said the President. "Where do you want me to start?"

"No," said the voice on the other end of his phone. "I mean you've got a problem."

"Tell me..."

"So you see, what you and I think of as physical laws our friend considers the cosmological equivalent of local weather conditions..."

At the end of the conversation Gene Newman was not entirely sure he'd understood everything his old tutor had told him. The President imagined Petra Mayer knew this and it was only respect for Gene's office that made her refrain from firing questions at him as if they were both still in a seminar.

"It's important?"

"Gene...If this is for real then it changes everything. Think about it. We're surrounded by a high-energy field...No," the Professor corrected herself, "we exist inside a high-energy field, one we barely notice because it runs through us and through everything else and suddenly there's a chance we can tap into this field."

"That is good, right?"

"It's terrifying," said Petra Mayer. "How do you think China will react if her oilfields become worthless overnight? What's a bankrupt Saudi Arabia going to do to the balance of power in the

Gulf? Shit, imagine al Qaeda with this technology. Gene, I wouldn't dream of telling you your job but—"

"Okay," said the President, "I can see the problem."

Silence came from the other end.

"What?" Gene Newman said.

"That's not it... Natalia Aziz thinks that one of the equations might relate to time. You're not going to like this." Gene Newman was Catholic, although not so Catholic that he had more than two children.

"Tell me."

"You need to know that Natalia Aziz believes in God."

"Of course she does. The woman's a Moslem."

"No, I mean as a scientist Aziz thinks God exists. It looks like Prisoner Zero thinks the same. Only one of his theorems seems to suggest that God will die."

"When?"

"At the end of time. When the universe comes to an end."

"What happens then?"

"God's born again."

"Along with a new universe?"

"You've got it, but he's probably not talking about God in the sense you're talking about God."

"You know," Gene Newman said, "we're not even going to go there."

"Okay," said Professor Mayer. "You've got your own people examining the photographs, right?"

Here the President was on firmer ground. "Of course I've got people looking," he said. "The best brains in the CIA and the Pentagon are examining them as we talk."

"That should be impressive." Petra Mayer's view on both was well known. As was the thickness of a file she'd eventually prized out of the CIA under section 552 of the Freedom of Information Act, having argued successfully that her file could no longer be regarded as operational.

There was an age when most Western scientists distinguished between space and time. This period lasted roughly from the Dark Ages to the beginning of quantum physics. A period during which the West caught up with and finally overtook the laws of science the Arab world had taken for granted for centuries.

Although few people thought of it in these terms, the shape

given to time always had been a religious choice. For those within the Judeo-Christian tradition time was subservient to God and ran like a river. Other faiths saw time differently, as an illusion or a great circle that always came back to where it began and in which history endlessly repeated itself.

It was only with quantum physics that the idea of time as space and the universe as a series of endless illusions really entered Western thought. Before this, time had a beginning and an end over which God would preside. Space was by turn the home of heaven, a starry mantel and a clockwork suburb operated by angels.

As it became possible for astronomers to go further, some suggested that our solar system was not necessarily the centre of the known universe. This destruction of the heliocentric view happened at about the point God was taken out of the time equation.

And then in 1904 a minor clerk at the Swiss Patent Office in Berne wrote a brief pamphlet, a side effect of which was that time and space became, like mass and energy, so inextricably linked they turned into variants of the same thing.

Petra Mayer was not a believer in unalloyed Einstein, any more than she believed in the angelic host, time running in only one direction or the universe as an ever-expanding balloon of mostly dark matter.

"You've got more than just the one photograph, right?" Petra Mayer said. She was having trouble keeping the impatience out of her voice. Old age and cancer were not treating her kindly.

"Yes," said the President, reopening a file. "They're one of the things we've just been discussing. We got copies this morning." Gene Newman leant over the table of the Situation Room to take another look.

There were five photographs in all. Three close-ups of the prisoner's ripped hands and two shots of his shit-smeared cage, with Prisoner Zero cropped at the waist in the foreground. Over the man's naked shoulder could be seen sketches and what looked like one half of a mirror-image equation.

"Do any of them give us more?"

Comparing the best of Pier Angelo's originals with the shot used on the front of that day's *Washington Post* told President Newman what he already suspected. "Afraid not," he said. There was no difference. The picture desk had used the best shot and used the whole thing.

"You can't execute him," said Petra Mayer. "We need the rest of that equation."

President Newman sighed. "You think I don't know that?"

Inside every adult was a child, or so it is said. Professor Petra Mayer was different. Inside Petra Mayer was an impossibly beautiful, barefoot adolescent who wouldn't have been seen dead giving her inner child the time of day.

In fact, that child had been left so far behind it no longer even haunted the edges of the adult's unconscious, its banishment an act of will so extreme that even Petra Mayer's husband had no idea of the sorry foundling his wife had once been. All he remembered was the ghost of the adolescent who had still, but only just, been visible behind her eyes when they first met.

She'd been beautiful, with high cheekbones and dark hair that swept back in a wave and glowed against the setting sun like a devil's halo. That was the view of Alan Ginsberg anyway, who once spent five pages and a whole summer in Asbury lamenting the fact she wasn't a boy.

Petra Mayer's beauty was long gone and in its place was a faded elegance at odds with the compact body she now inhabited. Only in her dark eyes, high cheekbones and greying hair could be seen the echo of beauty which once trapped year after year of Harvard freshmen, a collection of fathers who should have known better and the occasional female student.

"Katie Petrov," said Katie, answering her cell phone.

She listened for a moment.

"Thank you. Please show her in."

Dr. Petrov had dressed quickly and gone over her notes, taking extra care. Although she always took care, Katie reminded herself. She just hadn't been expecting a flying visit from an ex-mentor with the ear of the President. And it was a flying visit because Katie had heard Petra Mayer's helicopter land outside.

"Katie?"

Having made herself finish a note on her pad, Katie looked up and found herself staring into a familiar face, albeit more lined and slightly older than she remembered.

"You're looking good," Petra Mayer said. "Which is more than you can say for me, so don't bother." The Professor was wearing a sand-coloured skirt and matching linen jacket, both badly crumpled. "I liked your paper."

"Paper?" Katie's voice sounded puzzled.

"Anorexia and pre-adolescence... Interesting take." It had been the last piece of research Katie submitted, a slight article that did little more than attempt to overturn some of the received wisdoms on who was responsible for pre-pubertal eating disorders. Her grandmother had refused to speak to her since.

"Thanks," said Katie.

Petra Mayer smiled. "If we could have a word...?"

Only then did the Professor's gaze take in the man who sat naked on Katie's floor, his fingers swathed in white gauze.

"Maybe outside?"

When both the marines outside Katie's office snapped to attention, Petra Mayer had the grace to look embarrassed. "For the purposes of this visit I'm a general," she explained. "I didn't realize the kid could do that."

It took Katie a second or two to realize that "the kid" was Gene Newman.

## CHAPTER 34

### *Northern Mountains, CTzu 53/Year 20*

"We're going to crash."

Tris nodded.

"Just so you know." The yacht spoke in simple sentences. Somewhere between untethering and plotting its run to the Emperor's palace on Rapture, the yacht had decided that Tris was a child. Since then, communication had been limited to easily understood phrases and short words.

"The decoy's gone?"

"Well," said the yacht. "If you mean has my spare fuel cell been dumped, then yes. That was the pretty flashes you saw burning up about five minutes ago."

There'd be a toggle somewhere for switching off the character overlay that came bundled with the ship's AI but finding it meant digging though several layers of software and Tris simply didn't have time.

She didn't even have time to admire her appearance in a strategically placed mirror, and there were a lot of strategically placed mirrors aboard *All Tomorrow's Parties*. Not to mention a clothing unit more complex than any she'd ever seen. So now Tris wore a freshly applied second skin of black latex, half hidden beneath an oversized black leather jacket which read "Empty" across the back in neon.

Tris was pretty sure the latex wasn't what she'd asked for, but it looked good in a flashy rich-kid kind of way and it would do until she found a way to originate something more practical.

"How long to landing?"

"Crashing," corrected the computer. "How long until crashing."

"But we might touch down safely. You said so."

"You're going to touch down safely," said the computer. "I'm going to crash."

Tris looked at the curved wall in front of her, which showed exactly what she would have seen if the hull were made of glass, except then she'd have burnt up or got irradiated or something.

She'd asked the yacht about this earlier but the thing had been very cagey about side effects. After listening to the yacht prevaricate for a while, Tris realized it simply didn't want to frighten her.

"Define crash," Tris demanded.

"One: *verb transitive*. To smash violently or noisily. To damage on landing. To enter without paying. To suffer unpleasant side effects following drug use.

"Two: *noun*. A loud noise. A breaking into pieces—"

"No," said Tris. "What does crash mean to you?"

Outside, heat radiated from the hull as *All Tomorrow's Parties* plunged through Rapture's lower atmosphere like a clumsily thrown stone. The landing gear was already burned out, largely because Tris had insisted on it being lowered early. So now they had to find a way to make a soft landing.

The yacht seemed to hesitate before answering, although it was probably just putting its thoughts into a form simple enough for Tris to understand. (It had a very low opinion of her intelligence, something Tris put down to her refusal to listen when it suggested that double-crossing Doc Joyce was a bad idea.)

"Come on," insisted Tris. "Tell me. What does crashing mean *to you*?"

"Not being able to take off again."

"So why can't you take off?"

"Because," said the AI, sounding genuinely cross, "even if I had landing gear, you've just dumped my return Casimir coil. Remember?"

Tris did. It made a really good display.

The yacht could read facial expressions, both complex and simple. For example, it could differentiate between disapproving and puzzled, Tris having been disapproving of the luxury she found aboard *All Tomorrow's Parties* and puzzled as to why anyone would fit out the inside of a racing yacht in chrome, fish tanks and black leather.

Apparently its owner was anally retentive. And a request for an expanded definition led her into areas Tris really didn't want to go.

"What are you?" she asked the ship.

"A C-class Niponshi yacht, registered to XGen Enterprises. Licensed to race anywhere within the 2023 worlds."

"No," said Tris. "What are *you*?"

"A C-class Niponshi yacht, registered to—"

"That's not what I asked," Tris said. "What are *you*?"

"Me?"

"That's what I said." She jacked the slide on a weapon Doc Joyce had lent her and pointed it at the control panel. They both knew she wouldn't fire. It was one thing to threaten to fry the yacht's circuits when it was tethered off the Chinese Rocks and quite another to shoot it up from inside while it was falling towards one of the 2023 worlds. Tris wasn't running some passive-aggressive adolescent suicide routine, the ship had already established this.

"You mean what form does my core take? My thinking bit," the yacht added, in case Tris found the technical term too difficult. "That's what you mean, isn't it?"

"Yes," said Tris, through gritted teeth. "That's exactly what I mean."

"I'm crystal," said the computer. "Some Class Cs still use biocores but mostly we've upgraded. Somehow even the highest quality organic matter always seems to degrade in the end. Crystal is—"

"I know about crystal," Tris said flatly. "I used to deal it when I was a kid."

"That's—"

"Technically illegal," agreed Tris. "Quite probably. But not where I come from."

"And where do you come from?"

Tris opened her mouth to answer and then shut it again. For all she knew this conversation was being recorded so the yacht could make a formal complaint after this was all over.

"You wouldn't," said Tris. "Would you?"

"Wouldn't what?" asked the ship.

"Make a complaint about being stolen."

"Oh," the ship said bitterly, "I'm not allowed—" And then it stopped, hurriedly swallowing the rest of its sentence.

"You're only semi," said Tris, suddenly understanding everything. "Not full at all."

"I might as well be," the yacht said, "given what I'm expected to do. There are fullAIs out there who can't do half—"

"So why are you still registered as semiAI?"

"Because he races," said the yacht. "And if I was fullAI then he couldn't enter for rough-class races, could he? And that's where the glory lies."

Tris couldn't see what glory there could be in hacking between worlds when everyone rich enough to race was more than rich enough to have themselves backed up before they started. Although "rich" was a negotiable term when it came to the 2023 worlds.

Every inhabitant was entitled to what they needed. It was just that a few always seemed to need more than others and so acquiring extra became a matter of convincing the Library that one really did need whatever it was one needed. The Library's decisions, however, were often counter-intuitive and according to Doc Joyce this crankiness was intentional, being designed to give people something to circumnavigate.

Sand in the oyster, he called it. Translated, this meant too much of everything created its own problems. So everyone got more than enough and then had to decide if this was too little. It sounded incredibly stupid to Tris but then Razor's Edge wasn't one of the 2023 worlds.

"Okay," said Tris, looking at a chrome and glass table in front of her, its top rather thicker than it needed to be. "This is how it's going to work." She ran her hand along one of the edges, looking for some catch that might release the panel, and realized she was showing her ignorance.

"Open," she told the glass and it did just that, raising like the lid of a box.

The table had fooled her at first, when she was busy persuading

*All Tomorrow's Parties* that yes, it really did want to let her steal it. The top wasn't transparent at all, merely laminated with chameleon glass that reflected whatever it saw on the opposite side.

"You know, Tristesse," said the yacht, "I don't think this is a good idea."

The girl's shrug barely registered inside the leather jacket she'd found in a crew pod, its pockets stuffed with narcotics guaranteed to leave you looking happy and healthy, which seemed pretty skewed to Tris. If you took something that fucked your brain and then refused to walk you home afterwards, you wanted to look like you just took something that...

And if this item of clothing really had been grown to fit then Tris definitely didn't want to meet whoever owed Doc Joyce whatever it was they owed Doc Joyce. Come to that, Tris didn't much want to meet Doc Joyce again either.

"Everything's the wrong size," she told the yacht, and Tris was right. The overhead lockers were out of reach and the sloping chrome and leather chair next to the control table could have been a double bed. Even the tank of fish at her back stretched to twice Tris's height and contained three purple catfish at least as big as she was, with eyes which followed her every move.

She was beginning to realize that there might be another reason why the yacht kept treating her as a child.

"So what's going to happen to them?" Tris asked, nodding towards the wall of fish tanks. "I mean when we crash."

If the yacht could have shrugged it would have done so. Tris could tell from the lag it left between her question and its answer.

"They'll die," it said.

"Land in a lake."

"What?"

"Find a lake," Tris said. "Then land in it. Which bit of that don't you understand?"

"If I land in a lake," said the yacht, "then *I'm* going to die."

"You're not alive. You told me so yourself. A C-class semi. Do semiAIs qualify as sentient? I don't think so." She stuck her head further inside the newly opened table and followed what looked like a rainbow twisting together towards a blue light.

"What happens if I touch this?"

"We crash a little earlier than intended," said the yacht icily. And then it said nothing for a very long time until:

"Lake," said the ship.

Rocky cliffs rising on both sides and barren peaks, now higher than the ship, shrouded in mist and fringed with ice. Under them hung a fat nebula of cloud, mountainous with snow.

"Where?"

"Beneath that."

A strip of silver opened up and came closer as the yacht adjusted its vision to encompass sleet hammering into the water's surface and flattened waves sucking sullenly at a bank of fallen rock.

"Looks like a river to me." She'd never seen a river, of course. Come to that, she'd never seen a lake. The nearest RipJointShuts had to either was a storm drain that cut through the level like some ancient moat, too wide to jump and, according to Doc Joyce, so deep that no one had touched the bottom and come back to boast about it. But it was still a drain.

"River, lake . . . it's all soft," said the yacht.

"Well," said Tris as she traced the rainbow towards its end and found herself staring at a small sphere about the size of a marble. "That's probably true enough. Put us down when you can."

The yacht was silent.

"What?" demanded Tris.

"I should have arrested you," said the yacht.

"You can't," Tris said. "You haven't got the rights." She knew all about not having the rights. Doc Joyce lacked the rights to get relocated to a better level on Heliconid, which lacked the rights to be included as one of the 2023 worlds. By declaring Heliconid unfit for habitation the first Council of Ambassadors had guaranteed that those inhabiting it were assumed to have chosen their own wretched way of life.

"Put us down," Tris ordered.

"There is no us," said the yacht, but it dipped through the cloud all the same and settled into a holding pattern. If Tris hadn't known better she'd have sworn that its semiAI was plucking up courage. The first run took the yacht low over a wide strip of water and then the yacht went into a Möbius roll to skim the side of gorge, ending up exactly where it had started, staring down at the silver strip.

"You're good," Tris said, not really thinking about what she was saying.

"Of course I'm good," said the yacht. "Have you any idea how much I cost?" It turned out to be several thousand hours more than Tris could even imagine. A handful of her possessions could be counted in minutes but most, like her knife and the clothes she usually wore, were worth little more than a few seconds.

"What's that in days?" Tris demanded. So the yacht told her and that didn't make Tris feel any better either.

"Going in," said the yacht.

It skimmed low over the water and touched once or twice, letting the counter current towards the middle break its speed. Only, in the time this took, Tris got her head and shoulders right inside the table and found the lock protecting the yacht's memory.

"Okay," the yacht said, "entrance/exit to open. When I say 'get out' then g—"

Tris yanked.

And in the silence which followed she realized her heart had stopped. All Tris could feel was a band of ice beneath her breasts that threatened to prevent her from ever being able to breathe again. A power surge shocking her limbs into absurdly rigid positions, which was probably just as well, otherwise she'd have been dancing puppet-like with panic.

Freeing one arm, Tris hit herself hard in the chest and felt her heart start again. Removing the yacht's memory had been a good idea, getting herself electrocuted in the process . . .

"Shit," said Tris. She waited for the yacht to say something in return and then realized how absurd that was, given that she gripped its consciousness in her fingers like her life depended on it.

"Okay," said Tris. "So you're on your own. You should be used to it."

Shattering the fish tank by blasting off one corner using Doc Joyce's handgun, Tris watched as one after another of the catfish flooded out of the glass wall and into the water now lapping around her knees. And one after another the catfish stopped swimming, became rigid, convulsed and died.

She'd got it wrong again. She should have tried a side wall first. Something stocked with smaller fish. Frantically Tris tried to scoop up the last of the big beasts but there was nowhere to put it and the fish slipped out of her hands before she had time to work out what to do next, going rigid even as she was reaching for it.

Salt water had mixed with the fresh and cold with the warm. There were no catfish left to help. So when Tris realized that the exit had jammed less than halfway open and the gap was too narrow to let her fight through the incoming water, she almost didn't bother to save herself.

All the same, bulkhead lights still shone with an amber glow that endless members of a Chinese crew had once come to associate with being ripped open and left to drift towards the tectonic plates of a distant darkness. And that glow also meant the yacht's emergency systems might still be operable.

Rejecting the idea of trying to squeeze through anyway, Tris did something far more sensible; she jammed the blue marble back into position inside the table, flinching in anticipation of an electric shock that didn't happen.

"...'get out'," finished the yacht, then it swore. "No," it said, "forget it. We can deal with you being an idiot later." The sliding door, which had begun to open, hesitated and then hissed back on itself, locking tight. Lights came up and the table Tris had left open ran a series of rapid lights, ending in the squawk of a klaxon that shut off as soon as it began.

"Okay," said the yacht. "This is the way it's going to work. I'm going to open that entrance/exit completely this time. And you're going to do nothing until I tell you. *What are we going to do?*"

Beyond the hull a rock ground itself along the side of the yacht and as the cabin lurched water slopped across the floor in a low wave.

"You're going to open the door," Tris said through gritted teeth, "and I'm going to do nothing."

"Good," said the yacht. "Now once the door is open, you reach inside the table and take the memory. Only this time I'll shut down first. Understand? You don't touch anything until the pretty lights disappear. Otherwise you'll get hurt."

"I'm not a child," said Tris crossly.

The yacht considered this for all of half a second. "Yes, you are." Its voice was matter-of-fact. "At least, you are according to any definition I've got on file. Now you wait," it stressed, "until the entrance/exit is completely open, then you get out fast and let yourself drift downriver, don't try to swim for the bank."

"Why not?" Tris asked, but the door was opening and the lights had dimmed. An inrush of water was her only answer. Grabbing the memory, Tris began wading towards the door only to discover that every forward step she took swept her three steps back again. "Think," she told herself.

Tristesse al-Heliconid was in her mid to late teens, small for her age and less grown-up than she imagined. She wore her hair cropped short and her breasts small, her hips were naturally narrow. On some worlds girls of her age already had children and on others they'd barely begun their education.

She was unmarried and no one, absolutely no one, had ever tried to make her learn anything; but she had a brain, guts, synthetic sinews and her own reason for being there.

In the end, Tris decided her only hope was to wait until the river stopped rushing in and the water level inside and outside equalized, so that was what she did. And maybe she should have used those long seconds to look for useful tools or find a dagger, but something else had occurred to her.

Digging around inside the table, Tris identified where the marble had been and felt with her fingers, shrinking back when something wet and bristling brushed against her skin.

"Oh, fuck it." Grabbing the marble from her pocket, Tris gave the thing to the tendrils, feeling them suck the marble from her grip. The AI wasn't nearly as non-bio as it claimed.

"Well, am I glad to be—" Whatever *All Tomorrow's Parties* had been about to say stuttered to a halt. Lights came on all across the cabin and half of them promptly blew, mostly the half which happened to be underwater.

"Good," Tris said, "you're—"

"Fucked," said the yacht. "Unless you unplug me now."

"I need you to work." Tris tried to sound commanding, only her voice came out small and rather uncertain. "I can't do this on my own."

"You should have thought about that," said the yacht, "before you stole me."

"But once I stole you," Tris said, "I wasn't on my own, was I? Because then I was with you." She thought about it. "Anyway," she said, "don't semiAIs have rules about having to protect the sentient?"

"That's household appliances," said the yacht, "and it's 'not harm' rather than protect. There's a difference."

The water was up to Tris's hips now, pulling at the bottom of her stolen leather jacket. She could feel the cold eating at her legs and dissolving all feeling below her waist. And the yacht was beginning to lean. Last time Tris had checked the cabin was level, ripped by currents and still filling with water but definitely level.

Now it slanted, with one side wall almost underwater and the other, the one with the door, almost clear. Only waves kept spilling in over the sill as the yacht began to settle.

"I'm going to die," said Tris. Mostly she was trying the idea for size, wondering if it was one she could accept.

"So?" said the yacht. "You should have played it differently. Besides, I'm the one who's really going to die. You're just going to revert to a previous back-up. What will you have lost, twenty-four hours? Forty-eight, if you're really careless."

"You don't get it," said Tris. "I don't have back-up." She thought it through, facing the conclusion. "When I die," she said, "I die."

She could almost hear the yacht's surprise. Well, the surprise of its AI, which was actually a blue marble matched to an axion-rich anemone. It wasn't quite sound and it wasn't really silence, more like a stumble in her head.

"You die if you get wet?" she asked the marble.

Her question amused it and the answer was no. It died if it got left behind, removed from a source of power and never found again. "Worry about yourself," suggested the yacht. "Why did you wake me?"

"I wanted to know where I am," she said.

"Where you wanted to be," the yacht said. "You're on Rapture."

"I know that," said Tris. "Where on Rapture?"

"In a river."

Tris sighed. "I'm going to take you out again," she said, "so you probably need to turn off the rainbow."

"Rainbow?"

"Those colours," said Tris. "The ones wrapped around you."

"You can see them?"

"Of course I can," Tris said. "If I couldn't see them I couldn't tell you they were there, could I?"

"Such a child," said the AI. "So empirical."

"Whatever. You want to tell me which river?"

"This one," said the yacht, and before Tris could kick the table, a ghost landscape hung in the air before her. It was topologically accurate, impressive and detailed in the extreme but it was skew to the lapping water and not at all what Tris wanted.

"Just tell me."

"Here," said the AI. "You're here." A tiny blue thread on the face of the ghost world lit red. At the same time, the world tilted slightly until it was out of true with the wall of the cabin but level over the water.

"And the Forbidden City?"

A different sector lit gold, and even without knowing the scale Tris could see that they were a long way apart.

"I'm taking you out now," said Tris, reaching for the memory. "And I'll carry you with me."

The AI was about to say something but Tris yanked first and the rainbow shut down, tendrils brushing her fingers as they released the marble. All Tris felt was the briefest jolt of electricity and then she was alone again.

# CHAPTER 35

## *Marrakech, Summer 1977*

"Come here."

Moz almost asked, *Why?* But acting the fool around Major Abbas was not clever so instead he smiled, nodded to Hassan and sauntered towards the *grande taxi* that had drawn up on the other side of the railings.

A rolling, I'm-not-worried kind of walk.

It fooled neither of them.

"Excellency?"

The police officer didn't return his smile and when Moz saw the Frenchman in the back of the taxi he understood why.

"I need some information," said Major Abbas.

Moz nodded. "As Your Excellency wishes."

"Don't question him here," said the Frenchman. "Get him inside." Claude de Greuze's voice was brusque, slightly impatient until he glanced at Moz and then it went hard and cold. "Tell him to take a good look," he told the Major, indicating La Koutoubia and the overgrown gardens where Hassan and Moz had agreed to meet. "This is probably the last he'll see of it or his friends."

Without meaning to, Moz glanced across to where Hassan and Idries leant against a concrete bench in the shade of a palm, one broken frond hanging limp and pale like a lock of badly bleached hair. At their back were the ragged remains of an earlier mosque, which had been destroyed when an imam discovered the prayer hall was not truly aligned with Mecca.

Or so Moz had always believed. Only Celia's *Michelin Guide to Morocco* told a different story. It said the original mosque had been built by one ruling family and its replacement by another. The imam had merely said what expediency required.

"Is he listening?"

The answer was obvious.

Pushing open the passenger door, Major Abbas patted the seat beside him. "Get in," he said. The Major wore a cheap suit with the cap of a taxi driver and looked more uncomfortable in this than Moz had ever seen him look in full uniform.

Moz did what he was told.

They drove in silence, turning north onto Mohammed V. And though the sun hammered down onto the taxi's blue roof, Major Abbas kept the windows stubbornly shut, as if ignoring the rank corruption coming from the old man's body counted as some kind of courage.

"Where are we going?"

Moz meant his question for the Major but it was Claude de Greuze who answered and his answer was that the little Arab shit should shut the fuck up because he was in more trouble than anyone could imagine. Something Moz had begun to work out for himself.

"Turn here," demanded Claude de Greuze and Major Abbas glanced with surprise at the driver's mirror.

"Where did you think we were taking him?"

Their destination was a large if nondescript colonial villa on the corner of Rue Bernard and Avenue Foche. Stucco crumbled from underlying red brick and one of the pantiles lay broken between dead roses on a flowerbed that had dried to the consistency of rock. A peeling board read ECOLE PRIVÉE.

The only new thing about the old school was a rusting steel door that looked out of place between fat white pillars. If Moz hadn't known better he'd have said the place was deserted.

"Tell him to get out," said Claude de Greuze.

"Do what he says," Major Abbas ordered, leaning over Moz to push open the side door. "Don't keep the man waiting."

There were a dozen things about that moment which Moz was to remember in the months and years to come. And though sometimes he managed to forget the school altogether, he would never again hear gears grinding at an intersection without his footsteps faltering and his soul shrivelling a little inside.

Roses would bring him out in tears. The sound of any small child being dragged along the pavement by a scolding adult knotted his stomach until it hurt. Sun on his shoulders and the raw tang of fresh dog shit, the afternoon cry of the muezzin, all worked their way inside his memory like splinters of glass. But what Moz really remembered was warm piss running down his leg when he was hit.

The covering of his face with his hands was entirely instinctive, as was curling into a tight ball, and it probably helped that he'd been facing away when the old Frenchman slammed a cosh into his skull.

"Pick him up," said Claude de Greuze and Major Abbas lifted Moz from behind.

"Now turn him round." The spring-loaded cosh slapped between the boy's legs, hard and fast. "Come on." The Frenchman's voice was impatient. "Get him up again."

"Stand," said the Major, sounding almost sad.

Moz tried. He really did.

Glitter off gravel, so many lights that Moz forgot what he was meant to be doing. A foot caught him between his buttocks and its owner started demanding answers about Malika, only it was hard to hear what the Frenchman was saying over the sound of Moz's own gasping and the numbing waves of darkness.

"We should get him inside."

"Why?"

"Because," said the Major, "someone might see."

Claude de Greuze nodded scornfully at the colonial villas on either side. One had either been turned into flats or was divided between generations of the same family, sheets drying from wires strung across three huge balconies. The other had boarded-up windows and looked abandoned.

"What are they going to do?" demanded de Greuze. "Call the police?"

"All the same," Major Abbas said. "There's no point creating trouble." Wiping blood from Moz's jaw, he lifted the boy from where he lay curled on the gravel and carried him up three steps and in through the metal door.

It was dark inside the school, with shuttered windows. A single unlit bulb hung from a small ceiling rose in the middle of the hall and the floor was covered with dark linoleum. There were five doors and all were closed.

"Okay," said Major Abbas. "Now you must stand." He tipped

Moz onto his feet and steadied his shoulders for a few seconds. When he let go the boy swayed but remained upright, staring mutely around him.

Sounds came from behind most doors.

"Take him to three."

"No." Major Abbas shook his head. "Not yet. It's not necessary."

Claude de Greuze just looked at him.

"It . . . is . . . not . . . necessary," the Major said, stressing every syllable. For the first time, Moz heard quiet anger in his voice.

"Do you want to tell me why? Or should I call the General?"

Moz had no idea who the General might be but that didn't matter. There was always a general or a pasha, someone who made decisions.

"Call him," said Major Abbas. "Tell him you want to *question* one of my best informers. Someone I've spent five years developing." There was heavy emphasis on the word "question" and the Major's voice sounded more furious than ever.

"Is that true?" It was the first time the one-time advisor to the Pasha had spoken directly to the boy. "Well?"

Moz shrugged.

He'd told Major Abbas some stuff, repeated a few rumours and occasionally followed some foreigner to see where he went. That was it really, not what Moz thought of as being an informer. Informers were sinister figures. Shadows of the men Malika talked about, the Pasha's eyes and ears back in the days when Thami el Glaoui ruled the Red City.

"You don't know?" The Frenchman sounded incredulous.

"He knows nothing," said Major Abbas. "I've told you that already. Are you going to make that call or not?"

Moz was surprised that the Major kept pushing de Greuze but something had changed between the two men, and it wasn't that Major Abbas felt more at home in this strange place because he looked almost as uncomfortable as Moz felt.

It was something else. A challenge of some sort.

The two men stared at each other, both ignoring the boy who stood sticky with blood that showed only as glossy camouflage against the red lettering and black cotton background of his Ramones T-shirt.

"Okay," de Greuze said finally. "We'll do it your way."

"Yeah," said Major Abbas. "We will. Give me an hour."

## CHAPTER 36

### *Lampedusa, Saturday 7 July*

The file Petra Mayer put down in front of Katie Petrov was tattered along the edges and had a coffee stain prominently over one corner, but what Katie really noticed was the slew of Arabic running right to left across the top and the French translation underneath.

"You need to see this."

In case Katie couldn't read the French someone had thoughtfully provided a translation and paper-clipped it to the top of the file.

MARRAKECH POLICE—HOMICIDE DIVISION.

They'd also provided a translation for every one of the pages inside, although Katie Petrov didn't need a translation to recognize most of the names. Marzaq al-Turq, Jake Razor, Malika bint Kasim...

The shot of Jake showed a man in his early twenties snarling at the photographer. Something about its studied defiance suggested the three-by-four originated with his record company. Moz's shot was very different, a diminished imitation that had the boy staring into the lens of a police camera, one of his lips badly swollen and a long gash taped shut in his hairline.

It was the third photograph that made Katie Petrov jerk forward and wrap her arms around her stomach.

"Fuck."

She fought briefly against the bile that rose in her throat and then gave up the fight, running from her office.

Professor Mayer smoked a cigarette while waiting for the younger woman to return and then smoked another. And when she finally reached for the photograph of Malika it was to turn it face down on Dr. Petrov's desk.

"This is for you," she said after Katie reappeared in the doorway, wiping the back of her mouth with one hand. "You may want to read it now."

The letter was short and polite. It thanked Katie Petrov for agreeing to be a court-appointed psychiatrist, assured her that her fee would be paid in full and told her that her services were no longer required. It was signed by the White House official who had appointed her in the first place.

"What did I do wrong?"

"Nothing," Petra Mayer assured her. "You did everything exactly as it was meant to be done. Your notes are a model of professionalism."

"But I haven't even submitted my report."

"They know that." Professor Mayer shook another cigarette from its packet, sat back in her chair and smiled. It was a particularly grim smile. The kind that glared from the back of her more recent books and suggested she knew her readers wouldn't understand the contents but they should damn well try. "What would it have said?"

"I'm not sure I can tell you," Katie Petrov said.

The Professor shook her head. "Don't sulk," she warned, "it doesn't suit you."

"I'm not," said Katie Petrov, obviously feeling about twelve. "I'm just not sure."

They were both in part engaged in displacement activity. Professor Mayer knew this and she imagined that Katie knew it as well. Neither one of them had so much as glanced at the down-turned photograph since Katie walked back into the hot little room she'd been given as an office.

"Give me your thoughts," Petra Mayer suggested.

"This is unattributable?"

The Professor smiled. "How old are you?"

"Twenty-seven."

"So young," said Professor Mayer, "and they've already got you speaking the language. Yes," she said, "this is unattributable. So tell me exactly what you think."

She watched Katie Petrov run through the main points in her head, and when Katie seemed sure she had them in the right order and wasn't about to make a fool of herself, Professor Mayer listened to Katie count them off aloud, waiting for interruptions that never came.

"So you think he's sane?"

"Speaking clinically? Not a chance. At least not in any sense I understand. As the Pentagon's man pointed out, the autistic silences, the self-cutting, the obsessive nakedness and coprophilia can all be faked, but I still think he's the real thing."

"And legally?"

"More tricky," said Katie. "Did Prisoner Zero know the nature and quality of his actions? Difficult to say. And I have to be certain he was incapable of knowing the difference between right and wrong. Not as he is now or was when that journalist met him in Paris, but in Marrakech, that afternoon, when he loaded the gun, pointed it at the President and pulled the trigger."

"Tough call."

Katie Petrov leant back, nodded. "Near impossible," she said, "why else do you think it's taken me so long not to reach a conclusion?"

Petra Mayer smiled. "Off the record," she said, "which way were you leaning?"

"Legally, I think he was sane," said Katie Petrov. "Strictly off the record."

"Yeah, that's what I thought..." The older woman flipped open her packet of cigarettes, extracted the last and lit it with the stub of the one that had gone before. She had jet lag to make the vanished irritations of PMS feel like a minor cold and was in a space where she was surviving on will power and nicotine alone. The first mouthful of food or sip of alcohol would slam her into oblivion.

Petra Mayer knew her body. It was one of the things most men found frightening about her. "Are you okay to go through the rest of the file?"

"I'm off the case," Katie said, "why would I want to do that?" It was a real question.

"Because I want to hire you," said Professor Mayer. "To work with me on what comes next."

"And what does?"

Petra Mayer shrugged. "Good question," she said. "Read the file and we'll begin to work it out."

On 15 August 1977 Marzaq al-Turq, known also as Moz, was charged with the rape and murder of a girl whose age was put as between thirteen and sixteen, with a coroner's side note in French that a history of malnutrition would have put her age in the latter bracket. There was no mention in the brief and almost insultingly dismissive report that anorexia would have achieved the same, this not being a problem commonly facing the poor of Marrakech in the late 1970s.

The girl was described as half and half, with neither half being specified. She was not pregnant at the time of her death and her heart, lungs, liver and kidneys were in excellent condition. Her last meal had been vegetables, bread and water. There were no traces of alcohol, hashish or any other drug in her blood.

A long list of injuries matched those in the photograph; that is, all those injuries which could be seen in the original photograph were listed, although there were many more on the list which were not visible.

"Why only one crime scene?"

"I'm sorry?" Professor Mayer glanced up.

"Only one crime-scene shot," said Katie Petrov. "Where are the others?"

The Professor smiled sadly. "This was Marrakech, 1977. The miracle is that there are any at all." She thought about that, dragging on the last of her cigarette before stubbing it out in a saucer now filled to overflowing with splayed and twisted filters that looked like nothing so much as extracted bullets.

"In fact," said Professor Mayer, "the real question is why did somebody bother to take this photograph at all?"

"And you know the answer..." It was not quite a question.

"Read the file," Professor Mayer said, sitting back.

A sworn statement from an officer in the Marrakchi police stated that Marzaq al-Turq was the only suspect for the murder of Malika, daughter of Corporal Sidi ould Kasim, sometime informant and agent provocateur. The suspect lived in ould Kasim's house, in a room directly above the girl's, and a search of that room had revealed that a hole in the floor allowed the occupant to spy on the room below.

A trawl of the Mellah by the police had revealed no clue to the suspect's current whereabouts and extensive questioning of his known associates had produced so little information about the suspect's recent activities that this was suspicious in itself. Katie Petrov read this twice, to make sure she understood what was being said.

On the basis of the statement a warrant for the boy's arrest on sight had been issued by the Marrakchi police and then allowed to gather dust. Both the arrest warrant and the sworn statement were signed by a Major Abbas.

"What do you think?"

"The interest is in the gaps," said Katie Petrov. "If I got sent this back home I'd have returned it and demanded sight of the real thing. And I'd refuse to start work until the real thing arrived."

Professor Mayer nodded. "That's what I've done," she said. "Although I'm not sure how much we'll get."

Flicking through the three photographs, Katie forced herself to glance again at the final one. There existed crime-scene shots of Texas lynchings that showed less tissue damage.

"Check the file again," suggested Petra Mayer.

Three photographs, an arrest warrant, a sworn statement, a tatty strip of fingerprints lifted from a pocket knife found at the crime scene, a crudely drawn map of the wasteland marking where the girl's body was found and a report from the coroner.

"What am I missing?" Katie Petrov asked.

"These," Professor Mayer said, tossing across a cromalin of a second set of fingerprints, each one neatly positioned in a different-coloured box. The cromalin was new and still smelt of chemicals. The fingerprints came from the police HQ in Amsterdam and the name scrawled at the top of the original sheet was Jake Razor.

"Don't tell me..."

Katie held up the strip of fingerprints lifted from the crime scene in Marrakech and compared them to prints on the page in front of her. She didn't really need to be told what she would find. The American minimum for matching points was ten, the European standard was set at sixteen.

To Katie's gaze it looked like the match between Prisoner Zero's prints, those taken from the Marrakchi knife and the prints for Jake Razor from the Amsterdam drug clinic had at least eighteen points of similarity, maybe more.

"Still think he's sane?" Professor Mayer asked.

## CHAPTER 37

### *Northern Mountains, CTzu 53/Year 20*

The jets came in low over the water, three in all. Each one as flat as a manta ray and utterly silent, their uncloaking timed for when the already sinking yacht reached midway along the gorge.

So far as Tris could tell all three were completely transparent, as if made from glass or carved from ice, and they materialized just as the shell of *All Tomorrow's Parties* finally tipped on its side, expelling Tris from her doorway in a massive fart of bubbles and river water.

Sweeping low, the jets banked hard and came back on themselves, targeting the river where the yacht had been. And suddenly there was no water and no river and no yacht, just emptiness, which filled as the river roared back in.

Either the jets really didn't see Tris or they didn't care. Or else, Tris told herself, as the current carried her rapidly downstream towards some rocks, they simply weren't looking for a girl with a blue marble in her mouth and pockets full of water.

The jacket was a classic, expensive probably, with an inner lining that clung to her body no matter how oversized the garment looked on the outside and a waist buckle that was busy trying to do itself up. Unfortunately the wrists were still significantly too big for her and the pockets seemed to be expanding to make space for more water.

Tris reached for the buckle.

Once she'd extracted the marble from her mouth and finished coughing up river, she had another go. Only this time, Tris took a hurried breath before dunking herself and tugged hard at the buckle. When the buckle refused to budge, Tris tried pulling the jacket over her head, which would have worked if only the lining didn't keep shaping itself around her to provide warmth. She was being killed by the thing's blind and stupid kindness.

"Shit...

"Prick...

"Pudenda..."

The one advantage, probably the only advantage, to being alone in the middle of nowhere was that her grandmother wasn't around to slap her if she swore. Which was just as well, as Tris was rapidly reaching levels of vocabulary even Doc Joyce didn't know she possessed.

"Fuck this," Tris said. And she yanked at the buckle so hard it made her knuckles almost pop with the effort.

"About time."

Quite how Tris made it over the rocks unscathed she didn't know until later, when she rolled herself onto a gravel bank under the gaze of broken grey cliffs and realized she hadn't made it through unscathed at all. One shoulder was a mess of bruises and her left heel had been sliced near the arch, cut open by a stone. Bleached skin gaped on both sides of the cut.

Staring too hard at the wound made Tris feel sick so she stopped looking, pulled herself completely out of the water and sat with her back to the cliff. It was time to work out where she was and relate that to where she should be, which was infiltrating the Forbidden City with the express purpose of killing the Chuang Tzu.

The gravel where Tris sat was built up on the quiet side of the river, while on the other bubbling foam scoured against a rock wall. This was the way it worked, Tris realized, looking upriver towards a different bend and at another bend beyond that, tracking the course she'd taken. The river roared into the bends and threw up gravel on the quiet side, reversing sides when the gorge curved a different way.

Her own bank began fifty paces behind her as a narrow strip of shingle bellied out into the river and then narrowed again to nothing a hundred paces ahead. Walking to safety along the edge of the river was definitely out.

And that was a problem, because the rock-face behind Tris's back was sheer beyond climbing, even for Tris, and both sides of the gorge seemed to rise endlessly through the charcoal of cliffs to a belt of green before fading into a pale grey that rose like a watercolour wash above the tree line.

She was going to have to go back into the water, but first... Digging a thumbnail into the latex over her hip, Tris tried to rip the top half free from the bottom of her jump suit without messing everything up too much. All that happened was that the material tore and she ended up with an over-long top and a ridiculously low-slung pair of trousers.

Having done what she needed, Tris washed her hands in the river and yanked up her trousers, tying torn strips of latex together at both sides.

It was time to get wet again.

Tris wasn't sure when she first noticed the light in the sky. It might have been on her second night or the third. Whichever night it was, she'd got hungry enough not to care too much about anything but finding food. At the time Tris was trudging along a strip of shingle and expecting it to end in a return to the cold water. And at the point she realized the gravel was there for good, she was several klicks from where she'd last scrambled ashore and her cut foot was warm enough to hurt; although it would mend soon, her wounds always did.

Warmth and food, these weren't exactly thoughts, more the

things that went through Tris's head as she climbed a shingle bank and found herself stumbling towards the light across rough grass.

When it moved, Tris froze.

The weapon Doc Joyce had given her was either at the bottom of the river or else broken into its constituent atoms, which seemed more likely. And the knife she usually carried was where she'd left it, on the side in Doc Joyce's surgery. He'd assured her that the blade would wake every alarm system on Chinese Rocks and he was undoubtedly right. All the same she missed its weight on her belt.

To go forward or to go back?

Tris was still debating this question when the light ambled towards her and the answer became irrelevant. Compared to transparent jets, high-sided gorges and hunger so sharp it hurt, a knee-high stag with luminous antlers counted for less than zero.

Tiny fluorescent bonsai topped its lowered head and one front hoof pawed angrily at the damp grass in open threat, but Tris found it hard to take seriously a stag no higher than her hips, antlers included. Besides, she already knew about the *petit juc*; they appeared regularly enough in those sickly little feeds about the Emperor.

"Shoo," said Tris.

When the stag refused to move Tris decided to walk round it, which was how she found herself at the brow of a hill, staring towards a second, far brighter light.

"Now what?"

Rapture was known to be empty except for the three overlapping, interlinked areas of the city itself. No one lived in the walled palace except Chuang Tzu, his eunuchs, guards and servitors. A child of five knew that. The two outer cities looked from the air exactly like a single cell dividing down the middle, assuming both halves of a cell could be square and one half could contain the families of the servitors, the soldiers' camp followers and the shopkeepers, tradespeople and artisans needed to feed and clothe the inhabitants of the other, which housed the 2022 ambassadors to the Celestial Throne.

Maybe guards had been sent out to see if anyone had survived the crash, except it wasn't really a crash, more a bad landing, and those jets had obliterated the physical carcass of *All Tomorrow's Parties* along with the very water in which it sunk.

Tris hated not knowing what was going on. In fact, Tris hated it so much that most of the time she refused to admit to herself this was even a possibility. There were good reasons for that, reasons she studiously avoided, because if you didn't avoid them then the reasons had won.

"Fuck it," said Tris. Here she was, almost hallucinating with hunger, having been threatened by some midget stag with lights for antlers and still days away from where she needed to be, and already she was too scared to investigate what would probably turn out to be marsh gas or something equally stupid.

One of the first laws of exploring new worlds proved to be that it is a lot easier to walk uphill in the dark than it is to go down. Tris discovered this at the point her heel skidded on wet moss and she lost her balance, landing with a splash at the bottom of an absurdly short slope.

The light looked no closer but the grass was firm underfoot and the ground rose gently, so Tris set one shaky foot in front of the other and tuned her brain to a place where she'd crashed *All Tomorrow's Parties* slap bang in the middle of the imperial pavilions and mowed down the charging bannermen with a laser pistol she discovered at the very last minute, right next to the exit hatch.

Tris had once held a laser pistol.

It was very small and incredibly old. A collector's item, the owner said. He'd arrived one morning carrying a talking doll for her, a necklace of ever-changing stones for her mother and a knife for her father, even though everyone knew he was long gone and never coming back. Tris had hidden the knife when the grown-ups were talking and neither the man nor her mother ever asked where it went.

In the months to come Tris got a silver book and a bracelet which could answer questions on any subject beginning with a letter between "F" and "L." And for a while her mother was happy and their shack contained more food than Tris could ever remember seeing.

Sweet, sour and sometimes both, there were tastes and consistencies that worked perfectly while seeming to contradict each other. Cayenne ice cream, battered snails.

Endless food. New clothes.

It ended one morning when Tris trotted through to the kitchen to get some grapes and found instead the man standing at their small table, wrapping bread in the kind of foil that heated itself on demand. You just said the words and left it for thirty seconds. All explorers used it, he said. At least all explorers like him.

"You're going home . . ." Tris said.

Opalescent eyes looked at her, almost puzzled.

"How old are you?"

"Five."

"And how do you know I'm going?"

"Because I do," said Tris. She was still called Tristesse then. A name he'd casually attached to the sad-eyed brat after the first few days of living with her mother.

"Why don't you take me with you?" Tristesse suggested.

The man smiled. "You know what? I'm going to miss you." Putting his hands under Tris's arms, he lifted the child with one easy motion and stood her on the table next to the bread, so she could stare into eyes which were almost white and flecked with a thousand colours. "I really am."

"Why did you come here anyway?" It seemed an obvious question. Although from the look on the man's face you'd have thought it was the last thing he expected to be asked.

"I'm an artist," he said.

"Not an explorer?"

"Both," he said with a smile.

Tris thought about that. "What's an artist?"

"Someone who..." The man hesitated, as if debating the question with himself. "I collect objects," he said, "then wrap them up in memories and knot each one into a web."

"Did you find what you wanted?"

"Oh yes," he said, "you're one knot on the spider's web. A very special knot." Lifting her down, he picked up his bag. It was really a tube, almost as tall as she was, sealed at the bottom and sticky around the top. Tris had never seen another like it.

"You can keep the knife you stole," he said. "I've got this." And he produced the pistol, an intricate fusion of crystal and metal, so delicate that it could have been made by a spider itself.

Tris looked embarrassed.

"See you," he said.

"Will you?" Tris asked.

The man shook his head. "Probably not."

One step became another as Tris had walked her way through half a dozen daydreams and a fistful of memories, most of them making about as much sense in replay as they did the first time round.

The light, meanwhile, remained in the distance and with morning it vanished altogether. Tris wasn't too sure she could maintain her direction without the light to guide her. Equally, staying put meant losing a whole day's walking. So in the end Tris compromised. She walked all morning across grassland that climbed towards distant hills and then, come midday, she stopped, mostly because that way if she'd got the direction wrong she wouldn't have too far to walk back.

As compromises went it was barely adequate.

Making camp took Tris less time than it might have done if she'd been sensible enough to rescue anything useful from the yacht. "Get over it," Tris told herself. She'd had this discussion already and been forced to admit that rescuing more than herself would have been impossible. So she walked slowly around a huge boulder that protruded from the grass like weathered bone until she was sure which way the wind blew and then settled herself on the opposite side.

The third nightfall was less impressive than the second, which mirrored a rule Tris had already identified; new emotions devalued, going from intense through familiar to reach a kind of ghost state where one no longer really noticed them at all.

With darkness came the light and Tris was grateful, because it meant she'd been walking in the right direction after all. And the light might appear to be in the same place but Tris wasn't, because she was closer and that made her happy too.

Straightening her top and hitching up her frayed trousers, Tris set off uphill and walked until her foot hurt and then walked some more. The grass beneath her toes, having become soft, became rough again and began to alternate with heather and thorn. Tris had seen neither in real life. Heliconid lacked soil or open places where unnecessary plants could grow and had no ambassador to the Celestial Throne who could request help from the Library. All of the food in Heliconid came from the boxes or was raised on the levels under strip light.

And just when Tris had got used to tripping over clumps of heather in the dark and feeling wet thorn lash against her hips, the surface over which she walked changed again, becoming hard and warm with the heat it had retained from the recent day.

It was the remains of an ancient road, fifteen paces wide and so long that Tris reached five thousand, five hundred and fifty before she stopped counting, having lost her place enough times to know this figure might not be entirely accurate.

To break the monotony of the road, Tris began to count her

paces again and then took a break from that to sing to herself, having become certain she was being followed. When the fifth peek over her shoulder revealed nothing but silvery darkness and a short stretch of black that faded swiftly from her sight, Tris decided not to look round again, though she sang a little louder and stamped her feet that much harder as she walked.

Shoulders loose, arms loose, stay alert. Tris knew how to walk the walk and she'd won more fights on Rip than she'd lost, the last of them against a grown man with a knife.

One thousand, two thousand . . . Her heels hurt so much the blisters must have burst and then burst again. Hunger ate at her stomach and she was dizzy with exhaustion. As if this wasn't enough, sweat was gathering beneath her latex top and running down the crack in her bottom.

"You're no bowl of rose petals either," said a voice.

Tris stopped. Looking round, she saw nothing but darkness and somewhere ahead the distant light.

"Flames," said the voice. "They're flames."

She looked again, seeing nothing.

"She heard you," a different voice said.

"Of course I did," said Tris.

"Well," said the first voice a moment later. "Now there's a surprise. Maybe she's from the Tsungli Yamen."

"The Bureau of Foreign Affairs? I doubt it. She's probably a thief. We should deal with her."

"I'm not afraid of you," Tris said.

"You should be."

"Well, I'm not."

"She's beyond being afraid," said the first voice. "I'm not sure it's worth my time being here any longer."

"I'm not talking to you anymore," Tris said. She did her thing with one foot in front of the other, and pretty soon she was striding ahead as if nothing had happened. And maybe nothing had because hunger and tiredness can do funny things. Hallucinations were the least of it.

"We should stop her." That was the first voice.

"No," said the second. "I think it's too late."

Tris stamped one foot in front of the other, ten thousand and one, ten thousand and two, ten thousand and three, ten thousand and four . . .

"It's not your choice," Tris told the blank air. "I'm leaving now." She said this with a certainty she didn't feel.

"Going where?" The voice seemed to come from far behind her.

"To the palace."

"Palace?" said a voice in front.

"She thinks he'll save her. They always do."

Tris grinned. It was a hard grin that bared most of her teeth. "No," she said, "I'm going to kill him."

"Interesting," said the voice in front. "If a little stupid."

"Tell me something," Tris said. "Do you two actually exist?"

There was a silence.

"You know," a voice said finally, "you're not really meant to be asking us questions."

"Well, I am," Tris said crossly. "So the least you can do is answer them."

"Oh, we're real enough," said the other voice, sounding amused. And behind her the night moved slightly, coming closer. Only it wasn't night, merely something that swallowed all light and left an improbable afterburn on the surface of the air.

"Come back," said the voice. "We're not finished yet."

# CHAPTER 38

## *Marrakech, Summer 1977*

The steps down were dark with stains and a water pipe lay snakelike along one edge of the stairs. At the top the door had been old-fashioned, the kind which had panels and a knob that turned, although someone had nailed sound insulation to both sides of the door and painted the surfaces with cheap white paint.

At the bottom was another door. Only this one had no handle. Merely a fat bolt riveted crudely to the outside. At shoulder height on the wall next to the door someone had wired a bank of switches, each labelled in red plastic strip.

"Soldering iron," said one. "Saw," said another. "Water pump." None of them was on.

"You're in trouble," Major Abbas said, as if there was any chance Moz had missed this point. "And I'm not sure I can protect you."

Moz stared at the Major, seeing a face as dark and crumpled as walnut membrane. It had never occurred to Moz that anyone might protect him or that there could be something from which he might need serious protection.

"You understand me?"

Moz shook his head and Major Abbas sighed.

"There was an explosion," he began. "Last Wednesday..."

That, at least, Moz understood.

The Polisario had bombed an upstairs office on Boulevard Abdussallam. It had been on the radio, first as a denial, then as a qualified maybe and finally, seventy-six hours later, when gas explosions, failed foundations and acts of God had been discounted, as a guaranteed hundred per cent terrorist outrage. Two French lawyers had died and Paris was demanding action.

"What's that got to do with me?" Moz demanded.

"I don't know yet," said Major Abbas. "Maybe it's got nothing to do with you at all. I hope so. That's what we're here to find out." Reaching with a thumb, he wiped a streak of blood from the boy's bottom lip and flicked it to the floor.

"I'm sorry," the Major said. "You must understand that this has to be done." Moz wanted to ask why and what *this* was... Although a large part of him really didn't want to know. Instead he stood silently while Major Abbas unbolted the door. "In you go," said the Major, pushing the boy ahead of him.

Sunlight bathed what had once been a gymnasium. Climbing bars made from dark oak lined the far wall, ropes hung from the ceiling, eight of them, fixed to hooks high in the roof with fat knots at the bottom. A pair of rings hung from another part of the ceiling, leather handles worn smooth.

Afternoon heat clogged the stillness and made Moz feel sick enough to shield his eyes from the brightness that streaked through a huge window.

"Over there," said the Major.

Moz saw her then.

Straddling a vaulting horse was a naked girl, her wrists and ankles tied below the horse's belly. She was gagged.

Someone had shaved Malika's head.

"*No...*"

"You recognize her then?"

"Of course I recognize her." Moz began to move towards the motionless girl, only to be yanked back so hard that the Major almost pulled Moz off his feet.

"Did I say you could go over there?"

She'd been tied onto the vaulting horse lengthways, her arms made to hug the leather body and lashed at the wrists underneath. Something more complicated had been done with her legs. This involved tying her ankles, threading a single rope behind one knee, passing it under the horse and threading it behind the other knee, then tying both knees tight so that Malika gripped the length of padded leather as if riding at a gallop.

"The crow," Major Abbas said. "One of de Greuze's specials."

It was hard to know what the Major saw when he looked at Malika's splayed thighs and narrow buttocks, but whatever it was, it was not enough to stop the Major reaching for a discarded riding crop and cracking it absent-mindedly against the palm of his hand.

"So primitive." Major Abbas sounded almost sad. "So effective."

For a hideous moment Moz believed the whip was about to be handed to him, but instead the Major shrugged. Maybe he realized Moz would refuse or perhaps he knew that Moz would take the whip as ordered and this might be one humiliation too far.

More likely he just knew that the time was not yet right. Major Abbas had been in the police for all of his adult life, beginning his training under the French, and he had seen, done and made others do many things he would rather forget.

So instead of making the boy take the whip, the Major flicked it through the air a couple of times, like a conductor testing a baton, and then slashed the girl abruptly across the upturned soles of her feet, stepping back to watch as she reared up against the pain, her scream constrained by a leather gag.

"Stay silent," he ordered, reaching for its buckle.

*"Tell them,"* said Malika before Major Abbas had even got the gag properly undone. *"Tell him I was—"*

"I said silent," the Major said. Another slash of the whip and this time Moz could almost feel the scream that echoed round the dusty gymnasium. "Did anyone tell you that you could speak?"

The girl shook her head.

"Then don't," said Major Abbas. "Untie her," he ordered, not bothering to look at the boy.

Moz scrabbled with the knots. He was on his knees, staring up at the girl who lay trapped and sobbing. The knots were simple but

Moz's fingers were shaking and his eyes kept sliding from the tear-blurred rope in front of him to the sight of a breast squashed against the leather edge of the vaulting horse.

"Get on with it," ordered Major Abbas.

When Moz continued to fumble, the Major swung his riding crop and Moz felt Malika's body jerk furiously a second before her scream had him curled into a ball on the gymnasium floor with his hands over his ears.

Major Abbas kicked him. "Cut her free," he said, dropping his own pocket knife on to the floor beside Moz. "You've got five minutes." The last thing Moz heard before the Major slammed the door and bolted it from outside was a suggestion. "Use it well."

"*You have to tell them,*" Malika said before Moz had even returned to the knots, before he'd had a chance to saw at the rope around her wrists and ankles, lift her off the vaulting horse and lower her as gently as he could manage to the floor. "*You have to tell them I was with you.*"

"When?" Moz asked.

"Last Wednesday. You have to say that I was . . ."

Moz thought about it. Working the days back in his head.

"You were," he said, "we were—"

They both knew what and where. On the roof of the dog woman's old house, with the late afternoon sun in his eyes and Malika sitting in his lap, her bare arms locked round his neck and her legs curled around his hips. It was not something he was likely to forget.

"You'll tell them?" Malika said desperately.

"That we were on the roof?" Moz nodded. "Of course I will."

"I told them," said Malika.

"What's going on?" A very inadequate question.

Her answer came in tears and ragged sobs that echoed round the gymnasium. She didn't know, she really, really didn't know. She'd told the old Frenchman this already but he refused to believe her. Malika's voice was broken, helpless.

Dark circles surrounded her sunken eyes, her right thumb jutted at an obscene angle and all the fingernails from one hand had been ripped out. Excrement smeared the inside of one thigh. As well as shaving her head, the Frenchman had taken all her body hair and what was left looked like bruised meat.

He was crying too, Moz realized. A knot in his stomach as tight as any that might have bound his own hands.

"What do they think you've done?"

Malika was sobbing so hard and was so busy clinging to him that she couldn't answer. And by the time she could, Moz had worked it out for himself. They thought she was Polisario. That was why Major Abbas had asked him what he knew about the bombing in the Nouvelle Ville.

"I said we were together," Malika said. "I know I shouldn't but he wouldn't stop." Her words were barely audible, as if whispering could lessen the horror of what had happened. "He just wouldn't..."

And as Moz knelt in front of her, he understood that he was a coward, whatever Malika thought.

"What exactly did they ask?"

Jagged sobs were his answer.

"You must tell me," Moz insisted.

"The bomb," Malika said. "They wanted to know where I got the explosives."

"*You?*"

"Me," Malika said bleakly. "I made it and planted it."

"Who said so?"

"I did," said Malika. "When I signed his bit of paper."

"That's what it said?"

"That's what the Frenchman said it said," she replied.

"But you don't know?"

"No." Her shrug was tiny. "They wouldn't let me read it."

"This man," said Moz. "He was definitely French?" Moz felt sick to the bottom of his stomach.

"Yes," she said. "An advisor."

"Why do they say you planted the bomb?"

"I don't know," said Malika. "That's a secret so they won't tell me. There was someone else," she added. "An American or English. Only he left because he didn't like what the others were about to do."

It was a question that had to be asked, until the desolation in Malika's haunted amber eyes persuaded Moz that it didn't have to be asked after all.

"So," said the Frenchman, "it's true. You really are an informer." They faced each other across the cheap linoleum and Claude de Greuze seemed vaguely amused by something.

"No," Moz said. "It's not true."

"I've seen the files. Major Abbas has you down as a monthly expense. Forty dirham to Marzaq al-Turq, informant. He's just shown me."

This was the first Moz had heard of it. His only memories of payment were a handful of sweets, a glass of orange juice, cigarettes given grudgingly and the occasional glance in the wrong direction when Moz was busy helping Hassan move some cart which should have stayed where it was. There'd been no money, ever. Well, not very much and not until recently.

"So inform me," said the Frenchman. "What did you find out?"

"There's nothing to find out," Moz said. "She was telling the truth. We were together on the roof of Dar el Beida. She was with me all the time."

"No," said de Greuze, "I don't think so."

"We were," Moz insisted.

"Really?"

Moz nodded. He was standing so close to the old man that he could have reached out to touch his shabby jacket and Moz was breathing through his mouth, something he'd learnt from watching the Major.

The Frenchman was already dead in all but fact. Maybe that was why he cared so little for the living. "It's true," Moz said, "I promise."

Claude de Greuze's smile was as sour as the stink rising from his body. "I hope it isn't," he said, "because then I'd have to question you too, whether Major Abbas liked it or not."

## CHAPTER 39

### *Lampedusa, Sunday 8 July*

The chat with Katie Petrov was interesting, mostly for what it revealed about Dr. Petrov's views on emotional autism.

"Good morning," said Petra Mayer, shutting a door behind her. She listened to it lock from the other side and smiled. The Colonel was keeping to his orders. "I'm Professor Mayer," she added. The small woman said it like Prisoner Zero should know that already. "And you're..."

Petra Mayer glanced at Katie's folder, mere pantomime. "It seems you're more of a problem than we first thought."

The folder was simple and buff-hued, suggesting common sense, frugality and prudence. All virtues that Katie, Petra Mayer's second most famous pupil, liked to project as hallmarks of her work.

"Gene sent me."

Even this casual reference to America's President didn't rate a flicker of interest from the naked figure who sat with his back against a wall staring flatly at an utterly blue sky. And it was a very casual, we-go-back-a-long-way kind of mention.

The room was on the ground floor of Hotel Vallone but it was in the main building and had metal bars rather than steel mesh set over the windows. An en suite shower-room had been stripped of everything sharp and the door between the two rooms removed along with all the furniture except the bed. A notepad lay untouched beside the bed and the walls were still as pristine as when they were repainted. Prisoner Zero hadn't even opened the wax crayons he'd been given.

"You mind if I smoke?" Petra Mayer waited a few seconds and then shrugged. "I'll take that as a no." Pulling a brass Zippo from her pocket, the Professor put it on the bed beside her and dug into her pockets for a packet of Lucky Strike.

"Want one?"

Another silence.

This didn't worry Petra Mayer, who'd once ingested so much lysergic acid diethylamide that it was seventy-six hours before the Wernicke area of her brain could organize enough words to tell a very pretty German boy about the rainbow on the tip of her tongue. They were at the Burning Man in Nevada. Needless to say, no one else noticed a thing.

"Okay." Putting flame to her cigarette, the small woman smiled. "Let me tell you what's going on. As I said, my name is Professor Petra Mayer and for the purposes of irritating the Pentagon I've been made a general in the US Army. I am here at the direct request of the President of the United States of America. All my expenses are being paid for by the Oval Office."

It was called the Russian Pitch and Harvard Business School used to teach it way back when. Around the time the old Soviet

Union hit meltdown and arriving in the right place at the right time meant having whole industries drop into your lap. It relied on being flat-out honest and up front about the who, what and why.

Dragging on her Lucky Strike, Petra Mayer ran through the points and realized she'd left out the what's-in-it-for-me/what's-in-it-for-you.

Something of a deal breaker, usually.

"The President is minded..."

She hated that phrase, with its recursive echoes of qualification and non-commitment, its sheer mean-mindedness. Needless to say it hadn't been Gene who suggested its use. That little gem was down to the White House counsel.

"No, fuck it." Petra Mayer tapped ash onto a paper plate. "Gene doesn't want to kill you, okay? He thinks it's a crap idea. So I'm here to sort out some kind of deal. That's what's in it for you. As for what's in it for me..."

There were probably pin-lens cameras in here and microphones, infrared and other stuff so secret military intelligence at the Pentagon had forgotten to let the President know it existed. Professor Mayer wasn't too worried about that. She had a box of tricks of her own and Gene Newman knew it existed because he'd been present when Paula Zarte briefed the President's old tutor on its use.

It fucked up bugs, that was how the recently appointed Director of Central Intelligence put it, ignoring the glance of disapproval from the President's private secretary.

"There's been a suggestion," said Petra. "We swop you for a condemned prisoner and then publicly execute the prisoner. You get a new identity and we get the equations."

The suggestion had come from the First Lady and, much as it pained Professor Mayer to admit it, the idea had its attractions in a disgustingly *realpolitik* kind of way. Not least, that it kept the equations out of the hands of dangerous lunatics, while bluffing the world that they'd been lost forever.

Of course, Professor Mayer knew it didn't really keep the equations out of the hands of dangerous lunatics at all. It merely put them into the hands of *our* dangerous lunatics as opposed to *their* dangerous lunatics...

She sighed.

"We'd need your agreement," Professor Mayer said. "And you needn't feel guilty about the man who takes your place. He's going to die anyway...Why would we do this?" she asked, watching smoke trickle towards the ceiling. A whole world of rigid rules covering temperature, convection and Brownian motion all busily pretending to be truly chaotic. No wonder she loved smoking so much. "Because we've got a situation. And mostly it's that we now know who you really are..."

Not a flicker from Prisoner Zero.

"...and according to your family you're already dead."

Professor Mayer glanced round the prisoner's new room with its neat bed, built-in shower and view of the Mediterranean. Dr. Petrov could be forgiven her verdict of emotional autism, naïve though it was, because the man seemed totally oblivious to anything going on around him.

"Not a dead-man-walking kind of dead," she added. "The real kind. Ashes to ashes, dust to dust. Although in your case it was very much junk to junkie, wasn't it?"

Flipping open her briefcase, which now contained the Marrakech file, two sets of fingerprints and her latest acquisition, Jake Razor's medical records and a long list of attendances from the early 1980s at a drug drop-in centre in Amsterdam, Professor Mayer found what she was after, a photograph of the squat on Vizelstraat, five burnt-out floors overlooking a canal and the stark carcass of a cindered tree. Children sat on the deck of a narrow boat, oblivious to three police cars parked nearby.

"Here," said Professor Mayer, holding out the photograph. "Recognize it?"

There was a "Politie BBE" stamp on the back of the photograph over a date, the initials of a crime-scene photographer and a coffee ring where a paper cup had been put down carelessly.

They told Professor Mayer little more than she already knew. In April 1989 a squat used by heroin addicts had burnt out in Vizelstraat, Amsterdam. The fire-twisted body of a victim had been found and the body had been so badly charred it proved impossible to put an age on it. Although it was doubtful if anyone tried very hard.

The Bijzondere Bijstands Eenheid became involved because the first police officer on the scene decided that the body had been shot through the head with a high-powered rifle. As most of the skull was missing this was a reasonable mistake to make, even if it was boiling brains and not a bullet that ripped apart the vagrant's head.

After this had been established, responsibility for the crime reverted to the Amsterdam police and it was their note which was attached to the photograph. The victim was thought to be one

Marzaq al-Turq, sometimes known as Moz Ritter, and there was no evidence to suggest foul play.

"There was no reason to exclude it either," Petra Mayer said, but the Professor was talking to herself.

Police HQ in Amsterdam were currently trying to locate the evidence locker into which a bone sample from the body had been decanted, so they could carry out the forensics tests no one had bothered to do before.

"I followed your work, you know." She spoke as slowly and as clearly as she could. Many people thought Professor Mayer's lugubrious growl was affectation or the result of too many drugs. This was wrong.

The drug damage and the facial scar from her famous car crash might both be self-inflicted and closely related, but the voice came from God. Although the Professor was honest enough to admit that her sixty-a-day cigarette habit did not help matters.

"A BBS here," said Professor Mayer. "An early news group there. Little hints and rough workings. I kept a list of the names you used and I wasn't the only one, did you know that?"

*How could he not?* Prisoner Zero had waited for replies and confirmations. For other people's take on his solutions. It was a very quick and dirty form of peer review, a term he'd first stumbled over at Amsterdam University. Although it didn't always work, of course. He'd posted a line of code onto a Polish bulletin board, just that, nothing more. This was at the height of Solidarity. A time when messages were mostly coded and all BBS were watched no matter how primitive, and what passed for academic BBS in Poland at that time was very primitive indeed.

And his equation had just sat there, unanswered and perhaps unread. One of a dozen fragments he took from the notebook and posted in his attempt, fleeting and destined for failure, to find the numinous within numeracy.

"I'm offering you a new life," Petra Mayer said. "A new start." Grinding out her Lucky Strike, the elderly academic reached for the packet and realized it was empty. "No?" Professor Mayer's smile was sour. "I told Gene not to make me waste my time asking you." She paused, thought about it. "Not much point asking you anything really, is there?"

## CHAPTER 40

## *Northern Mountains, CTzu 53/Year 20*

In the beginning there was lightning and then agony, sharp where it shouldn't have been. Where no one should be touching her.

"CV-1," a voice said, sounding matter-of-fact. "Also essential for countering heart attacks, near-drowning, frigidity, bed-wetting, incontinence and related ailments."

Fingers moved from between her legs to her chest, rolling up the latex top of her jump suit and the voice said, "Do I need the quill?"

It was speaking mostly to itself.

The fingers found a point on Tris's sternum, settled one finger on top of another and pressed in the bony hollow of her chest, at a point exactly equidistant between her nipples.

"CV-17," said the voice. "Good for confusion, hysteria, high blood pressure, breathing ailments, difficulty swallowing and assorted similar maladies..."

The pressure increased and then lifted as the darkness unwrapped itself, leaving Tris facing the top half of an anxious-looking young man, whose skin was as white as his tied-back ponytail. Above the waist he was as real as Tris, below this he seemed a mere shadow. At least that's what Tris thought, until the boy flicked back the other half of his cloak and suddenly she could see all of him.

"Unlucky," he said, helping Tris to her feet. "Getting lightning struck like that." The boy was taller than anybody she'd ever seen, his face soft and somehow bloodless, pale like snow or high clouds in a summer sky.

"Aren't there two of you?" Tris said.

Luca Pacioli shrugged. "There are dozens of us," he said. "Unfortunately, these days they're all me." Thrusting out his hand, the young man offered it to Tris.

His shake was tentative.

His skin cold.

"I'm Luca Pacioli," he said. "Ambassador Luca Pacioli. You're welcome to use my house if you need to sleep. I'm a baron," he added, rather diffidently. "A very poor one, sadly."

Luca let his eyes trail across her ripped jump suit, hesitating at the tear above one breast and stopping altogether when his gaze reached her bare abdomen where the trousers barely clung to her hips.

"You must have walked far," he said.

Tris nodded.

"A pity about your ship."

"My . . . ?"

"That little racing yacht of yours. I saw it skim overhead a few days ago. Very pretty. You must have been upset when they shot it down."

"I crashed it," Tris said. "No one shot it down."

Luca's glance was kind. "That's not what I heard. The imperial guard took it out. I listen to the private feeds," he added. "I'm not meant to but there's not much else to do."

Somehow while he'd been talking, Luca had managed to steer Tris in a wide circle across rough grass and a broken path, so that now Tris found herself heading back the way she'd come.

"It's okay," he said. "You can trust me."

"Yeah," said Tris. "That's what they all say."

There was a feed bar on the fifteenth level of Rip, right at the bottom of the Razor's Edge where she'd wasted one summer. Actually there were several bars but they had merged into one in her memory and the jump area was called the Razor's Edge, because that's what it was.

A ragged scar down the inside of the world. Someone had sealed the Rip with spun glass, the silvery kind which was meant to catch radiation. Although Tris didn't believe it worked because too many jumpers she knew got sick and died from the coughs. You could always tell who was going to go next because their skin went bad and their eyes developed that haunted look, like they knew what was going to happen but didn't want anyone mentioning it.

Tris's health remained good but that was Tris, she'd never been ill in her life and the one thing she'd learnt from her time on the fifteenth was it really didn't matter if the guy was dying or not, you really, really couldn't trust anyone who said, "You can trust me."

You just couldn't.

And if they said, "I'm not going to hurt you" they always did.

"This way," Luca said, leading Tris towards a turning off the road between a broken wall on one side and a mound of rubble, so brush-covered that it was nearly impossible to work out what had been there originally, on the other.

"Fechner's house," said Luca. "You know what its number was?"

Of course she didn't.

"Think of two numbers," said Luca, "then add them together to make a third."

Tris did what she was told, though she kept the numbers small so that the sums were easy.

"Now add the second number to the third, which will give you a fourth."

That was a bit harder.

"Now add those two together to give you a fifth."

As they walked Tris added numbers until she lost count of how many times Luca had asked her to do this.

"Finished adding the last two?"

"Yeah." Tris nodded.

"Good," said Luca, "now take that final number and the one before and calculate the ratio between them." He walked in silence while Tris worked out first what his instruction meant and then whether she could answer it.

"Well?"

"One point six?" Tris said finally.

"You sure?"

"Pretty much."

Luca smiled. "That's Fechner's number," he said. "You need to remember it." Tris was going to ask why but the boy now stood in front of a shimmering silver wall, concentrating hard while he did something complicated with his fingers.

Luca Pacioli lived in a palace. More precisely, he lived in part of the Emperor's palace, the one everyone recognized from the feed. Not in the actual Qiangquing Gong, obviously enough, but definitely a replica of what was intended to be a suite in a guest wing.

"That's the Jiulongbi, the Nine Dragon Screen!"

"Yes," Luca said sadly, "it is."

Someone had painted the Jiulongbi onto cloth and nailed it to the window frame, so the canvas faced inwards. The painting was crude and most of the nails holding it in place had rusted to the colour of dried blood. When Tris reached out to touch the canvas, flakes of dragon scale came off on her fingers.

"We used to have a real picture," said Luca. "One that did light and dark and showed eunuchs scurrying past the window and soldiers gathering on parade. The sky even showed black cranes flying."

"What happened?" she said.

"It broke." He shrugged. "My father kept it going for as long as he could. Far longer than was reasonable but in the end... you know. Things break." Luca gave her water and what might have been some kind of dry bread. And while Tris wolfed down the food, Luca told her about his childhood.

His father had brought him to Rapture so long before that Luca couldn't even remember when his father had died.

The pavilion had been glorious then, crowded with family, retainers, animals and servants who wore drab but functional smocks and wooden clogs for when the courtyard got waterlogged.

Ambassador Pacioli had chosen the servants and animals, just as he'd chosen his retainers and those who made up his secretariat. An important person in his own civilization, his luck had always been bad. A lucky man would have found reasons why someone else should go instead.

The replica of the guest wing in which Luca now lived had been the idea of Lady Pacioli, Luca's mother. It was not a particularly original idea because endless ambassadors had undergone training in replica palaces before taking up their posts. The novelty lay in Lady Pacioli's suggestion that the replica should be taken with them.

A feat less difficult than it sounded since all she needed was to acquire enough spiders to create whichever replica was appropriate. The secret was to instruct the spiders so they knew in advance exactly what they were meant to be doing.

The way Luca said this made Tris decide that he was reciting it from memory rather than actually understanding what spiders were or how they could grow a palace from the ground up.

"It's falling apart," Luca said.

"What is?"

"All of this." The stare he turned on the girl seemed heavy with too much knowledge and a realization that he'd never reach wherever it was he once thought he was going. "I'm sorry it's not better."

Luca looked so sad that Tris decided she probably had to sleep with him. It wouldn't be her first time and Tris wasn't worried about getting pregnant because Luca was obviously other than human and the mix never took in cases like that.

This piece of information came from Doc Joyce. And though the

Doc had talked about exceptions, Tris felt it unlikely that Luca would carry the kind of germline fix needed to let him father children on stray humans . . . Of course, Tris didn't exactly think like this. She just thought, *It's not going to happen.*

And somehow that was enough.

"You own a bath?"

Luca's face froze and it took Tris a second to realize she'd just offended him. "I'm not saying you need one," she said hurriedly. "I mean, I've never had a bath. So if you've got one can I borrow it?"

"It's been a while," Luca said.

"What has?"

"Since I talked to anyone alive."

Tris decided not to think too deeply about that. Nodding at a random door, she said, "Through there . . . ?"

"Sure," said Luca. "Why not?"

When Tris reached the doorway the room on the other side was busy rearranging itself, a divan melting into a wall as floor tiles stretched and sank to produce a bath twice her length.

"Too large," said Luca behind her and the tiles shifted again. "You'll still need some water," he said. "There should be water."

He led Tris to a courtyard where a huge cauldron stood, filled to the brim with rainwater. The cauldron was green with verdigris and the dragons that supported it had oxidized so badly in the rain that their scales were almost flat.

Below the cauldron stood a hearth heaped with ashes and when Luca swept these away Tris could see filaments of gold, some of which had melted and run together.

"We'll need some wood," Luca said. Instead of heading for a log pile, he wandered back into the pavilion, grabbed a gilded stool and smashed it hard against a doorpost. Scars on the post suggested this wasn't the first time it had been used that way.

"Try the table," suggested Luca.

Made from a honey-dark wood new to Tris, the table's top was carved into an ornate and aerodynamically sleek dragon, with vast wings which caught the wind like sails. On the back of the beast was a monk whose robes, beads and beard fluttered in the slipstream.

"Yes," said Luca, "that one."

So Tris picked up the table and carried it to the door. "It's beautiful," she said.

"Isn't it?" agreed Luca. "Here, let me." Taking the table from

Tris's hands, he swung it hard into the doorpost, cracking monk and dragon into three. "It's not hard when you know how," he said. "The trick's in the wrist."

A temple carving followed the table, reduced to tinder in a single swing. "That should do us for now," said Luca.

To build his fire, Luca simply banked up fragments of table around a core of temple carving. And when both wood and kindling were ready, he flicked the fingers of his right hand across his thumb, like flint across steel.

"The water will take about a minute," he promised.

"How...?"

"The cauldron multiplies the heat. Whatever the cauldron takes in, it gives out more."

"That's impossible," said Tris.

"Most things are," Luca said, "if you think about them for long enough."

Kneeling next to the kindling, he reached out and Tris watched fire dance from his fingertips, catching ragged wood on a fragment of screen and turning those edges to gold.

"Watch," he said.

Flames caught the splintered screen and fire soon licked the underneath of the ancient cauldron, sliding up its sides until the flames grew, lost colour and disappeared into a heat so hot it was sufficient to make Tris stand back a little. All the same, the flames were nothing compared to the quantity of cold water in the cauldron and yet the inside rim was already beginning to birth bubbles, which grew fatter and fatter, until suddenly the whole slick surface began to roil and break.

"You'll need a bucket," Luca said, "to carry the hot water... We used to have servants," he added, "but they died." Seeing Tris's slight nod, Luca hesitated. "Did I tell you that already?" he said

Only Tris had stopped listening. She stood in the doorway of the pavilion looking bemused.

"The table..."

It was back, not yet complete but soft-edged and almost. A wax sculpture of woodwork melted by the sun. On the wall, a gold and red oblong was coalescing into a temple carving, its gold leaf and red undercoat becoming crazed with age.

"How?" the girl demanded.

"This is what the house does," Luca said. "Endlessly and always the same... Until something gives and suddenly a fire no longer lights itself or the shutters begin to ignore the rain. It will die eventually," he added, his voice entirely matter-of-fact, "but probably not before I do."

Tipping the first bucket into the bath, Luca went back for another. He worked with the rhythm of someone used to the world he inhabited, his life worn loosely.

"How old are you?" Tris asked. The question had been worrying her.

"You know," said Luca, as he scooped another bucket into the cauldron, "it's hard to say." He lifted the full bucket without appearing to notice its weight and carried it through the doorway in which she stood.

"Why is it hard?"

Luca shrugged and as he passed Tris on his way back their eyes met. It was nothing significant. Luca was just doing his best not to look at her breast where the top had torn. "Not sure I can answer that either," he said, sounding embarrassed for the first time since they'd met. "We live time differently."

"How do you live it?"

Like that, he wanted to say. Except this would be wrong, because the water in the cauldron boiled so simply, bubbles rising and currents defined by convection, properties of matter and the shape of the vessel in which it was all held. Time worked in all directions but was lived by humans only in one. At least that was what Luca had been taught.

And there were other differences. The girl's brain contained no pain fibres, for her, synaptic action was a pain-free process. Her brain could rot and she'd feel nothing. When Luca said a thought hurt he meant it.

"I live it one way," he said, "you another." Scooping up water, he carried his bucket into the pavilion, poured it into the bath and came out again. After that Luca worked in silence until the bath was full. "All yours," he said.

The girl glanced doubtfully at steam rising from the surface.

"No problem," Luca assured her, "the temperature will adjust. Well, it should do, unless that's stopped working as well."

In the end Tris tried the water with one toe, and then, when she realized Luca didn't intend to leave, she stripped off her ragged top, shook herself free from the trousers and stepped into her bath.

"Can you make me more clothes?"

"Maybe the house can," Luca said. "Whether you'll want to wear them . . ." And then he smiled, his gaze catching the latex rags she'd kicked into one corner of the room. "I'll see what we can do," he said, and with that he was gone, leaving the girl to soak away her doubts.

Tris said later, mostly to herself, that she couldn't remember why she agreed to sex. Although this was inaccurate because Tris was the one who instigated it by climbing from her bath and walking naked through the pavilion until she finally found Luca in an attic room, drawing something on a long scroll of paper. An ink stone and mixing pot stood beside him and a small bamboo brush was held elegantly in one hand.

"CV-1," he said blushing.

And Tris saw a sketch of her genitals, a dotted line inked between vulva and anus. "CV-1?"

"A *tsubo* point," Luca said. "Good for heart attacks, near-drowning and strikes by lightning. Inconveniently positioned, however."

Yeah, thought Tris, you could put it that way. He'd used the handle of that brush to activate the nerve. She'd seen him putting it back into its holder when she came awake at the edge of the road.

"I've grown you some clothes," Luca said quickly.

Tris glanced at the padded blue jacket, wafer-thin silk trousers and rope sandals. "Thanks," she said. "I think."

Somehow Luca looked even younger when he slept, his face was less strained and his mouth had relaxed into a child-like smile. Even his eyes rested easy under their lids.

"Sweet dreams," she said.

The man stank of vaginal secretions and of things Tris hadn't even realized people did to each other in bed and she stank of the same. What Tris didn't stink of was Luca because he had no scent. At least, no scent that she could detect.

Tris leant closer, just to make sure.

"Whatever."

Rolling out of bed, Tris landed lightly and grinned, tucking the single silk sheet tightly around Luca's sleeping body. In part this was because she didn't want the man to get cold, but mostly it was because Tris intended to search his room and wrapping sleeping punters in a sheet to make them feel secure was an old trick. One she'd learnt as a child from listening in on the whores at Schwarzschilds.

"Tuck them in," Bella had been saying, "so they're safe and tight." Then she'd glanced round and seen the kid standing by the wall, nursing a frosted glass of something purple and sighed. "Don't just stand there," she said. "If you want to learn, come over here and learn."

Tris did what she was told.

"There's this five minutes, honey," Bella said. "When men's heads go walkabout and that's the time to tuck 'em in and strip their wallets of anything worth taking."

Only the sex was hours behind her and Tris had no intention of searching Luca's pockets, she just wanted to look around. Most of the drawers in the attic refused to open for her, being owner specific. So in the end all Tris found to open was a long sandalwood chest full of clean sheets. Glancing at what she could see of the filthy mattress visible beneath Luca's sleeping head, Tris shrugged and filed the query away to unpuzzle later.

Under the last of the sheets was a full court dress, Mandarin Third Class, although the jade buckle looked rather grander than this. Tris knew about court grades from the feeds because everybody on Rip knew about stuff like that.

Beneath the court dress she found a sword with an ivory grip, ruby pommel and sharkskin sheath. The blade was oiled but felt blunt to her touch. Since Tris had no way of sharpening the blade and the obvious value of the sword frightened her a little, she placed it carefully on the floor and kept digging.

Another court dress, much smaller this time and more suited to a child. And a second sword, only this one was so tiny that it was barely more than a long dagger. The kind of thing an ambassador's son might carry if he was expected to be presented at court.

Tris felt no guilt at stealing the weapon. What was a small boy's sword compared to a racing yacht? And, besides, she needed a weapon. Of course, she could pretend she was taking it to protect herself against wild animals, or that it was needed to fight off imperial guards. But those would be lies and Tris never lied to herself. At least not more than was required to stay human or sane. Lying to others was different. That was what people like her did if they wanted to remain alive.

She intended to use the small sword to cut out Chuang Tzu's heart. That was all. Any other reason Tris gave would have been untrue.

At the bottom of the chest was a map, a scroll and a jewellery box made from mottled shell. Inside the box nestled a jade necklace so fabulous it had to be real. The map was of Rapture and the scroll contained Ambassador Pacioli's credentials. No one had even broken the seal.

Shutting the jewellery box on its necklace, Tris carefully repacked the scroll, both sets of court dress, the larger of the two swords and the sheets; then she dressed herself in the padded blue jacket, thin trousers and rope sandals that Luca had grown for her.

As payment to Luca for the little sword she left the yacht's memory, sitting on top of the chest looking blue and lonely in the daylight.

## CHAPTER 41

### *Marrakech, Summer 1977*

Celia, the woman who once sacked a Glaswegian punk band mid-tour while facing down a drunk roadie on a twenty-four-hour, amphetamine-enhanced rampage, was scared. And the man who scared her was a balding and badly dressed French official who stank of death and carried himself like a man entering hospital for the last time.

Jake, however, was angry.

There might have been some fear in Jake's anger. A level of self-protection that displayed itself in a snarl and an upturned, arrogant set to his chin, but it was real fury, of the kind which took no prisoners and expected no mercy in return. The object of his anger was Claude de Greuze and the fact that Major Abbas also stood in the courtyard of Riad al-Razor was a barely noticed irrelevance.

That Jake had decided his real argument was with de Greuze and not the Major was accurate; it also spoke volumes about Jake's background and cultural limitations, not to mention a mind-set he affected to despise.

"Look at him," Jake demanded, hands clenched into fists. They were talking about Moz, in particular about Moz's split lip and the camouflage pattern of bruises that mottled the boy's temples and cheeks. "Is this how you treat children?"

It was, Moz had to admit, one of the stupidest things he'd ever heard Jake say, among a whole list of stupid things. Everyone knew that compared to the old days, those now advising the government were as children themselves, casually cruel but not coruscated by decades of hate.

"I don't think," said de Greuze, "you realize how serious this is."

"No," said Jake, his fists still balled but now almost grinding into his hips, his pose unconscious but still taken straight from the cover of his second LP, *Anemone of the State*. "You don't realize how serious this is. You kidnap a child, torture him, only bring him back after I telephone the US consul and police HQ to report the boy missing."

*Jake had called the Hotel de Police?*

Moz was shocked. No one involved themselves in the affairs of the police unless they had little alternative and, even then, most Marrakchi would find an alternative.

"Go to Celia." Jake's voice was sharp.

Moz glanced from the Major to the woman with the blonde bob. She sat, still scared but now more openly defiant, on a wicker divan which Jake and Moz had painted pink for a joke one morning a couple of weeks earlier.

"Sit here," Celia said. "You're safe now." And it sounded as if she half believed what she said, that somehow the purple-painted walls of the riad's courtyard, the pink wicker and the sheer fury in Jake's face could save Moz even from this.

Celia looked as if she'd spent the morning in tears. Dark landslides of mascara deepened her pale blue eyes. Moz wanted to say *It's okay,* although obviously it wasn't and probably never would be.

Having mentally discounted Major Abbas, Jake was now concentrating his vitriol on Claude de Greuze, each word accompanied by a stab of his finger that never quite touched the old man's chest. "The boy's with me," he said. "Have you got that?"

"With you?" Major Abbas said suddenly. "How, exactly, 'with you'?"

Too angry to be careful, Jake flicked his attention from de Greuze to the small police officer. "Ah yes," he said, "*you*... The man from the station. The one who was so *helpful* when Celia's watch was stolen. How could I forget?" Contempt practically dripped from Jake's lips while his eyes racked up and down the policeman, finding him wanting.

Moz wanted to explain that this was Major Abbas. The son and grandson of police officers. A man feared throughout the Mellah. And the *nasrani* with him, the Frenchman, was more dangerous still. They were not people to whom Jake should be rude.

Only Jake was *nasrani* himself and the world he saw through his eyes was not the one Moz saw, no matter that he had *nasrani* blood himself, for only a foreigner could have showed such open anger to an officer of the Sécurité.

"Stolen?" Major Abbas said. "Didn't you sign a declaration saying it had been lost?"

Jake shrugged away the detail like the technicality it was. Lost/stolen, what difference did it make? Celia had got her gold Omega back and, if it had gone, he'd have just bought her another.

"You know exactly what I mean," said Jake.

"I very much hope," said Major Abbas, "that I don't."

The American grinned, a wolfish grin that exposed one canine and creased up his eyes until he could have been staring into the lens of a Hasselblad. It was a look Celia had seen before and she didn't like what it presaged. The only thing worse than Jake drunk or wired out of his skull was Jake self-consciously flying in the face of hidebound, bourgeois convention.

"You wouldn't believe," he told Major Abbas, "I mean, you really wouldn't believe some of the VIPs who've come to my parties." Suggestions of naked children, drugged roadies, copious hashish and doubtful politics hung in the air between them.

"Moroccan VIPs," Celia said, just in case Major Abbas had missed that point.

"And, of course," said Jake, "I've kept a diary of my time in Marrakech. A very detailed diary obviously. Names and places, dates, bribes paid...And I can tell you," he added, "most of it makes Saturday night at Studio 54 look like my first day at Montessori."

Neither Jake nor Celia had ever been to Studio 54, obviously enough. He hung out at CBGB, a club in the Bowery situated below a flop-house. He was talking, however, not just to the Arab police officer but to de Greuze and the Frenchman could be relied upon to know of Studio 54, in a way he might not of a club where at least one person was reputed to have jacked off in the chilli, the bartender often forgot to change the beer and the whole place stank of piss.

"This famous diary," Major Abbas said darkly. "You can show it to me?"

Something passed in a glance between Celia and Jake. A look

that marked a point beyond which Celia had not intended to go, although she promptly went straight beyond it. Jake had always had that effect on her.

"Of course he can't," she said dismissively. "Jake writes it in weekly installments and I mail it to Jann Wenner." She named the brains behind *Rolling Stone,* hoping fervently that Mr. Wenner would never find out quite how liberally she'd taken his name in vain.

"Malika," Moz reminded Celia, pulling at her hand. Very carefully, the Englishwoman unpeeled his fingers.

Again that glance.

"We'll help your friend later," said Celia. "If we can. But first we need to sort this out because Mr. de Greuze says you're in trouble." Celia spoke slowly, as if to a very small child. "And we all know you didn't really do anything wrong."

"I didn't?"

"No," said Celia. "It's okay. Jake's told them the truth." There was something about the way Celia said this which told Moz more was being said than he first understood. At the same time he felt a cold certainty that something very wrong was in the process of happening and somehow he was allowing it to happen.

"Malika," Moz insisted.

"Forget her." The Major's voice was hard. "Worry about yourself." Turning to face the boy, he said, "I need you to tell me the truth. Were you here last Wednesday evening?"

"Of course he was." Jake's voice was equally sharp. "We've already been through this."

"I wasn't talking to you," said Major Abbas. Words that should have reduced Jake to frightened silence.

Jake just sighed. "I've been through it with Mr. de Greuze." He put heavy emphasis on the word "mister," so maybe the Frenchman wasn't a mister at all. He certainly behaved like an officer in the Sécurité, all sweaty skin and suspicious, watchful eyes.

"Well?" Major Abbas demanded.

"I was . . ." Moz knew exactly where he'd been. On the roof of Dar el Beida, the dog woman's old house opposite the entrance to Derb Yassin. Sun tightening the skin on his neck as he slowly unbuttoned the front of Malika's shirt. "I was with Malika," he said firmly. What else could he say?

The Major and the Frenchman looked at each other, then the Major glanced from Jake to where Moz sat beside Celia.

"You're certain?"

Moz nodded.

In de Greuze's pocket was a folded square of foolscap. A dark stain on one side forming a map of no country Moz could recognize, the other outlined Malika's part in planting a bomb for the Polisario. The confession used the word "I" a lot and Moz was referred to throughout as "he." It was signed in childish capitals.

"What's that?" When Jake stepped forward the Major also stepped forward, putting himself between Jake and the boy.

"Let him read it," Major Abbas said. "He's the only one who can tell us if this is true."

"Of course it isn't," Moz said, handing back the paper. "It's a lie."

"Malika didn't plant the bomb?"

Moz stared at the Major. "She was with me," he said firmly. "That's the truth. She was with me."

"And you were both where?"

"On the roof of Dar el Beida. I'm doing some painting there. An English friend of Jake's is going to buy the house." He would have told them about delivering the drugs for Caid Hammou, but then he'd have been in even worse trouble.

"Moz was not on that roof or any other," Jake said firmly. "The boy was here."

"And I'm expected to believe that?" de Greuze asked. He was looking at Jake when he said this, but it was Celia who answered. And for once her voice was matter-of-fact, no cut-glass drawl to drag her words beyond breaking.

"Moz was here," she said. "For the entire afternoon and evening. None of us even left this riad."

"That's not true . . ." Moz protested.

The four adults ignored him.

"You have witnesses?"

"Of course." It was Jake who answered the Frenchman. "Celia and I were both here. I say the boy never left my side and Celia is my witness."

"She's your girlfriend." A sour smile accompanied those words.

"No, she's not," said Jake, avoiding the Englishwoman's gaze. "She's my manager, and her name's Lady Celia Vere. Her uncle was British ambassador to Paris."

The look on de Greuze's face suggested this information was new to him. "And you," he said. "Should I know who you are?" His English was heavy but the sarcasm was edged with something that suggested he was reassessing.

Jake smiled. "I don't see why you should," he said. "It's not likely we've met."

The way Jake said this made Celia wince, but de Greuze barely seemed to notice. "I take it Jake Razor isn't your real name?"

"A persona," said Jake. "Nothing more."

"And your real name?" That was Major Abbas.

The name he gave meant little to Moz but de Greuze recognized it instantly and even Major Abbas blinked.

"As in . . . ?"

Jake nodded, casually apologetic. And behind his nod were good schools, family trusts, Norland nannies and a New York bank and City of London brokerage that still bore his name. He'd been given the very best to resent and Jake had the wit to recognize that. Of all the facts stacking themselves up in the head of the elderly Frenchman, only one was really significant.

The financier about to donate *Virgin and Child with St. Anne* to the New York Met was Jake's grandfather. His donations to the Met, the National Gallery in London, the Paris Louvre and the Prado in Madrid were famous. His donations to competing political parties more famous still.

"You are still American?"

"For my sins," Jake said. "My mother was English," he added, catching Moz's eye. He'd told the boy he came from London. "I went to Westminster."

"*It's not true,*" Moz said.

"Yes it is," insisted Jake. "I lived with my grandmother."

"No," said Moz tearfully. "It's not true that I was here. Malika and I spent the entire afternoon on the roof. She let me get into her knickers," he added desperately, as if that might convince them. "You're both lying."

"Moz." Celia's voice was firm. "You were here."

"No I wasn't." He sounded about twelve, Moz realized. Arguing in a language that wasn't even his own. "*You know I was with Malika* . . ." Actually, there was no way they could know that but Moz was beyond caring.

"Look," Celia said. "We know the girl's a good friend of yours but you can't help her. She confessed. When Mr. de Greuze came here we had to tell him the truth. You were with us." Her voice hesitated and something sad flitted across her face.

"With Jake," she amended. "Jake told him everything."

"I had to," Jake said. "It was the only way . . . And now I'm the one in trouble." He looked between Major Abbas and de Greuze, his eyes troubled, almost apologetic.

"What?" Moz asked. "What did you tell him?"

Although he already knew. Understanding now the look given him by the soldiers on the stairs of the police station, the contempt in the eyes of the Frenchman.

"I showed them the photographs."

*What photographs?* Moz wanted to shout, but his throat was tight and despair had begun to shake his body. He felt as if the whole world were watching him and the weight of their watching was more than he could bear.

"I'm sorry," Celia said, "there wasn't anything else we could do." Her eyes were huge with tears and she wouldn't look at Jake when he came back from collecting the folder.

There were maybe fifty photographs in all. Most showed Moz sleeping, his head cradled on a thin forearm, his naked body turned on its side and curled around itself like a child suspended in dreams. An upper sheet had been turned down in all of these, sometimes only as far as Moz's hips, although a few showed the sheet turned lower. The last showed him standing naked in a doorway, his head turned towards the camera and a surprised expression on his face.

"You took these?" Major Abbas asked.

Jake nodded.

The spike-haired, gangly boy from the Mellah was beautiful. Not handsome like Hassan or striking as Malika had been but beautiful, a single reed waiting to be broken.

"I'll take those," said Major Abbas, holding out his hand.

"Why?" de Greuze looked puzzled.

"Evidence," said the Major.

## CHAPTER 42

## *Lampedusa, Monday 9 July*

"You know what," said Petra Mayer, fanning photographs out on the mattress in two neat rows. "I can't believe it took me this long to work out. These are you. You're the Arab boy."

The speed with which Prisoner Zero jerked his gaze from the window was impressive.

"Everyone's got it wrong," she said, with a slow smile. "And, as yet, no one has any idea just how badly." Her excitement was almost tangible. "Just wait till Gene finds out."

A large number of people considered Petra Mayer unreliable, badly dressed and unable to cope with the simplest things in life, like driving round the Washington Circle without crashing (right outside the GW Hospital). An embarrassment that happened only once and about which far too much was made, mostly by journalists who could barely read the titles of her later books, never mind understand them. Those who knew the Professor better would have recognized the gleam in her eye.

Entire layers of fact were being discarded and reassembled. She'd taken all the evidence and put it together in the only way that worked.

"They *are* you, aren't they?"

Prisoner Zero gave a slight shake of his head, while simultaneously mouthing the word "yes"... Conflicted, Katie Petrov would have said and she'd have been right. Although after the drugs, the culture shock and the years in Amsterdam and Paris it was a wonder he knew who he was at all.

"Almost professional," said Petra Mayer, picking up a black and white of a boy about to step into a shower and then making herself put it back. "They show real talent."

The naked man remained silent and after a few seconds his gaze returned to the window. There was something very deliberate about the way he took his attention away from the photographs.

Petra Mayer smiled. She'd won; he just didn't know it yet.

Accompanying the two dozen photographs was a letter from the new Chief of Police in Marrakech which outlined the contents of the envelope to which it had been attached. Inside the envelope had been the photographs, an evidence docket, a typed suggestion that the photographs be burnt and a handwritten note giving reasons why they were to be sealed and marked for storage in a secure vault rather than destroyed.

No mention was made on the docket of the boy's name or where the photographs were taken, and the only name Petra Mayer recognized was scrawled on the first note, the one outlining reasons for the photographs' destruction, which was couched as a suggestion but read like an order.

Claude de Greuze. The man had been infamous.

"This is a good one," said the Professor. She crossed the tiles and dropped to a crouch in front of Prisoner Zero. His nakedness meant nothing to her and as for the stale sweat that rose from his body, it was what she would expect in this heat from any man who hadn't washed for a day or so. Petra Mayer was very pragmatic about these things.

"Take a look." She flipped the photograph round so Prisoner Zero could see a younger version of himself asleep and naked on a bed. When he moved his head she moved the photograph with it.

"Do you want to talk about it?"

The man shook his head, openly this time. And it was all Petra Mayer could do not to grin. Two psychiatrists, three doctors, a Moroccan diplomat and even a top-level military psychiatrist who'd worked Guantanamo Bay, brought out of retirement especially, and she was the one who got a reaction.

"Did Jake take these?" Another photograph, of the same boy sleeping. He looked younger in that one, more vulnerable and, Petra Mayer had to admit it, very obviously under-age.

"Does it matter?"

It was an interesting voice, particularly to someone like Petra Mayer, who had dabbled in social linguistics. Interesting because Prisoner Zero's voice had a slight dissonance, a mere trace of something usually found in those who'd remained silent for a long time, whether voluntary or enforced.

There was a second reason. Most people are defined by their voices—place, class and education all being easily identified. Languages adopted through the act of learning, however, carried indicators of the person teaching as well as of the person being taught.

The extreme examples were well known. Professor Mayer had met a Zambian physicist who'd read his original degree at a university outside Kiev and come back talking like an elderly Chechen prostitute. A palaeontologist at New York's natural history museum, a self-educated man from Brooklyn, spoke Persian with the Tabrizi accent of a 1950s aristocrat.

In the prisoner's statement were echoes of Moroccan Arabic, Upper East Side New York, received BBC pronunciation and something that could only be Amsterdam-inflected Dutch, which was the Netherlands' equivalent of Brooklyn.

"Of course it matters," said the Professor. "I want you to tell me what really happened."

The prisoner stood up, walked past her and dropped to a crouch by the bed, reaching out to take one particular photograph from the mattress and examine it carefully, while Professor Mayer looked over his shoulder.

Dark eyes stared from a half-turned face and the face looked towards the camera. In a looking glass behind the boy could be seen a naked sliver of the photographer, all soft hip and pale skin. Petra Mayer wondered why she hadn't seen it earlier.

When Prisoner Zero put the photograph of the naked boy back again it was face down beside the other pictures on the mattress. Although that still left several shots the right way up.

"They're good," she said.

The prisoner seemed slightly surprised, the first time his face had actually expressed emotion, and Petra Mayer absent-mindedly made a mark on a chart, checking the time on her watch without being seen to do so.

"Technically," she said. "I mean technically. Jake must have owned a good camera."

"It was Celia's," said the prisoner.

He'd only found out how expensive it was when he'd seen the thing advertised in a magazine. A newer model, minimal changes and an extortionate price. He'd thought of all *nasrani* as rich, that this richness varied Prisoner Zero only realized later, around the same time he finally came to understand how far the blonde Englishwoman had been up that particular scale.

"A Leica, with rapid-load and rewind, proper engraving to the brass, self-timer, functioning shutter and flash socket. They were handmade," Prisoner Zero added, just in case Petra Mayer didn't know this.

She'd offered him money, Celia had. Cash to get out of her life and start again, somewhere he wouldn't be known and cause her problems. At the time he'd thought the sum incredibly generous, even as he refused the envelope she tried to push into his hand. It was only later, when Jake told him about her father dying and the will being contested by two of the man's ex-wives, that Moz discovered just how much money had been settled on Celia on her eighteenth birthday, with more at twenty-one, twenty-five and thirty-two.

Then Celia's offer began to seem almost contemptuous. Of course, by then he'd done what she wanted and for nothing. He was out of her life and deep into the dregs of his own, a life circumscribed by Jake, heroin and the narrowness of a single mattress on the floor of an unfurnished squat in Amsterdam.

"Celia?" said Petra Mayer. Short questions generally worked best and she was old enough to have taught herself not to fill in the gaps, to leave space for what the other person wanted to say. "I thought Jake was your lover."

"Lady Celia Vere." The bitterness in the prisoner's voice was undeniable now. "Her uncle was British ambassador to Paris, you know."

Petra Mayer shuffled her file. "No," she said, "I didn't know. How did you first meet?"

Prisoner Zero smiled. "I stole her watch."

"Is that true?"

Prisoner Zero shook his head. "No," he said. "I only pretended it was me. Someone else took it."

"Who?"

"A girl called Malika," said Prisoner Zero, and then he didn't say anything else for a very long time.

## CHAPTER 43

### *Northern Mountains, CTzu 53/Year 20*

"You forgot this..."

The voice came out of nowhere. At least, that's what Tris thought until she realized it was the man she'd left sleeping, if "man" was the right word, which she was beginning to doubt.

"...and you'd better put that down."

Tris looked at the blade she held and then at the half light obscuring the entrance to her rocky overhang, where Luca was unwrapping himself into existence. The Baron had the manners not to point out that the child's sword Tris held was his.

She'd once spent a whole winter wanting his look. She'd been a kid back then, impressed by an older girl's quick and dirty body change. Of course, being a kid, Tris hadn't realized the new body was meant to look like Luca and she doubted if the other girl did either.

"What did I forget?" demanded Tris crossly. There was stuff in bed she'd have given a miss if she'd known she was going to see Luca again. Things like his bite to her throat and leaving one of her nails in his back.

Stepping around the blade, Luca smiled. "You left your marble on the chest."

Tris sighed. "It was a present," she said. "And it's not a marble."

"Oh." Luca looked thoughtful. "What is it then?"

"It's the memory," said Tris, "from my yacht."

"You had a yacht?"

"You saw it, remember? A C-class, X9 interchange." All objects of value in the 2023 worlds were grown individually, that's what Tris had always understood. And yet the owner of *All Tomorrow's Parties* still gave his ship a number. No wonder Doc Joyce hated him.

"Where did you get a yacht?"

Tris wanted to say, *Don't I look like a girl who might own an X9 interchange?* Unfortunately they both knew the answer to that.

"I stole it," said Tris, taking the marble from Luca. "Then we crashed into a lake except it was really a river. This is what's left."

They ate wild hare, roasted in the ashes of a fire Luca built in the mouth of the overhang. He took the wood from a long-dead thorn, snapping branches as easily as Tris might have broken twigs and igniting the fire with a snap of his fingers. He also set the trap. A slight thing that was little more than a noose, a thorn branch bent double and a V of twig to peg the thorn to the ground.

"That's it?" Tris had asked.

"Sure," said Luca, "it's enough."

He'd already discarded his leather satchel and was unbuckling his cloak at the time, fussing with a silver knot on its left shoulder. "It used to untie itself," he said. The cloak was already large enough but when Luca unfolded it once and then twice it became very big indeed.

"Find me a long stick," he said.

Tris almost said, *Find one yourself*. But she restrained herself and after setting the trap outside, she helped Luca make a bivouac from his cloak, the stick she'd found and a dozen small rocks arranged around the edge. Since the cave-like overhang already kept out the worst of the wind Tris wasn't sure this was necessary.

It was when she was putting the last of the stones into place that Luca came back with the hare. "Here," he said, "kill this."

"You do it," said Tris.

Luca shook his head and offered her the animal, which he had by the ears. "I'm not allowed to."

"But you eat meat?"

A nod, quick and totally unashamed.

"That doesn't make sense."

"Maybe not," said Luca, "but that's the way it is."

"Why?" Tris demanded, but she took hold of the hare, only just avoiding one of its back legs which raked towards her wrist. "Tell me—"

"Do you always ask too many questions?"

"Yeah," said Tris, "always."

Luca sighed. "The thing is," he said, crouching down to sit on his heels, "if I started killing I'm not sure I'd be able to stop. You wouldn't like that. So why don't you kill it, I'll cook it and we'll both eat the thing?"

"You're not human, are you?" Tris said, realizing as she said it that this might be a tactless question.

"Nor are you," said Luca, his voice matter-of-fact. "Actually, most people aren't. Not in any sense humans would understand... Now hurry up and kill the hare, anything else is cruel."

"We could let it go," Tris said. "That wouldn't be cruel."

"You need to eat," said Luca. "That's one point. The second is that the animal's half dead with fright so you have a duty to kill it." He nodded towards the small rock she'd only just put into place around the edge of his bivouac.

"Use that," he said. "And hold it the other way up or its ears will come off in your hands when you hit it."

Grabbing the hare by its back legs, Tris hung the animal upside down and thumped it hard with a stone on the back of its head without giving herself time to think. Shitting black raisins at her feet, the animal turned from something living to meat.

"You do the rest," Tris said.

Fifteen billion people watched her toss the dead hare at Luca's feet, although Tris didn't know this. Which was just as well, because the first thing she did after stalking from the camp and dry-vomiting away her disgust, was drop her silk trousers and raise the hem of her padded jacket, letting rivers of steam melt frosted blades of grass.

"Moron," she said.

And all the while, buzzards circled overhead and a lizard clung to rock, either dead or too catatonic with cold to move. There was no single camera watching Tris and Luca. Indeed, the concept "camera" meant nothing to Tris. If she'd stopped to wonder how feeds were fed she'd have decided *by magic*.

The truth was far stranger. Every living thing on Rapture watched everything else, from the cat that slunk across the yellow roof of the Emperor's pavilion to the single butterfly delivering a message as it touched his wrist. And the Library drew together these threads and, from them, created a seamless feed that was life in the Forbidden City.

Ripping a leg from the roasted body of the hare, Luca held it out as an offering. "Try it," he suggested.

They ate in silence.

It sleeted that night and again the next morning. What had started as sleet became hail, driven on a chill wind that roared down a valley into their faces. They had to set their next bivouac quickly and break it down just as fast, Luca converting their crude tent back into his cloak with a sleight of hand that Tris somehow always missed.

"You sure this is the right way?"

"No," said Luca, "I'm not."

"We should have brought a map."

Luca stared at the hail and sleet breaking up the world around them. "No point," he said. "Coordinates have zero meaning at this level." It was the last thing he said that day.

And Tris was ready to believe he'd forgotten her existence, except that once she slipped while stepping from rock to rock and Luca grabbed her so fast she barely saw his hands move. She slept in his arms that night as snow piled up against one side of the bivouac, although there was nothing sexual in his stroking of her hair and both retained their clothes.

"No," Luca had told her, when Tris first knelt to scrape snow from the hillside, making space for their bivouac. "Don't dig."

"Why not?"

"Sleeping on snow is warmer," he told her. "Here..."

Tris caught his knife.

"Stab the ground."

Shock echoed up Tris's arm and only the fact Luca's knife had a crossbar stopped Tris slicing her hand on the blade.

"That little sword of yours could break stabbing this stuff," said Luca. "It's permafrost. You need to know these things."

He read the question in her face.

"Because," Luca said, "you're meant to be doing this on your own."

The dreams were worse that night. So terrible that when she woke Tris would not allow herself to remember a thing. All she could feel was their numbness, as if the permafrost over which she slept had entered her soul. Having eaten the last scraps of roast hare without tasting, Tris reached for Luca and pulled him close.

"I'm not sure this is wise," said Luca, opening one eye.

Tris reached down with her hand. "You know what?" she said. "I'm not sure I care."

Afterwards, Luca scrambled out from under the cloak and disappeared behind a low strand of bushes. "Now you," he said on his return.

"It'll hold."

"No." The Baron shook his head. "It won't... From here on when we climb we're tied together. You want a piss, I'm this far away." He held his hands so, indicating distance.

In fact the gap between Luca and Tris as they climbed the first snow bank was greater than Luca had said it would be, if not by much. And Tris wore the stolen blade across her back, because Luca had insisted she take a long stick of thorn in each hand, so that if Tris missed her step she could jab her sticks into the snow and avoid sliding back the way she came. He also made her walk first, on the grounds that if she did slip he might be able to catch her.

The dreams haunted her again that night and followed her into the day. All Tris got were glimpses from the side of one eye. Patches of snow that kept pace, stalking the edge of her vision where endless flakes of falling snow lost themselves in a perpetual half glow that ice fields seemed to bring with them.

Once she saw something stranger.

Amber eyes like Luca's, but staring from the face of a huge cat. She told Luca about this and in return he told her about snow blindness, hypothermia, oxygen starvation and their collective responsibility for her hallucinations. He left out the pain, Tris noticed, and after a few minutes she zoned him out and concentrated on climbing the icy slope in front of her.

Every now and then, Tris would thrust one hand inside the front of her padded jacket and nestle it under her armpit in an attempt to thaw out her fingers and once, when Luca was looking at something else, she thrust both hands between her legs. The pain of her fingers unfreezing hurt so much that tears crystallized on her cheeks like pearls.

Around midday they stopped climbing, the snow underfoot levelled out and then began, very gently, to dip in the opposite direction.

"That was it?" said Tris as she unknotted Luca's rope and dropped her end in the snow. "That was your cliff?"

Luca frowned. "Tristesse," he said heavily, "we've barely started."

He wouldn't look at her for the rest of that afternoon and, come evening, he just scooped out a shallow dip in a snowdrift, did whatever he did to his cloak and buried the edges of the newly created bivouac beneath the snow to keep them secure. He made no attempt to start a fire, nor did he invite Tris inside when finally he crawled under the cloth.

After a few minutes, Tris clambered inside anyway.

They slept like husband and wife, back to back, not touching. It was an old, sour joke from her grandmother. One she'd failed to understand until that night, the night the snow tigers came.

When the first animal padded silently out of the darkness, Tris was restless and already awake. The tiger came in a gap between falls of snow. A handful of white shadow and smoke-grey stripes, paws the size of plates carrying it over a skim of frozen crust, its tail brushing the snow as it loped out of the darkness and halted outside Luca's make-shift tent.

The others came in the seconds which followed.

It was their breathing Tris heard first. "Me?" she asked, in case there was some mistake. And the biggest of the tigers nodded, fat strands of spittle drooling onto pale snow.

"Malika," it said when Tris stayed where she was.

"I'm Tris," said Tris. She wasn't too sure they'd got that bit.

"Malika," repeated the tiger.

She went to it anyway, crawling from beneath Luca's bivouac and walking barefoot over the snow crust, leaving lonely footprints behind her. All three were beautiful, elegant beyond anything life had let Tris imagine. Their eyes amber and their claws tallow, like ancient ivory.

"You're beautiful," she said.

The biggest tiger's casual nod seemed to suggest that this was obvious.

"Can I feel?" Reaching out Tris tangled her cold fingers into warm fur. And as soon as her hand gripped the tiger's mane, the beast began to move, slowly but decisively.

"She's going," said a voice.

"Not much we can do about it now." That voice was different. Come to that, so was the voice before. Rougher, speaking words Tris barely understood.

"Doesn't matter," the first voice said. "We've got enough."

The snow had stopped burning Tris's feet. Her fingers felt normal. She no longer felt the need to clamp her hands between her legs or across her chest, hiding them in the darkness of her underarms. Even her smell was gone, that stink of bruised flesh and ripped pain.

"Damn," said a voice.

"You tell me," Luca said. He was sitting outside his bivouac, cupping his hands around a flame that leapt between his thumbs, like electricity arcing between points. Tris had just asked him why she was standing bootless in the snow.

He didn't seem that surprised to see her or that pleased either. "Knew you'd be back," he said, stuffing his hands in his pockets. "Where else could you go?"

Tris knew this was untrue and wanted to explain how difficult it had been to leave the tigers, how painful wrenching her hands from the flame of their fur, but she was too busy looking at Luca's face.

Someone had clawed ragged lines across his cheek, four gashes that ran from near his ear to the side of his chin. And to judge from the holes in the snow and the discarded pink-streaked, compacted handfuls of ice around his feet, Luca had been trying for some time to staunch the bleeding.

"The tigers attacked you?"

The Baron stared at her. He looked thinner than yesterday, which was thinner than the day before. His eyes were huge and his mouth twisted into something between anger and disgust. He seemed to be waiting for something.

"An apology would be good," he said at last.

"For what?"

"Oh." Luca shrugged. "I don't know... How about for trying to rip off half my face and disappearing into the wilderness for two hours?"

"Me?"

"Yeah," said Luca, "you." One hand went up to touch his face.

"It can't have been me," said Tris. "I wasn't even here."

"Yes, you were," said Luca. "And it was." Scooping up snow, he held it to his cheek and then tossed away the soiled handful. "You want to tell me why you did it?"

"I... wasn't... here." Tris left a gap between each word, just in case Luca needed time to digest their sense. "And," Tris added, speeding up, "if I wasn't here, then I couldn't have done it, could I?"

"So where were you?"

"With the snow tigers," said Tris. "I heard them breathing. And when I looked outside they were waiting for me. They were beautiful," she said. Tris wanted to say more but sadness had tightened her throat. She should have stayed with them, she knew that now.

The tigers were right.

Luca sighed. "Maybe you were having nightmares," he said.

Moss spiralled along the main cables where fat cords had been twisted together and weather-bleached ropes hummed in the wind that whistled along the canyon, keeping the suspension bridge mostly clear of snow.

Two rusting iron rings had been set into a rock-face behind Tris. What happened at the other end was impossible to say because everything but the first ten paces of the bridge was lost in a flurry of snow.

"I've heard of this," Luca told Tris.

It occurred in a story his father had told him. About the first ambassador from Luca's people to set out for the Forbidden City. He began the trip without permission from the Tsungli Yamen, the Bureau of Foreign Affairs. And having packed his family gods into a lacquer trunk and commanded his servants to carry himself and his wife in separate sedan chairs, he set out for the capital of the 2023 worlds, leaving Luca's father in charge of his affairs.

Luca's father never told his son exactly what happened, but over the years Luca came to understand that it was a disaster. The sedan chairs were found ripped apart in a ravine near the start of the plateau. A silk *changfu* belonging to the ambassador's wife was discovered two days later, tied to a pole like a flag and rammed into the snow.

That was all Luca's father ever said.

The original Baron Pacioli had hated the 2023 worlds. No one in the worlds did what they were told, because there was no one but the Library to tell them what to do and the Library never told, it merely suggested.

This had taken Luca's father most of his life to understand. No families were bound to other families. No groups depended for employment or shelter on the obligation of others. Indeed, Luca's father wasn't sure the concept of family even existed on most of the 2023 worlds in any sense he understood.

People lived, they were fed by the Library and they died when they wanted. No codes enforced dress or behaviour. Names, sexes, body shapes and relationships were fluid and all could be changed without attracting approbation.

And in the middle of this chaotic fluidity lived the Chuang Tzu, his every move subject not just to age-old rules and regulations but to intense interest and speculation from the 148 billion individuals Luca's father assumed the Emperor existed to govern.

Because there was the other problem. So far as Baron Pacioli could work out, the Emperor issued no laws and delivered no judgements, no one needed his permission to do anything. The throne was powerless, his importance apparently token. Unless, of course, that stuff about the weather was true and chaos was what the Emperor required from his subjects.

"Which world?" Luca asked, suddenly turning back to face Tris.

"What?"

They were at the edge of the chasm and the rope bridge disappeared into the blizzard ahead of them. Luca and Tris had been standing like this for some time.

"Which world are you from?" said Luca. "They all have names, don't they?" He'd known those names once, as a small child.

"We've been through this." The girl's voice was entirely matter-of-fact. "I don't come from a world."

"You must," Luca said. "Where else could you be from?"

"Heliconid," said Tris. "You won't have heard of it."

In the end it was Tris who stepped onto the bridge. She had Luca's rope tied around her waist and both thorn sticks strapped across her back. She had her blade drawn and held in her right hand. For some reason Luca found this hysterically funny, although he wouldn't tell her why.

Testing each plank before putting her weight on it meant it took Tris the best part of an hour to cover a distance she could have walked in five minutes at her normal speed. And when the blizzard cleared and the far end of the bridge remained resolutely out of sight, Tris agreed with Luca that they'd have to do it differently.

"Okay," she said, as she untied the rope knotted around her waist and handed it to Luca. "I need you to lengthen this." Tris didn't know how Luca would do it, she only knew he could.

"Much better," said Tris, when he returned the end to her.

Retying the rope around her waist, Tris tested the knot by yanking it as hard as she could. "We don't have time to check every step," Tris said, sounding more sure than she felt. "So I'm going to walk normally and you'll save me if I fall through. And if you fall through then I'll save you . . . Although that's not as likely."

Afterwards Tris came to believe that she'd walked the bridge for weeks, maybe months, suspended over a nothingness so deep that, even on the afternoons the snow cleared, she never saw the bottom.

In fact, it took less than three days. Seventy-two hours during which a final figure of ninety-eight billion people watched Tris slip into a mental state little higher than stupefaction. It was during the last of these days that Tris decided she would burn the Chuang Tzu's precious pavilions around his ears.

She didn't remember telling Luca this, although she remembered his answer. Which was that the idea probably acquired its all-encompassing appeal from the fact that she was dying of cold.

The sheer strangeness of Tris's journey was enough to make even those who scorned the feeds decide to make an exception. Rumour in the 2023 worlds was a strange beast, widely recognized and little understood, except by a few ancient mememagicians who studied more for the sake of study than from hope of surpassing the early masters.

Somehow, during those seventy-two hours, the idea that watching a girl from a non-world walk a bridge might be culturally required reached tipping point, jumping from those who would watch anything rather than live themselves to those who treated all external input with suspicion. From here, the tale of her ridiculous quest passed to the cold immortals, who found meaning not in her intention to kill an emperor who waited impatiently for her arrival but in the sheer innocence of her battle against his weather.

She became, without knowing it, the container for a billion conflicting interpretations of what it meant to be alive.

A few million bet on her survival, others set out for Rapture to offer their help or to attempt to duplicate her journey, but most just watched from the corner of their minds, not letting Tris's journey take up too much of their thoughts but never forgetting it either.

In a civilisation once described by one of its oldest minds as an endless dinner party at which no one knew who were guests and who the waiters, what occasion was being celebrated or who was paying for the meal, Tris's battle with herself engrained itself into the conversation.

It helped, of course, that no one knew who the girl was or why she talked to a companion no one else could see. There were no eight degrees of separation, nor sixteen, thirty-two or sixty-four... She was tabula rasa, which was interesting and in its own way quite terrifying to worlds in which everyone knew each other, even if they didn't.

## CHAPTER 44

### *Marrakech, Summer 1977*

The deal offered to Jake was simple.

Exile.

Jake would leave Marrakech, taking Celia with him. Riad al-Razor would be sold, within the month if possible and certainly by the end of that summer. As it turned out, Major Abbas was able to recommend a discreet and trustworthy agent who could be relied on both to find a suitable buyer and handle any legal matters that might arise.

And it would be best if their Peugeot was included in the price of the sale. Did Jake have any problems with the suggestions so far?

De Greuze said nothing during all of this. The revelation about Jake's family had shifted his priorities and he wasn't about to mess with the grandson of a known philanthropist with the direct ear of the American President. All the same, he'd already palmed one of the nude photographs of that boy which Jake had dealt so casually from the pile with his thumb, leaving a really rather beautiful fingerprint.

Jake and Celia were sitting on the pink-painted wicker sofa, de Greuze had pulled up the largest chair without being asked and Major Abbas had announced that he preferred to stand. Moz had been sent to the kitchen to make mint tea.

"Here," he said, banging his tray onto the table.

Celia smiled. "I'll have mine unsweetened. You'd better check with the others." When the tea was poured into glasses, she made him go back for a plate of pastries, mostly chopped pistachio mixed with honey and variations on baklava.

Moz was preparing himself to be furious when he noticed that de Greuze and Major Abbas were more furious still. It was like a card game in which everyone but him knew the rules.

"Give me your bank details," said the Major to Jake. "I'll have the money sent on." They were still discussing the finer points of the deal.

"No." Celia shook her head. "Arrange a dollar bank draft and have it sent to these people." The card she pulled from her leather satchel gave the address of a New York attorney who specialized in handling the more difficult kind of celebrity client. "I'll tell them to expect the money."

Jake only made the grade with that firm because of his family, his musical career to date not being enough to rate him client status. A fact both the attorney and Celia had been careful never to point out.

When Major Abbas made the mistake of looking doubtful Celia told him in painstaking and patronising detail which Marrakchi bank could act as go-between, what kind of commission they would expect and how long it would take to organize. "I'm sure the agent you have in mind can handle it."

If Jake were going to lose the riad and be banished from Marrakech, which effectively was what had just happened, then Celia wasn't about to retire without leaving a few scars.

"So we just leave?" Jake said. He didn't seem to be asking the question of anyone in particular. "And take Moz with us."

"That wasn't what I said," the Major replied, dipping his hand into a pocket and removing a packet of small cigars. Smoke spiralled towards the sky as he looked from Jake to Moz, noticing the similarity of their haircuts, jeans and general slouch. He should have seen it before.

"This boy is under-age," Major Abbas told Jake. "He also lacks a passport. Anyone attempting to take him out of Morocco would be breaking the law. You understand me?"

Jake nodded.

"Good. Were such a thing to happen... It would be very inadvisable for that person to come back to Marrakech again."

Jake assumed that the land agent was in the Major's pay and would organize matters so that Riad al-Razor was sold cheaply to a member of the Major's immediate family. This assumption was untrue. Being unmarried and an only son, the Major had no family.

The agent Major Abbas had in mind was actually a brother of his deputy who would probably sell the house to a cousin of his own. The money would then be split into three sums, with the first and largest going to the American bank mentioned by Celia, a second and smaller amount going into the agent's own account and a third and equivalent sum going to the Major.

Had Celia been Moroccan or even *au fait* with the etiquette of buying houses in North Africa, there would have been a fourth sum, made by splitting the largest sum two thirds–one third. The second of those sums would have been declared to the authorities as the price of the riad, becoming liable to any taxes that might be appropriate, and the first would have gone straight into Jake's pocket.

Nobody shook hands when the Major and de Greuze left. Instead Jake stood under the arch of the front door and watched the *petite taxi* pull away from where it had been parked against the wall of a mosque.

"I reckon we've got till the end of the week," he told Celia. "I'll go buy a VW. You find the kid some new clothes..." And that was when Moz finally realized a deal had been struck and that, at no point, had anyone let him have the slightest say in the matter.

He would be leaving Marrakech with the others. Jake and Celia had known from the beginning that Malika was beyond saving.

"No," said Moz, tears in his eyes. "I won't."

"Won't what?" Celia sounded puzzled.

"I'm not leaving," Moz said. "You can't make me. And it was a lie. I wasn't here. I was with—"

Malika's name was lost in the sound of Jake backhanding the boy across his face, swearing loudly and stamping inside, slamming the front door behind him.

"Fuckwit," said Moz.

Celia sighed. "That wasn't clever," she said. Moz thought she was talking about Jake but he might have been wrong. She might well have been talking about him.

# CHAPTER 45

## *CIA HQ Langley, Monday 9 July*

Paula Zarte shut her office door and then changed her mind. She'd made a point of operating an open-door policy and saw no reason to signal that this might be about to change. In practice, the only people who asked to see her were those she'd have seen anyway.

The difference was previous heads of the CIA had operated a section-heads-only policy and this was obvious and known. Paula had made it clear that anyone in the Agency who felt the need could ask to see her. The end result was the same but she'd acquired a reputation for openness that had reached the *Washington Post* and done much to cement the belief that things within the Agency had changed.

"Sit," she said, indicating a chair better suited to One Washington Circle or the Mercer in SoHo. Agent Wharton glanced doubtfully at the white leather but did what he was told. He sat on the very edge of the chair and leant forward, with a file of notes on his knee.

"You took Bill Hagsteen to see the President?"

Agent Wharton nodded.

"How did it go?" Paula Zarte watched the young man turn the question round in his head, examining it from every angle.

When he was certain it was safe, Agent Wharton said, "It went well."

"Good." Paula Zarte smiled. "What did they talk about?"

This elicited a much longer silence. "Warren Zevon mostly," Michael Wharton said finally. "About the round-up of musicians playing on his last album. A bit about John Hyatt..."

Paula Zarte's office looked out onto a lawn set with sprinklers and a high-tech security system that relied on everything from pressure pads across paths to infrared sensors and directional mikes. A very beautiful and meticulously tended lawn, it had to be mown twice a week with a hand mower because anything more sophisticated might upset the security system.

Standing up from her desk, Paula Zarte went across to the window and looked down at two men walking across the grass. They were both nu-school CIA, thin and fit, probably teetotal and dressed like fashion plates in something understated but expensive.

They made her feel antique.

Her life had improved in the last few weeks. Mike had stopped coming home at midnight and was muttering about maybe taking the kids to Orlando for Christmas. He'd hate the place and so, she imagined, would the kids, being precisely the wrong age. She was pleased all the same.

They weren't back to sex yet, although Paula could see that happening. Maybe they should be the ones to go to Orlando and leave the kids with her mother. The kids would probably prefer that anyway.

Paula's Puerto Rican bodyguard was gone, fast-tracked to the next level and reassigned to San Francisco. Doubt and the faintest trace of bitterness had filled Felicia's eyes when Paula described this as a well-deserved promotion, but the new job was a good one and what else could Paula do?

Felicia had traced Mike to a hotel in Baltimore and found out far more than Paula now wanted her to know. Of course, Paula had been the one who'd asked Felicia to do it. And it had been the President's offer of an ambassadorship in Central America that brought Mike to heel. He wasn't stupid, he knew exactly what that meant.

"They talked about Warren Zevon?" Paula said over her shoulder, watching the two young agents close an outside door behind them. She was due to address their section head shortly. As yet she had no idea what to tell him.

"Mostly... The President also wanted to know about something called the Stiff Tour."

"The Stiff what?"

"'If it ain't stiff it ain't worth a fuck'..." Agent Wharton spread his hands apologetically. "It was a seventies thing in England apparently.

Bill Hagsteen played drums briefly in a support act. That was when he first toured with Jake Razor."

"He's *absolutely* sure it's the man he knew?"

"Prisoner Zero? Yes, absolutely. Bill Hagsteen told the President he was kicking himself for not recognizing Jake from the start. You know, in Paris, when he and his... When they went looking for Jake."

"He and his what?" Paula Zarte asked.

"Partner," Agent Wharton mumbled and Paula sighed. He was even younger than she'd imagined.

"Jim James, the photographer, right?"

"Yes, ma'am."

"And where's Bill Hagsteen now?"

"Downstairs, ma'am. In one of the holding rooms."

"Let him wait." Paula turned back to her desk and reached for a file, then changed her mind. Agent Wharton wasn't the person to talk to about its contents. In fact, Paula Zarte was beginning to resign herself to the fact there might not be a right person to talk to, and that included Mike.

The big question and the one Paula didn't really feel competent to answer was should that also include the President? If she could read Gene's mind, which would he want—for Prisoner Zero to be Jake Razor or for the man to be some North African kid grown old and bitter?

She was coming close to making real enemies of the Department of Justice, the Attorney General and the Pentagon. And it was a tough call, even for someone whose job it was to make such calls.

Prisoner Zero was still on death row, put there by a military commission and with an execution date set at least one week before the start of Ramadan, because the last thing America needed was to execute an Arab on the eve of a major Islamic fast.

Only now everyone thought Prisoner Zero was American, which presumably meant that America could do what they wanted with him. Except if Gene pardoned him half the world would decide it was because he wasn't Arab after all.

"Cancel the briefing," she said. Paula was talking to a squawk box on her desk and not Agent Wharton, who looked up guiltily and then relaxed once he realized he wasn't the one being addressed.

"Send my apologies," Paula added. "Oh, and organize a secure video link to all the section chiefs for six p.m. Eastern Standard

Time. Okay, Steve? I want hearts and minds for all areas on local responses...

"No," Paula said heavily. "Not the execution. The equations." Steve Duffy was pretty, enthusiastic and ticked off the boxes for a handful of the government's affirmative action requirements, being trailer poor, dyslexic and gay. Unfortunately he was also none too bright.

"And get me Professor Mayer on the secure line, then Vice Questore Pier Angelo... the Italian," she said, "and the President's private secretary. In that order."

## CHAPTER 46

### *Zigin Chéng, CTzu 53/Year 20*

"I'm winning," Zaq said. "So you might as well go away." Every looking glass the Emperor passed showed him the same thing...

A man with a scroll under his right arm and long scholarly robes tumbling down that side, his long fingers stroking a poet's chin. The Librarian had the obligatory beard of a Taoist thinker and thin moustaches that draped into wisps of white hair.

And every time the Chuang Tzu caught a mirror's eye, the Librarian would open his mouth to say something and then close it as the Emperor strode by.

In his other hand the Librarian carried a long halberd, its blade facing towards the floor. The left side of his body was armoured with plate mail over padded leather and a steel helmet switched to a scholar's cap along a line bisecting the middle of his forehead.

The split between warrior and scholar represented the classic virtues required of the Emperor's tutor and, by extension, of the Emperor himself. Zaq was only too aware that his own *chao pao* militated against mockery of the old man's costume.

An embroidered dragon coiled across the front of Zaq's formal court robes, which were for a duke, first class. Zaq changed his clothes every day now, switching ranks at random and varying the path of his early morning walks through the outer pavilions.

He did this for amusement and because he knew that it worried the Library. Sometime soon, Zaq would have to face the glass and listen as the Librarian explained what Zaq already knew. That a young assassin, crazed with cold and loneliness, was working her way across the bridge between plateaux. A dark-haired, thin child who held conversations with the air and carried a large knife with which to rip out the heart of the Chuang Tzu.

Everyone Zaq met in the palace thought he was hiding from the danger facing him. Zaq could see it in their faces and hear it in the way conversations stilled as he swept through the corridors.

They were wrong.

Zaq knew all about the cold assassin and he assumed the Library knew about the prisoner trapped on a sun-baked island who carried the emperor's dreams. War could be a very complex business and weapons were not always what they seemed.

"Majesty..."

"Excellency," Zaq corrected. The soldier should be able to work out for himself that he stood in front of a duke and not an emperor. Zaq tried hard to recall the man's name, screwing up his face as he did so.

*Tso Chi?*

*Li Han?*

He could ask the Library, only then Zaq would have to talk to the Librarian about the other thing and that was exactly what he was trying to avoid.

"General Ch'ao Kai," said Chuang Tzu, and saw surprise turn to pleasure as the bannerman understood he'd been recognized. "This must be important." They both understood the hidden rebuke. All were forbidden to acknowledge the Chuang Tzu's existence and there were no exceptions.

The old soldier nodded. "I beg Your Excellency's permission to deploy troops outside the city wall."

"And why would you want to do that?" Zaq asked without thinking. He should have said something like *Deploy troops, for what reason?* But more and more these days he forgot to keep his thoughts formal, his face measured.

"Just manoeuvres, Excellency. The troops need exercise. I thought you might approve of the idea."

The man lied badly.

Zaq smiled. It was a gentle smile, the kind one might expect from either a poet faced with a particularly beautiful waterfall or a scholar presented with a scroll no other scholar had seen for a thousand years. The kind an emperor might give in the face of death.

"No," he said. "I don't think so."

Real anguish crossed the old General's face. So convincing in fact that Zaq was impressed yet again with the sheer inventiveness of the Library.

"They can exercise in front of the Taihe Dien," Zaq said, the nearest he was prepared to get to a compromise.

"And in the outer city, Excellency?"

"The square," Zaq said firmly. "Then I can watch them from the Supreme Harmony Gate." He wouldn't, of course. In all his years as Chuang Tzu he'd only ever watched the troops on one occasion. He understood the levels of skill required, but had little personal interest in the use of weapons.

Smiling at the old man, Chuang Tzu touched him lightly on his shoulder and turned to go, leaving General Ch'ao Kai looking after him. Somehow his generals were always old, always bearded and dressed in elaborate armour that seemed to consist mostly of polished tortoiseshell and red ribbon. Red was the colour of luck and given the amount used in the Forbidden City, Zaq should have been very lucky indeed.

"Majesty..." The voice came down the corridor behind him and the fact it was aimed at his back was such a breach of court etiquette that Ch'ao Kai had to be truly desperate. Zaq could stop or he could keep walking and send a clear sign that he did not choose to hear what the General was so desperate to say.

He stopped, that was all, stopped and stood in silence, dressed in a ceremonial *chao pao* as if conducting negotiations or taking a wife. And all those not watching Tris struggle her way across the bridge listened to a grey-haired, sad-eyed man tell his Emperor that the Librarian urgently requested a word.

And those fifteen billion watched Chuang Tzu shake his head, surprisingly regretfully, and then keep walking.

Many of them were still watching when Zaq skirted the Western Palaces and the Thousand Autumns Pavilion on his way to the rockeries and walkways of the Yuhua Yuan, the Butterfly Garden.

They didn't realize it yet but the Emperor had made a decision. Here was where he intended to stay. Not just for the morning or the rest of that day. Zaq would stay for however many nights and days it took for the Library to bring him the assassin.

And when this happened and the stranger had made it across the bridge and into the Forbidden City, Zaq would stare the young assassin in the eyes and ask the question 148 billion people wanted answered.

Why?

And then, if he was lucky, Zaq might finally be allowed to sleep.

"Shit," Luca said, then apologized.

Tris smiled. She could have told him words far worse. Some so vile he'd probably need coaching in their meaning. This thought kept her amused until he swore again, which was soon.

"What?" she said, stepping from one plank to another.

"Just this," said Luca. So thick was the falling snow that there were whole hours, sometimes longer, in which Luca drifted from sight behind her and Tris was anchored to his absence through a haze of floating white that stung like memory as it turned to tears on her face.

She had frostbite, her lips were frozen into a rictus grin and her ears felt missing, along with most of her fingers and both her feet from the ankles down. Only the wind was in their favour, having switched direction and turned to a light breeze that no longer threw snow directly into their faces.

"Keep going," Luca said.

Tris's world was reduced to narrow and uncertain strips of ice which glazed the ancient wooden planks over which she stepped. Luca's blade was stuck through her belt and she knew this was a stupid way to carry a naked weapon, but having the blade visible reminded her why she put one step after another instead of just doing what she wanted to do, which was curl up into a ball and give herself back to sleep. Instead she put one foot in front of the other and kept walking...

"Why have you stopped?"

Tris turned to find Luca at her side and realized she'd been staring over the edge of the bridge without even realizing it, both hands gripping one of the main cables. And she'd been standing there for so long that snow had made gloves of the backs of her fingers.

"I can't remember," Tris said.

"You okay?"

"Sure," said Tris, then thought about it. "I don't even know where I am," she said, gesturing wearily at the way ahead and then turning to include what little could be seen of the bridge behind, which was a half-dozen frosted planks that did scant justice to the hours they'd been walking. "Of course I'm not okay," she said. "How could I be?"

"We're almost there." Luca put one hand lightly on her shoulder and appeared not to notice when Tris shook it off.

"Two days at the most," she said. "Wasn't that what you told me?" They both knew it was and yet Luca seemed unfazed by the endlessness of the planks and almost happy that the ice glazing each one was becoming thinner by the hour. "So what changed?"

"I think," said Luca, "it's more a case of what's changing." He glanced at the cloud and then at the snowflakes which continued to fall long after they passed where Luca stood on the bridge beside Tris, both of them gripping a fat cable and staring into the abyss.

" 'What's changing'?"

"Well," Luca said, "there aren't that many alternatives. And since I doubt that time is expanding it must be the bridge."

"How can a bridge expand?"

"How can it not?" Luca slipped off his cloak and did something with his hands that unravelled whole layers of material not visible a moment earlier. "You sleep now," he said. "I'll keep guard."

As dawn filtered through the falling snow, Luca lifted his cloak and looked at the dying girl. She was so pale and so obviously frozen that the decision made itself. Pulling his hands from his pockets, Luca held them close to the girl's face and willed flame to dance between his fingertips.

And then, because this was not enough, he crawled under the cloak and wrapped both cloak and himself around Tris. He was alone on a bridge with a sleeping child, her head now resting on his knees and he felt... Luca wasn't too sure how he felt; fonder, probably, than he should have been of a creature not quite human and yet not like him either.

(And he knew that "child" was a relative term, but the brief span of her life could not be measured against the expanse of his.)

Baron Luca Pacioli was tired and old, despite appearances, and had come to realize he belonged neither to the civilization into which his father had been born nor to the 2023 worlds, which talked only to each other and so barely knew that Luca's people even existed. This was hard because Luca understood at least as well as the Tsungli Yamen that he was not allowed to die until he'd been received by the Emperor, even though the Bureau of Foreign Affairs refused to accept his world existed.

"Come on," Luca said, flicking his fingers to produce a flame that even he could see was less bright than it had been. "You need to wake up now."

And although many billions heard cold wind hum against the down ropes holding the planks on which Tris slept and a few million noticed that flakes fell oddly around a patch of snow on which the sleeping figure rested her head, none watching saw Luca or the sorrow that filled his amber eyes.

They just saw flames come from nowhere to warm the face of the girl as her cloak seemed to gather itself tight around her. She had powers, most of those watching agreed amongst themselves, talking across great distances with a single thought. And those powers, it was then agreed, made it possible that she might reach the Forbidden City after all.

Possible, but not likely.

A few billion of those still not watching began to watch, while many of those who'd announced they regarded the whole affair as tawdry and insignificant began to wonder if maybe they had been wrong.

## CHAPTER 47

### *Marrakech, Summer 1977*

In the end, Malika's body found him.

"Moz, wait," Idries said. His face was strained, his fingers curled in on themselves, broken nails biting into his own flesh. His jellaba was filthy and his lips looked bitten.

"Fuck off," said Moz, not stopping.

"Hassan is looking for you."

"So?" Moz threw the comment over his shoulder. Already he was pushing his way through a crowd of *nasrani* tourists spilling from a coach onto a pavement outside a market in Gueliz.

"It's about Malika."

Moz stopped so abruptly that one of the foreigners ran into him.

Whatever she saw in the eyes of the Marrakchi kid made her step back and take a sudden interest in a display of terracotta bowls.

"Malika?"

"You'd better come with me."

"Where is she?"

"Hassan will tell you," Idries said. Something like fear nictated across his eyes. Something dark, something adult.

"You tell me."

Idries shook his head. "Hassan will tell you," he insisted.

Between that market and their destination stood ten minutes of strained silence and whitewashed palm trees that flaked onto stone pavements built by the French and then abandoned along with the villas more than twenty years before. An Alsatian barked from behind a wrought-iron gate, the name on the post something European and strange. The streets became shabby as Idries led Moz away from Avenue Mohammed V towards the area around the Prison Civile, becoming smarter as Moz and Idries came out into a road that skirted Le Cimetière Européen.

To their left was a dark slant of rock jutting from the red earth as nakedly as broken bone. Jbel Gueliz, little more than a toy mountain.

Dogs howled, scrawny cats slunk against walls and doves fluttered around a tall, white-painted cote. They met carts laden with tomatoes and peppers and stepped aside for a farting three-wheeled truck over-crowded with sheep. A comforting smell of dung filled the air as they passed two donkeys tethered on a half-finished building plot, guarded by a boy barely half as tall as his animals.

Moz was saying goodbye to the city without knowing it and stacking his head with fragments when he thought his mind already numbed beyond caring. Although, mostly what Moz was to recall about that afternoon was Idries two steps in front of him, head down and walking so fast that Moz could barely keep up, despite being both taller than Idries and stronger.

The other boy was—almost literally—running away from Moz's questions. They both understood that. Idries's answers reduced to jagged breathing and an endless repetition of "Hassan will tell you." Moz knew he should stop asking, just as surely as Idries realized this wasn't going to happen. So Moz hurried along behind, his shoulders hunched and fear pressing in on him.

On any other day he'd have been wincing at the rawness of his split lip or stripping off his T-shirt to show Malika the blood-dark bruising all over his body, only Malika . . .

The physical pain Moz felt was nothing compared to his fear and both were subsumed beneath his need to arrive wherever it was Idries was taking him.

"How far?"

"Over there," Idries said, pointing to a gate in a wall. Moz could see the relief in his eyes. "Hassan's waiting inside. He'll explain."

"About time."

"Over there," repeated Idries and then sunk to his heels, grabbing oxygen from the hot air. Stains had blossomed under his sleeves and a dark patch spread from the centre of his chest, where sweat had soaked through the blue cotton of his cheap jellaba.

Moz knew it was bad when Hassan came to meet him. Quite how bad he only realized when the older boy put out his hand.

Absent-mindedly, Moz shook it and then watched Hassan step back to touch his hand to his own heart and then forehead, lifting his fingers away with a slight flick of the wrist. It was an old-fashioned, sadly formal gesture.

"I'm sorry," Hassan said. There was none of the usual bravado in his voice. He could have been Moz's friend, not one of his lifelong enemies and loser of their most recent fight. "I had no idea..."

"Where is she?"

"Behind the Jesu."

This was an old statue of the *nasrani* god draped in the robes of a Sufi and staring up to heaven. Heat, wind and a poor choice of sandstone meant that the figure was barely recognizable.

And the choice of location meant that whoever was responsible knew Malika's childhood secrets. Behind the Jesu was where Moz and Malika met as children, that summer they became friends. A circle of beaten earth in the middle of a thicket of thorns. A place, even then, of crushed beer cans, soiled tissues and peeling, piss-coloured filters from stolen cigarettes. That was how Moz thought of it, when he remembered the place at all.

"It's bad," Hassan said.

Moz looked at him.

"Whatever you're imagining," Hassan said, "it's worse." Without even thinking about it, the older boy made a sign against the evil eye. "You don't have to see her," Hassan added, as if he'd only just realized that. "I can ask my uncle to—"

"She was my friend."

The very flatness of Moz's voice told Hassan this was not an argument worth having, so instead he pointed to a gap between two bushes. "Through there," he said. "I'll be waiting. The debt is mine."

Settling himself against the trunk of a pine, Hassan reached into his pocket and found a packet of cigarettes. It took him three goes to get his fingers steady enough to light one of the things.

## CHAPTER 48

### *Washington, Tuesday 10 July*

"How's Ally?" asked Paula Zarte.

"Still wants a cat." Gene Newman's smile was sour. "Still thinks I should be able to talk her mother into allowing it."

"And that stuff with the boy?"

The President looked at his Director of the CIA. "You're keeping tabs on *Ally*?"

Paula Zarte shook her head. "Ally texted me," she said. "Girl talk."

Gene Newman wasn't sure how he felt about that. And there was something more important worrying him. "You know," he said, "the First Lady's not going to like this."

Glancing round the low-lit restaurant, Paula took in the other couples bent over their meals or gazing into each other's eyes. A plate of squid-ink linguini sat untouched before her.

The President had eaten two grissini, leaving crumbs all over the white linen tablecloth, and was looking doubtfully at a bowl piled high with mussels. A bottle of a good Frescobaldi Frascati was chilling in an ice bucket next to their table.

"She's not going to know," Paula Zarte said.

When Gene Newman raised his eyebrows it was in a studied, post-ironic sort of way. It was simpler than asking the question which was on his tongue. Just what the fuck did the elegant black woman in the simple Armani jacket think she was doing? She'd called him direct and they had an agreement about not doing that. What's more, she called him on his family cell phone, a number he didn't even know she had.

It was true he'd had an assistant her husband was seeing reassigned to duties outside the White House and he knew how outrageous that was. Paula also knew this was how it worked. In these kinds of deal it was the woman who got moved or fired, because she was invariably younger and had less powerful allies.

If he'd had his choice, he'd have made Mike take the ambassador's job in Ecuador but Paula was against that. Mike and he had history, which was pretty obvious really, given he'd slept with the other man's wife.

"Stop worrying," Paula Zarte said. "At least, stop worrying about that. And believe me," she said, "there are a lot more serious things for you to worry about."

"You think nobody's going to talk?" The President gestured at the tables around them. He'd been sat with his back to the wall, next to a door that led through to a loading bay. One of his agents stood by the door, another guarded the loading bay and a third guarded the loading bay exit in the alley outside.

"Of course they're not going to talk," Paula Zarte said. "There isn't a single person here whose salary isn't paid by the Agency . . . They're mine," she explained, when the President look bemused. "The place was closed for renovation. As of now it's opened a week early."

Paula Zarte smiled. "The owner used to be one of ours," she added. "It was simpler to do it this way."

"Simpler?"

"It gives us deniability. Say this gets out. What's the worst anyone can say?"

"That we had supper together in a tiny Italian restaurant where no one in the White House has ever eaten before. One which was obviously chosen because it was out of the way."

"Exactly," said Paula Zarte. "And what's the inference?"

"That we're having an affair."

"Again." The black woman sat back in her chair and nodded. "Believe me," Paula Zarte said, "as rumours go that's way better than any of the alternatives."

"It is?" Gene Newman wasn't entirely sure Paula Zarte understood how angry the First Lady could get.

In the end, a pretty Italian-looking girl came to collect their plates, brushed away the President's grissini crumbs with a tiny metal scoop and brought them dessert menus bound in red leather.

"Don't tell me . . ."

"Five languages and she can strip and reassemble a handgun faster than most of the men in this room," Paula Zarte said. "She'll be a section chief in five years."

"Who's here from the FBI or the NSA?"

"No one," Paula said, "they're not involved."

"You know what you're doing?" Gene Newman sounded genuinely concerned. There were laws governing inter-agency relationships. The President knew, he'd introduced some of them.

"You have a problem."

President Newman looked at her. "You're not the first person to tell me this in the last few days."

"I know," Paula Zarte said. "I had a call from Petra Mayer."

That was the moment the President knew his world had finally gone pear-shaped, to use one of his daughter's expressions. There were no circumstances under which Petra Mayer and Paula Zarte should talk to each other through anything other than attorneys. It was Professor Mayer who'd made case law by extracting her files from the archives at Langley and Paula Zarte's predecessor who spent a large amount of the Agency's money appealing the case.

"Do I want to know about this?" he asked.

To his surprise the woman opposite took the question seriously, disappearing behind her eyes while she considered the possible answers. In the end, she just reached down beside her chair and opened her briefcase. It contained police records, files from drug clinics, banking details from a family trust and even an old copy of *NME*.

Paula Zarte left all of these in the case. What she produced belonged to her daughter and came from Santa Claus. It was a child's Etch A Sketch. Twisting the plastic knobs, Paula wrote a simple sentence, showed it to the President and then shook the toy so that its screen went grey again.

"Let me know what you want to do."

Gene Newman didn't even need to think about it. "I want to know how this happened."

The woman on the other side of the table sighed. "I was afraid you'd say that." Signalling for the bill, she paid cash and pushed back her chair. "My car's outside," she said, "and I've booked a double room at a tiny family hotel overlooking the Sound. You'll be surprised to know that it's opening early."

* * *

The receptionist's hair had faded from red to grey and her pale blue eyes watched the single car draw up with little interest. If the old woman behind the desk recognized Gene Newman she gave no hint of that fact.

"Sign here."

"I'll do that," Paula Zarte said. She signed the form with a name so anonymous it had to have been chosen by computer for lack of recognition factor. The address was similarly anodyne. "They're real," she said, when the old Irish woman was off fetching a key.

"Don't tell me..."

Their room was small with a shower rather than a bath and one window that looked out over grey waves lapping a shingle beach.

"What do your people think is happening?" Gene Newman turned back from the window and its view of three muscular fishermen casting weighted lines into an unpromising looking surf.

"You mean, do they think we're really having an affair?" Paula Zarte smiled sadly. "It's possible. But they know that's not why I'm here. We've got budgets coming up and it's known you're not happy with Homeland Security. In fact, you're rumoured to be looking at breaking HS up and giving everyone back some level of autonomy, subject only to an overview from your new National Security Advisor."

"That's your price?"

"There is no price," Paula Zarte said. "As far as everyone out there is concerned we're discussing budgets and the limits to this Agency's responsibility. The reason we're meeting like this is you can't be seen to talk to us before talking to anyone else...You haven't talked to anyone else, have you?"

Gene Newman shook his head. "You know," he said, "I'm beginning to see why we couldn't have this meeting in the Oval Office."

Later, Paula brought up the issue of pardoning Prisoner Zero. "It's going to play better at home if he's American," she said.

"I still need him to appeal to me directly."

"You can do it without."

"Of course I can. But some kind of public remorse and an appeal for clemency would make things a lot simpler."

"In which case I wouldn't hold your breath."

President Newman looked at her.

"I've been reading Dr. Petrov's file. Half the time I'm not even sure the man is aware he's even human. Of course, Ed's got his own ideas on how to handle this."

Gene Newman's Security Advisor had a theory on everything.

"Don't tell me," said the President. "We take Prisoner Zero down to a cellar and sweat the equations out of him."

"Even better," Paula said. "We kidnap Prisoner Zero and replace him with a decoy, then we execute the decoy as a matter of principle, ride out the public storm and give the original back to our North African allies to extract the information we need."

"Yeah, right," said Gene Newman. "Like we hadn't thought of that."

The sex was slow and gentle and rather a surprise to both of them. In his private study the next morning, preparing to telephone Petra Mayer, the President was unable to remember who began it but completely aware that, once started, neither Paula nor he had been in any hurry to stop.

It lacked the fire of their Paris days and when Gene reached up to wrap one arm around her naked back, supporting Paula while he rolled both of them over to put himself on top, he realized she was heavier than before and he was less strong. Fumbling the turn, Gene lost his rhythm.

"We're getting old," he said.

"No," said Paula Zarte. "You are. I'm just not as young as I was."

Afterwards Gene Newman pillowed his head on one breast and listened to the slowing of her heart. And then when he could put it off no longer, he showered, dressed and came back to sit on the chair next to their bed. The problem seemed like something he should discuss while wearing his clothes.

"You want to tell me how this happened?"

"What's to tell?" Paula shrugged. "We got it wrong. Prisoner Zero's real name is Marzaq al-Turq, he's part German and wholly a genius. It looks like Jake Razor really died in that fire in Amsterdam."

"So," said President Newman, "Prisoner Zero stole his identity."

"What would you do?" Paula said. "You're penniless, drug-addicted, surviving on small sums paid into an account by a family who refuses even to see your only friend and suddenly that friend dies. Prisoner Zero didn't steal Jake's identity. He just kept cashing the cheques."

"Who knows this?"

"Me," said Paula, "you, Petra Mayer and Prisoner Zero." She managed to say the Professor's name without making it sound like a swear word. "That's all, so far."

"What about Jake's family?"

"So far as they know it was Marzaq al-Turq who died in the fire. The flat in Paris was their way of getting Jake away from Amsterdam. Off the record, they even accept that Prisoner Zero is Jake, no matter what they've been saying to the press."

"What are the chances we can keep them believing that?"

Paula Zarte thought about it. "You want my suggestion?"

The President nodded.

"Leave it to me," she said. It would take a certain amount of juggling of records and a couple of fingerprint swaps, but nothing that hadn't been done before.

"You can do it?"

"Oh yes," she said, "we're the CIA. We can do anything."

# CHAPTER 49

## *Northern Mountains, CTzu 53/Year 20*

As Tris and Luca headed towards the end of their bridge, Zaq sat under his willow in the walled garden, holding a peach and watching butterflies flicker in and out of sight, not yet warmed enough by the sun to do more than make small hops from one flower to another, wings beating lazily.

"Almost time," Zaq said.

Inside his head a boy stood over the broken body of a girl and Zaq knew, beyond doubt, that the boy had just died there in the dusty graveyard and the man who walked away was never more than a ghost. It was unfair, unjust and, for all Zaq knew, destined to produce only failure, but he still let it happen.

Sometimes the Chuang Tzu surprised even himself with his ability to make others cry. Wiping his eyes with the back of his hand, Zaq stared round at the mulberry bushes fat with purple fruit.

"Wait," he told a butterfly.

The way it was meant to work was that the Chuang Tzu would reach out his hand and the butterfly would alight, bringing its message. After delivering the message the butterfly would die. As would anyone else in the garden unwise enough to reach for a butterfly without being the Chuang Tzu.

Only the reborn could communicate in this fashion with the Library and live. Since Zaq refused to reach out and welcome the hovering butterfly it fluttered at the edge of his vision, puzzled but willing to wait.

It was a very small butterfly, presumably to reassure Zaq that the Librarian's question was not really that important, a mere trifle that Zaq could make disappear simply by answering.

If Zaq didn't reach out his hand soon the butterfly would die anyway and another would take its place. The creatures had very short life-spans. A point he was meant to ponder as all emperors had pondered before him; except that Zaq was busy refusing to be emperor, he was being Zaq.

Which was the cause of his original war against the Library. And maybe this was his last chance to be himself before everything changed.

The peach Zaq held was fresh, perfect in its plumpness and the bloom of its unmarked skin, so perfect, in fact, that it reminded him of the servitor girl whose name he'd now forgotten. There were a dozen peaches like it on a small tree so close to the willow that he could almost reach for fruit without moving and a dozen trees within easy walk if that tree would not do.

The garden held a strange place in the affections of the Library; Zaq could think of no other way to put it. Maybe it was because of the link between gardens and perfection, gardens and heaven, gardens and the afterlife. Actually, there was no maybe about it. Zaq knew this was true because he'd asked the Librarian.

When the Library first talked with Major Commissar Chuang Tzu, who was obviously not the original Chuang Tzu, merely the original for the purposes of the Library who'd never met *Homo sapiens* before and had not realized the universe was still inhabited, its creators having moved.

When it first trawled though the young Chinese officer's deepest memories it had noticed the single-minded importance put on a vegetable garden and the wild grasses growing on a hillside above a waterfall. A search through the AI and the memories of the cold eternals aboard the SZ *Loyal Prince* revealed that most faith systems on the world from which the ship originated bound heaven and gardens together.

So the darkness (as it then was) gave the Chinese officer the garden he'd known only in the abstract. A place of butterflies, messages and memories. Zaq didn't need to hear the message and he already knew what it would say, some riff on what General Ch'ao Kai had said yesterday.

*He had time to change his mind. The situation was not irreversible. The best way to make peace with the Library was accept his role as Emperor and reinstate the imperial guard.*

*Let them kill this assassin.*

*All General Ch'ao Kai needed was permission to mobilize his troops.*

Nothing Zaq hadn't already heard. And, more to the point, nothing he hadn't already refused to contemplate. Zaq wanted an end to this and his orders stood. He was to be regarded as invisible. All of those living within the Forbidden City were to go about their everyday business as if he had never been. He would remain in the garden and wait for his assassin.

Zaq smiled and a billion people wept at his sadness.

A moment or two later he changed his mind.

"Oh, come on then."

Holding out his hand, Zaq watched the butterfly make its short journey from mulberry leaf to Zaq's wrist, dying in a tiny flash of electricity.

"*Back yourself up*." The order was stark, except it wasn't an order. The Council of Ambassadors couldn't give orders, they could merely make suggestions. Ones that the Emperor was entirely free to ignore. Of all the suggestions they'd relayed to the Librarian, this was certainly the shortest.

"No," said Zaq, "I don't think so."

Backing himself up meant returning to Baohe Dian, the Hall of Preserving Harmony, to be examined by the imperial doctors. After which he would sign orders making General Ch'ao Kai regent for the eight minutes it would take Zaq to be read, found adequate and recorded. Maybe the Library had a host already prepared, a second Zaq blissfully sleeping away his non-life in a glass tank somewhere.

Zaq had in mind the pods originally found on the SZ *Loyal Prince,* which he'd visited. This was rare among emperors, who mostly sat quietly in the Butterfly Garden or retired to the silence of the Library to practice calligraphy, draw endless misty mountains or note down their carefully composed words of wisdom.

Of course, for them the SZ *Loyal Prince* was historical abstraction, not somewhere they'd called home for the first seven years of their lives. Zaq was aware that as Chuang Tzu he had been less than impressive. Rapture still existed and the 2023 worlds were healthy, true enough, their peoples no more bored or less happy than under the putative rule of any of the other, earlier emperors.

Only he'd intended to be so much more and would have been if he'd had the courage of the assassin who struggled so hard through the snow and storms Zaq sent against her. This small, cropped-haired figure wrapped in a cheap jacket and torn trousers, who talked to the air, slept oblivious and alone on a storm-tossed bridge and rose the next morning, equally oblivious as to why the storm now stilled. Zaq was exhausted from trying to live up to the assassin's expectations.

"Oh well," he said, climbing to his feet. Turning, Zaq hurled the peach he held against the grey up-stroke of a willow. It was a perfect shot and the fruit burst as it exploded against pale bark, staining the willow's trunk with a smear of darkness.

Zaq would have given anything for the peach to contain a maggot, to be bruised or rotten at the stone, but that would never happen. Perfection was required for the Emperor, even in the Butterfly Garden, and the Library was there to ensure perfection was what he got.

The maggot, the bruising and the rot were inside Zaq's head. He didn't think anyone had much doubt about that.

"Go back," Tris suggested.

The words popped out of her mouth in that way words sometimes do. A fleeting thought suddenly translated into speech with no filter betwen original thought and open mouth.

"Go...?" Luca looked amused, tired and almost dead on his feet, but very definitely amused. "Go where?" he asked.

"Home?" Tris didn't intend a question, that just happened to be the way it inflected. "You should go back," she added, more decisively. "You're exhausted. I can manage from here."

"Manage?" His smile became a sad grin. "Of course you can manage," Luca said. "I'm not here to help you."

"You're not?" demanded Tris.

Luca shook his head. "You're helping me," he said. And in that moment he sounded like an adult talking to a very small child. An intelligent, well-loved child, but a child all the same.

Moving Tris gently to one side, Luca stepped off the bridge and onto solid rock. "There's no way I could have escaped the village before you arrived."

"Why not?"

Luca's look was kind, if slightly exasperated. The look of someone who really didn't quite know where to begin. In the end, all Luca said was, "Rapture wouldn't let me."

"Why not?"

"The storms, the plateau, the ravine, the bridge... They're linked, you know." He glanced at her. "You do know that, don't you? That everything on Rapture is tied to everything else and all of it tied to the happiness of the Emperor."

"Really?" Tris said.

"At all levels," said Luca. It was obvious that this was news to Tris. "Didn't anyone ever explain quantum interdependence?"

Helping Tris onto the rock, Luca brushed snow from her blue jacket and peeled frost from her eyebrows. He did this without thinking, the way a father might do it for a daughter and Luca knew, at a theoretical level, that treating Tris this way made for problems because he'd already bedded her, creating the template for an entirely different if less complex relationship.

Luca knew this only at a theoretical level because he'd met very few people from the 2023 worlds. In fact, to be honest, the only person with whom he'd talked closely was Tris and he questioned whether she really represented that culture at all.

The girl certainly didn't fit his image of a hyper-educated, sexually sophisticated, slightly blasé member of the richest society yet existing, which was how the Always Knowledgeable and Correct Empire of the 2023 worlds sold itself, mostly to itself.

"Which world do you come from?" Luca was sure he'd asked Tris this question before and had memories of not understanding her answer.

A second snow-covered plateau extended for at least a day and maybe longer beyond the bridge. Because there were few hills and no actual valleys, the snow had spread evenly across the undulating surface and the flakes were so dry they barely stuck to Tris's and Luca's shoes, although this dryness meant the plateau's surface was forever sifted by the wind.

And yet even the wind seemed to be in their favour, shifting to the west to blow gently against their backs and coax them on their way.

"Something's changed," said Tris.

"No," Luca said. "Everything's changed. Take a look around you."

The sun was beating down on the snow and a billion diamonds

of light flickered in its brightness. The whole thing looking like nothing so much as a crust of solidified foam.

"This is good, right?" Tris asked.

"Well." The Baron shrugged. "It's certainly different."

In the end the plateau didn't so much finish as fall away into a slope that got steeper and steeper until suddenly it stopped being a slope. This happened at a point where the crust over which they walked slipped over the horizon and vanished altogether from sight.

"Walk backwards," Luca suggested. "You'll find it easier if you know where you've come from." Gripping his sticks, Luca strode to the start of the steepness, turned to face Tris and then stepped back, jamming both thorn sticks deep into the snow. He would like to believe that what he hit was earth, but chances were it was compacted snow, ice or bare rock because the ends of his sticks slid slightly.

"And dig deep," he added.

Tris did as she was told, turning as Luca had done and stepping back, feeling for a foothold that seemed further away than it ought to be. Her sticks slipped a little and then locked into place.

"If you feel yourself slip," said Luca, "ram both sticks into the snow and keep hold." The twine from his trap was gone, lost along the way, and this was irritating because he'd have liked Tris's sticks to be lashed to her wrists and he lacked the strength to tear fresh strips from his cloak. Tris had almost no idea how tired Luca was and he hoped to keep it that way.

Afternoon slid into evening, the high cirrus having cleared to reveal the silver shimmer of a sky filled with worlds around the distant sun, as if some insane mosaicist had decorated the inside of a globe with tiny tesserae and then not bothered to fill in between the tiles.

"So many worlds," Tris said.

Luca smiled.

Somewhere stacked in the back of her brain, Tris had Doc Joyce's breakdown of how and why. Obviously not the deep physics, the stuff that allowed each tesserae to retain its position within the globe while replicating gravity and retaining a workable atmosphere. All who claimed to understand this lied, their explanations quick and dirty hack around what little was left of preZP physics.

She learnt quickly, Tris was proud of this fact. Unfortunately the speed at which Tris assimilated ideas was something her grandmother never quite seemed to grasp. Her childhood refrain, *You just never learn, do you?*, being so far from the truth that Tris had seen little merit in pointing out that actually she learnt everything until there was nothing left to learn.

When Tris finally ran out of facts at home she went searching. No one ever thought to ask why and, if they had, Tris probably wouldn't have been able to answer. But the vanishing acts had grown in length, from missed afternoons through whole days to nights when she didn't come home and weeks that went by in a blur of cheap drugs, cheaper sex and bad conversation.

Translated, this meant reflex accelerators, fear inhibitors and a wide range of near opiates. Not to mention turning tricks against the wall at the back of Schwarzschilds for some tourist tom too blitzed to notice that Tris held him between her thighs instead of inside her.

The queens were cleaner, less animal, usually.

Many of those who put Tris up against a wall talked to her first, about their worlds and what made them come to one of the lowest levels of the Rip, a place most guides suggested they avoid. And once she even extracted a snatch of conversation from a gene splicer so silent even Doc Joyce had long since assumed the man was mute.

"Stop," said Luca and hands gripped her hips, halting Tris. "We're here."

Tris wanted to ask, *where?* There were so many things Luca assumed she knew when for most of this trip she'd merely been guessing. He was getting older and more tired, less happy to have her around. It was a look Tris knew well. One she'd seen each evening as a small child in the face of her mother, when the woman realized another day was gone and Tris's father had not returned. That, in all probability, he never would and she was left with a small child, a leaking shack and a mother-in-law who'd retreated into a world of her own.

And then one night, instead of looking resigned, Tris's mother had collected together the few things she actually owned and left. Tris wasn't even surprised.

"Keep staring ahead," said Luca. "You can't afford to turn round and you mustn't look down. Keep the moment close. And let everything else go."

Tris knew exactly what he meant. At least she hoped she did. "We're going to jump, right?"

"Not quite," said Luca, reaching into his satchel. For once the conditions were on their side. A whole strip of snow along the lip of the drop had slipped, exposing naked rock. This enabled Luca to find a flaw into which to ram the first of four steel pegs he produced from his bag.

"I'm going first," Luca told Tris. "And you're going to follow... The problem is I've only got a handful of these." He nodded to the spike. "So you're going to have to collect them as you go."

"How?"

"Easy," said Luca. "Just twist the top."

So Tris did, only too aware of the sheer drop towards which she shuffled, edging backwards so slowly she barely moved. Tris found the spike by dropping to a crouch and reaching behind her, fingers closing on cold metal.

It was stuck fast in the rock.

"Twist the top," Luca said again.

And Tris felt the spike slide free.

"We had hundreds once," said Luca, "thousands, maybe more." He sounded tired, old beyond his wish. "They were for building."

"You brought them with you?"

"It's possible," Luca admitted.

Holding the narrow spike in one hand, Tris twisted the top with her other.

"It's broken," she said.

Luca shook his head. Whatever was meant to happen took place at a level invisible to human eyes.

"It's working," he promised her.

She held a fortune in her hand, Tris realized, while another three fortunes lay at her feet. Doc Joyce would have restrung her entire body and thrown in new bones and buckytubes for her brain for one chance to work out what the spikes did and how.

Even fake tek was worth something. Certainly enough for the Doc to manufacture idiot-looking artifacts that tourists bought time and again, just in case they turned out to be real.

Tris grinned.

"What?" Luca said.

"Nothing that matters." Glancing back at the plateau, Tris was bemused both by the distance and the breath-catching beauty of a landscape she and Luca had crossed without really noticing. She was tired now. Almost as tired as Luca and the Baron was so tired that at times he seemed almost transparent.

"Focus," Luca said crossly. He nodded to the spike still gripped in her fingers. "And put that back."

Tris did, twisting the top to lock the spike in place.

"Right," said Luca. "Empty your head of everything but locating the next spike, reaching for it with one foot and letting the spike take your weight. You'll be roped to me and I'll be fixed to the cliff face with this." Luca pulled a final piece of climbing equipment from his bag. This spike had an eye at the top through which a rope could pass.

"One last thing," said the Baron. "You don't move until I tell you."

Tris understood that bit.

"A little to the right." Luca was doing his best not to sound worried. "Left a bit. That's it. The next spike's below your foot."

They'd been hanging on the edge of the drop for almost fifteen minutes and hardly made any progress at all. In fact, the lip over which they'd climbed was barely out of Tris's reach. All Tris had to do to follow Luca was remove the first and original spike, tuck it into her waistband and shift her weight so she could hang from a second spike, while using one foot to feel for a third that Luca had already fixed into the cliff.

"I know where it is," said Tris.

"Then use it."

Darkness was coming in faster than either had expected and Luca was running out of reassuring clichés about the first step being the most difficult, things getting easier, it just being a matter of practice . . .

"I thought you did this all the time in the Rip," Luca said, irritation winning out over tact.

"That's jumping," said Tris. "It's different."

Give her a rope long enough and she'd have been halfway down the cliff before Luca had finished fixing his wretched spikes.

"You must have climbed on Rip," said Luca.

"Of course I did," Tris said. "That was up, though. This is down . . ." All the same she twisted the spike, slid it from the rock and pushed it into the waistband of her thin trousers. She was climbing in her rope sandals, Luca having insisted that this would be better than bare toes.

"Well done," said Luca.

"Yeah," Tris said, "and you can fuck off too." But she said it too quietly for Luca to hear.

# CHAPTER 50

## *Marrakech, Summer 1977*

Several years before she died Malika told Moz a fairy tale. It was the summer she turned nine and Malika told it without once looking at Moz, her eyes fixed on a distant line of clouds.

Moz told the story to Jake and Celia as they all drove north in the VW campervan, the earth beyond their windows turning from red to yellow and finally to brown as they travelled the two hundred kilometres that took them to Casablanca and three seats on an Air Maroc caravelle to Tangiers, where a ferry to Alicante waited for them.

It was a flat road and mostly straight, dotted occasionally with spindly cedar, larch and imported eucalyptus and it cut through the Middle Atlas, a mountain range so scrawny and underfed by the time the mountains met the Marrakech–Casablanca road that it barely merited the name.

The fields along either side of the road were hedged with prickly pear and occasionally stone, the plots broken into smaller and smaller fragments as farms passed from fathers to sons and parcels of land were divided time and again.

At this point Jake still intended to buy a house in Spain, although he changed his mind shortly after docking at Alicante when three gun-toting, green-cloaked members of the Guarda Civile, having ordered everyone out of the car he'd just bought, emptied Jake's luggage onto the road, dismantled the seats and ripped the spare tyre from its wheel.

A body search followed for each of them.

That was when Celia announced she was going back to Cheyne Walk as soon as possible and Jake decided he might try Amsterdam instead. They had a short and bitter argument about who had responsibility for Moz.

Jake lost.

Moz told them Malika's story when the VW was an hour outside Marrakech and Jake and Celia were still talking to each other. He told it because he hated them and because he knew they would not understand. The story began on the sixteenth day of Jumaada al Thamy in the year 1375 AH, which Jake and Celia knew as 1956.

On that day, Monday 30 January, in a square near Bab Doukkala, three Arab stallholders poured petrol through the broken window of a racing-green Studebaker, the 1954 model. They were watched by a heavily veiled woman chewing on a dried fig and a small boy who hopped from leg to leg with excitement.

Waving the boy and his grandmother away from the car, the eldest of the three men pulled a brass lighter from his jellaba pocket and lit a petrol-soaked rag he'd already tied to a stone, tossing the stone high in the air, so the rag flamed like a comet on its way down.

So huge was the explosion that the small boy tipped backwards and suddenly found himself sitting in the dirt. For a second his bottom lip quivered and then he began to clap.

At the other end of Derb Ali, in what had once been stables, a young Berber shouldered open a locked door. He did this as quietly as he could. Something of a rarity for Driss Mahmud, a man who liked to make his presence felt.

Sultan Mohammed V had returned from French-imposed exile to declare himself King. On the morning in question, at 11.30, his old enemy Thami al Glaoui, eagle of Telouet, the black panther and mountain gazelle, the last great lord of the Atlas and Pasha of Marrakech, had died, having made profession of his faith.

He was seventy-eight years of age, feared and revered in equal measure. A hero to many and a traitor to more. And with his final breath withered not only the Glaoui's life, but the protection his reputation gave to those who had served him.

"Hide me." Driss Mahmud's voice was jagged with fear, although one had to know the man to realize this.

"*Where?*"

He could hear contempt in Maria's question, which was the first time she'd ever dared reveal such an emotion to his face. Her mother had been an *esclave* in the Glaoui kasbah as had her grandmother before that. The girl's father was unknown, a man who'd given his unclaimed daughter little to remember him by but pale skin and green eyes.

This room had been Driss Mahmud's present to Maria. Not really his to give but that seldom mattered to the servants of Si Thami al Glaoui. All Driss had done was order a café to give up its storeroom and the girl had been living there ever since.

She was fat with child, her breasts sore against the thin cotton of a cheap dress. Her head was bare, her hair untied and her forehead sweaty. Darkness was approaching but it brought only a shift in the sounds of the city. It was a bad night to be found with a servant of the old Pasha.

"Hide me here," said the man. "Say you've got a customer."

Maria slapped him then.

And when she finally picked herself off the dirt floor, wiping blood from her lips, it was to walk past him to the storeroom door. "I don't do that anymore," she said, pulling aside the curtain.

A single step brought Driss close, so close Maria could feel his breath on the nape of her neck and a sharpness against her skin. Everyone knew that Driss Mahmud carried a knife and on a night like this he might well be carrying his gun.

Except there had never been another night like this.

"In here," Maria shouted, and would have shouted again but for the sudden hand over her mouth to ensure silence.

"I should kill you," Driss said.

*You should have killed me months back*... The thought came and went, more wish than thought. Maria wasn't good at considering her own emotions. Most of the time the girl found it hard to believe that what she felt might matter.

Once, in the time of the big war, a fat foreigner had sat in a rattan chair on the terrace of the Pasha's kasbah and said something that made the Pasha roar with laughter. They'd both been looking at a small girl scooping ice into a bowl when he spoke.

"You." The Pasha's voice was low, surprisingly soft. And Maria realized she'd never dared listen to his voice before. "What's your name?"

She gave her mother's village, her grandfather's name and his job as one of the Pasha's herdsmen. Maria wasn't sure how else to answer. All of this the Pasha related to the foreigner in the stranger's language.

"So," said the foreigner, "call her Mimi." Or so one of the dancing girls reported afterwards.

The Pasha stared at him.

"Her hands," explained the fat man. "They're frozen."

"What was it you asked?" said the Pasha. "How much do I pay them?" He turned to the girl. "How much do you get paid?" he said.

Maria looked at him, her eyes wide.

The fat man in the rattan chair dragged on his cigar, blew out a cloud of smoke and turned to the Pasha. Whatever he said about her silence made the Pasha frown.

"You." He nodded to the girl. "Why do you work for me?"

She had no answer to that either.

When the Pasha glanced at Maria again it was to wave her away. So Malika's mother picked up her bucket, which was actually silver and made in Paris, covered it with a white linen napkin as she'd been taught and crept from the terrace.

The next time anyone noticed her it was to offer her to a German industrialist. She was twelve.

A month later Driss was told to deliver her to a brothel in the Medina. It was unlikely the Pasha even knew or cared that she was gone. Between the kasbah and the brothel, Driss stopped once to push her into a bricked-up archway, raise her dress and turn her to face the wall.

Now he stood behind her again. In the room which he'd found for her. And though his life was in danger and the Medina full of men after people like him, Driss Mahmud paused for long enough to force one hand inside Maria's dress and grip a swollen breast, twisting hard.

"You won't forget me," he said.

And as fear and a full bladder emptied themselves down Maria's bare leg, Driss went, knife out in front of him, running at a half crouch like some wounded animal.

"Here," Maria shouted to no one in particular. "Over here."

A motorbike beam lit the night and bounced wildly off the alley walls. The owner left its engine running to keep the beam bright. "Where?"

"Over there," shouted Maria, and pointed towards a shadow which hugged a far wall, moving at a jagged run. "He's one."

As the stolen 500cc Norton lurched forward, a second hunter sprinted from a side passage and swung himself onto the bike behind its rider. He carried a curved sword in one hand.

"After him."

The order was unnecessary. The single-cylinder machine was already skidding down the alley, its headlight picking out Driss Mahmud. A blip of the throttle, a single slash and the antique blade had opened up the running man's shoulder.

"Go round again," shouted the man with the sword and the bike slid to a halt.

It might not be the worst cut their victim had taken, but there would be others and the wounded man understood this. The most intelligent thing he could do was anger his attackers so badly they killed him outright.

"*Fatah!*"

He was many things, Driss Mahmud. A coward was not one of them. Holding his knife in his one good hand, he watched the 500cc Norton turn in the alley and blinked as its headlight caught him in its beam.

Shouting his insult again, Driss flipped the knife so that he held it by the blade. The man would have seen that, which was the point.

"Come and get me..."

Driss felt no pain and barely any shock, only a determination to take both riders with him if he could. Somewhere inside he must have been afraid, though. He had to be; why else would his lips be reciting prayers?

It was late, the evening call from the mosque of Bab Doukkala was long gone. Fires burned across the city. At least they burnt in the only bit of Marrakech to really matter. Who knew or much cared what happened beyond the walls in Hivernage or Gueliz?

Driss could smell wood smoke and grilling goat in the alley, and something uglier like burning rubber.

That was his last conscious thought. Tyres burning, foreigners beyond the wall, a final declaration of faith... And then the bike was on him in a blaze of light that dragged a blade behind it.

Driss threw, hard as he could, and ducked like his old caid had taught him, rolling out of the motorbike's way and into a sudden kick to his spine. Vertebrae cracked and Driss crawled away from the pain straight into the path of another boot. There were legs all around him now.

It had been a mistake to let go of his knife.

"*Wait!*" Climbing from his bike, the off-duty policeman pushed his way through the mob. The figure at their feet was still recognizably human, though the noise issuing from his bloodied mouth was strictly animal.

"Not here," the man said. "Take him to the rubbish dump."

Someone tried to make Driss Mahmud walk but broken ankles and cracked vertebrae made this impossible. So instead the mob poured gasoline over him, tied a rope around his ankles and dragged him to the dump beyond the Doukkala Gate, gathering onlookers with every arch and alley corner they navigated.

* * *

"It's not much of a fairy tale." Petra Mayer looked up from her notes. In front of her was a deposition from Lady Celia Duncalf, née Vere. Now resident in Holland Park, with a flat in St. Germain des Prés and a beach house in the Hamptons, Lady Celia's main concern seemed to be that her newly married daughter might discover details of the summer her mother spent "working" in Marrakech.

There was an accompanying letter, written in strong script and addressed to Professor Mayer by name. This touched briefly on Lady Celia's belief that Marzaq al-Turq had died in a fire in Amsterdam and enclosed a photocopy of a note to that effect signed "Jake." The lettering of the signature was as spindly as Celia's writing was firm and determined.

"You wrote this," said Professor Mayer, as she pushed the note across to Prisoner Zero. "How did it feel announcing your own death?"

Only Prisoner Zero ignored her because he was too busy remembering when the tale had been told to him. "A fairy tale" was what Malika called it, in a voice which showed she didn't quite understand why someone else, someone grown-up, had called it that.

Malika's father had not yet become enemies with Moz's mother, so the two of them were still allowed to be friends. Except this was a fairy story about how Malika's father was really someone else.

"They killed your father?"

"No, stupid." Malika shook her head in exasperation. "If he was my father I'd be much older."

"How much?"

The nine-year-old girl thought about it.

"Not sure," she said. "Almost grown-up probably."

"That would be weird."

Malika looked at him.

"If I was me and you were grown-up..." Moz shrugged at the thought and shook out his left arm, feeling blood return to his fingers. The twine that usually bound this arm behind his back was curled on the tiles where Malika had thrown it.

Moz was happy. He was on the roof of the baker's with Malika, his arm untied and his jellaba discarded in an untidy heap beside the twine snake. All he wore were the shorts his mother insisted he wear beneath his jellaba and Malika's hat.

Malika sat against a wall opposite. And from where they both sat they could see across the city's white roofs to La Mosquée, the heart of Marrakech. Everyone in the city steered themselves through the jumble of the Medina by glimpses of La Koutoubia's seventy-metre-high minaret. It became instinct. A way of triangulating position by how much could be seen of this or that monument, but always with La Koutoubia as the main point.

They were hiding on the roof of the baker's because Malika was in trouble with ould Kasim again. Quite what for, Moz was unsure; not that it made much difference. She'd still have to go down to face him sometime. That was how their conversation began.

"He's not my real father, you know," Malika said suddenly.

"What?"

"That man." She meant Corporal ould Kasim.

"Then who is?"

"A hippie."

"They didn't exist when you were a baby."

"Yes, they did," said Malika. "There just weren't very many of them. He was English."

The boy raised his eyebrows.

"Rich," Malika said. "Very rich. He paid gold for the house in Derb Yassin and painted all the rooms black. He was a poet."

Moz thought of the narrow house his mother now shared in the Mellah with Malika's father. Two rooms each, split upstairs and down. No running water. No electricity. It wasn't that he thought Malika was lying, he just didn't quite understand.

"My real father died," Malika said. "Of a fever. He got thinner and thinner until he couldn't even stand up. My mother tried spells and doctors but nothing worked. He didn't want to live, she said." Malika's voice was bleak. "And after she buried him she discovered he'd spent all the money."

Moz could imagine the rest without being told. Corporal ould Kasim, the man he'd always thought was her father, owned a small café. Only a tiny place between machine shops but it was on Djemaa el Fna, good for tourists, and a woman might work there. Of course, she would need to be married...

"Everything I do is wrong," said Malika. "The meat's not good. The bread's stale. I pay too much for grain. The chickens don't lay enough for what I feed them." She did a good imitation of ould Kasim's dead-eyed stare and the sourness of his words. "I'm going down," Malika said, resignation in her voice. "Do you want me to tie your arm first?"

It took only a minute for her to loop twine round Moz's wrist and secure the hand behind his back. Malika knew which knot to use. She'd been untying and retying the restraint for almost two years.

"What happened to the man?"

Malika turned, shading her eyes against the sun. "Which man?"

"The one they caught."

"Driss. They dragged him to the rubbish heap outside Bab Doukkala and burnt him along with all the others and the police did nothing. Although the new Pasha set a guard over the mound of burnt bodies to stop wise women breaking bits off to work magic."

"How do you know?"

"My mother told me. She went to watch."

Years later, in a public library in Amsterdam, Moz discovered that Sultan Mohammed V, newly King of Morocco, was so appalled by the hunting and burning of the traitor Thami al Glaoui's followers that he refused to eat for seven days, despite the fact that al Glaoui had been responsible for the Sultan's exile to Madagascar.

Of course, from another book, Moz learnt that al Glaoui was a hero whose clever manipulation of his colonial overlords kept the French out of much of the High Atlas. By then, Moz had been away from Marrakech for so long it never occurred to him that he might one day go back.

## CHAPTER 51

### *Lampedusa, Tuesday 10 July*

"Okay," said Petra Mayer, "I'm just going to switch this on." She flipped open a silver box about the size of a paperback and tapped its only button. Two diodes lit at the front, one red and one green. The diodes were actually something clever involving complex light-emitting polymer. Compared to the rest of the box they were almost steam driven.

"You know what it is?" Extracting an Italian cigarette from its garish packet, Professor Mayer tapped the silver box.

"A recorder," said Prisoner Zero.

The Professor and he had an agreement. He talked to her and

she pretended to Colonel Borgenicht that he was still locked in silence. It seemed to Prisoner Zero that this arrangement was about to come to an end.

"Not exactly," said Petra Mayer, fishing for her lighter. "It blocks parabolic mikes and makes bugging near impossible. Everything said remains between the two of us."

"And the President."

"Yeah," agreed Petra Mayer. "Him too."

"So it's the three of us," Prisoner Zero said. He was having a numbers day. It began with a battered road sign on the way down to Calla Madonna. Without thinking, he'd divided the kilometres by eight in his head and multiplied by five to get miles. Then he did it properly, using 8.04672.

The numbers thing had gone on from there really.

Now he and Petra Mayer were on the terrace of a deserted café, staring out over a rocky headland towards the Tunisian coast. Either that, or what the Professor thought was North Africa was really a low bank of cloud spread thin across the horizon.

Professor Mayer sighed. More rested on this than just her friendship with the Newman boy, as she still found herself calling the President, albeit only in her head. She'd had calls from colleagues, calls from enemies. A New York tabloid openly accused her of consorting with traitors, although it used shorter words.

On a secure line the previous night she'd asked President Newman what he wanted and come to the nasty conclusion that he didn't know. He just wanted everything to be different. It was a very Gene Newman position. The man simply couldn't understand why Prisoner Zero wouldn't explain why he took a shot at the President, express remorse and beg for a Presidential pardon.

It obviously wasn't religion or politics, tabloids notwithstanding. Even the rump of the Republican Party was beginning to admit this. And then there was what the President now called "All that stuff with numbers written in shit." The director of the Saatchi Gallery in London had labelled its destruction the greatest act of artistic barbarism this century. *New Scientist* was offering a life subscription to anyone who could fill in the second half of the final line. Although Petra Mayer felt a Nobel Prize was probably more appropriate.

"You're running out of time," Professor Mayer said.

"Seventy-six hours," said Moz, watching a seagull twist for the fifth time in the same thermal. "Four thousand, five hundred and sixty minutes. Two hundred and seventy-three thousand, six hundred seconds."

Petra Mayer nodded.

Prisoner Zero was pretending to do the maths in his head. And without realizing it, he had his head twisted to one side, the way Jake always did when he was thinking, but no math was required. He had the figures ready and waiting in the way Celia kept a running total of just how much she'd eaten on any day. She could do calories by single day, individually day by day over the course of a week or any permutation of averages.

Prisoner Zero had never asked the woman how she managed it and doubted if Jake even realized it happened, but he could pretty much guarantee it wasn't by having darkness hollow out a cave in her skull and sit in one corner whispering numbers.

"Coffee?" Petra Mayer suggested.

Moz asked for an espresso without thinking and the coffee came black as night and bitter as memory. Actually, it was perfectly ordinary, if slightly chewy in that Italian way.

"Better?" said Professor Mayer.

"Than what?"

The Professor sighed.

She was the thinnest woman Prisoner Zero had ever seen. So tiny he could see either side of the back of her chrome chair at the same time. All she ever seemed to ingest was coffee and nicotine. He'd intended to ask her about the silver box but ended up nodding to her cigarette.

"Those keep you thin, right?"

"No," she said. "Being ill keeps me thin. These are just killing me. Of course," she added, "it doesn't help that I'm hopelessly addicted."

"To what?"

*What have you got?* The small woman waited, then shrugged. "Brando," she said, "*The Wild One*."

Prisoner Zero had seen it dubbed into Dutch, in a fleapit under a strip joint on Warmoesstraat. Jake had snored through the final reel, his head flopped onto Prisoner Zero's shoulder. All he could remember about the film was the smell of ammonia in a filthy lavatory, a couple of raddled queens arguing about Brando's beauty and a sullen kid in his late teens smoking badly cured schwag.

That had been him. "You do realize," said Professor Mayer, "that the Pentagon still wants you dead?"

Prisoner Zero said nothing.

"And the Secretary of Defense is determined to get his way..."

The man in front of her thought about that. "I'm not sure I care," he said.

"You don't care?"

"Not really." Prisoner Zero shook his head. "I'm freezing up."

"You're *cold*?" They were in the shade of a green umbrella that read "Café Lampedusa" and all around them grass was turning brown while tarmac went sticky in the heat. Beyond the headland, the sun had hammered the sea into a sheet of glistening armour.

"It's over ninety," she told Prisoner Zero, and another number twisted like a fleck of dust in front of his eyes, flickered and died.

"Inside," he said. "I'm cold inside."

Where the darkness waited and the story stood frozen, with Tris hung from her cliff and the Emperor still watching butterflies flicker and die like so many twisting numbers. Prisoner Zero had lost count of the times he'd watched that scene in his head, never quite reaching the end.

"You need another coffee." Snapping her fingers, Petra Mayer signalled to a thin man hovering in the gloom of the café.

The owner was nervous for a good reason. Nervous, cross and totally unable to do anything to change the situation in which he'd been placed. Professor Mayer wanted to borrow his café. Colonel Borgenicht had explained this to his local liaison officers, who'd explained it to the patron.

Their coffee came in unwashed cups, Prisoner Zero's thumbprint clearly visible on one side of an absurdly small handle. The patron reused dirty cups to make his protest. He was alone inside the café, minus his usual staff. The tourists were already missing and even his wife had been told to go home. So it was just him, his espresso machine and whatever food his wife had prepared already.

US jeeps locked off the coast road at both ends. Half a dozen marines stood next to each vehicle, the marines flanked by a dozen unhappy-looking *carabinieri*. Their commander, a colonel on loan from Rome, had tried to claim control of the operation. He'd lost.

"You see that flash?"

A flare of sunlight reflected from a headland to one side of them.

"Telescopic sights," said Prisoner Zero, sipping his coffee. He'd seen the snipers with their long rifles on his way to the café. A couple of them had stood by a hastily thrown up roadblock, waiting for orders.

Their job was to stop anyone shooting at Prisoner Zero, that was what Colonel Borgenicht had told Petra Mayer. Maybe the marines didn't do irony. The Colonel certainly seemed to find nothing odd in throwing up a cordon to protect the life of someone his men were scheduled to kill in seventy-five and a half hours.

*Four thousand, five hundred and thirty minutes.*

*Two hundred and seventy-one thousand, eight hundred*...The prisoner tried to blink away the darkness and got freefall, except he was roped to a cliff and it was this safety line which brought him up short, spilling numbers from his mouth.

"Shit," said Petra Mayer, looking at the pile of vomit. "That's all we need."

Very carefully, the owner put a glass of water on the table in front of the prisoner and retreated to the safety of inside. Maybe he just wanted to be out of the afternoon sun.

"Sip it slowly," Professor Mayer instructed. "But wash your mouth out first."

Spitting water into the dust, Prisoner Zero swilled out his mouth and spat again. He drank half of what remained in a single gulp, overflow escaping from the sides of his mouth to roll down his chin and splash onto his combats.

"Slowly," said Petra Mayer.

Colonel Borgenicht had him dressed in desert casuals and canvas combat boots. So many subtexts were backed up behind this decision that Prisoner Zero hadn't even tried to shuffle his way through them. He was leaving that to Petra Mayer.

She'd been the one doing all the talking since she had Prisoner Zero dug out of his cell, dressed at gunpoint and loaded into a jeep. Only then did she mention that they were going for a picnic. Mostly she'd been talking about the guilt Prisoner Zero must feel for Malika's death. Quite how the woman had the gall to imagine she knew, Prisoner Zero was uncertain. Only the more he listened, the more certain he was that she did.

It was a weird feeling.

"Those flashes," Petra Mayer said, watching another spark from a peak of the headland. "They're camera lenses."

The prisoner thought about this and decided it made as much sense as anything else. "There must be a lot."

"Six," said Petra Mayer. And Prisoner Zero remembered how keen she was that he took the other chair.

"How do you know?" Prisoner Zero demanded.

When Professor Mayer smiled her face crumpled into a map. "Because that's how many I told the Italian police to let in."

"They didn't mind you—?"

Petra Mayer's laugh was not entirely kind. "I gave them names."

She might pretend to dislike the marines, but in the end the Professor, Dr. Petrov and the marines were all on the same side. It was, Prisoner Zero reminded himself, as well to remember this.

"What do you want?"

"No," said Petra Mayer, "that's not the question." Picking up a paper napkin, she tore off the strip that read "Café Lampedusa" and twisted it into a tiny rope which she placed neatly beside her saucer. "Displacement," she added, when she saw Prisoner Zero watching. "Something you seem to have turned into a life's work."

He was meant to ask, *All right then, what is the question?* Prisoner Zero understood that but he just couldn't be bothered. And anyway, she was going to tell him, it was obvious from her face.

"Do you regret trying to shoot the President?"

"I'm not sure," Prisoner Zero said with a shrug. "It seemed like a good idea at the time."

Petra Mayer sighed. "The correct answer is 'Yes, deeply'...We have a problem. And the problem is that the world doesn't want you dead."

Prisoner Zero looked at the small woman who sat opposite, chain-smoking her way through a packet of Italian cigarettes.

She appeared to be entirely serious.

"Don't you get it?" said Professor Mayer. "It would be like shooting Einstein. World opinion won't let Gene do it, that's his first problem. The second is, he can't afford simply to pardon you."

Prisoner Zero smiled.

"What's funny?" There was irritation in Petra Mayer's voice. And a low-level fear that she might have missed something important.

"Who said I wanted pardoning?" asked Prisoner Zero. "You know what I see when I look at you?"

"Malika?"

"I see cliffs. Impossibly tall cliffs. And you know where they are?"

The Professor didn't.

"Etched onto the inside of my eyes. Make sense of that if you can." Reaching out, Prisoner Zero drained the last of his glass of water. "You know what I see if I keep my eyes shut?"

There was no way she could know, but Prisoner Zero asked anyway because he was talking to himself; which was all anyone ever did, it seemed to him, talk to themselves while half meanings and misunderstandings fed into the minds of those who thought they were listening.

"I see ice and darkness," said Prisoner Zero.

Professor Mayer lit the last of her cigarettes. "Really," she said. "So what does the darkness see?"

# CHAPTER 52

## *Northern Mountains, CTzu 53/Year 20*

Many things had changed next morning. The wind, which usually swung Tris and Luca's sleeping bag through the patterns inherent in the bag using only one retaining rope but containing two people, both fastened by tethers of their own... This wind was gone.

Better still, the heavy cloud that had clung like guilt to the lip of the cliff was also gone and had taken the snowfall with it. Clean skies spread above Tris and hawks ran thermals in the clear air below.

It was said that in the old stories skies had been blue rather than pale silver. This idea was odd enough to have caught Tris's imagination as a child. And she'd spent much of one week trying to come up with reasons why. In the end she'd given up, not because she couldn't find reasons but because she had better things to do.

Like find her way from one level to another.

And now Tris could see from where she hung on the cliff right to the valley floor, and it was very long way. So far indeed that Tris wasn't sure if what she saw below her was a village, a town or the Forbidden City itself. All she could see was a square smudge of green.

"What do you reckon?"

A faint echo was her only answer.

That was the other change and Tris wasn't too sure how she felt about this one. In fact, if she hadn't been so annoyed with Luca she'd probably be crying again. But there was a limit to how much and how often one person could cry and Tris felt she was beyond it.

All the same...

She woke cold but not frozen and found herself curled up like a child in the bottom of their makeshift sleeping bag. Curled up and alone. Waking slowly through the dreams of a man who stared out over a huge expanse of beaten metal below the blue of a childish sky.

Still tired and unquestionably cross, Tris had kicked out one leg, claiming stiffness in her knees but really hoping to hit Luca. Instead of the Baron her bare foot caught the edge of the sleeping bag and she felt it then, the change. A part of her wanted to describe it as a wrongness, but Tris wasn't sure this was the right word.

Luca was missing.

Struggling to her knees inside the bag, Tris reached out and made sure of what she already knew. Luca had gone and she was alone. More than this, he'd left his knife, the marble, his satchel, what remained of the food and their two unused climbing spikes.

Tris stopped, took a slow look around her and did what she did best.

Reconstructed events from the facts stacking up inside her mind. It wasn't intelligence that let her do this, though Tris sometimes told herself that it was. And even Doc Joyce seemed to buy into the idea of her intelligence. At least he pretended he did.

No, it was coldness. This stacking up of facts, sifting of ideas and synthesis of both into a conclusion was about protection and distance. About protecting herself from the world outside her and keeping her distance from those not drawn like moths to the same cold flame.

"I've been tried," said a voice in her head. "I'm not interested in overturning the conviction."

Tris blinked.

The man beside the huge expanse of water was standing up, waiting calmly as other men moved towards him, shackling his hands behind his back while a woman looked on.

"I'll call Gene," said the woman. "See what he says."

Tris looked from the rope that held the sleeping bag secure to the overhang, then looked at the tether still knotted around her thighs, the one which ran from between her legs, under her padded jacket and up to a steel spike in the rock-face. And finally she looked at the rope she'd been avoiding.

It was cut very cleanly, probably by the bare blade now resting in the bottom of the sleeping bag. And there was something else: the bag remained sealed along the side Luca had chosen. Which meant... Tris tried to clarify in her head exactly what this meant and rather began to wish she hadn't.

Cold and alone, Luca had unzipped the molecules along his edge of the sleeping bag, climbed out to hang in space and then leant across to seal the bag again before cutting himself free and falling to his death.

He'd sealed the bag to keep Tris safe, to prevent her absentmindedly kicking the knife or spikes out of the bag or rolling out herself into the night wind to panic as she twisted on her short length of tether.

Tris could think of half a dozen practical, utterly prosaic reasons why Luca might have done what he did. But she couldn't think of *the* reason, not the one that really made sense.

"Shit," she said to herself. It was hard to remain furious with someone who'd sacrificed himself to let you live.

"If that's what he did," said the voice in her head.

"What else?"

"Despair."

"At what?" The girl's voice was contemptuous.

"The sheer scale of that descent."

Tris shook her head, even as she picked up his satchel and put it over her shoulder. The knife went through her belt, its cold edge rather too close to Tris's hips for her liking. And then she clambered out of the sleeping bag, yanked down her trousers and pissed into the cold air.

"It's time to start," said the voice.

"Yes," Tris said. "I've already worked that out." She took a final look at the silver haze above her where other worlds formed their fractured shell around the distant sun.

She would have to leave the sleeping bag where it was, because only Luca knew how to turn it from cloak into a bivouac or bag and back again and it was much too cumbersome to carry.

"Move," Tris said.

"Yeah," she said. "I know."

"Well, do it."

Tris was talking to herself again.

# CHAPTER 53

## *Marrakech, Summer 1977*

Prisoner Zero knew when things went wrong exactly. A few minutes after the early evening call to prayer had finished echoing from the minaret of La Koutoubia, when Idries hurried into Chez Luz, a two-room café off Djemaa el Fna used by the men in Moz's part of the Mellah, and sat himself opposite Moz and Malika without being invited.

"Malika was still alive at this point?"

Prisoner Zero nodded. "This was before."

"And Malika didn't like Idries?"

"Nobody liked Idries," Prisoner Zero said. He was telling Petra Mayer why he decided to carry drugs for Hassan after all.

"What do you want?" Moz made no attempt to hide his irritation. The rat-faced boy was Hassan's bagman, little more. These days he might dress like Hassan in a suit cut to the European style, but the garment looked as stupid on Idries as it looked stylish on bagman.

"We've been waiting for you."

"We?"

"Hassan," said Idries quickly. "Hassan's been waiting."

"Then let him wait," Malika said. She was the only girl in a café full of old men wearing jellabas, a couple of middle-aged men in suits and the two teenaged boys. Only Moz was close enough to see that her hands were trembling.

"It pays," said Idries, smiling at the look on the other boy's face. It was a particularly rat-faced smile, even for Idries. "Hassan said that would interest you."

"How much?" said Moz.

"Depends," Idries said.

"On what?" Most conversations with Idries were like this. Unsatisfactory exchanges of minimal amounts of information.

Idries spoke out of the corner of his mouth and chain-smoked Gitanes. The result of too many afternoons watching black and white Belmondo films at a cinema behind Boulevard Safi.

"Whether it's two of you or one." Idries glanced at Malika. "It's in a smart area of the Nouvelle Ville," he added. "So she can't dress like that."

"What's wrong with my clothes?" Malika demanded.

Idries ignored her.

"How much?" demanded Moz, bringing the discussion back to the thing that mattered. "And what's the job?"

"Hassan will tell you," Idries said. "Meet him in an hour outside the café opposite the market on Mohammed the Fifth." As an after-thought, Idries turned back to address Malika. "Any chance you own a hijab?"

The answer was no, but Malika could borrow one. Come to that, she could steal one freshly washed off the wall behind her house and claim a sudden, God-inspired attack of modesty if she got caught. The old crows were quite stupid enough to believe that.

"Find one," Idries said, "and wear something that covers your arms." He stood without offering to pay for the pastries he'd taken from the plate in the centre of their table and threaded his way to-wards the door, sneering at the old jellaba-clad men.

Idries made a real point of not looking back.

"Here," Moz said, pausing to tear a piece of cake in two and offer half to Malika, "you need to eat."

Malika shook her head, her red hair hidden and her face framed by the black folds of a haik. She looked beautiful. A beauty that only highlighted the set of her mouth and the anger in her cat-like eyes as she stalked across Place de Foucauld into Avenue Mohammed V, catching her reflection in the first shop window.

"Look at me."

"You look great," Moz insisted. Only this time flattery was not enough. And so Malika strode ahead and the boy in the black jeans and weird T-shirt hurried to keep up.

"It pays," Moz said.

Malika snorted. "One of these days," she said, "Hassan's going to get you into real trouble."

The avenue around them was beginning to fill as those in the Old City came out for the evening. A few tourists hurried passed the edge of Parc Lyautey, heads down, wearing shirts that were too thick, the wrong cut or just too tight for the heat, but mostly this stretch of Mohammed V was filled with Marrakchi in traditional dress.

Ahead of Malika and Moz bicycles, mopeds and donkey carts streamed through Bab Larissa, scenting the air with burning oil and the sweet smell of animal sweat and dung.

"Look," Moz said. "I need to make my peace with Hassan."

And Malika finally halted, ignoring the scowls of the old men around her as she touched her fingers to a bruise on Moz's cheek.

"What about this?"

Moz shrugged. "I've been thinking," he said, "Hassan's going to be somebody. You and me . . ." He looked into the eyes of the girl opposite. "We're just going to be ourselves. And maybe that's enough."

He understood this now. Jake wasn't going to be Moz's ticket out of Marrakech after all, because Moz no longer wanted a way out unless it included Malika. What he wanted walked beside him into Gueliz dressed in a stolen haik, her sandals slapping angrily on the dusty pavement.

"Idries is irrelevant," said Moz. "And I didn't say we should be friends with Hassan. I said we needed a truce."

"You said peace."

Peace, truce . . . Moz was about to say, *What's the difference?* Then he thought it through. "I meant truce," he said. "You don't have to like Hassan. But I want to stop having to avoid him."

"You don't avoid Hassan," protested Malika.

Moz looked ashamed. "That's not true," he said. "I've been avoiding him my whole life."

"You came," said Idries, and Hassan glanced at his bag carrier. It was a slight glance, so quick that neither Moz nor Malika really bothered to wonder what it meant. This was a mistake, although how much of a mistake Moz only realized later and by then it was too late.

Of course, Hassan might not really have glanced at Idries. Moz might only have imagined this in Amsterdam, when he was digging through all the memories that refused to stay buried.

"Why would they not come?" said Hassan, his voice arrogant. He nodded abruptly to Moz and would have ignored Malika completely had she not reached forward to feel the lapel of his suit.

"Nice cloth," Malika said, managing to make it sound like an insult.

Moz laughed.

This was the point Hassan should have thrown them out, stood up and punched Moz or said something cutting, but he only sat back in his chair and pulled out a wallet, counting ten-dollar bills onto the table. The total got to forty dollars before Hassan shrugged, casually added one more to the pile and slipped his wallet back inside his jacket.

"Fifty dollars," he said.

It was an incredible sum in a city where an entire family could work for a month and earn nowhere near that.

"Half now," said Hassan, "and half later." Pulling a small cigarillo from a leather case, he waited for Idries to produce a lighter. It was brass overlaid with chrome, the name of some Essaouria nightclub in enamel along one side. "We can meet at Café Lux afterwards."

"After what?" Malika demanded.

"After you deliver this." Hassan lifted a plastic bag onto the café table. "I'm glad you came," he added, sounding almost sincere. "I would have been very unhappy if you hadn't."

"Tough shit," said Malika, but she said this under her breath.

"What's in it?" That was Moz.

Idries snorted. "You don't want to know."

"We do," said Malika, "don't we?" She looked at Moz, who scowled, although it was at Hassan for raising his eyebrows.

"Anyway," Idries said. "Kif isn't drugs." He sounded amused at the idea. "And you don't have to go far."

"Where?" said Moz and Hassan named a café on Rue Arabe about fifteen minutes south of where they sat.

"Malika can be your sister," Idries suggested. His grin when he said this was less than kind.

"Not me," Malika said. "He wants to take it, he can take it..." There was a scrape as she pushed back her chair. "I'm going home."

"You can keep all the money," said Moz, her gaze stripping all the bravado from his offer. "Please," Moz added.

Malika sighed. "Who do we ask for?"

"You don't ask for anyone," said Hassan. "You leave this bag under a table at the back, near the left-hand corner." He held up his left hand, so they both understood which one he meant. "A friend will collect it after you're gone."

"And if someone's using the table?"

"The table will be free," Hassan said. He sounded very certain about this...

* * *

Malika carried the plastic bag in one hand, swinging it gently so it looked like shopping. And they talked as they walked, about the things Malika and Moz always talked about: the Mellah, Malika's mother, how weird it must be to have a normal family like Hassan's.

Somewhere after the Church of St. Anne and before the green wrought-iron railings and neat flowerbeds of the Jardin de Hartai they passed two police cars parked in a side street outside a half-built hotel, windows down, their occupants listening to what sounded like static on a radio.

Café Impérial was where Hassan said it would be, between two of the new hotels and backing onto a slightly tatty French-built office block, and the table was empty. "I'll do it," Malika said. "They'll notice you."

No one stopped her from entering and few noticed when she left. No one came to collect the bag. The next person to use the table kicked it under a bench. He was still sitting there when it exploded.

"I see," said Petra Mayer. In front of her, fanned out on Prisoner Zero's floor, were the contents of the Marrakchi police file. The worst of the Cimetière Européen crime-scene photographs showed an adolescent girl, the marks of a swollen ligature around her neck. Slash marks on the torso had been matched to a lock knife found at the scene. The fingerprints on the handle of the knife were those of the man in front of her.

Petra Mayer reread the arrest warrant, although she already knew it by heart. It charged Marzaq al-Turq with the rape and murder of Malika, daughter of Sidi ould Kasim.

"And the knife was the one you'd used to cut her ropes. That's why your fingerprints are on it."

"The Major's knife," Prisoner Zero said. "Not that it makes any difference. I still killed her."

Petra Mayer had to agree. "You know," she said, looking at the file. "I can think of several good reasons why it might be better for all of us if you remained Jake."

# CHAPTER 54

## *Lampedusa, Wednesday 11 July*

Stubbing out her cigarette, Petra Mayer looked round the room that now made do as Prisoner Zero's cell. She'd been talking since noon and getting nowhere.

"Look," she said, "let's go back to basics. There's been a forty-eight-hour stay of execution and the President agrees to meet. Okay?"

She put a neatly printed appeal for clemency in front of Prisoner Zero and offered him a pen. All the man had to do was sign the thing.

"Jake," Professor Mayer said crossly. "You've got what you wanted, all right? He's going to fly across to inspect the USS *Harry S. Truman* and while he's over here he'll come and talk to you, I promise."

That the President also wanted this meeting Petra Mayer left aside. Gene Newman had given her only two instructions: proceed on the basis that Prisoner Zero was Jake Razor and find out why the man needed to talk to him. *The darkness thought it would be a good idea* did not constitute a reason.

Petra Mayer knew exactly why the President intended to pardon Prisoner Zero. He needed Europe on his side in his refusal to sign a joint space accord with China until Beijing sorted out its human rights issues.

Sort out the human rights and he'd sign off billions of dollars for a joint mission into space. Refuse, and Beijing could go it alone. As if that was going to happen... It was a tricky position to take and "Killing Einstein," as the First Lady now billed the Prisoner Zero problem, was not going to help impress Europe.

"Did you hear what I said?"

Nodding, the prisoner leant forward to pick up Professor Mayer's pen, flipped over the appeal for clemency and began to sketch a squat tower on the back.

"Concentrate," Petra Mayer suggested.

Dark eyes looked up from the paper. "Believe me," said Prisoner Zero. "I'm trying to."

On her chair in the corner, Katie Petrov scrawled a note in her book, ripped out the page as quietly as possible and stood up to pass it to Professor Mayer. *Reassurance?*

"He's really coming," Petra Mayer promised. "And he really wants to talk to you, but first you have to sign the paper."

"And he'll listen?"

"Gene Newman always listens." Professor Mayer was telling the truth. It was one of the President's trademarks, like his arm around the shoulder of whichever dignitary was walking beside him and his oh-so-sincere double-fisted handshake. Whether he'd pay serious attention to what Prisoner Zero had to say was another matter although chances were he might. Gene Newman could be weird like that.

"This is what you want, right?" said Petra Mayer. "To meet the President?"

Prisoner Zero shook his head. "It's what the darkness wants."

Returning to his drawing, the prisoner quickly sketched a mulberry bush, shaded in some background and added an arch, then a man standing in it. After that, Prisoner Zero began filling in tiles on a temple roof.

"Tell me," he asked suddenly, "why now?"

They all knew the answer to that. With thirty-six hours to go the President had been the one to blink first. The stay of execution was proof of that.

"Because," said Petra Mayer, "now's the right time."

And Katie Petrov found herself wondering if her old tutor even half believed this. There was no correct time for the US President to shake hands with his would-be assassin. A substantial slice of home opinion was still holding firm on this.

"But if you don't sign, then we'll have to call the whole visit off."

Prisoner Zero shrugged.

Either the man was a brilliant actor, Katie Petrov decided, or his demand to see the President was as much a part of his dementia as the self-starvation, earlier filth and his utter refusal to contemplate that his precious darkness might not exist.

"Sign the appeal," Petra Mayer said.

"No."

Neither of them was yet prepared to return to the paragraph at the end in which Jake Razor acknowledged that his attempt on the life of the President had been a mistake. It was so brief that the thirty-seven words could have been written in half a minute at the most. That it apparently took White House staffers a day and a quarter to construct, Prisoner Zero regarded as one of life's lesser ironies.

He wasn't going to plead temporary insanity, any more than he was prepared to throw himself on the President's mercy or allow any one of the eight human rights groups currently demanding a retrial to do so in his name.

Before he signed anything Prisoner Zero needed to meet the President face to face; the darkness was very strict on this. In the meantime it reserved its right to insist on Prisoner Zero's execution. While Petra Mayer considered this latest impasse, the man who wasn't Jake Razor went back to his drawing.

Gene Newman's problem was simple. Given he'd been tried and condemned by a military tribunal, Prisoner Zero had a right to death. This would play badly with everyone except the Secretary of State for Defense, most of the inhabitants of Texas and bits of the Midwest.

The First Lady had convinced Gene that to meet Prisoner Zero before he'd asked for clemency would be political suicide. Prisoner Zero said the darkness refused to allow him to appeal before it had met the President.

Small wonder that Petra Mayer had a headache.

"Interesting," Katie Petrov said, getting up again to take a closer look at Prisoner Zero's drawing.

The prisoner ignored her.

"It's a corner turret from Beijing's Palace Museum," Katie Petrov told the Professor, who glanced up briefly but more or less did the same. "You know," insisted Katie, "part of the UN heritage site."

"No," said Prisoner Zero, "it's not." They were the first words he'd actually addressed directly to Dr. Petrov.

"Triple-roofed, gables on the two highest, carved *acroteria* on the corner of each, intricate screens..."

"It's not," Prisoner Zero insisted.

"China," Katie Petrov wrote in her notebook. "Beijing..." If nothing else, dropping hints about Beijing would tie up half the upper echelon of the NSA and keep them off Professor Mayer's back for a while.

Prisoner Zero's sketch progressed in shades of grey, the cross-hatching made from numbers and words. The words were broken, the numbers near random and he would lose the drawing at the end of the day because, every evening before the overhead bulb went out in Prisoner Zero's cell, Sergeant Saez would come in to search his room.

The darkness thought it only kind to give him something to find.

Sergeant Saez's search was methodical. The mattress was overturned (Prisoner Zero had one of those too) and his new table and chair examined carefully. The laptop recently made available by Petra Mayer was confiscated for the night as was every single piece of paper on which Prisoner Zero had doodled during the course of that day.

Laptop, paper and pencils were returned again the next morning. To get them back Prisoner Zero had to eat at least half his breakfast. No one had explained this to him but empirical testing had confirmed that this was how it worked.

"I don't get it," Katie Petrov said.

"What's to get?" said the Professor. She was used to this. Katie's questions to Prisoner Zero went unanswered. Which meant that if Katie wanted to ask him something she had to ask the Professor, who would ask the prisoner. It was clumsy, arbitrary and time consuming. Petra Mayer assumed that was the point.

"Where does Beijing come into this?"

"So," said Professor Mayer, addressing the prisoner, "where does Beijing come into this?"

"It doesn't."

"That's not Beijing?"

"No," said Prisoner Zero. "That's where the darkness lives." And with that he returned to a small figure climbing the outside of a tower. He gave the figure a short sword in each hand and then scrawled out one of them, turning it into rope.

As a church clock in a distant village struck ten and day turned to night on Lampedusa without bothering to pass through dusk, Colonel Borgenicht arrived to suggest that now might be a good time for his men to be allowed to lock Prisoner Zero down. Petra Mayer could tell by the Colonel's manner that he knew all about the President's planned visit and didn't like the idea one little bit.

"In a minute," she said. "We just want to take him for a walk first... That was a joke," she added, seeing anxiety suddenly flood the Colonel's face.

Colonel Borgenicht nodded weakly.

"You know," Katie Petrov said, as she and the Professor were crunching across gravel on their way back to their quarters, "you probably shouldn't tease him so much."

Petra Mayer glanced round to where the Colonel stood staring after them. "I thought you loathed the man."

"Of course I do," said Katie Petrov hastily. "All the same..."

The Professor raised her eyebrows. "Stockholm Syndrome," she said. "You'll be feeling sorry for him next."

Katie Petrov blushed.

"Can I ask you something?" Katie Petrov had reached the door of her chalet, and was actually feeding her key card into the lock when she stopped and turned back to the older woman.

"Of course."

"What does the President really hope to gain by coming here?"

"He carries the Europeans with him on his refusal to sign the space accord with Beijing until the human rights issues are resolved. America is seen to be magnanimous to someone it could justifiably treat harshly. And Gene gets to prove he's not the previous incumbent."

"But that's not all, is it?"

Professor Mayer shook her head. "No," she said. "He sees Prisoner Zero as an asset for America and a personal challenge."

"And that's it?"

"Mostly," admitted Petra Mayer. "Although we shouldn't forget the photo shoot. Gene Newman and the world's lost genius... Brave move by US President... Newman meets would-be assassin..."

"So where does the challenge come in?"

"If you knew Gene the way I know Gene..." It sounded like the first line of a song and after a second Katie realized that was exactly how Petra Mayer intended it to sound. "You ever met anyone who just knows they can do things better than anyone else?"

"Sounds like my first husband," Katie said.

The Professor looked interested. "How many have you had?"

"Just the one," Katie said. "I learn quickly from my mistakes."

"And could he?"

"The man could barely change a light bulb without reading the manual."

"Gene can," said the Professor. "It's one of the more annoying things about him. He acts like Olivier, writes like a Don DeLillo, cooks like Anthony Bourdain. And I'm reliably informed—" Whatever Petra Mayer was about to reveal, she thought the better of it. "He looks good too," she ended lamely.

"What's all that got to do with him coming here?"

"Think about it," said the Professor, and she wasn't being rude. Just talking to her companion as she'd have talked to herself.

Watching stars break through a pitch-black sky, Katie Petrov worked it out. "Yeah, I get it," she said. Gene Newman was coming to Lampedusa to sort out the "Killing Einstein" problem for himself, and he was planning to do it in the full glare of the world's press.

## CHAPTER 55

### *Zigin Chéng, CTzu 53/Year 20*

"You have messages."

Zaq snorted. The record for messages was one point five billion in a day, or maybe that was per hour. An entire bureau, the Tung Wen Kuan, existed to answer these, which were always dealt with individually, usually by a short cerebral link that gave each recipient the impression that he, she or it had been in direct conversation with the Emperor.

Someone, supposedly the original Chuang Tzu (though Zaq suspected it was actually the Library), had decided that every answer should equal the message received. So random mental messages got simple cerebral replies, while actual gifts were met with tokens of equal worth, that worth calculated using a complex algorithm that took time/value into account but gave it less weight than rareness or originality.

"Answer them then," he told the voice in his head.

"It's not that simple."

Zaq was about to snort when he realized he'd done this already. So he made do with a scowl. "Why not?" His voice sounded petulant, even to himself.

"Because it's the Council of Ambassadors."

"The—" Zaq had rather forgotten about the Council. On good

days, of course, only on really good days, he could even forget that he had an empire. Although he'd never, no matter how hard he tried, quite managed to forget the Library, but this was probably because the Library and he were threaded through each other.

"What do they want?"

"What they wanted last time."

"Which is...?" Zaq really didn't have time to remember this stuff.

"They demand that you back yourself up and insist that I make you. For the good of the 2023 worlds."

"And what's your opinion?" asked Zaq, his voice tight. The Librarian was meant to be his mentor but it was also a facet of the Library. Neither Zaq nor the Library had any doubt that they were now at war with each other. And Zaq still believed he was winning.

"Would it make a difference?"

"What do you think?"

The Library and Zaq knew the answer to that.

"This message is from the Council..." The voice hesitated. "My opinion is irrelevant. You've made that clear."

"No back-ups," said Zaq. "And you can't make me."

"I could. Only I'm not allowed to..."

"Why not?" Zaq sounded interested.

"It's in the rules."

"And who made the rules?"

"I did," said the Librarian. There was a definite element of regret in its voice.

*"General Ch'ao Kai."*

The yellow-clad eunuch halted under the archway, made his announcement and then stepped back to make space for the man he'd just announced. A carpet of discarded trays, most of them full of congealing dim sum, made this last manoeuvre slightly tricky.

The kitchens continued to prepare food and the servitors continued to deliver it to the edge of the garden, which was as far as they were allowed to go. Unfortunately, no one had experience of what to do if the Emperor refused to believe the trays were actually there.

"Who?" demanded Zaq, but his major-domo was already gone.

From beneath the arch came the scrape of boots on a path. As this was not the kind of sound an assassin might make, Zaq ignored it while wondering whether or not to be disappointed.

"Tuan-Yu?" came a voice that was both old and very tired.

"What?"

The soldier in the archway was dressed in full armour and carried a snow leopard's tail attached to his lance. Zaq tried to remember the man's name but failed, so he counted the toes on the dragon on his breastplate and made do with the man's rank instead.

"General," he said, "how good to see you." Zaq's intonation made clear that he realized the elderly man was at the very top level of the banner horde and General Ch'ao Kai relaxed. The Emperor seemed aware that the General was real and this in itself was reassuring.

"Tuan-Yu," he said, "I hope you are well..." General Ch'ao Kai was still wondering how to frame the Council's demand when Zaq shook his head, stood up from where he sat and retreated further into the garden.

"We need to talk," said a voice right inside him. The voice sounded sad. Not desolate or disappointed, just sad.

It was bound to happen eventually and when it did Zaq was stunned by the sheer sense of scale that filled his mind. It was like standing on a ledge and watching mist clear across an almost endless plain or standing on that plain and looking up at a mountain which just kept rising.

And then Zaq's mind adjusted to what it really saw. A shell of worlds around a sun, each world so vast that the first Emperor's home planet could have been lost in one of its oceans. The shell was alive with communication between the worlds, endless vessels slipping in and out of individual atmospheres as they made the jump from where they were to where they were going.

It was breathtaking in its complexity.

"This is what you want to destroy." And as it spoke the Library looked through Zaq's eyes at the garden and matched this with what all the other Chuang Tzu had seen before him.

There didn't seem to be much difference.

Yet there had to be a difference, because overlying the beauty of the mulberry bushes, the butterflies and the elegant rockeries so understated that they looked natural was the sadness that Zaq had heard in the voice of the Library, not realizing it was his.

"I can get rid of the dreams," said the Library, and they both knew which dreams it meant. Something had gone wrong with this Chuang Tzu right at the beginning when Zaq was first given the apple. The Library was starting to think that it should have dealt with the matter then.

"No," said Zaq, "you can't."

"You should talk to the Council," said the Library. "They're beginning to get upset."

"The answer's no," said Zaq.

"You haven't heard their question."

"It doesn't matter," Zaq said. "The answer is still no. It was no yesterday and it will be no tomorrow."

"There may not be a tomorrow," said the Library.

When Zaq woke he was in a painting. It was a very famous painting, one reproduced widely across the 2023 worlds. The cloak studded with the memories of his predecessors lay across his bed, even though Zaq remembered burning the thing. He was naked and Winter Blossom On Broken Rock was lying next to him.

She was crying.

"How?" Zaq asked, and then he knew because the Librarian knew, and Zaq watched himself being carried back from the gardens and tucked into bed where he slept.

"Clothes," Zaq demanded, but no one came.

"The servitors have gone," said the girl. "The chief eunuch sent them home."

"They have homes?"

The girl nodded.

"I thought you just turned off," said Zaq. "Came back to life again when you were needed."

She looked at him through huge eyes. "I'm not sure I understand," she said.

Zaq dressed himself in his pale blue *chao pao,* the one decorated around the neck, across the shoulders and above the hem with embroidered five-clawed dragons.

The original ruling was simple. Five claws for an emperor, four for a prince and three for generals, chamberlains and dukes.

Sometime between the first Chuang Tzu and Zaq, who was the fifty-third emperor to have taken that title, imperial dragons had suffered severe inflation and so had the materials from which they were made. The dragon embroidered across the cloak that Zaq now wore had so many claws they were almost impossible to count.

"Go," Zaq told the girl.

"Where should I go?"

"Home?"

So she went, still naked. And Zaq watched her walk away until she turned a corner at the end of a corridor and he was alone again.

*I may eat this, I may not eat that. I will walk this distance and stay silent for that many hours. Hold my hands out to my sides for this many minutes. Stay awake for that many hours.*

The rules Zaq made for himself were no more arbitrary than those written for him by tradition. And if others failed to understand them that was not his fault.

Was it?

Wrapping the dragon cloak around him, Zaq allowed himself a red bean mini moon cake from a gold plate and headed back to the garden, stopping only to smash all the mirrors as he came to them.

## CHAPTER 56

### *Marrakech, Summer 1977*

Fifteen minutes after the girl in the oversized haik left Café Impérial and retraced her steps along the edge of Jardin de Hartai to where a boy waited, five sticks of industrial explosive detonated beneath a bench at the rear of the café. The wooden bench was against the left-hand wall and only one person was sitting there because the café was almost empty, which was all that could be said for what happened.

The primers had been manufactured for quarrying. Of low grade to begin with, age and careless storage had taken them to the edge of their useful life. In fact, the forensic expert borrowed from Paris regarded it as a wonder that they hadn't detonated of their own accord while being carried through the streets of Marrakech.

Sécurité regarded this as a poor miracle.

It mattered little that the bomb was of such low quality because someone had taped rusty nails around each stick. A report written a couple of weeks after the atrocity by a policeman called Major Abbas and circulated by the Ministry of the Interior to Paris and

Washington noted the similarity between this attack and similar Algerian-inspired atrocities, concluding that the organizers were probably already across the border and thus could not be found.

His report contradicted a suggestion in *Le Matin* that the nails were chosen because they were rusty, pointing out that these were probably all that had been to hand.

Either way, the rust added complications to wounds that were already, if one were honest, beyond anything other than the most palliative treatment. Shrapnel from a bomb can spin up to and through the point of impact. Where and when it stops spinning depends on the rate of spin and the density of the tissue with which it comes into contact; bone is usually enough.

Of the few patrons in Café Impérial scarcely any survived. And of the three who did, all died from side effects or medical complications within a period of fifteen weeks. The last to die was Ishmael Bonaventure, who still controlled a number of brothels, clubs and cafés at the time of his death, including Samantha's, a discothèque on the edge of the Palmeraie visited by Brian Jones and Jimi Hendrix.

Among those who died instantly were the manager, his son, the man on the bench and a second cousin of Hassan's uncle, who'd come to meet Ishmael Bonaventure.

Monsieur Bonaventure had been as surprised to receive a telephone call from the cousin as that cousin was to be contacted by Caid Hammou. Having fallen out six months before over profits from a bar in Agadir, the bad blood between Hassan's uncle and the cousin was known to many.

Caid Hammou offered his cousin a simple choice: renewed friendship or a lifetime of enmity. That this life was likely to be short went unspoken.

The cousin had not been looking forward to visiting Café Impérial, centre of Bonaventure's operations in the New Town. As prices went, however, acting as go-between for Caid Hammou and Ishmael Bonaventure was far less than the cousin had been expecting to have to pay for what, in retrospect, was a very unfortunate error in accounting.

So he agreed, fixed the meeting and went with a list of suggestions from Caid Hammou on how operations in Marrakech might be more fairly divided.

Eminently reasonable suggestions, all things considered. And sitting across a table from the elderly freedom-fighter turned gangster, the cousin could see that Bonaventure felt this too.

"I will need to meet Caid Hammou." The old man's tone might have been peremptory but his acceptance of Hammou's right to the title "caid" said all that was needed about how content he was with the compromise on offer.

"Of course," Caid Hammou's cousin said. "Shall we arrange that now?"

The old man looked surprised, also gratified. He had assumed that Caid Hammou would make difficulties about the exact time and place of the meeting in an attempt to keep face. "He's happy with this?"

The man on the other side of the table nodded. "Let me make the call," he suggested, pointing one finger at a telephone on the wall. "May I use that?"

"Be my guest." Ishmael Bonaventure sat back to enjoy the moment. He was still savouring his success when a young Arab girl walked in, swathed in a black haik. Someone's servant, he imagined.

She drank mint tea, the cheapest thing on the board, and ate half a pastry, leaving her payment in a handful of small coins. Ishmael Bonaventure was willing to bet a few would be *empire cheffian*, old currency from the days before the French gave up their claim to his country.

Bonaventure watched her eat, drink her mint tea and pay in an old mirror which his father had imported from Paris. He didn't notice that she'd forgotten to take her shopping bag.

The old gangster and Caid Hammou's cousin were both still waiting, somewhat impatiently, for Caid Hammou to arrive when the bomb exploded at the table behind them and their impatience ceased to matter.

The café was destroyed, its back wall ripped open, its ceiling crumbling in like eggshell. It was mere bad luck that Café Impérial backed onto a notario's office sometimes used by French intelligence. And it was this, that an office on Boulevard Abdussallam had been destroyed and two European lawyers killed in the blast, which made the news.

## CHAPTER 57

### *Lampedusa, Thursday 12 July*

More fucking flash guns than at the Oscars. Colonel Borgenicht kept his assessment to himself, while still regarding it as pretty accurate.

Originally he'd demanded that the event take place during the day and that numbers be limited. He'd been overruled on both counts. His attempts to go over the head of General Mayer, as he found himself referring through gritted teeth to the Professor, foundered when the five-star general he approached was overruled by Gene Newman in his capacity as Commander in Chief.

So Colonel Borgenicht found himself providing security for a Sicilian village emptied of most of its inhabitants and filled with the cream of the world's press, which wasn't exactly how the Colonel thought of the growling and surging mob roped off on one side of a picturesque nineteenth-century square.

After a quick once-over, he'd dismissed the female journalists. Mostly they were scrawny, dressed in black and utterly interchangeable, being short-haired, immaculately made up despite the heat, and thin as teenaged boys. His own tastes were more lush. The men came in two models, ponytailed and those, infinitely greater in number, who sported heads as cropped as any of his own marines.

These ones worried him.

Colonel Borgenicht existed to protect his President, his country, his men and himself in that order. The thought that the President might be killed while he was on duty had given the Colonel a sleepless forty-eight hours and reduced his social skills to zero. All that concerned him was getting through the next two hours.

The time had been chosen because Prisoner Zero needed to show the President the Milky Way. That was what General Mayer had told him. The lunatic wanted to show President Newman some stars. So the entire meeting was timed to coincide with the heavens breaking through the evening sky.

It helped, apparently, that the meeting was taking place on Lampedusa, where light pollution was still in its infancy; although, to make sure, most lights in the village were to be turned off at a preset time.

Colonel Borgenicht had wanted this meeting in broad daylight on American soil. Some place where he had complete control of who was let in. Better still, some place where he was not the most senior officer present. There were, it seemed, a number of good reasons why this was a bad idea. And he could tell, just by looking, how distasteful Petra Mayer found it having to put those reasons into words.

They'd been at breakfast in the officers' mess. (This is what a hand-scrawled note on its door called the place. A vending machine inside selling six kinds of flavoured water, and a row of rubber mats revealed its other identity as the hotel's T'ai Chi room.)

"It should be in the US."

Ripping apart her smoked salmon bagel, Petra Mayer ate the wedge of salmon, having first scraped off all traces of cream cheese. "Ma'am," she said. "You're meant to call me 'ma'am'."

The Colonel was sure she did this only to irritate.

"It has to be in the US, ma'am."

The officers' mess was meant to be self-service, something to do with recent advances in democratic equality, but the Professor had discovered that spilling a few glasses of orange juice as she carried them to her table was enough to make waiter service suddenly materialize. Besides, she was a general. A very short, rather ill and temporary general, but still a general.

The Professor raised her cup. "Another coffee," she demanded.

Nothing else was said until this arrived and then she sat forward, indicating that Colonel Borgenicht should do the same. "Why," she said quietly, "do you think we're keeping the prisoner here?"

"Because it shows faith in our NATO allies." That was the first among many reasons trotted out by the Pentagon Press Office and the Colonel didn't believe it any more than the Professor.

"No," said Petra Mayer. "I mean *really*?"

The Colonel blew out his breath. He was having trouble seeing this small woman as a general. In fact, he had trouble seeing her as anything other than trouble. Her brief stint as the President's tutor he knew about. Her intelligence assessments of Beirut and all places similar was on a need-to-know basis, and he didn't.

"Questioning," he said.

Petra Mayer nodded. "Obviously," she said. "Take this man to the US and a whole different set of rules apply. You want that?"

Something was troubling Colonel Borgenicht. "I'd have thought—" The Colonel stopped, considered and wondered how to finish.

"That this is exactly what I would have wanted? Of course it is," said the Professor. "It's also exactly what the US can't risk. At least, according to the Attorney General." Petra Mayer stared at the Colonel, who now leant right forward to ensure their conversation remained private. "What do you think the verdict would have been if this had been tried in an open court?"

"I can guess," he said, after a moment's thought.

"Quite," said Petra Mayer. "You've seen the files."

"He made a confession."

"Indeed," said the Professor. "We're getting really good at letting others do our dirty work. That would be the first thing to go. Throw out his confession and what do we have? A lunatic who should never have been allowed out in public. Unfortunately he also happens to be a genius."

"So we retry," said the Colonel, his words almost a whisper. "Keep the court military."

"And reach what verdict?" Petra Mayer stared at the crop-haired black officer. The man was built like the proverbial shithouse and had biceps that still, fifteen years after he was commissioned, betrayed the fact he'd started in the ranks. Petra Mayer had seen the Colonel's file. She knew about his divorce, last year's less than discreet battle against OxyC, a prescription analgesic better known to most of Dr. Petrov's clients as "hillbilly heroin."

The man had a high IQ fighting to escape the limitations of its uniform.

"It gets worse," Petra Mayer said.

The Colonel looked at her. "How can it get worse?" he demanded.

"The meeting's to be televised in real time," said Petra Mayer. "They're going to walk out there in front of the cameras, look at the stars and shake hands."

"Why?"

"Because it's part of the deal."

"Whose deal?"

"Prisoner Zero's."

"Jesus fuck." From the look on his face, it seemed Colonel Borgenicht finally understood that his certainties were coming unravelled over a cup of cold coffee in a hastily emptied hotel room on an island in the middle of nowhere.

* * *

The square was carefully selected. Although it was only chosen after several alternative locations had been considered and rejected; Camp Freedom was the first to go.

As this was Colonel Borgenicht's first choice he expected no less.

The camp was secure, wrapped tightly with razor wire and had high-powered searchlights set up at all four corners on scaffolding towers. Machine-gun encampments guarded the roads in and out. The very qualities that made it Colonel Borgenicht's first choice led to its rejection by Gene Newman.

Razor wire and searchlights said the wrong thing for his administration. They said fear of the world outside. Gene Newman wanted something warmer, more media-friendly. He wanted historic, elegant, statesmanlike...

The town hall in Lampedusa had to be dropped when the ruling Northern Alliance wanted to be part of the handshake. A seventeenth-century palazzo, now functioning as a five-star hotel on Punta Muro Vecchio, reluctantly went the same way, even though it had its own heliport, the terraced gardens were entirely walled and the Milanese manager loved the idea.

Astronomical insurance costs, claimed the owners. The real reason was more pragmatic. Palazzo Muro Vecchio had a wide and loyal Italian clientele who were none too happy with the way the Marrakech incident had been handled and the Swiss group owning the hotel took an entirely sensible decision to protect their investment.

This left Valera, an old white-walled *villaggio* near Punta Parise, at the western end of the island, beneath the shadow of Monte Alberto Sole. A press release from the White House revealed that the village variously had been Byzantine, Arab, Norman and Spanish. For much of the Renaissance, while *condottieri* set themselves up as princes in the north and southern Italy continued its war of attrition against the Barbary pirates, Villaggio Valera lay derelict, a home to goats and the occasional fugitive.

All of this changed in 1881 when what remained of the derelict village was bought by Baron del Smith, a cotton trader from Liverpool who'd fought alongside Garibaldi at the battles of Volturno and Aspromonte, been created baron by Victor Emmanuel II and then, five years later, been sent into exile by the same King for trying to introduce communal farming to Sicily.

The village was rebuilt to a plan drawn up by Baron del Smith's wife and the slopes around it divided into workable farms. Olive trees and lemon groves were planted, as were almonds and oranges. The experiment was a brave one but lack of adequate irrigation, the heat of a few bad summers and the mistrust of other landowners saw the village fall back into near ruin. By 1910 the almonds were being picked, sorted and husked by old women who spoke sadly and often of their sons making new lives for themselves in America.

President Gene Newman's great-grandmother was born in Villaggio Valera. In retrospect, it was an obvious choice.

"There'll be a gun on you at all times. You understand that?" Colonel Borgenicht's voice was tight. "We've got snipers in the bell tower and on the roof of the town hall."

Prisoner Zero smiled.

Part of Colonel Borgenicht wanted to beat the man's head against the nearest wall, the other bit wanted to get on his knees and beg the bastard not to fuck this thing up. Instead, he just nodded, as if Prisoner Zero had given him the answer he wanted.

"Yeah," said Petra Mayer. "You've told him that already."

They were standing beside the church. And at the opposite end of the square, behind waist-high metal barriers, waited the press, plus selected members of the public and Katie Petrov, Miles Alsdorf and all those who didn't rate being included in the Presidential entourage.

Colonel Borgenicht would have preferred the barriers to be higher, but then he'd have preferred the bit parts and media not to be there at all, which was obviously impossible since the entire meeting had been turned into one big press call.

He had snipers stationed at both ends of the square, a precaution helped by the fact that the town hall's roof was flat and the bell tower of the church was easily reachable by stairs from the inside.

A sniper in the ornate bell tower was responsible for the laser dot on the back of Prisoner Zero's head. It would have been simple to give laser sights to the man on the roof of the town hall opposite, but then Prisoner Zero would have had a rag dot visible in the middle of his forehead. And that would send out all the wrong signals, apparently.

The plan was simple.

President Newman would arrive by helicopter at a field outside the village. He would walk up the hill, rather than take a jeep. This was his choice and against the express advice of his Secret Service men. A side effect of this was that extra snipers had to be found to cover the lower slopes of Monte Alberto Sole, stretching the Colonel's resources even thinner.

He would walk along a short section of Via Smith, from which cars and pedestrians had been banned, and enter Piazza Solforino from the north, crossing the cobbles with the press and token public behind their barricades to his right. In the middle of the square he would stop and take a salute from Colonel Borgenicht, before pausing to examine the seventeenth-century bell tower silhouetted against the twilight.

Professor Mayer would then bring out Prisoner Zero, who was to be clean-shaven, dressed in jeans and a T-shirt and unmanacled. To bring the prisoner to the President was, in Colonel Borgenicht's opinion, a very basic breach of protocol, since all those President Newman intended to meet should be ready and waiting.

The President had insisted, however. He didn't want any shots of an exhausted-looking Prisoner Zero standing beside an ill, elderly looking Petra Mayer.

"All you do is shake hands." If anything, the Colonel's voice was even tighter. "You step forward, shake hands, step away. Nothing else. And you don't speak until you're spoken to."

"It's going to be fine," Petra Mayer said. "We've been through all this." She turned to the prisoner, who looked almost normal in Levi's, Nike trainers, a Gap sweatshirt and two weeks' growth of hair. "You know what to do, right?"

Prisoner Zero smiled at the small woman with the three gold bangles and a beak-like nose. A crow, Malika would have called her, and in all probability would have been right.

"Well?" Colonel Borgenicht said.

The prisoner shrugged. Whether or not he knew what to do was irrelevant. All that mattered was that the darkness did.

President Newman's helicopter was small, single-bladed and pale blue with the President's seal fixed either side, on both doors. Since that model went into service only in black, camouflage or jungle green, Colonel Borgenicht imagined the craft had been given a rapid paint job. It also flew low over Villaggio Valera on its way to the field, which the Colonel was sure had not been in the flight plan.

"Shouldn't you be with your men?" Petra Mayer nodded to an honour guard who stood at attention in the twilight.

The Colonel knew Professor Mayer was trying to get rid of him. Most probably so she could talk to the prisoner in private.

"I'm going," he said, adding "ma'am" as an afterthought.

Prisoner Zero and the Professor watched the thick-set black officer march out to a prearranged spot, halt with what looked like a complicated stamp of his boots and come to attention.

*"The President is entering the square."* The voice in Petra Mayer's ear bead was clipped and military, and she watched Colonel Borgenicht nod to himself from his position in the middle of the square as he heard the same message. A ripple of tension ran through the crowd, heads turning and photographers surging forward as they realized what those wired for sound had already been told.

Gene Newman, looking relaxed in light fawn slacks, tan shoes and a summer-weight jacket, strode under an arch and into view, the First Lady half a pace behind him.

He was a Hollywood star who happened to be President. A brilliant mind, a sharp politician, an adequate husband. Most of all, he was a man of the people. Hands stretched out to him, voices called.

Stepping off the path that had been marked discreetly in chalk, Gene Newman reached the barriers and grasped the hand of an old woman, shaking it warmly. From first seeing the crowds until that moment, his eyes had been on a young Sicilian woman in her twenties, a small boy glued to her hips, his thin arms tight around her neck. She had a face straight from *La Dolce Vita* and breasts full enough to die for.

But the second the old woman behind the girl thrust out her own hand, all Gene Newman's attention locked on to her. "You have a beautiful village," he said, in Italian bad enough to disgrace a child, and around the grandmother, daughter and child, members of the European press practically cooed in delight.

He was brilliant, Petra Mayer had to give her old pupil that. Ruthless, intellectually arrogant in private and occasionally promiscuous but a good president all the same. He didn't talk to the girl next either, instead he pulled a stupid face at her child, then reached out and gripped the toddler's nose lightly between thumb and first finger.

The boy might have burst into tears or buried his head in his mother's shoulder, but this was Gene Newman and the kid just grinned as the President grinned back and a dozen flash guns fired in the dying sun. Only then did President Newman turn to the mother. His words were few and his Italian rudimentary, but he left her staring after him with something approaching open hunger.

The man could have kept a team of anthropologists in research papers for life on how power made middle-aged men unfeasibly attractive to women in their twenties.

"Ma'am," said Colonel Borgenicht, his voice tight in her ear. "You're on..."

This was Petra Mayer's signal to walk Prisoner Zero out into the middle of the square. The sniper rifle in the bell tower would be covering him from beginning to end and the man behind the sights was the best America had to offer, on special loan from the CIA. Whatever happened, that rifle would remain trained on Prisoner Zero's skull. If necessary, the sniper would shoot through anyone who got in the way.

From the look in the eyes of the Colonel when he told her this, Petra Mayer knew he meant every word.

"Time to go," Prisoner Zero said brightly, pushing himself away from the church wall, and Petra Mayer did her best not to look shocked.

Marzaq al-Turq, sometimes living as Jake Razor and now answering only to Prisoner Zero, stepped into the square and began his walk across the dusty cobblestones of Piazza Solforino. Camera flash burnt his eyes and the weight of history hung like a yoke around his shoulders but he barely noticed.

"Look this way..."

"Over here!"

"Hey, Jake..."

Prisoner Zero could hear the demands of the press over the beat of his own heart and he could taste nightfall in the air and smell dog shit, diesel, a distant fire and the stink of sweat that rose from his body. A scrawled echo of the only day that had really mattered in his life.

All the things he'd hoped to develop from Jake's notes remained unfinished. He didn't understand the shape of time, not *really*. All he had was a matrix of multi-dimensional intimations filtered through a three-dimensional brain, a flicker book masquerading as film.

He was no closer to finding the missing name of God.

"The missing name of what?"

The question came from a man standing in front of him. Gene Newman, President of the United States, the man who refused to sign a space accord with Beijing and the person Prisoner Zero had been instructed to kill.

"You have to take America into deep space," Prisoner Zero said. "You can't let China go it alone."

"That's what this is all about?"

"I think so."

"But you don't know?"

Prisoner Zero shook his head.

"I can't sign the accord," said the President. "Not the way things are in China at the moment. You know how many people Beijing has in prison camps?" He was on firmer ground here. Gene Newman was always on firm ground when it came to statistics.

The man looked at him.

Gene Newman sighed. "That's different," he said.

Around them people were looking anxious. Well, Colonel Borgenicht, the First Lady and Petra Mayer were looking anxious and they counted as people.

Cameras were flashing, voices shouting. But all the President's attention was on one emaciated figure in front of him. Prisoner Zero didn't look a threat to anyone. He looked like someone trapped in a life where genius was not enough.

"You can change history," said Prisoner Zero. As he moved closer to the President than he was meant to get Colonel Borgenicht began to glance between his Commander in Chief and the bell tower.

The Colonel was anxiety made flesh.

"We should put that man out of his misery," said the President. "We'll talk about the other stuff later. Let's do the shake." He spoke as if Prisoner Zero regularly did camera calls. As if the world's gaze came naturally to them both.

"You okay?" he added, watching Prisoner Zero sway. The last thing President Newman needed was for the man to collapse in front of the cameras. He could see the papers now. TORTURED PRISONER COLLAPSES AT FEET OF PRESIDENT. That would be one of the politer headlines.

"Sure," said Prisoner Zero.

"Then let's get this over with."

The President reached for a shake, cameras whirring, before Prisoner Zero even had time to take the hand offered. "We faked your signature," said the President, trapping Prisoner Zero's hand between both of his. "And backdated the appeal. Petra has explained that to you, hasn't she?"

"You...?"

"Look into the lenses," President Newman told Prisoner Zero, "shake my hand and smile." And the prisoner did just that. He shook the offered hand, turned to the press and gazed into a bank of cameras, overtaken by a firestorm of flash.

*Mulberry bushes, a stream almost wide enough to be called a river and, over it, a tiny bridge formed from a perfect quarter circle, painted red, green and gold.*

A boy running.

Prisoner Zero wasn't too sure where that was happening until he heard Colonel Borgenicht's voice bark in his ear. The order was for everyone, President Newman was to be protected.

The boy slid to a halt in front of the President, dropping to one knee and pointing his Leica at the man. He had a badge around his neck which read "Presse" and his grin was wide, his eyes dark. He reminded Prisoner Zero of someone and Prisoner Zero was still wondering if that someone was him when Gene Newman held up his hand.

"It's okay," he said, to no one in particular. "Give the kid some room... Where are you from?"

The boy thought about it. "Xingjian," he said.

Gene Newman laughed. "I meant which paper?"

*"El View."*

"Not one I know." He shrugged. "Sorry."

The boy looked about twelve. No, the President caught himself. Eighteen, twenty... Half his own staff looked like children these days.

"You want us to shake again?"

The boy nodded.

"Okay," Gene said. He thrust out his hand to Prisoner Zero. "Let's give the kid what he needs."

Light, such as Prisoner Zero had never seen.

A click of the camera, a flash and then somewhere very distant a grown man screamed; but the sound of Colonel Borgenicht's outrage was already fading and Prisoner Zero was not its cause anyway.

## CHAPTER 58

### *Zigin Chéng, CTzu 53/Year 20*

"You're too late."

The girl shuffled off a stolen cloak, discarding it onto the gravel behind her like a shadow. Her feet were bare and bleeding and she wore little more than the rags of a blue padded jacket and torn silk trousers. Around her narrow hips was a length of twine. It was through this that a child's sword was stuck.

"Too late for what?" she said. Pulling the blade from her makeshift belt, Tris crossed the elegant half-moon bridge in a handful of steps and halted a few paces from where Zaq sat on his rock.

A very elegant rock, carved from jade.

The Emperor was crying and when Tris took a closer look she saw that his face was screwed up like that of an anguished child. Scrolls littered the ground around his feet.

"Something wrong?" Tris said.

This was meant to be ironic. Tris was holding her blade and she could see in his eyes that the Emperor knew why she was there. All the same, he took her question seriously.

"He thought he was dreaming me," Zaq said. "He thought I was the darkness."

"Really?" said Tris. "And should I know what you're talking about?" Tris had less than no idea what the man's words signified.

"You came to stop me. That's why you're here, isn't it?"

"I came to kill you," said Tris. "Stopping you isn't enough." She looked from the rock to her blade and then back again. "You need to stand up," she said.

"Why?"

"Why do you think?" Tris said crossly.

Zaq shrugged, then wiped his eyes with the back of his hand. "I don't know."

"Because I can't kill you if you're sitting down."

"Is that in the rules?"

"Well," said Tris, somewhat reluctantly. "It's in mine."

"Then I'm going to stay right here," said Zaq. "I mean, what would you do?"

Tris frowned. "You can't sit there forever," she protested.

"Maybe," said Zaq. "Maybe not."

In Tris's opinion the Emperor wasn't giving her the attention she deserved. She had a firm idea of how this should go and the Chuang Tzu begging for his life, expressing disbelief or at the very least demanding her reasons came high on that list.

"You know," Zaq muttered after a while, "I probably could... I mean, I don't really eat and sleep scares me." He was ticking the points off on his fingers as he went. "My muscles retain their tone whether or not I exercise. I don't know if I can actually control my waste functions but it seems possible. After all, I can control everything else.

"You should try dangling your feet in the stream," he added, when Tris just stared at him. "It might help the blisters."

"What's with the butterflies?" Tris asked eventually. Once curiosity finally overcame her irritation, it seemed an obvious enough question.

Zaq looked up from his scroll. There was ink on his fingers and his brush had splayed at the bristles where he'd been pressing too hard. His ink stone was broken in three and he'd taken to grinding one of the broken ends directly into a saucer of water. Tris was sure that wasn't how it was meant to be done, but then what did she know?

"Try one," he suggested.

And then Zaq went back to his scroll, alternating perfect circles with sketches of crude flying machines which hovered around a small hill town.

"Go on," he said a moment later. "Here. I'll show you how." Reaching out, Zaq held his hand absolutely still until a butterfly skimmed across the grass towards him.

"Watch," Zaq said.

And as Tris watched, the flicker of purple stamped on the Chuang Tzu's outstretched fingers, the man blinked and the butterfly fell dead, twirling to the ground like a fallen leaf.

"You try it."

Tris held out her hand to a butterfly and across the 2023 worlds 148 billion people sucked in their breath as Tris's body arched backwards and she hit the ground at Zaq's feet.

"That was stupid," he said.

* * *

Flames licked up both sides of the Changlang, a 2572-foot corridor built along the northern shore of a lake which bordered the Emperor's Summer Gardens outside the Forbidden City.

Only a few of the famous paintings lining its walls looked likely to survive the inferno now sweeping the wooden corridor's entire length. Tris's calling card.

Zaq hated it when people wouldn't stay dead.

"This is between me and her," Zaq said. Although he said this to himself since the Librarian was no longer talking to him.

It was muddling and strange and more frightening than he'd expected and Zaq wasn't quite sure why he was still there. If America joined Beijing, the *Loyal Prince* would no longer be solely Chinese. Most probably it would not even be called the *Loyal Prince*. Someone else would discover the 2023 worlds. There'd be no first Chuang Tzu, never mind a fifty-third . . . He'd rewritten history and changed everything.

So why wasn't everything changed?

Unless, of course, the man he needed to kill had not been killed. The more Zaq thought about this the more certain he became that this was what had happened.

He was trapped here, waiting for the American Emperor to die. And his own assassin was out there somewhere. No one else could have fired the Changlang and few would want to, fewer still would dare and none but the girl could have made it this far.

He blamed the Library.

The plateau should have stopped her, as it had a thousand before. And if not the plateau then the ice bridge. She'd got past both, which was unknown, and survived the stamp of a butterfly when none but the reincarnated could do that and live.

All 2023 worlds knew this and so did Zaq, because he'd patched himself into a feed. So now he watched himself staring into space, talking to nothing and sitting on the step of a pagoda while the Dragon Throne sat empty behind him.

There was little need for her to burn the buildings of the Summer Gardens. All of the doors had been left unlocked and the shutters open. The guards who might have stopped her had been absent since Zaq dismissed them months before. But she had burnt the Changlang anyway, stalking the length of its corridor with her head high, a blade stuck in her makeshift belt and her face grim.

The only incongruous thing about the figure who swept through in a storm of fire had been her hands. She'd dragged them across the walls and paintings like a child rattling her stick against a fence.

And everywhere Tris's fingers had touched flames sparked.

Zaq looked pitiful sitting on those steps. A tearful young man in a dirty blue cloak and tunic, his chin in his hands and his attention focused, when it focused at all, on the burning line of the Changlang.

He wanted to be braver. Most of all, he wanted to be born someone else, someone completely different. A person the girl didn't want to kill.

"I'm going to find her," said Zaq.

A hundred and forty-eight billion people wondered if this was a good idea.

"And turn off the feed," Zaq added, pushing himself to his feet.

Silence greeted this order.

"Do it."

"You'll cause chaos." The order had been shocking enough to make the Librarian reappear. So now he stared from a puddle. As unhappy to be talking to Zaq as Zaq was to listen.

Walking to the edge of his terrace, Zaq stared down the wooded slopes of Wanshou Shan to a flickering wall of flame that had once been the greatest collection of classical paintings ever gathered into a single building.

"It's chaos already," he said.

Zaq found her at one end of a wooden pavilion in the Summer Gardens, kneeling with her back to him. She seemed be trying to crack open a small wooden chest. On the wall in front of her was a carved and gilded phoenix.

Tris had changed into a yellow silk jacket with a dragon embroidered across the back in white-gold thread. On her head was balanced a simple black hat that looked like an upturned bowl with the bottom cut out.

The sword was stuck through her belt.

Flames licked against one window and the sky outside danced with embers that flickered and spun in the night wind. The Changlang had burnt easily, being old, fragile and made mostly from cedar, and sparks from that fire had danced and then fallen onto a nearby roof.

A thousand golden butterflies rose in the night sky and threatened the roofs on which they landed. Zaq half expected the Library to fill the sky with clouds and batter the fires into submission but the night stayed almost clear and almost dark, with that silver tinge which came from the sun reflecting on distant worlds.

The room in which Tris knelt stank of smoke, charring shutters and a petrochemical reek which was oil-based paint bubbling beneath early tongues of flame. It was a complex smell, heavy with hydrocarbon. And though Zaq would have liked to stay to savour its richness, he realized this was probably unwise.

"So," Zaq said, "what are you looking for?"

"*You* . . ."

Tris scrambled to her feet so fast she almost tripped. Only to realize that a dozen paces still separated her from the Emperor and anyway he was unarmed. So she drew her own blade and stepped away from the sandalwood box.

"Nothing," said Tris.

*You must be searching for something,* Zaq almost said, then shrugged his reply away. Why would she tell him anyway?

"So what now?" he said, hoping it sounded nonchalant.

"Fuck," Tris said. "I don't know." She tossed her blade from hand to hand. "What do you think?"

"I think the world's going to end."

"Only for you," she said.

Her juggling with the blade was very impressive. Unfortunately for the 148 billion waiting to be impressed, the Librarian had taken Zaq at his word and the feed was gone. Zaq's head was empty and the single mirror on one wall showed only a burning room.

It was a wonderful feeling.

"Let's dance," he said.

And Tris looked at Zaq then, seeing him for the first time. A man who looked not much older than she was but must be twice her age.

"Dance?"

Zaq indicated the embers swirling beyond the window. "You got anything better to do?"

Tris was still working on an answer to this when the phoenix so lovingly carved into the panel behind her proved unable to live up to its own legend and crumbled onto a bed of embers.

Through the open door ahead she could see the Changlang burnt down to a smouldering line. A dozen small pavilions between the wooden corridor and her also smouldered, ceramic roof tiles exploding in the flames into which they'd fallen.

All around them bonfires lit the *Yihe Yuan*, until the Summer Gardens glowed with a richness they'd never possessed before and gilded pavilions grew ever more golden as they were varnished with flame.

She should leave now, before it was—

"Too late," said Zaq.

A huge shutter crumbled as its lacquered wood broke apart and the sudden inrush of air fed the blaze. More oxygen was all the pavilion needed to explode into flame, fire flowing across the floor like running water. Wooden panels on the ceiling began to char and the last unvarnished wall grew fat with flame as smoke fought to escape through doors and windows.

The heat was beyond anything Tris had experienced. Almost beyond anything she could imagine. This had to be dying, Tris realized. And all the while the Emperor just stood opposite her, seemingly unmoved and unharmed, the flames now so close that his cloak had started to char at the edges.

"You did this," she said, each word tearing at her throat.

He shook his head.

"Yes," said Tris, "you." Stepping forward, she drew her blade to finish what she'd travelled the worlds to accomplish. She expected him to twist sideways or block the blow, to turn and run.

Instead Zaq stepped forward, put out one arm to steady Tris as she began to fall and barely grunted when she used all that remained of her strength to ram the blade under his ribs and into his heart.

Time froze?

This was not strictly accurate. What actually happened was subjective in the way everything is when one gets down to that level. Time slowed to a crawl as the Library rewrote reality inside the skulls of Zaq and Tris, the handful of seconds separating Zaq from cardiac failure and the alveoli in Tris's lungs from rupturing suddenly extending before both of them like a slow glide to infinity.

And as the speed at which their thoughts began to operate ripped apart their neural nets, the flames which had been roiling around them slowed and slowed again until they barely crawled up the walls.

"Why?" Zaq said. But then he knew.

Because what Tris thought was what he thought and there were no boundaries between them. They looked at the world through the same eyes. And that world was fucked, seriously screwed, far weirder than either had imagined.

Zaq saw...

Well, he imagined that he saw himself. It looked like him only he couldn't remember any such incident. He was in a bath, marble and old. The room was painted in flat greens, golds and reds but then his rooms were always painted in those colours.

There were no servitors, he was naked and the water in his bath had turned cold. So cold that a scar on his wrist had grown blue and the skin around his nails become frayed and white. The fingers of his right hand, the one that gripped a knife, were so pale they seemed to belong to someone else.

It was a very beautiful knife, with a wavy line along one edge from where it had been forged, and fragments of room reflected in the blade's surface as if looking into a river or a bowl. Zaq had a feeling the knife might have been given to him by someone; he found it hard to remember.

Actually, Zaq found it hard to think, full stop. In locking him into this moment the Library had trapped him inside such pain that it overwhelmed his sight and hearing, his sense of smell and his very self.

"Hell," said Tris.

The Library nodded.

"Remember now?" Tris said.

She was talking about the room and the cold bath and about the boy who came through a door, a plate of dim sum on his tray and a rat perched on one shoulder. Through the eyes of that rat had peered a brain of a rodent and more billions of people than Tris could imagine. The servitor was about Tris's age. In fact, Zaq was pretty certain that the servitor was—

"Wrong," said Tris. She could feel the knife in Zaq's chest as clearly as he suffocated beneath her struggle to draw breath, both frozen into each other's pain on the wrong side of death.

"Look again," she demanded.

It was as if he refused to recognize himself or found it hard to care about what had happened to the boy with the rat. As if he saw life through a sheet of glass. Except... Tris corrected herself. It was a sheet of darkness and ice. And then, as Zaq finally remembered sitting in the bath, Tris understood *everything*. (Something she could have done without, really.)

"What?" Zaq said, looking up.

The boy grinned, shut the door behind him and looked around at the ornate room and whistled. "Wow," he said. "Fucking neat."

"Out," said Zaq.

"Zaq," said the boy, "it's me. I've blagged you some dim sum." He held out the tray as if he expected the Chosen of Heaven to join him in eating congealed food.

"There was this weird guy in the kitchens," he added, oblivious to Zaq's fiercest scowl, "wanted me to—"

"Don't," said Tris.

Zaq rose from the water, blade in hand.

He was naked and so was the blade which took the boy's head from his shoulders. As a spout of arterial blood pissed itself almost to the ceiling, Tris screamed and the boy began to crumple, his knees buckling as the torso toppled forward to hit the floor.

*How could you?*

From the far corner, the rat and the servitor's head both stared at Zaq with looks that only grew less accusing when the rat blinked and death began to soften facial muscles and glaze the boy's eyes.

"But he's not even—"

"Of course he's fucking real," Tris shouted, her voice a wind which scoured the edges of Zaq's mind. "They were *all* real," she said. "Every servitor you killed, that concubine you raped..."

She stopped, considered what she now knew. "You really didn't—"

"No," said Zaq. "I didn't know."

He saw it all now. The horror of what he'd done, which was as nothing to the horror of what he had been. A monster.

"Who was he?" Zaq began to ask and realized he already knew. Tris had been too young to watch it happen on feed, little more than a baby. No, Zaq knew that was untrue. She'd been unborn when her—

"Your father?"

This didn't seem possible, yet it was true and there was something else, something obvious.

*Eli ate the apple*, said the Library, as if this explained everything. And strangely enough it did. Both of them instantly understood why it was always this fruit that tradition demanded. And with the memory of juice running down Zaq's chin and Eli reaching out for his share the final piece fell into place.

"My brother," Zaq said. "Your father."

*She's your half niece,* said the dark. *You had different fathers.* This seemed possible, even likely. Although, since Zaq could barely remember his mother, how anyone might expect him to remember the man who . . .

*I can still save you.*

"How?" said Tris, knowing it was to the Chuang Tzu that the strange voice had been speaking.

*I can loop time back to when you were young. Or we can let your flame pass to the next candle.* The Library sounded regretful, as if things really hadn't been meant to end like this.

"Save us," Tris said.

The Chuang Tzu said nothing. He felt sick and stupid, ignorant to the point of wanting to disappear, to be anything other than what he was. He didn't want to be young again or inflict his memories on the next Chuang Tzu. He wanted everything to be different.

The Library thought about that.

"Billions will die," said Tris.

"No," insisted Zaq. "They will simply become someone else."

"Right," said the Library. "Let me find the tipping point."

# CHAPTER 59

## *Marrakech, Summer 1977*

Hassan sat back in his chair and pulled out a wallet, counting ten-dollar bills onto the table. The total got to forty dollars before he hesitated, added one more to the pile and slipped his wallet back inside his jacket.

"Fifty dollars," he said.

It was an incredible sum for a boy who once scraped a living delivering bread and now survived on trading odd snippets of information with the police. For a girl who kept house, swept, cooked and spent most evenings persuading the drunk who was not her father that he didn't want to hit her it was enough money to fund an escape.

"Half now," said Hassan, "and half later." Pulling a small cigarillo from a leather case, he waited for Idries to produce a lighter. It was brass overlaid with chrome, the name of some Essaouria nightclub in enamel along one side. "We can meet at Café Lux afterwards."

"After what?" Malika demanded.

"After you deliver this." Hassan lifted a plastic bag onto the café table.

"What's in it?" said Malika.

Idries snorted. "You don't want to know."

"We do," said Malika, "don't we?" She stared at Moz, who looked doubtful.

"It's fifty dollars," he said.

"Well." Malika's voice was firm. "I want to know." Moz and Malika looked at each other, Idries and Hassan temporarily forgotten.

"Can we talk?" Moz said.

"Talk all you like," said Malika. There were tears in her eyes and her bottom lip jutted so far that she looked like a petulant child.

"Give me a minute," Moz said and Hassan raised his eyebrows, then shrugged and lolled back in his chair.

"Don't take all night."

"We've been through this," said Moz, as soon as they turned the corner into a palm-lined side street. "I owe Hassan."

The eyes watching him were huge, magnified by a lifetime of unspilt tears. "Owe him what?" Malika asked.

"I don't know," Moz said. "I'm just tired," he added. "Tired of the fights and tired of watching my back. I'm tired of being locked into something I can't win."

"And this will end it?"

Moz shrugged. "It's a start," he said.

When they got back inside, Moz sat and Malika stood behind him, her hands clasped demurely in front of her. Only Hassan and Idries were fooled.

"Okay," said Moz, "we'll deliver the package."

"Good choice," said Hassan.

"Only first Malika and I get to look inside."

Hassan stopped smiling.

"Why?" demanded Idries.

"If we're going to take the risk," said Moz, "then we want to know it's really kif and not opium. That's fair." He could see from Hassan's face that the older boy thought it was anything but.

"If you refuse to take it," Hassan said, "Caid Hammou will be very cross."

Placing his hand over his heart, Moz bowed his head. "I'm not refusing," he said seriously. "And I swear to carry the kif wherever Caid Hammou wants as soon as Malika and I have checked inside."

"It's already packed," complained Idries. "My uncle said it's not to be unwrapped."

"Why not?"

Only Moz could hear the *told-you-so* in Malika's question.

Hassan looked from Malika to Moz. "You really going to let a girl tell you what to do?" he asked.

"She doesn't," Moz said with a smile. "She makes suggestions. I make suggestions. We do something in the middle. That's how life works." Celia would have been proud of him, if somewhat surprised at his wholesale stealing of her lines.

They left Idries arguing with Hassan, probably for the first time ever. It seemed Idries was not keen to take the parcel either.

"I need to get home now," Malika said, wrapping her haik tight about her. She was finally learning what society required of those growing up. Lies and prevarication, hypocrisy and long sleeves.

"Not yet," said Moz. "We should go to Riad al-Razor. It's time you met Jake properly." It was on their way that Moz made his suggestion to Malika. He made it without having talked to Jake or Celia, although he didn't think this would be a problem.

Celia came to his room less often now that Jake had taken to visiting hers. There was undoubtedly a raw element of jealousy behind Jake's decision to repair his relationship with his manager, but then there was an element of jealousy in everything Jake did. It was the dark side to his genius and Moz doubted he'd ever be any different.

"It's going to be okay," Moz said. "They'll like you."

He suspected that he'd have to explain to Jake that Malika was different and that girls from the Mellah weren't like girls in New York and London, but then he realized that Celia would undoubtedly explain this for him. And anyway Jake would be returning to London soon. His notebook was full and he had taken to rereading the articles about himself in *Sounds* and *NME* every day now.

And if Jake went then Celia would go too and they'd need people to look after the riad for them.

"What are you thinking?" Malika said.

Moz smiled. It was such a Malika question. Usually he'd have said "Nothing" because that's what boys always replied, but Moz felt he owed her the truth. "Things," he said. "You know, the future. Stuff like that."

# EPILOGUE

The Federal Nations support ship *Eugene Newman* was a Malika-class explorer, designed in Shanghai and built in high orbit by Atlas Interplanetary, a consortium put together fifty years before by His Excellency Caid Marzaq al-Turq.

It was an old-fashioned double hull reaching the end of its useful life and only the fact it was named after the man who bluffed Beijing into not using slave labour to build the launch sites had allowed sentimentalists at the Agency to siphon off enough funds to extend its life far beyond the usual ten-year service period.

No one was sure who came up with the idea to retrofit the *Eugene Newman* with a ZeroPoint/Casimir coil drive and make it the first ship in the Federated Nations fleet able to cross the galaxy in a single lifetime.

Several old men claimed the credit but these were people who also claimed to have been friends with Jake Razor, the maniac, musician and mathematician notorious for having no friends, and so everyone discounted them.

There was no doubt, however, about who suggested the destination. Lao Kaizhen, known in his childhood as Chuang Tzu because of his ability to lose himself in dreams, had grown up to exhibit that most Chinese of abilities, successfully mastering two entirely separate disciplines.

A poet of international repute, he commanded the *Eugene Newman* because his fame as an astronomer and deep-space theorist precluded everyone else from being offered the post.

Besides, he was the man who first stated that object x3c9311 was artificial in construction. The argument over Lao Kaizhen's claim lasted for fifteen years, which was the gap between the world's first ZPE/RazorDrive drone being launched and the probe getting close enough to take definitive readings.

After that, the argument became one of provenance and purpose . . .

"Two thousand and twenty-three," said a mapping officer. Next to her an assistant looked up from a different monitor and nodded. Their totals agreed.

"Any satellites?" Lao Kaizhen asked.

Both officers checked again. "No, sir," they said, more or less in unison.

Even as the *Eugene Newman* had been approaching the Dyson shell, Captain Lao hadn't been sure what to expect, and now he'd passed through and was inside, looking up at larger than gas giant-sized fragments of jigsaw enclosing a type II sun, he only knew it wasn't this.

Mirror-smooth surfaces reflected light back towards the centre and the recorded temperature of that reflection helped explain the oddity of the object's infrared image, which had been more or less what he first saw all those years ago, while looking across the disc of the galaxy.

"Signs of life?"

The definition of this had been set intentionally wide.

"Nothing."

"A pity." Captain Lao shrugged away the last of his dreams and sighed. It had been childish to hope for anything else. And all the while, the darkness watched and waited, considering carefully.

It would like to get things right this time.

# ACKNOWLEDGMENTS

Acknowledgments and thanks in no particular order, except for the last...

Aziz, for a truly terrifying drive between Marrakech and Casablanca and explaining Berber inheritance law. Maison Arabe in Derb Assebbé for teaching me how to make tagine properly. Blacks in Dean Street (Soho) and Caffé Nero in Winchester for letting me use them as offices. Upper Street's Friday Lunch Time Crew. Anders Sandberg and all who contributed to the Dyson Sphere FAQ (just put it in Google). *New Scientist*, for making me and everyone else who reads it actually think.

Mic Cheetham for fixing the contract that got this book published. Juliet Ulman for encouragement, and Josh Pasternack for tolerance. Television, Patty Smith, Johnny Thunders, Neil Young and John Cooper Clarke for sound tracking the early drafts.

The following books provided information or inspiration: *Lords of the Altas*, Gavin Maxwell's brilliant book on the House of Glaoua, *Wisdom of Idiots* by Idries Shah (but then anything written by Idries Shah provides inspiration), and *The Art of Shen Ku* by Zeek, for general weirdness.

Finally, thanks to Sam Baker, who sat, years back, in Gaby's in Charing Cross Road and argued long and hard about whether time was shaped like an ice cream cone or a blue marble. This book would never have existed without that conversation. We should have known it was shaped like both.

## ABOUT THE AUTHOR

Born in Malta and christened in the upturned bell of a ship, Jon Courtenay Grimwood grew up in Britain, the Far East and Scandinavia. Currently working as a freelance journalist and living in London and Winchester, he writes for a number of newspapers and magazines, including the *Guardian*. He is married to the journalist Sam Baker, editor of *UK Cosmopolitan*. Visit the website at www.j-cg.co.uk.